The Tarian shoved through the doorway, his bulky frame too big for it, forcing him to duck under to keep from hitting his head. Then he reached out one of those massive paws he called a hand, the palm raised upward as if he were the most refined gentleman asking to escort the heiress of Allay onto a dance floor. The idea of it on such a rough man was, of course, ludicrous. As was the idea of her willingly putting her hand in his, and effectively signing her own death warrant.

The Tarian saw her hesitate, saw her entire body draw back in fear, although by only a minute movement.

"One day you are going to have to cross the line, Princess," he said quietly, his eyes such a deeply intense amber, an overall tinge of rose coloring making them seem so rich and so surprisingly beautiful. It was almost like looking into a warm, moving golden flame instead of the fiery orange one might expect. They were steady on hers as his accent lightened again by half. "You're going to have to take action to get what you want. To claim what's rightfully yours. Why not take that action today?"

By Jacquelyn Frank

THREE WORLDS
Seduce Me in Dreams
Seduce Me in Flames

NIGHTWALKERS
Jacob
Gideon
Elijah
Damien
Noah

SHADOWDWELLERS
Ecstasy
Rapture
Pleasure

SEDUCE ME IN FLAMES

A Three Worlds Novel

JACQUELYN FRANK

BALLANTINE BOOKS • NEW YORK

A Ballantine Books Mass Market Original

Copyright © 2011 by Jacquelyn Frank
Excerpt from *Seduce Me in Dreams* copyright © 2011 by Jacquelyn Frank

Published in the United States by Ballantine Books, an imprint of The Random House Publishing Group, a division of Random House, Inc., New York.

BALLANTINE and colophon are trademarks of Random House, Inc.

This book contains an excerpt from *Seduce Me in Dreams* by Jacquelyn Frank. Available from Ballantine Books.

ISBN 978-0-345-51768-5
eISBN 978-0-345-51771-5

Cover illustration: Craig White

Printed in the United States of America

www.ballantinebooks.com

9 8 7 6 5 4 3 2 1

Ballantine Books mass market edition: August 2011

For Donna and Natalie,
without whom my life
would fall completely
apart

PROLOGUE

Fire burned everywhere. Cinders clung to long grasses that had been obliterated by it but, by some miracle, still held together. The smell of accelerant was still in the air because it had been poured on the field in such a massive quantity. Along with it was the unmistakable stench of char and smoke. Nothing could possibly have survived.

But in the center of all that destruction, something stirred. There was a cough just before the young man sat up and spit. He was charred as black as everything around him, making him blend in perfectly with his surroundings. He took a breath, his first in what seemed like ages. Well, he thought, it shouldn't surprise him that they had tried to kill him. After all, he had accidentally exposed his power in the center of the town square during a damn festival.

Shit. He'd kept it secret from everyone for all of his twenty-one cycles. And it hadn't been easy. Adolescence alone had been a trial for him, and he'd had something of a temper back then. Still, he'd managed to keep it all under wraps.

He ought to have known this was coming. There was no way a mutation such as he was could go an entire lifetime undetected.

But if it hadn't been for that girl . . .

Yet, how could he have turned his back? She would

surely have died at the hands of those self-serving sicko bastards.

He shook his head, shook away the memory for the uselessness that it was. There was a bitter taste in his mouth and it had nothing to do with the Axiom fuel they'd dumped on him in hopes of burning him like all the rest of the char and ash around him. He had let them think they were successful. What choice did he have? If they didn't "kill" him to their satisfaction, they would keep on trying until they actually figured out a way to succeed.

Had he truly thought at one time that his lifelong friends and family in his own village would be the ones most likely to understand and accept him? How many times had he come close to revealing himself before, thinking they would love him anyway? He had been so naïve. Such a fool. And yet, why did this shock him so much if he'd felt so driven to keep it hidden?

He looked around carefully before getting to his feet. It was dark now, the only light coming from the flames that burned so powerfully on the horizon. The damn fools had burned him, yes, but in the process had started a fire on the plains that had quickly raced into the village. The screaming had long since died down. He figured they were all dead, if not mostly so.

His secret was once again a secret.

He brushed layers of ash from his bare skin, the remainders of his clothing no doubt. Now he was naked, disenfranchised, and utterly at a loss as to what to do next. Still, he began to put one foot in front of the other, began to move. He had learned new things about himself, he could say that much. But he wasn't sure if that made things worse or better. He was too angry, too hurt to care.

It would take him a very long time to get over both of those feelings.

CHAPTER ONE

Her heart beat harshly, her breath rasping in the back of her throat. *What could it mean? What could he want?* The same questions swirled around in her head again and again as she strode through the palace hallways with an air of confidence she did not feel. There had never been a sense of confidence, a sense of security in her life. Even when her father had supposedly loved her, she had never felt that sense of cocooning comfort that a child was supposed to feel when in the presence of her protector.

She supposed his treatment of her these last years had proven her very intuitive, even at toddling age.

He had once professed a magnificent love for her mother. There were those in her household who swore, to this day, that her mother had been the great love of his life. But then his eminence the emperor had tired of his favorite concubine. Some said it was because a newer, younger woman had caught his fancy. Others said her mother had overstepped herself with him one too many times, that she'd grown proud and arrogant, making the mistake of thinking that being the mother of his heir apparent made her as good as being empress.

Whatever the reason, Emperor Benit Tsu Allay had put down his common-law wife like a dog. Unafraid of the possible repercussions he might face at the hands of the Interplanetary Militia, he'd had her tried for treason, proclaiming her an enemy to his crown and a conspirator in a plot to have him killed. Her mother's trial had been a whirlwind of, some said, overwhelmingly damning evidence, spurious accusations, and her execution one of the cruelest and most horrific in the history of their realm. Then, before she could understand that her mother would never touch her again, hold her or hug her, Ambrea had been declared fruit of a poisonous tree and packed off into the back of nowhere, and there she had been languishing ever since.

More or less.

She'd been called into her father's presence twice since her exile at the age of four—once at the age of eleven and once when she was thirteen. Both times he had hurled accusations of treason at her, accused her of knowingly plotting with his enemies to overthrow him and take his throne. However, lack of evidence, or, perhaps more likely, his unwillingness to slaughter a child, had spared her life—but not before she had spent over a year each time in his prisons.

Then there had been an almost chilling quiet.

After some time news had filtered down to her that the emperor had sired a male heir. Her brother, and her only living sibling. This decided lack of proliferation the emperor had blamed on his weak-blooded concubines; however, with medical technology at such an advanced state that in vitro fertilization could have been performed at any time with any viable uterus, it was widely believed that Emperor Benit was the one with the problem. However, Benit wasn't about to prove anyone right by having himself tested.

All of this swam through her mind in a ceaseless stream as she was led by a cadre of guards through the grand halls of Blossom Palace, the emperor's most favored of his seven residences. The astounding opulence of just the corridors took one's breath away, but she could still remember playing in these halls, running the maze-like lengths day after day, her rich little gowns inlaid with Delran platinum. Her bed had been so big and soft that she had needed help getting in and out of it, and all six of her body attendants could lie on either side of her comfortably.

Now her bed was narrow and serviceable, the sheets a bit worn in places. She had only two personal attendants (one of whom was, she suspected, her father's spy) and a household totaling four when the maid and cook were taken into account. Her gown was threadbare at the seams, her father having neglected her household stipend, and when he did remember to pay her servants, there was nothing left over for new clothes. She balanced the books herself because years earlier, she had been forced to let go her secretary. As it stood, her servants stayed purely on the basis of their love for her, because they certainly did not stay for the value of the living she could provide.

Still, it was a damn sight better than the cold, bleak dampness of the emperor's prisons.

The fact of the matter was, she was the emperor's daughter, whether he wanted to acknowledge that or not. The blood in her veins meant that his enemies could use her to stage a coup. So, he had to control her and have her close enough to keep an eye on her. At least, she believed, until he could contrive a way to be rid of her as he had done with her mother.

Now she was twenty-six cycles old and more than adult enough to be a threat to her twelve-cycles-old brother, whom Benit considered his new heir apparent. She was also old enough now to be executed without making her father look too much like the monster he was. Truthfully, ever since her previous incarceration, she had been living in anticipation of this day—the day when she would be called into his presence for the last time.

When she reached the presence chamber, the guards before her threw open the doors. She had expected to see her father at the end of the bamboo runner that led through a sea of courtiers and ended at the foot of the throne, where he was usually sitting in much state and pompousness. After all, when he handed down his abject humiliations to her, he enjoyed doing so publicly, to make an example of her, to make sure everyone knew that even his own daughter's acts against him, be they perceived or real, would not be tolerated.

But the throne sat empty, and there was an eerie quietude amongst the courtiers. Her chin rose proudly as she realized that all eyes were upon her. She might be terrified of what the emperor had in store for her, but she would be damned if she would let anyone else see that. No matter what he decreed, as far as she was concerned she was the heir to his throne. She was his first-born child. The law of their land demanded that she be his heiress. She did not recognize the laws he had hastily passed in order to put her aside.

But neither would she raise a hand against her innocent half-blood sibling. She knew there were factions willing and able to overthrow the young prince, should he ever ascend to the throne, if she so much as nodded in their direction, but she would not banish another to the fate she had been exiled to. And the alternative of eliminating him entirely was out of the question.

Out of the corner of her eye she saw Prelate Kitsos step to the edge of the runner as she was being hurried past the roomful of prelates and paxors. He tried to catch her eye, his look full of some kind of meaning and intent. She remained staring full ahead, not wanting in any way to be associated with the man's plots and plans.

He was too obvious in his avarice. He would be the death of them both if he were not more careful.

Now her heart seemed lodged firmly in her throat and it felt as though it was beating twice as fast. She was led past her father's throne and into his private visitation chamber. The difference in the brightness from one room to the next was shocking, and she was nearly blind in the sudden darkness. She clutched the prayer book she held between her hands, hoping the Great Being was watching over her. As her eyes adjusted to the darkness, she was grabbed roughly around each of her arms and shoved hastily forward. She tripped over the skirt of her gown, making her fall to her knees in an obeisance she did not truly feel, may the universe forgive her for her angry heart.

She was now kneeling at the feet of the man who had tormented her throughout her life in one way or another. She would have bowed to him under her own power, but she would never have groveled before him. She clenched her teeth in anger, forcing her countenance to remain cool and serene. She could not afford to be prideful. She could not risk any show of backbone in front of an emperor who had no compunctions about killing off anyone who angered him.

Silence ticked by, the only sound in her ears the rasp of her own breathing. She kept her eyes trained on the bamboo runner that ran through this room as well. The woven, decorative mats were used to protect flooring and, in this instance, hand-malleayed carpeting. Artisans created malleay rugs on great looms, teams of people working in some sort of concert of creativity. She had not seen one of the rich creations in completion since childhood, and even now the mat thwarted her. True, the bamboo in itself was cleverly wrought, colorful threads and Delran platinum decorating the plain tan fibers and creating something quite spectacular, but she would much rather see the rug beneath it.

Far more than she wished to see her father just then. Even now, all she could see of him was his slippered feet.

"Sister."

The pubescent voice startled her, as did his address, and she forgot herself and looked up. Instead of her father, she found herself at the feet of a brother she knew only from images in VidMags and other media. He was tall and gangly, all sharp joints and a physical awkwardness that rolled off him even though all he was doing was standing still. But he also had that imperious air and confidence of a prince born and raised. The luxurious cloth-of-platinum robes he wore were robes of state and, though they seemed to weigh heavily on his narrow frame, he wore them perfectly straight and with the exactness of someone used to such finery.

"My good brother," she said, inclining her head again. "I am honored to meet you at last."

"Are you?" he questioned her. "Or are you as much a traitoress as your mother was? Now that our father is dead, will you drive a knife in my back at the first opportunity?"

"Our father is dead?" The shock was so tremendous, so unexpected, that she forgot she was not allowed to acknowledge the emperor as her father.

"*He will be long remembered*," everyone in the room said solemnly, the ritual confirming the fact.

Beyond the shock there was also such a stupefying release within her psyche, the relief of almost a decade's worth of stress and tension, that she immediately felt light-headed. Blackness rode over her, forcing her to drop her prayer book and brace her hands on the floor. She fought off the faint that was tugging at her and used her seemingly obeisant position to touch her forehead to her brother's slipper.

"My great lord and emperor," she said shakily, "I am so utterly sorry for your loss."

"So, you acknowledge me to be our father's heir?" He was clearly fishing and she had learned to tread carefully around such dangling worms.

"I have always done so, Your Eminence. Is it not so decreed? I am the fruit of a treacherous woman who conspired to murder our lord and master, the late emperor. Her shame is my shame. I do not deserve to be heir or empress according to the laws he passed against me."

"Then you will not mind signing this documentation to that effect."

Her brother's hand swept out to the left. She raised her eyes to see a secretary reach down with a carefully drawn up document, its gilt edges obscenely bright as she quickly read the contents.

I, Ambrea Vas Allay, do swear from this day forward that I renounce my blood and any connection to the Allay throne. Thus, I will now be known only as Ambrea Vas, a commoner and subject of this realm. I sign this of my own free will with both signature and retinal scan to prove beyond a shadow of a doubt that these are my wishes and desires. Any attempts on my part to take the Allay throne, from this day forward, will be considered an act of high treason and will result in the immediate forfeiture of my life.

—Ambrea Vas

It meant Ambrea . . . "daughter." Ambrea Vas Allay meant "daughter of this realm." In all these years, her father, though he had alienated her and stripped her of her rightful place in the succession, had never taken this step, stripping her name. She had always wondered why. Perhaps there had been some part of the former emperor that had been, after all, loath to deprive himself of his spare heir while his only living son was still young and susceptible to many illnesses and the dangers of youth. Perhaps he had not, in the end, wanted to leave her without any claim to anyone. But clearly her brother had no such reservations.

To sign such a document would mean she could never, even in the event of her brother's death, lay claim to the throne. She would be cut loose. Set free. She could then do anything. Go anywhere. Her brother would be renouncing all ability to hold power over what she did or where she went, except that of a sovereign over his subject. He would no longer be responsible for her upkeep. She would, in essence, be her own woman.

The rush of the idea was a heady one. The thought of it, of being able to walk away, perhaps leave the planet altogether, where she could explore any part of the Three Worlds—it was remarkable. She could hear her blood rushing against her eardrums. She was a signature and a scan away from turning her back on this stifling existence forever.

Except . . .

"I beg you to forgive my hesitation, Your Eminence," she said quickly, not wishing to anger him, knowing nothing of his temperament that she didn't see in the media. But all hints thus far had pointed to a spoiled, rich, and powerful youth who was used to getting his way, just like his father had been. "I am merely in shock at the news of the emperor's death."

"*He will be long remembered*," her brother's attendants chorused respectfully. But there was a decided lack of enthusiasm in their voices. The fact was, Emperor Benit had been a tyrant, and these attendants who were now flocked at her brother's back had been the previous emperor's attendants and advisors. When Emperor Benit had raged, which he had often done, these were the people who had borne the brunt of it. Now they were eagerly supporting a child they probably felt would be far more malleable than his father had been. There was power to be found by being the advisor to the boy sovereign. These vultures would be clawing at one another for the best position.

"He had been ill for some time," her brother said, faltering.

There was emotion there. Genuine emotion. Despite how he was portrayed in the media, young emperor Qua Tsu Allay had feelings. And now his insecurities were also showing. Suddenly those robes of state looked far too big for the boy. And, in truth, they were. He was hardly old enough to rule himself, never mind the second-largest continent on Ulrike. What would happen to her country, her place of birth, and, truthfully, the land she greatly loved, under the rule of this boy? Or rather, the proxy rule of these attendants behind him. She had had many dealings with these greedy men and women. True, they must have had enormous courage to brave Emperor Benit's wrath from one moment to the next, but their avariciousness had far outweighed their sense of self-preservation. Many of them had come to her over the years, spearheading the accusations against her and machinating her terms of imprisonment. Her contempt for them was powerful, and well they knew it. But now they all seemed smug, secure in their power of the moment, sure that all the abuses they had suffered had been well worth it for having brought them to this moment.

She could be very sure that the idea of this document was theirs. They knew that she was the one thorn in their collective heel. There were many people who would not feel secure in the idea of an adolescent ruler. Many were as wise as she was and would realize that the boy would quickly become a puppet to those not of royal blood. Perhaps even to those *of* royal blood.

Ambrea noticed her uncle lurking in the shadows at the back of the room. Balkin Tsu Allay had lived in his imperial brother's shadow all of his life, seemingly content to be there. Her father had never felt threatened by his younger brother, an odd thing considering he had felt threatened by her as a mere child and by just about everyone else of noble blood. No doubt Emperor Benit had named Balkin Regent Tsu Allay, guardian over the young emperor until he came of age.

This press to have her sign this document, forfeiting all her rights to the throne, would mean that, should anything happen to her brother, her uncle would be next in line to inherit the throne.

It was these thoughts that stayed her hand. Fear gripped her, for she knew that to refuse to sign the document could be tantamount to treason in her brother's eyes. But she looked around the room and saw the dire future her country was in for. As much as she craved her freedom, craved to drop the chains that the country held her in, she also craved an end to the reign of terror that the imperial Allay line had been subjecting the Allay people to for so very long now.

"My most beloved brother," she said, picking up her prayer book and holding it tightly between her hands and pressed to the place beneath her breasts. Perhaps she was trying to keep from losing her breakfast more than being devotional, but whatever worked in the moment. "I would do anything to please Your Eminence, I beg you to know that. However, if I sign this document I will lose something that is very precious to me. Not my succession to the throne, because I have reconciled that loss, along with my mother's loss of grace and loss of life, since I was four years old. Our . . . *your* most esteemed father—"

"*He will be long remembered.*"

Ambrea had paused for the response, though she did not join in it.

"—saw fit to outlaw my rights to the throne that same year. To sign this document now would surely be redundant. And even our father never asked me to give up the right to my name. I am still the Princess of Allay. I am still of his blood. The blood of this line. Take from me what you will, but I beg you to leave me my name."

"Insolent girl!" Her uncle surged out of the shadows, glaring down at her as rage shook through him. "You talk so prettily, but what you say is ripe with sedition. You bear no love for your brother."

"That is not true!" She rose to her feet, unwilling to kowtow to a man who did not deserve her obeisance. In the scheme of things, disinherited or no, she was his better and regal law dictated that he show her respect. "Where is your proof, my lord? Why do you hurl these accusations at me? What have I done to deserve them?"

"Do not think this crown is not aware of your plots to seat yourself on the throne. Your father had no stomach for ordering your execution, but this regency does not have such scruples."

"My father knew me to be innocent of all the charges laid at my feet! He knew he would one day have to answer to the Great Being, as he now most certainly has, and our Divinity has surely seen the wisdom in the emperor's ways and has shown him mercy."

"Your throat will be slit and your seditious tongue cut out before you can even reach that door, girl," he threatened her coldly.

"Will it? And how will you answer the charge of political assassination when the Interplanetary Militia comes looking for you?" She was just as cold and seemingly fearless as she stood up to an uncle who was clearly as bloodthirsty as his brother had been. "Will you so easily put my brother's new rule in jeopardy by making such a hasty mistake?"

Her brother paled and looked anxiously at his regent.

"Uncle, we cannot risk being censured by the IM," he said nervously.

There were many countries on the Three Worlds, each boasting an individual political structure. Long ago all of those countries had signed a treaty that had created the IM, the Interplanetary Militia, an elite armed force that operated independently of any of the countries or planets, yet within an agreed upon set of laws and parameters. The militia did not interfere in the political growth and changes of any individual country, but there were limitations to what the rulers of a country could do. Anything considered a crime against humanity or a blatant crime as set out in the IM's charter would evoke a swift retaliatory reaction, and the IM would then have the power to restructure the political scene according to the legal succession or the democratic guidelines put in place by that particular country.

That could mean—

Ambrea shook the thought away before it could even be born. She had no energy to waste on fruitless supposition. Right then, she was fighting for her life. Her uncle did not hide his fury, but neither did he lose control of it.

"The IM has no power to judge who we throw in our prisons." He smiled meanly at Ambrea before instructing the guards. "Throw her in the catacombs. Let her rot in there for a while. She will quickly become more malleable when she no longer has her daily comforts. I promise you, Your Eminence, she will be forgotten as many before her have been. Most think the banished princess long dead already. But for those who entertain otherwise, let them see just how little power she has. Her precious name will mean nothing in the wet rooms."

Ambrea drew in a sharp breath, then forced herself

not to react in any other way. She would not give that snake the satisfaction of seeing her fear. The catacombs had become quite infamous under her father's reign, and it looked like their reputation was destined to grow.

The guards did not lay their hands on her. For all of her destitute state, she was still a princess of the realm. Political climates changed constantly. There was no wisdom, especially in this currently shifting monarchy, in making enemies with someone who might become more favored on the morrow.

Ambrea held her head high, her spine ramrod straight, and her shoulders aligned in regal elegance. The simple gown she wore was clean and crisp, its frayed seams invisible under the shine of her personal brilliance. She turned in the midst of the guards who surrounded her, but at the last moment she turned back to meet her brother's eyes.

"I regret that we have not known and loved each other throughout these years. Perhaps if we had, you would know me better and you would know that I would never wish any harm on you, that I have no aspirations to your throne, and no desire to unseat you. I am, and ever will be, your sister by blood and your sister in my heart."

She made no further pleas or arguments. There was really nothing more to be said. Strangely, the first rush of fear she had felt at being ordered to the catacombs was now faded, leaving resignation and practical acceptance in its wake. It wasn't the first time she'd been unjustly imprisoned, but it was a far more fortunate fate than her mother had met.

At least today she wasn't going to die.

"Out! All of you mutts, get out!" raged Balkin, Regent Tsu Allay.

The attendants, long familiar with the previous emperor's similar temperament, and knowing just as well the kind of man the regent was, made almost comical haste to do so. The boy was left alone with his seething uncle and no choice but to stand there and watch Balkin pace a furious circuit around him.

"It's no matter, Uncle," he said with a shrug, pausing to scratch at the tight collar of his robe of state. "As you said, no one even remembers her anymore. There hasn't even been a picture of her in the VidMags for years."

"Of course they remember her, you little idiot. And as long as she is alive, this throne will be called into question."

"Uncle, you will not address me with such disrespect," Qua said with a spoiled bravado. He was used to being catered to and having everyone tell him how excellent he was in every way. The whelp's attitude burned at Balkin's very last nerve.

His uncle's explosive reaction made Qua stumble back away from him as the older man let out a roar and leapt at his face. Balkin's hands were raised into violent fists, and his entire frame shook with the power of his barely checked rage. But he did check himself. Held himself. He took a breath and lowered his hands, brushing gently at his nephew's shoulders, resituating Qua's robes with care and seeming attention to detail.

"Of course, you're right," Balkin agreed gravely. "Forgive me. That girl has been a canker on the ass of this realm all of her life, and then her mother the whore before her. I watched for years as your father was wounded time and again by that entire line of blood. Anything associated with her tends to make me run hot."

"O-of course. I understand." Qua recovered his composure as his uncle did. "But what can we do? We cannot force her to sign. We cannot k-kill her. I . . . I don't think I would be comfortable with that."

"No. No, of course not." Balkin smiled at the boy, hoping it hid his contempt for the little weakling. Truth was, the boy was nothing of any depth. He was hardly bright enough to remember the steps in certain official rituals. He had more verve for games and wastrel pastimes than he did for the wondrous power he had just been handed. On the other hand, that made him the perfect shell, the perfect puppet. Balkin could pull his strings with little to no trouble at all, he was certain of it. The child was completely dependent on him. The only irritant was that he had been raised with extraordinary privilege. He knew exactly how everyone ought to treat him. He knew exactly how far his demands could extend.

"After all, she is utterly powerless and disinherited," Qua said.

"Mmm. Disinherited, yes, but not necessarily powerless. If the people doubt your ability to rule, Your Eminence, they might search for loopholes and try to usurp your position on the throne."

"That would be illegal," Qua dismissed with a sniff.

Not necessarily, Balkin thought. His brother had disenfranchised his daughter on very thin precepts. While he was alive, no one had dared to question him. Now that he was dead and the people were faced with an overindulged boy child as their imminent ruler, they might be far less afraid of picking apart the details.

"Nephew," Balkin said as he turned to busy himself with pouring a drink, trying to regain control of his composure and use his head better when dealing with this child, "it is very crucial that you make the people feel . . . secure. You need to do things that will prove you are your father's son."

"Such as?" Qua wearied of standing in state now that there was no one to see him, and he worked the collar of his robe free and took a seat on his throne. The seat of state was enormous and swallowed up the underdeveloped boy.

"You have to put a little fear in them. Show them your backbone. Throwing that whore's child in the catacombs is a good start. Perhaps we ought to have her tortured until she does what we want her to do."

"Uncle!" Qua was aghast. "She is still a princess of the line. It would be a high crime to injure her so cruelly. And in truth she hasn't done anything."

"She's pissed me off. She drives me mad and drove your father mad as well. She needs dealing with. But you need not decide on it right away. Let the wet rooms soften her up a little. Let her feel her memory refreshed as to what it's like to be in all that dark and cold."

Qua relaxed, much preferring the more passive approach to dealing with his sister. It frustrated Balkin. The boy had never met her before today. He owed her no allegiance and could not possibly feel any love for her. Why was he being so squeamish as if they'd grown up together, sharing an affection?

It was because of what the clever little bitch had said just before leaving. She had meant to tug on Qua's conscience, had planted the idea in his mind that they could have had some kind of great sisterly and brotherly bond with each other if given half a chance. She had perhaps even intended to sow a seed for a future reconciliation between them, to work her foot in the door.

That would be a disaster. If Qua ever looked favorably on his sister, she could interfere with all of Balkin's plans; she could drive a tremendous wedge into the grip he planned to grasp the boy with.

"No matter," Balkin said dismissively, "get a good meal in you, nephew. Dress more comfortably. The issue is dealt with for the time being."

"Thank you, Uncle. I think I will."

Balkin went to the door and called in Qua's servants,

instructing them in the feeding and caring of the new emperor. Then he excused himself and walked down the palace halls. He rubbed at his aching temples as he did so, unable to help resenting his brother for leaving him with this entirely ruinous mess. Benit's death had been a horrible shock to Balkin. The suddenness of watching his brother simply drop midstep as a vein in his brain exploded was something he simply could not get around. For years he had been Benit's right hand, the two of them of a like mind on almost every matter. He had never resented or coveted Benit's imperial position in life before now. Why should he have? Balkin had all the power and money he could ask for, and his brother had trusted him implicitly and often followed his advice on matters of state and political maneuvering. If someone crossed Balkin, all he had to do was speak of it to the emperor. They would then put their heads together and devise an appropriate retaliation.

Ah, Benit had had such a beautiful touch with vengeance. Balkin's temper often made him hot and quick and less elegant in dealing with those who crossed him. It had been Benit who had shown him the grace in turning a screw slowly and with deliberate viciousness.

It had been a wonderful relationship.

Balkin reached his quarters and pushed his way in. The smell of burning Ayalya spice struck him, the luscious scent warm and exotic. Sunlight streamed in the wall of windows in the center room, highlighting the curls of smoke that filled the space. There were at least half a dozen burners lit at once, but the Ayalya's nature was such that it didn't overwhelm the senses.

The patrician style of the open rooms allowed Balkin to sense where everyone was in the apartments almost immediately. The servants who were currently unoccupied immediately knelt and bowed their heads to the floor as he moved past them. He barely took notice. In the next room, however, where there was a sprawling bath set into the intricately etched stone floor, the two female servants were busy attending the woman in its waters. One was crushing thick, fragrant masse petals before tossing them onto the water's surface. The other was pouring a thin, slow stream of hair oil into her mistress's hair while at the same time working the oil into the lush curls with her free hand. Balkin, as always, was astounded by the perfection and beauty of his lover even in what could be considered a state of dishabille. She had rich, dark chocolate colored tresses with strands of sparkling silver running throughout. Her eyes were a warm, fathomless gray, with lashes so dark she needed no cosmetics to enhance them. Her lips were a creamy fair pink, the perfect touch to accentuate the smooth and healthy complexion that only someone so young could have.

"Well, that was quick," Eirie noted as she watched him approach the edge of the bathing pool. "Did the little tramp sign her rights away?"

He smiled even though the topic was a sore point with him at that moment.

Eirie smiled back. "I told you she wouldn't," she said. She picked up some of the petals floating near her and rubbed them together between her fingers. "I certainly wouldn't if I were her."

"Call me an optimist. I thought after all those years of exile she might be grateful for an escape clause."

"I suppose it all depends on a person's nature." She tilted her head and narrowed her eyes on him. "So what do you plan to do now?"

"I sent her to the wet rooms, where she can rot for all I care."

"Hmm."

Balkin knew her well enough to know that those non-committal sounds meant she thought he had made a tactical mistake or that she would have done something differently.

"Why? What would you have me do with her? I can't have her running around out there. Someone like Prelate Kitsos or Paxor Morick will find her in exile, prop the bitch up, and start a civil war behind her."

"I am aware of that. But imprisoning her could make her an object of sympathy."

"I am willing to take that risk. But no one even knows she was here."

"Oh, so you brought her in secretly? Not through the main receiving room where everyone could see her? Whether they know her face or not, they need only see all of that hair of hers and they would know who she is. The law is clear, no one may have hair longer than the blood princess."

Balkin shifted, giving himself away easily.

"Ah, I see. And I'm willing to bet she didn't bind her hair up. She wore it down and long and fully on display so no one would mistake her identity."

"By the Great Being's balls, she did exactly that!"

Eirie chuckled. "She's a clever one. And she's outmaneuvering you, Balkin."

"But she didn't even know her father was dead. There was no fabricating the shock on her face when she saw her brother standing there in state. She fully expected to see her father today. The emperor's death hasn't even been announced to the press yet. She's been living in isolation. She couldn't have plotted these things on purpose. No. These are my mistakes, not her victories."

"Perhaps." Eirie turned up a hand to dismiss the servants. Once it was just the two of them, she gave him a slow, luscious smile and an inviting look from sly eyes. "Why are you still dressed?"

"Eirie, I have a busy day ahead of me. My princely puppet is, to be kind, a moron. He hasn't the slightest clue as to how to manage this realm." He coughed when his stomach soured at the thought of spending all the rest of his days subservient to an idiot who would likely be completely dependent on him for every single move he made.

"So you will manage it for him. You will make certain everyone knows who it is exactly they are dealing with. They will learn very quickly who the real emperor is." She prevaricated, "Unless . . ."

"Unless?"

She moved across the bath to him, pushing through the water like some kind of divine creature too beautiful to bear, and stood up slowly. She tilted her head all the way back so she could see him, her long neck so elegant, her oiled hair shining and curling down her back.

"Unless," she said softly, "the new emperor was to fall ill. Be victim of some terrible accident. These things happen all the time. And then you would be next in line."

He squatted down before her, reaching to encircle her neck with a single hand.

"I would be the first person they would suspect in just such a mysterious happening. Especially since I was by my brother's side when he died."

"Bad luck that. Bad luck tends to run in streaks." She stretched up to brush a butterfly kiss against his cheek. "You've spent all your life in your brother's shadow. Here is fate whispering to you the opportunity to take your turn in the sun."

"My brother's son and his succession was everything to him. He made me regent because he trusted me implicitly to protect Qua. To guide him. What would that make me if I were to betray my brother's desires after all he has done for me?"

"I think it would make you wise. Self-respecting. Not to mention it would be for the good of the country. Benit is beyond this realm now. He is beyond caring about the machinations of this country and his family. You paid him allegiance when he was alive, and no brother could ever do more. But you cannot be beholden to him forever. Even into the Great Beyond? That asks too much."

"Eirie, you are much too ambitious, I think," he warned her even as he covered her mouth with his and kissed her with the fire only she had ever inspired in him. She had been in his bed every night for the past five cycles, ever since she had been nineteen cycles old. But still every moment with her was new and like a fierce dream that never ended. He no longer wondered when he would find her boring. He was convinced it was impossible. The worry was, when would she become bored with him? He was nearly twice her age, far from being a young, vigorous man in spite of how she made him feel. She was vital and vivacious and, as he had just pointed out, very ambitious. "And you forget, I am not next in line for the throne should something happen to Qua."

She scoffed at that, pushing back from the side of the bath and gliding through the water. "Oh. Her again."

"Yes, her."

"She is easily taken care of. Poison her food. People die in prison all the time."

"Poison can be discovered."

"Not if it's done well." She smiled wickedly. "I have learned a great many things from socializing with the emperor's concubines. I must say, they are some very clever, vicious bitches. Did you know there is a potion of easily gettable herbs that prevents conception just as well as modern medicine can? It can be administered on the sly, in a simple glass of nectar or lemon water and the person drinking it would never know she was taking it."

"Are you telling me that they were poisoning one another of their ability to conceive?"

"Why do you think the emperor had so few children?

A child meant power. Successive children would put the heir in threat. A concubine's power is attached to her abilities as a lover and mother. Rob them of motherhood and what is left? A skilled lover can hold her own in the emperor's favor for only so long before he would become disgusted with her inability to conceive. You know your brother. His barren concubines infuriated him. He threw them over for something fresh the way one might discard a dress that has gone out of fashion. The only reason the princess was born so quickly to him was because he had only two concubines at the time. Not so much backbiting. Not so much danger."

"It's a wonder the prince was ever born," Balkin said, his astonishment clear.

"A wonder indeed. There is also a potion to purge a womb. Anyone could have slipped this to the prince's mother at any time during her pregnancy. But your brother had the foresight to isolate her, remove her from the House of Concubines. The story goes that Irinia, the prince's mother, would drink only from fresh running water sources and only eat whole fruits and vegetables— methodical practice designed to avoid all attempts at poisoning her."

"Clever indeed. I don't know if I should be fascinated or disgusted."

"The point is, there's always a way. A drop of poison, the slip of a knife, or perhaps catching a trifle of a cold."

He laughed at her then. "Germ warfare now? Will you stop at nothing?"

"Nothing," she assured him vehemently, standing once again so he could see the water rushing down her voluptuous body, the stark darkness of her nipples compared to her otherwise fair flesh. "You are the mighty Balkin Tsu Allay, brother to the most revered and most feared emperor of all time. His blood is in your veins and his temperament runs through you just as strongly.

Why should you have to play second to an idiot boy or be held back by a scrubby little redheaded black-blood? You could be emperor," she said passionately. "*Emperor*."

"And you empress, I suppose." Eirie could see that he was toying with the possibilities.

"If you but command me," she said with a gracious lowering of her eyes.

"I have asked you to wed me all of twenty times, Eirie, and you've always said no. Yet if I were emperor, suddenly then I would be worthy of you?" His tone was sharp and bitter.

"You are not emperor now, and you cannot command me to wed you. However, as your lowly citizen I would have to submit to your demand. You would be ruler of all. I could not expect to say no and leave with my life intact. I am not a foolish woman."

"No," he agreed. "You are too clever by far."

The metal clang of the door shutting at her back made Ambrea cringe inwardly, but she showed none of that fear to the gaoler. She knew very well that he would be ordered to report every move she made, every reaction she had. Her uncle would be looking for any sign of weakness, any sign that she would crumble or cave to the demands being made upon her. And as strong as she was in that moment, she knew she was not without weaknesses. She knew, as they did not know, how oppressive and terrifying she found being locked in a small room to be. It had been that way ever since her first imprisonment. She remembered how confused she had been, how utterly panic-stricken. She'd been ripped away from her governess, the only woman she'd ever known as any other child might truly know a mother. Blay-ana. Blay-ana had taught her everything. From her first letters to her first clumsy steps into womanhood.

Although the governess had not been affectionate by any stretch of the imagination, she had been wise and steady and the only friend and confidante the exiled princess ever had. Ambrea was too "common" to be deemed a worthy and worthwhile friend to her peers, yet too royal to be allowed a common companion. So it had been just her and Blay-ana.

Then her father had gotten it into his head that her burgeoning womanhood went hand in hand with some ephemeral power to command and coax factions to her side. He had severed her from Blay-ana, making sure they never saw each other again. They never even had the chance to say farewell to each other. He had thrown Ambrea into the catacombs, keeping various weak charges hovering over her so he could justify the long term of her imprisonment.

It was well over a year later before she was released and given back her own household. All the faces had been strange, though, and for the longest time she had not dared to trust anyone.

"Ah, hello my old friend," she said wryly to the cell around her. She gave her uncle credit for consistency. She'd been given the same cell as her last time there, as well as the time before that. She could tell by the little waterfall dribbling along the cracked, mildewed stones in the far left corner. The cell was now a little older, the wearing of the water paths a bit deeper, but it had little charms that made her certain it was the same cell. There were no windows, since the entire catacombs were just as the name suggested, completely underground. The cot against the wall made her bed at home look luxurious. As poor as her household had become over the years, she had never thought to complain. She had always known it could be worse. And even these accommodations were probably considered highbrow. She knew well that there were deeper levels to the catacombs. Darker levels. Though torture was outlawed in the IM's charter, the emperor, her father, had made a poorly kept secret of his dealings with those he considered enemies of his throne. He had imagined himself above the laws of the IM, merely by privilege of his exalted birth.

Feeling eyes on her back, knowing that the guard was peering at her through the small window in the door, she lowered herself to her knees, closed her eyes, and said a hasty prayer for her delivered safety. Futile or not, the Scriptures taught that she should never give up hope, because that was tantamount to losing faith. Even if her uncle did manage to find a way to justify her future death, even if she were to be murdered by his hand for all to see and revel in, she could never lose hope. Not even in those last moments could she forsake her belief in the Great Being's power.

She glanced up at the cameras that were trained on her from either corner of her cell. Holding her book of devotionals close, she opened to a worn, familiar spot. But instead of the prayers that filled the book on every other page, this one held a sheet of paper-thin Vid. The Vid was a rotating picture, three images only, of the woman who had given birth to her.

Ambrea knew little of Junessa Vas Allay that had not been told to her with vicious condescension from her peers or those who had raised her after the concubine's downfall. However, while Blay-ana had been one of those strident, rote voices who spoke of Junessa's ill qualities and the pridefulness that had led to her downfall, she had also been the one to slip this Vid to Ambrea on a seemingly innocuous night when they had been alone in the gardens where no surveillance could reach them. Then she had softly said:

"Do not take all that is said about your mother too much to truth. While it is true she was willful, and her own actions led to her fall from grace, there were many who plotted against her and desired to see her fall. There are some who believe your mother's worst crime was her ambition. She wanted to win the sole love of the emperor and to be made empress at his side. She thought she had charms enough to coax your father into one day sharing his ultimate power with her. And, indeed, your father was much enamored of your mother from the first moment he caught sight of her. As you can see, she was quite beautiful."

Ambrea had seen very few images of her mother over the years because her mother's name was forbidden to be spoken and her image had been struck and outlawed from public records in Allay. To have this Vid was a high crime. Blay-ana could have lost her life for giving it to her, and Ambrea could suffer for it should she be caught. But she had more of a desire to treasure the images of the fine-boned brunette than she had a fear of being caught with them. Although it was uncanny how much she looked like her mother in the pretty, feminine contours of her face and the regal elegance of her neck and shoulders, the brilliance of her fiery red hair and the strength and height of her body were all obvious gifts from her father. The teal shade of her irises was a perfect blend of her mother's stunning green and her father's cerulean blue eyes.

It was hard to believe he was dead. As hatefully as he had treated her, she had always held him in her mind with a measure of awe and respect, her sharp intellect recognizing that he had wielded his absolute power with a magnificence that equaled his tyranny. His reign had fathered a great deal of prosperity for the country of Allay. He had wrought new trade agreements that should have the governmental coffers overflowing. Allay was a jewel in the crown of the planet Ulrike, and her father had made it shine very brightly.

But he had been young—not even fifty cycles old. How had he died? What sickness was there that modern medicine had failed him at such a young age? Had there been a violent accident? Or perhaps an assassination?

Ambrea closed away her mother's images. She pressed the book to her heart and wondered, as she had many times before, what her mother's true flaw had been. Had she really been a traitor, as everyone insisted she was? Or had she simply displeased a spoiled man who wanted his way in all things and resented anyone gainsaying him? If that was the case, what had been the terrible boundary that she had overstepped? What had she done that had warranted her topple from first lady of all Allay to its most despised criminal?

There was a loud clang behind her as the bolts of the door snapped open and the portal gave way with a pneumatic hiss. She stood and turned to face whatever destiny was coming toward her.

There was a gliding sound, a rustle of fabric, and suddenly Suna was there.

"Suna!"

Pride and bearing were forgotten as relief washed over Ambrea, and she rushed to clasp hands with her trusted friend. This was her companion who had stayed with her these many years, even through her last imprisonment, even though no glory or riches were to be found as the companion of a fallen, destitute princess. It was customary for a prisoner of great station to be allowed a companion, provided one volunteered. Suna had been left behind at Blossom Palace when Ambrea had been called before her brother. The guards must have returned to her and informed her of her mistress's fate.

"Oh, I am so glad to see you," Ambrea breathed. But in the next instant she released the hands of her best friend and gave her a stern frown. "You can't be thinking of staying with me. I forbid it absolutely."

"And I refuse to obey your command," Suna said firmly. "We have been jailed before. It is of little consequence to me. I will always serve you as best I am able, my good lady."

"Oh, Suna," Ambrea sighed, turning away from her as sadness weighed all around her. "I am afraid that there will be no freedom for me ever again. Not unless I do as they ask."

"I have already been told what they asked of you. I've been commanded to 'work' on you, to make you see sense and the errors of your ways. I am to talk you into freedom."

"Hush now," Ambrea warned, glancing up at the cameras. "Don't give them fodder for taking you away from me. Your disrespectful tone could be seen as traitorous."

"Forgive me, Princess, but if I farted it would be seen as traitorous."

Ambrea laughed in a sharp, undisciplined burst. She covered her mouth and took in a breath through her nose, regaining her composure. Her eyes shot warnings at Suna, and her companion nodded in acquiescence.

The two women took their seats across from each other at the rickety old table provided for them in one corner of the room. There was only the one cot between them; her servant was expected to sleep on the floor. In a day or two, when things had settled a bit, Ambrea would be able to make small demands. Suna would get a decent bedroll, perhaps even a cot of her own. It would all depend on where the guards' politics stood.

A great many Allayan people would see Ambrea as the rightful empress of Allay. To see her treated in such a manner would rub them very much the wrong way. They would do whatever was in their power, perhaps just shy of treason, to see to her comfort. Then again, there were those who were not afraid of taking even treasonous action. But Ambrea was not comfortable with putting others too much at risk. Perhaps there would be a time and a place for her to take part in the orchestration of a shift in power, but she had not seen the right opportunity and had never been comfortable with the idea of unseating her father who was emperor by birthright.

But now that her brother was emperor, that made for a very different game. For in her heart she knew she was empress of Allay. The hastily passed laws of a bitter tyrant could not change what blood had dictated. Since time was time the firstborn child of the emperor or empress in power was automatically and by right of that birth, heir.

Her heart beat in a rapid rush as she understood for the first time what her father's death truly meant. Unless she was foolish enough to sign away all her rights, as her uncle and brother were demanding, she was empress of Allay.

CHAPTER
TWO

Ambrea felt incessantly cold. Her clothes were always damp. She could feel the weight of the water the fibers now held. And after endless days of imprisonment, they smelled of the must and mildew that infused every corner of the catacombs. *She* hardly smelled any better. These cells were crafted when personal hygiene had not been taken very seriously. A vibratory shower had been installed against one wall, the small nozzle pointed in such a way that the bathers would have to shove themselves up against the mildewed rock in order to partake of its effects, thus defeating the purpose of the shower. However, the nozzle was faulty, and there were no curtains or privacy doors. She refused to strip herself before the cameras in her cell. She was certain the film would show up in some trashy VidMag faster than she could spit. When she was younger she had not thought much about it, but now she would not give her brother the fuel he needed to denigrate her in the eyes of their people.

One of the guards was kind enough to bring her a bucket of clean, warm water every morning, so she was able to fumble around her clothes with her back to both cameras and make a semi-decent job of maintaining personal hygiene.

Another of the gaolers had brought in a second cot for Suna. He had also brought them warmer blankets and plenty of them. It would perhaps help stave off the inevitable chill-colds that she and Suna would be subjected to during their incarceration in the wet rooms. She recalled that during her last visit in the catacombs she had not been able to shake the first chill-cold she had caught, and it had quickly morphed into something that had nearly killed her. Of course modern medicine would have quickly cleared up the whole thing but Emperor Benit had not seen fit to offer medical care to his daughter until it had become clear she was going to die. It baffled her, as it always did, that he had not simply let her die. Once again he had spared her life, keeping her around despite the threat he perceived her to be.

The guards had also taken to sneaking her VidMags. Normally she didn't read that kind of fame-hounding trash as Suna was wont to do, but at the moment it was her only connection to the outside world. Of course most of them were only fifty percent accurate, so she had to choose carefully what to believe and what not to believe.

The topic of all interest, of course, was the death of the emperor and the ascension of his son to the throne. They were spinning him to seem older than he was, picking apart his behaviors in order to accentuate those that made him seem more mature and capable. No doubt these were her uncle's machinations. The free press on Ulrike was not something even the regent could buy, but he had a cadre of public relations experts who could influence general opinion. And they were doing a bang-up job of it so far.

She felt sorry for her brother. Unlike when their father was alive, now he would not be as accepted for making mistakes as he had been. His childhood had been hard enough as a royal heir, with all the expectations due him, but now his entire adolescence had been stolen from him. That and the fact that their uncle was no doubt sitting on the boy's chest, whispering words of fear and sedition to him. Perhaps the regent was even being abusive of his charge. There was no telling. Ambrea knew from personal experience that the former emperor had not been above laying a personal hand on his offspring. Why would his brother be any different? And if Balkin wanted to wield any true power, that would mean yanking the royal progeny completely beneath his reins, or eliminating him entirely.

The thought made Ambrea restless, and she began to pace her cell. She much preferred to project an air of quietness and peacefulness to the camera's unceasingly watchful eye, not wanting to give her uncle the idea that she was frustrated by her captivity. In fact, it gave her great pleasure to sit peacefully with Suna playing a game or twist-stitching, especially when she knew it would miff her uncle to watch her behaving in so unruffled a manner. After all, it was a contest of wills. And she simply needed to prove herself the stronger will between them.

The very thought helped calm her, helped bring her into focus. She reminded herself that she could not spend her energies worrying about a brother who was by far better off than she was at that moment. Regardless of the pressures he might suffer, he at least was warm, dry, and, above all else, free.

Then a loud crash sounded in the catacombs beyond her door, the noise echoing forward and back, followed quickly by an uproar of shouts and cries. Ambrea couldn't help her curiosity and quickly crowded with Suna to see out the small window in their door. The hand-excavated tunnels beyond the door had been shored up with steel frames, the walls covered in pitch and pyorite to harden them for centuries to come as well as those that had already passed. The yellow lights along the tunnels gave them a ghastly color, leaving them in more shadow than illumination.

But in the midst of all that darkness was a bright burst of daylight as the outer doors were opened, allowing a cascade of bodies to tumble down the short flight of stairs. It was a contingent of guards, all well armed and armored, and all being tossed about like tin soldiers. There were clatters and crashes as gun belts and shock vests banged against walls. In the center of the fracas, and the cause of it, was a tremendous brute of a man. He was locked into cuffs, his arms pinned behind his back. He was also well outnumbered, but clearly none of this mattered to him. Even the slam of the outer door and the clanging of its lock didn't discourage him from gnashing at the nearest guard with the only weapon he had—his teeth.

Well, actually, he had his amazingly bullish size as well. He was easily double the size of any one of those guards, the straining of the arms locked behind him flexing an impressive display of muscle. He growled out a shout, then another, fighting his captivity tooth and nail. However, Ambrea couldn't escape the feeling that he was playing with them, toying with the men and women milling around him trying to get him under control. The thought made her smile a little. He threw back his head and howled, his golden hair gleaming with sweat at its short ends. At some point he had lost the better part of his shirt, baring his chest and those massive arms, showing off the distention of the veins in his neck and, more distinctly, his biceps. Not to mention the tattoos that ringed them. One was very obviously a Tari tribal tattoo.

"Bad luck for you, my friend," she whispered.

Tarians were not very welcome in Allay. The IM charter prevented any world or state from closing its borders to members of another world or state, but it was another one of Allay's poorly kept secrets that they looked on Tarians as little more than savages. They were treated in such a way that Allay was not exactly considered a hot destination spot for Tari vacationers. This was the first time Ambrea had ever laid eyes on a Tarian . . . at least that she could remember. It was hard not to fear him as he savagely knocked about the gaolers. However, that fear was laced with a strange sort of excitement that doubled her heartbeat. He was clearly savage, yes, but in spite of that she found him strangely erotic, strangely compelling. Her skin turned unusually warm over her entire body, and the most peculiar sensation of discomforting heat flooded through her. Discomforting, but not wholly unpleasurable. The understanding made her blush, and she ought to have moved away and composed herself; however, she did not. She couldn't seem to pull her attention from the flex of fine muscles and the sculpture of a truly exquisite male body.

But then he looked up at her as he struggled, bumping and dumping those who tried to hold him. The moment he met her eyes, the corner of his lips drew up on one side, and amusement bled into his russet eyes. Part of her was afraid that he was somehow aware of her inappropriate thoughts toward him, but just the same Ambrea couldn't help smiling back. He was, she had to admit, very handsome. With angular cheekbones and a rugged squareness to his jaw, he appeared roughly beautiful. The way his gaze held hers was stunning, and it felt as though he could see her in her entirety, straight through the solid door that kept her bound to her cell. Her hands reflexively came to her shoulders, her arms crossing her chest and protecting the racing heart that thundered beneath her breast.

But she wasn't repulsed or offended. Just connected in a way she had not felt before. In a way that was utterly ridiculous. He was a stranger. A random, beastly man. She should not be feeling like this.

Perhaps it was because he was fighting so hard for his

freedom, she thought. She very much understood how he was feeling as he was faced with the notorious wet rooms. Were she as big and strong as he was, she too would have fought tooth and nail against being brought into that place. Every time he threw off one of the guards, she wanted to cheer him on. It took everything she had not to shout out.

Then one of the guards got a clean shot with a stunner, and that big body jolted in pain and surprise. Anybody else would have hit the floor in a mewling ball of discombobulated pain, but not this Tarian. Instead he turned to the gunner and gave him the coldest, deadliest look that Ambrea had ever seen. It even outstripped those that her father and uncle had given *her*. Probably because their power had been an ephemeral thing, whereas this prisoner's power was far more tactile and all but bounced off the walls.

"Come try that again, squirt," the beast goaded the gaoler.

The young gaoler looked as though someone had just stripped him naked and thrust him into Blossom Square. He was still armed, still aiming the weapon straight at the prisoner, but his hands and body were shaking fiercely, and Ambrea wouldn't have been surprised to see him standing in a puddle of his own wet any second now.

Fortunately for the frightened guard, his compatriots were not as scared. They began to take aim at the prisoner in twos and then, when that had no effect, in threes.

"Surely not even a Tarian can withstand three stunners at once," Suna whispered. But the tone of her voice was eager and delighted. She, just like Ambrea, wanted to see the Tarian kick them all straight to the Great Being's doorstep.

But there was truth to what Suna said. Stunners attacked the nervous system, discharging jolts into it that disrupted the electrical impulses of the nerves. Not even a savage Tarian could shake off that kind of disruption. When three stuns filled his body with electricity all at once, there was nothing he could do to withstand it. He staggered at last and fell to his knees, cussing in a garbled sort of way when he couldn't even think straight enough to form words.

Ambrea hated to see him fall. It made her sad in a way that her own imprisonment had not been able to do. She leaned closer to the bars and could imagine she could smell the out-of-doors and the wild places of Tari on him, not this endless wet mustiness she knew too well. She saw the clench of his jaw, the ticking fury of what had to be an incredible amount of frustration. He was looking directly up at her again, so she clearly saw him make a conscious decision to stop fighting. His big body relaxed, even went limp. Strange, she thought, that it wasn't already both of those things after being hit with three stunners. Sure, at the time of the stun all the muscles tensed up, and then immediately following would go lax when all normal impulse in the body disrupted the ability to flex or contract, but this was afterward by a good twenty seconds. It was clear to her that he went lax because he had decided to do so.

Oh, to be so powerful a man, Ambrea thought with no little envy. She had seen some strong, dogged women in her time, even female fighters who could excel beyond some of their male counterparts, but not a man like this. This giant was something Ambrea could only dream of being in another lifetime. She was willing to bet there were few others who could push him around or tell him what to do. He was, no doubt, in command of his own destiny.

Although, she realized wryly, he had still managed to end up in exactly the same place she was.

She watched as they quickly bundled him up into a

cell only a couple of doors down and across from hers. They were afraid to give him too much time to recover by bringing him down deeper into the wet rooms. That was how the Tarian managed to spare himself the Allay torture chambers, for the time being anyway. Perhaps that had been the method to his seemingly wild madness. Perhaps that had been the source of that playful smile he had shared with her.

She wondered what his crime had been. Had he crossed a line legitimately, or had his tattooed arm and chest made a mark of him, goading the Blossom City guards into fabricating charges or provoking him into breaking city law? Still, not every common criminal or trespasser was given the inestimable experience of the wet rooms. Usually it was an experience reserved for those of higher rank or those who crossed someone of higher rank in a political gambit.

Ambrea's curiosity ate at her, resulting in her lingering at the door long after Suna lost interest and went back to her twist-stitching. Ambrea got some amusement out of watching the guards regroup after their tussle with the Tarian brute.

"By the Great Being's ass, he was a strong son of a bitch," one noted breathlessly to another as he rubbed at a sore shoulder. "I don't know how we're expected to transfer him into the deep tunnels."

"Going to have to knock him out, I guess. Maybe the feel of three stunners will mellow him a little bit."

The eldest guard, one who was sympathetic to Ambrea's situation and had proven to be quite wise and intelligent for his position in life, just smiled and shook his head at the younger, less experienced gaolers.

"The only way to mellow out a Tarian is to kill him," he remarked. "I don't know what it's like on that planet, and frankly I don't want to know, but that hell-acre spits out some of the worst and some of the toughest prisoners I've ever dealt with. But I'll tell you this, if I was caught in a bad spot, I'd want a Tarian fighting on my side."

"They're savages," a younger guard scoffed, looking at his senior coworker as though he'd lost his mind. "Just as soon eat you as fight for you."

"Don't be ignorant," the older guard warned him with a frown. "You know all that crap about them being cannibals is just that. Crap. Don't you?"

The younger man agreed halfheartedly.

The senior guard looked Ambrea's way and noticed her at the door window. He gave her a gentle smile. "I guess for these few minutes you were actually glad to be locked safely away, great lady."

"I doubt that would ever be true," she rejoined. "I'd much rather be out amongst you fighting a Tarian than locked 'safely' away."

He inclined his head and body in respect and then followed the guards back up the stairs, where they sent a shot of daylight into the darkness before leaving the floor abandoned. Well, hardly that, since they had cameras watching every nook and cranny of it and the doors were locked with the latest security devices. Besides, she knew that the guards weren't far away. The exterior guardhouse was situated right at the mouth of the catacombs entrance. And there was only one way in or out of the wet rooms.

Even if every prisoner escaped their individual cells, the guards could lock down the catacombs at that single armored and reinforced door and wait for the mob to tire or starve to death. They could shut down all the water and food dispensers. They could completely control the climate.

No one had ever successfully escaped the wet rooms, and no one ever would. Not even the brutish Tarian. Once they'd dumped him down those stairs, fighting for escape was a lost cause. Perhaps he wasn't aware of that. Perhaps he hadn't cared one way or another. He didn't look as though he was much impressed by those finer details.

Before long, Ambrea's persistence at the door paid off. The Tarian male stuck his face against the small aperture in his own door and began to look up and down the tunnel. Then he looked across to her and that smile came back, crinkling the corners of his eyes. She noticed then just how tan he was, as though he had spent a great deal of time under a hot sun. She imagined him to be from the plainslands of the planet Tari, where the only true savages might remain. Most Tarians actually came from the clannish space platforms. Like stepping-stones, these colonies were each successively farther away from the actual planet of Tari but still in the same orbit. The closer to the actual vastness of space, the wealthier the platform was, since space traders preferred to go the shortest distance with their goods and found the external colony the easiest to trade with. The goods would then be marked up and would filter from platform to platform, each step adding its own tariff, until by the time they reached planetside it was impossible to afford anything.

This was why Tarian natives on the actual planet—"true Tarians" they liked to call themselves—tended to live nontechnological lives and lived solely off the natural products of the planet. However, it also meant living without modern medicines and food cultivators, which left crops vulnerable to common blights and the ravages of insects and animals, and the populace vulnerable to the devastation of the simplest of diseases. It was said that a true Tarian never left his homeworld in his entire lifetime, so a true Tarian could not be found anywhere but on the planet Tari.

That meant that in the eyes of his own people, this Tarian was no longer "true."

"Hey Blue Eyes," he greeted her, his voice sounding like a rolling rumble. His tone made it easy to imagine him riding a djit beast bareback over vast rolling prairies, his body bare and painted in tribal patterns. He would not be a simple farmer. No. She imagined him as nothing else but a warrior in defense of his own tribe. "Can't imagine what you did to earn a stay in the emperor's famous wet rooms."

The guttural vibration of his accent made him almost impossible to understand, but in a few moments she caught on. Unlike most people her age on Ulrike, she had not been fitted with a standard translator in her preadolescence. Such things were expensive, and her father had seen to it that she couldn't afford the standard tool. Even if she could have afforded it she imagined she would have been forbidden to get one. The more she was isolated from others, including alien others and outside sources of information or media, the more crippled she would be. He figured it would keep her from hearing what other worlds thought of Allay, or keep her from petitioning others for help.

"I'm here because I was born," she answered him wryly. She sighed and leaned her forehead into the cold metal of her door. "I'm willing to bet you could say the same. Tarian's are not treated well when they come to Allay."

"Aye," he agreed, momentarily curling his lip. "But I don't imagine I helped things much by being caught smuggling a wee bit of this and that into the country."

A wee bit of this and that? "There isn't much outlawed in trade in Allay," she mused aloud. "Certainly not much that would be considered enough of an infraction to earn you imprisonment in the catacombs." But there *was* one thing. "Unless you're a Delran smuggler."

The supposition made him smile, and she felt her heart clench with a sudden rush of excitement. The one thing the emperor of old and, very likely, the emperor of new tried to keep a tight grip on was the entrance and exit of Delran platinum through the Allay borders. Delran platinum, mined most successfully and in the most abundance on Tari, was the most expensive and valuable metal in all the Three Worlds. And although it was the most beautiful decorative metal, known for its easy malleability and subsequent strength after being heated, it was also the most conductive and most widely used in just about any and all technology. To control the flow of Delran platinum was to control every single industry in Allay. In a complex series of trade agreements, tariffs, and controlled avenues of import and export, the royal house managed to earn a sumly portion of every Delran platinum purchase that took place.

Unless, of course, it was being smuggled into the continent and completely bypassing all federal fees. Under her father's rule it was an offense punishable by public execution. An offense that the IM charter left to individual countries to adjudicate—unless, of course, that country asked for their help. Allay would never ask for that kind of help. It would open up the government to too much scrutiny—perhaps enough scrutiny to draw attention to the ways the ruling house used to dispose of its enemies.

"Allay does not take kindly to those who would take money out of its coffers."

"Its coffers are fat and overflowing enough. Meanwhile, your merchants are being tariffed into starvation. Your technology is lagging behind because it costs too pretty to make new, innovative machines."

"You sound very passionate about a land that is not your own. Far from it, in fact."

He tried to shrug it off, but she was unconvinced. "I'm just about the money, Blue Eyes. And maybe a wee bit about the danger. It's fun trying not to get caught."

"With 'trying' being the operative word. You might work more on the succeeding part."

That made him chuckle, whereas another man might take offense at having his skills called into question.

"You might be right about that. But it's always about a weakness. Mine's always been the damsel in distress. I stopped to help a woman in need and it turned out she was a damn cop. That should teach me a lesson. Next time, I won't fall for a pretty face asking for help."

"There won't be a next time," Ambrea scoffed. "You'll be sentenced to death. And apparently whatever it was you were doing was enough to earn your being held in the country's most notoriously inescapable prison, so you might put escape out of your head if that's something you're hoping for."

"Ah. You're a real cup-half-empty kinda girl, now aren't you? Are you an expert on this place? How long have you been in here? You have some color to your skin and face, so you haven't been underground that long."

"This time, only a couple of weeks, I think. Time moves so differently in here, and they don't exactly give us a clock to watch. Not unless they want us to watch it. It can be hard on you to see the minutes of your life slowly ticking away, or the moment of your execution quickly ticking toward you."

"This time? You've been in and out of here before?"

Ambrea exhaled long and slowly. She didn't feel like discussing her periods of incarceration. It was better not to think about it. It would only depress her. If she let her mood flag, it would make it easier for her uncle to weaken her. In a low moment, she might end up throwing it all away.

She liked to think she would never do that. That she was stronger than that. That she cared too much for the future of her country. But interminable darkness and wetness and having all your rights stripped away for no apparent reason other than the question of your birthright—it could wear on a person's spirit. Honestly, she didn't know how Suna could bear it. How she could volunteer for it. Perhaps it made it easier, her knowing that at any time she could just get up and walk away. Then again, so could Ambrea. All it would take is a signature and a retinal scan.

"Once you're here for any length of time, it seems as though you are here forever. It never leaves you. I don't think there is any such thing as freedom from this place."

"I think that it's all in the strength of your mind," he said with a sudden soft seriousness, his eyes penetrating through the dimness and distance between them. It even seemed as though his accent lightened up and he spoke very clearly to her. "And whether or not you are willing to give up. Are you the sort to give up easily?"

She felt a flash of anger. He was talking about things he didn't understand. Give up easily? Her whole lifetime had been about struggling to survive. She had fought for it in one way or another ever since her mother's death when she'd been four. She was bone weary from it. But if he had any idea of who she was and what she had put up with, then maybe he wouldn't be questioning if she were a quitter.

"I've never quit. I'll never quit. There's far more than my well-being at stake. It wouldn't be right for me to just throw it all away and look for an easy out."

And that was when she realized she would never sign that renunciation. She had questioned herself, had toyed with the idea, had gone back and forth about it in her head as she spent these hours pacing a dark, wet cell and staring her potential death in the eye. But when it came down to it, she would never give up on what was rightfully hers.

But neither would she sink to her brother's level and

do him any kind of harm. It would be up to fate to play out the cards that each of them held.

Unfortunately, in her passion, she forgot about the cameras watching them. It was one thing for her uncle to keep her alive when he thought prison might soften her resolve, might encourage her to sign the renunciation, but if he watched the passion in her declaration to this other prisoner, he might realize just how futile that hope was and be forced to take more drastic measures.

"I shouldn't speak to you anymore," she said to him, and went to push away from the door.

"Wait a second there now, Blue Eyes!" The call made her hesitate, and she leaned back into the window so she could see him.

"Yes?"

"I was just noticing, you're not like the rest of your people. You talk to me like I'm a person. Not an idiot or some dumb hunk of brutish muscle."

"We're all equal in here," she said softly. "I can't say how I would have acted if we'd met on the street."

"You're terribly honest. Even when it makes you look bad. You shouldn't ever go into politics."

She gave him a wry little laugh. "There isn't much I can do about that."

"And hand in hand with your honesty are your cryptic comments. You're intriguing as well as pretty. Clearly a damsel in distress. You're my downfall in a perfect package."

"Only I don't expect you to rescue me. Rescue would be a fool's effort."

"Call me a fool then," he said sotto voce.

CHAPTER THREE

She barely heard him, but when it became clear what he meant, she felt her entire body clench with a combination of dread and exhilaration. She felt it well up in such a way that she was ready to burst with questions, wanted to demand he clarify, but they both knew that she could not ask any more than he could answer. All she could do was reach up a hand to grip the cold steel bar crossing the window. She watched as he reached into his mouth and, with a chilling pop, yanked out his tooth. Only it wasn't a tooth. It was white and encapsulated and close to the shape of a tooth, but the bloodlessness of the extraction and the way he snapped it in half told her it wasn't a tooth and he wasn't performing random dentistry on himself.

She wanted to call for Suna, but the less attention she drew, the better. Great Being, was she actually entertaining the idea of the impossible? No. It was insane.

He disappeared behind his door for a second and then he was back.

"Back away. I don't want you to get hit."

Hit?

She did as instructed, but only to the edge of the distance that still allowed her to see out the window. Ambrea almost jumped out of her skin when a violent bang echoed into the hallway. She leapt forward toward the door instantly afterward, ignoring Suna's exclamation of surprise. She could hardly believe her eyes when she saw that the locking mechanism had been completely blown out of his door. He kicked at the door, and only then did she realize that during their conversation earlier he had been working his way out of the cuffs they'd left on him. How had he done that? The electronic bracers were notoriously hard to decode, never mind doing so with your hands behind your back. His kick was resounding, the locking panel flying off the door and crashing into the opposite wall. He didn't hesitate. He came straight to her door and then reached down to pull a seemingly decorative stripe off his pant leg. He carefully and quickly shaped the stripe around her lock.

"Back away, Princess. You've got five seconds."

"And in three they'll be pouring through the door," she said as heart-choking panic began to grab at her. She couldn't take part in this! Not in any way! When he was captured, and he *would* be captured, her uncle and brother would cite her escape attempt as proof positive of treasonous intent. For all she knew, that's what all this was. A huge setup to coax her into doing that one thing they needed to justify giving her a death sentence.

And yet, like some kind of numb soldier, she stepped away from the door, grabbing hold of Suna's arm and preventing her from going to the door to look out and see what the noise was all about. Coldness walked down Ambrea's spine. He'd called her "Princess." Though she had not identified herself, he knew who she was. Any ideas she might have that he was a random smuggler making a random escape attempt with a total stranger were utterly dismissed. He had come for her. He had purposely allowed them to catch him, to bring him down into this hole, to attack and shock him. He had orchestrated all of his behavior so they would place him on the top level, the level where she was being held.

Then he had been forced to act quickly, she realized, for they were not going to let a Tarian remain in the upper levels for long. They would want to move him down and away from her.

Although the explosion around her lock was far more shaped and controlled, it also sheared it off completely from the rest of the door, as if someone had punched a hole through it and left burnt edges. The lock dropped to the ground with a clang. The Tarian shoved through the doorway, his bulky frame too big for it, forcing him to duck under to keep from hitting his head. Then he reached out one of those massive paws he called a hand, the palm raised upward as if he were the most refined gentleman asking to escort the heiress of Allay onto a dance floor. The idea of it on such a rough man was, of course, ludicrous. As was the idea of her willingly putting her hand in his, and effectively signing her own death warrant.

The Tarian saw her hesitate, saw her entire body draw back in fear, although by only a minute movement.

"One day you're going to have to cross the line, Princess," he said quietly, his eyes a deeply intense amber, an overall tinge of rose making them seem so rich and surprisingly beautiful. It was almost like looking into a warm, moving golden flame instead of the fiery orange that one might expect. His eyes were steady on hers as his accent lightened again by half. "You're going to have to take action to get what you want. To claim what's rightfully yours. Why not take that action today?"

"Ambrea, no!" Suna gasped, her shock at what was happening finally wearing off. "You'll never make it out of here! If you do, you'll be a fugitive! They'll kill you on sight." She must have realized she was sounding hysterical, so she ratcheted down her fear and narrowed her eyes on the Tarian. "What if it's a trick?"

"And what if it's the solution you've been looking for?" he countered.

"Who sent you?" Suna demanded, puffing herself up and pushing between the two of them as if her tiny stature could do anything to stop the Tarian. "This is Balkin's plotting, isn't it?"

"Nothing I say will convince you otherwise," he said quietly, meeting Ambrea's gaze once again. "Ask yourself one question." He paused for a beat, a significant beat considering the jeopardy they were in. "Ask yourself, 'Why has no one come through that outer door yet?'."

That was when it sank into Ambrea's head just how unhurriedly he had done everything so far. And he had done it with such a quiet, knowing confidence. He wasn't alone. This wasn't a random, impulsive act at all but something well thought out and well planned. So far it was well executed, but she could tell by the way he briefly glanced down the tunnel that they were quickly losing whatever advantage he felt they had. Had he been completely unworried, she would have known that this was something of Balkin's staging. But although there was no denying his steady confidence, it was clear that time was ticking away in his mind.

What if he was right? What if this was her one and only chance to do something? To commit herself to her course? She was always thinking about how it would have to happen one day. What if that day, that moment, was right now and here? Even if she refused to take action against her brother, refused to throw the country of Allay into a civil war that made the people choose between siblings, she could at least escape the oppression of her long life of captivity. She wouldn't be turning her back on Allay for good—she didn't have the heart to do that—and she wouldn't be signing away all of her rights to a throne she felt in her soul belonged to her, but she would be taking a step of strength. A step toward freedom. A step where she was putting her foot down and saying to all who watched that she refused to be treated this way any longer.

Ambrea turned away from him quickly, leaping for the devotional book resting on her cot and her mother's picture within. She pressed the worn leather cover to her lips, the smell of it reassuring and comforting. Most carried around the thin, lightweight VidPads these days, the pocket-sized things resistant to wearing and aging and able to be used for multiple purposes rather than just containing Scriptures. But this had been from her nursery, from back when her mother had been alive. From back when she had been a fully entitled princess and had been treated as her birthright had demanded she be treated. Even now she recalled her mother coming to her bedside at night and reading from the beautiful, thoughtful stories in the book. The night she'd been packed off into exile, she was told she could take a single favorite toy, and this book had been her choice.

She wasn't about to leave it behind now. Not when she most needed the Great Being to look after her. Not when she needed her mother's attention from wherever she was in the Great Beyond to focus on her and get her safely through this.

She turned to face the Tarian, whose presence seemed to overflow the tiny cell that had before been adequate enough for the two smaller women. Ambrea lifted her hand and placed it in his. She drew a soft little breath when she felt him snatch her up tight in his grip, the hard calluses of his palm so coarse and overwhelming compared to the simple softness of her own hand. His palm swallowed her entire hand, and she became immediately aware of the heat of his skin and the kinetic strength and power she had just turned herself over to.

It somehow strengthened her decision, and she turned to look at Suna.

"Are you coming?"

Suna snorted at that. "Or get left behind and hung as a traitor in lieu of my mistress? Do I seem daft to you?"

"Ladies, we must move with haste now."

Ambrea let him draw her out of the cell. Her heart thudded with a mixture of fear of what could happen next and the thrill of shaking off that damp, miserable hole.

Neither anticipation would prove worthwhile. To her shock, he drew her past the outer doors and the promise of daylight, and instead guided her into the guard elevator. He latched the door and rapidly yanked out the control panel and began to rewire it, whistling all the while as if he were busily going about a day's work and didn't have a worry on his soul. She tried to let his attitude infect her, especially when the elevator jolted into movement, and she tried not to question him when it was clear he had a distinctive plan in mind.

"We're going deeper into the wet rooms," she noted ridiculously after a moment, trying hard not to make it sound as though she was questioning his judgment, and just as hard not to make the observation sound as stupidly obvious as it was.

His only reply was to give her that half-baked smile again and touch it off with a mischievous lift of both brows.

"I'm going to need you to keep quiet for a moment," he instructed her as the elevator slowed to a stop on the lowest level. "And if you could just take a little step backward." He nudged her toward the wall on the right, and her back touched the cold metal planking just as the doors hissed open.

"Freeze!"

The command was followed with the cock and whine

of what seemed like a half-dozen stunners at once, all of them pointing into the elevator. *Of course*, she realized. The guards on the lower levels had been alerted by the cameras to their unauthorized access to the elevator. All the guards had to do was sit and wait for them to come to them. Dismay and dread sank deep into her gut. What had she been thinking? She'd been out of her mind to attempt the impossible and to trust a total stranger. She had just thrown away her entire life.

And then he was bull-rushing the entire lot of them, yanking two of them into the elevator by the muzzles of their guns so hard that they were pulled right off their feet. They passed so close to Ambrea that one of the gaoler's gun belts snagged the skirt of her gown for an instant. And then both guards were planted face-first into the metal planking at the rear of the elevator so hard that the distressed pinging of the metal echoed loudly all around them. Blood streaked the shiny surface as the men collapsed unconscious at Suna's and Ambrea's feet.

Meanwhile the Tarian had toppled three other men outside the lift, and before they had finished hitting the ground he had disarmed another and used that gaoler's stunner on the final standing guard. Then he methodically cranked up the stunner to its most painful setting and shot every guard left conscious. The setting was brutally painful, but it was also the most expedient way of robbing them of consciousness without doing them further lasting physical harm. The memory of the pain would last only about as long as the pain itself before they were completely out.

Ambrea was speechless at his efficiency and speed, but also grateful that he was not going to subject the gaolers to undue violence. After the way he'd been stunned, she might have thought he would extract some kind of revenge. But perhaps, she thought as she read his enigmatic smile, stunning them back at such a high level was its own satisfaction.

"My lady," he said politely as he reached into the elevator to help her pick her way over the carpet of fallen men. He had hooked the stunner's strap over his shoulder and kept it aimed down the corridor. "How much are you willing to bet they sent every last guard on the floor here at once?"

"I wouldn't take that bet," she hedged.

"Neither would I," he agreed cheerfully. He made sure that she and Suna were both out of the elevator and heading down the right-hand tunnel. Then he paused to yank the unconscious men, two at a time, several feet down the corridor to the left. He pulled at another stripe on his pant leg, bent to slap it onto the floor of the lift, and then strung it over the saddle of the elevator door and all the way across to the opposite wall. He straightened and then herded them ahead of himself and quickly to the right.

The explosion followed immediately after, but they were already around the next bend in the tunnel. Still, it was easy for Ambrea to imagine the elevator being blown out of use and perhaps the tunnel collapsing at their backs. If that were the case, they wouldn't have to worry about anyone coming up behind them.

Clearly that was the Tarian's intention, because he kept all of his focus straight ahead of them, moving from one side of the corridor to the other like a pacing Hutha lion, a gigantic wilderness cat from Ebbany that easily outweighed and out-bulked the man in question. It wasn't lost on her that he was keeping his big body between her and any potential dangers that might pop up.

They were truly in the worst section of the wet rooms now. The lighting down on this level was below substandard and not at all dependable. It flickered if it worked at all, the electrical connections buzzing unsteadily and noisily. Every last wall gleamed with wetness, small rivers having formed at the creases where the walls met the floors. All the tunnels graded downward, so the water was running that way as well. There were the telltale squeaks of hair rats, and before long the creatures were dashing side to side over their feet and under her skirt. Everything in her wanted to scream at the idea of the filthy rodents coming near her, but she was even more afraid of further two-legged dangers than she was of the four-legged ones, so she swallowed her would-be cries and danced quickly around the vile little creatures. She assumed that Suna was equally determined because her companion didn't bat an eye, pausing only to kick one of the critters off her shoe with such violence that they heard it smack into the wet wall.

They met no further human intervention, however. That didn't surprise her because the tunnel they had chosen was clearly unused and had fallen into heavy disrepair. Furniture littered the hallway where it had been shoved out of the way into temporary or permanent storage.

It began to rain as they moved deeper into the bowels of the catacombs, the walls so wet that the ceilings dripped heavily. The small rivers on either side of them now melded into one large one. Before long their feet were entirely under water.

Ambrea couldn't take it any longer. She had to know.

"Where are we going? How can we possibly escape this way?"

That earned her a smile that wasn't exactly directed toward her and wasn't exactly not, either. It was hard to tell in the increasing darkness and with all of his attention facing forward.

"What do you see around you, Blue Eyes?"

She was being baited. She decided to bite. What else did she have on her plate at that moment?

"Darkness. Cold. Wet."

"And it smells like some of those hair rats have died down here, too," Suna joined in. Ambrea didn't correct her about that being a smell, not something she could actually see, as he had requested.

"Wet. A lot of wet. And it's all going in the same direction," he noted. "Makes you wonder why these tunnels don't all just fill up and drown out every last room, doesn't it?"

It was such a simple point, one she ought to have considered on her own. She was smart enough for that. Unfortunately, she wasn't exactly functioning in her comfort zone.

"The aqueducts. Allay is made up of solid bedrock with natural aqueducts networking through it. The aqueducts are probably what formed all of these lower tunnels. They bored through the stone over many thousands of years and have changed their path over time. When the upper tunnels were originally dug out for the catacombs, the workers stumbled onto the lower tunnels and decided to connect all of the tunnels. But the pressure of the aqueducts all around them and the coldness of the water is why the walls are constantly wet down here and why they can never be made warm enough no matter what kind of technology is tried to regulate it."

"Not that the gaolers are interested in the comfort of their guests or anything," Suna noted dryly.

"More likely it was an effort to make the guards more comfortable. Can't imagine many people lining up to volunteer at working the catacombs," the Tarian mused.

"This is the duty you get when you're new and just starting to make an impression on your superiors, or older and having screwed up at your last posting," said Ambrea.

"At least that's the case under the current regime," the Tarian noted.

And that was when they stumbled into foot-deep water. It rapidly became knee high and then mid-thigh as they took a few more steps. The Tarian shouldered his stunner and then looked around.

He closed his eyes for a moment, almost as if he were doing an internal check of his own brain. Then he pointed down a right-hand branch of the tunnel.

"This way," he said.

"How are you so sure?" Suna demanded suddenly as she gripped the skirt of her sodden day dress. "It's only going to get deeper, and I hate to break it to you, but I can't swim. This is a bad idea. A bad idea all around. You should never have let him lead you away like this, Ambrea!"

"Hush, Suna," Ambrea scolded, in spite of being riddled with doubts herself. The fact was, she had thrown all-in with this man, and she had no choice now but to play the hand she had through to the end. Griping about doubting her choices wouldn't help any of them now.

"Look at it this way," the Tarian said with a smile that touched coldly in his eyes. "No one else is going to think you've survived this any more than you think you're going to survive it."

He had a chilling point.

The right-hand tunnel was also so full of water that the lighting had long since shorted out. Debris floated darkly on the surface. Ambrea knew it would be impossible to see. Tarians were reputed to have keen eyesight, but she imagined he would be unable to make out anything any better than she could.

He moved forward, reaching to grasp Suna by her upper arm, effectively controlling the only factor he must feel he had unsatisfactory control over. Ambrea didn't know if she should be insulted or not by the idea that he was confident she would follow him like a meek little sheep. In any event, what choice did she have? He was the one in control of all this. The one with a plan. A plan he didn't think was necessary to share with the two of them.

But she wasn't a meek little sheep.

Was she? That she had spent an entire lifetime obeying all the rules that her father had imposed on her did not make her meek. She'd truly had no choice. She would have been long dead if she'd done anything else.

But now was not the time for her to inspect her possible shortcomings. The water was quickly becoming breast high and was bitterly cold. Her teeth began to chatter. She would have wrapped her arms around herself to conserve her body warmth, but there was so much debris in the water that she had to constantly push her way through and around it. As it was, it was banging into her the moment she released one piece to grab for another. She would be pretty bruised come the morrow.

Provided there even was a tomorrow.

She didn't want to think so fatalistically. At least now the water was cool and clean. It was washing away a world of sins and stink from her body. After appeasing herself with that silver lining, she tried to play a game with herself in the darkness, attempting to identify what each item in her way was or once had been. Most of it was furniture or bundles of wiring, its insulation making the metal float.

"Stop."

His command was so sudden—disturbing the almost rhythmic quiet of moving through water and the sound of their own breathing that had descended on them, that she startled and lost her footing on the slick floor under her feet. She went completely under. The moment she did so the panic she had been pushing aside all this time came bubbling to the surface. She became completely disoriented, unable to figure out which way was upward because the water was too dark to see even an air bubble rise. She thrust out both hands, forcing herself not to open her mouth and scream again as she had when she'd first gone under. The water was only a few feet deep. How could she feel so lost?

Suddenly a bright orange light streaked through the dark water. The brilliance of it was fast and fierce, blinding in its intensity. Then she felt a strong hand locking onto her arm, dragging her sharply to the surface, where everything was just as dark as ever. Still there was nowhere to put her feet down. Through water-filled ears she heard Suna crying out for her, understanding that she and the Tarian had traveled quite a distance from her companion. That was when Ambrea realized there was a powerful current in the water, one that was even stronger now that she had no foothold and they had come so much farther into the tunnel. The current dragged on her so powerfully that she was certain, had it not been for that hand on her arm, she would have been swept away.

"Hold on to me," he instructed calmly, pulling her arm up and around his big neck.

Ambrea had never been so grateful for the warmth of another body. In truth, it was a terribly unfamiliar sensation. No one ever had or, she imagined, ever would touch her with such familiarity. She was a princess of the blood, whether she was approved of or not, and no one was allowed to touch her in such a way, nor would they even think of doing so. The last person to touch her so fully had been, she realized, her mother. She remembered her mother hugging her brutally hard because, Ambrea now knew, they had been about to take Junessa away to the wet rooms, from where she had never returned. Perhaps this was the real reason why Ambrea felt such suffocating dread whenever a command was handed down that sent her to the catacombs. The catacombs' reputation had begun for her long before her first childhood incarceration.

But the Tarian did not give Ambrea any chance to dissemble about the familiarity in his handling of her, nor did she want to as her heart raced with fear. If she had been cold before, now she was freezing. The cold, wet weight of her hair dragged behind her in the water as he hoisted her up against his chest, seating her backside onto his forearm and guiding her legs around his thick waist. Her skirt was wrapped around her thighs and she was still submerged up to her chin, but clearly he had his feet on the floor of the tunnel and was pushing against the current to bring them back to Suna.

"For the love of Kintara, will you stop screaming?" he bellowed down the tunnel. "Would you draw them a map to find us?" He spit out water. "You'd best hold on tighter than that," he warned Ambrea.

She awkwardly tried to do so, but she was hyperconscious of how close in contact they were. She didn't care about propriety in these circumstances, but it just felt so alien, as did the strength of his radiating body warmth. On the one hand she wanted it because she was about to shake out of her own skin with the coldness of it all. On the other hand there was something so indelibly strange about being this close to him. The heat he exuded was only part of it. It was the peculiar burning sensation from within herself that truly baffled her. She had never felt anything like it before, and it was overwhelming. She went hot with a blush, feeling embarrassed without knowing exactly why.

"I'm s-s-sorry," she shuddered, fumbling at his wet, bare shoulders. His skin was so slick, and he had done away with the stunner apparently in his bid to come after her, so she couldn't find the strap to hang on to.

"Like this," he instructed, making her lock both hands together at the base of his neck.

And just like that she was able to settle down against him. She was amazed that he wasn't shivering as much as she was, or maybe she couldn't feel it because she was shaking so hard herself. Maybe the fact was that everyone was tougher and more stoic than she was.

"I thank you," she thought to say. For years she had been punished for thanking anyone of lower rank, but once her governess had been taken from her and after her first incarceration, she had been in charge of her own household. She had felt more and more compelled over the years to be grateful to those who served her. Especially when they did so in spite of her being in arrears of their payroll for months, once even as long as a year. In those times she had fed and housed those servants and their families, selling her Delran platinum plate and jewelry to do so. She had been indebted to them for their loyalty and services. The least she could do was thank them for those services.

This man had just saved her life. Of this she had no doubt. It remained to be seen what his motives were for everything else he had done. But she at least owed him thanks for his rescue of her.

"You'll be warm soon," he promised her.

"It feels like I'll never be warm again," she confessed.

"Are you calling me a liar?"

"Oh! No!" She was horrified for a moment until she realized he was teasing her. *How did he do it*, she wondered. How did he remain so calm and at ease given the circumstances?

"You should be an old pro at this," he noted as he pushed them through the water.

"Old pro?"

"Cold and wet. You've been in here for long periods

of time before. I hear that's what it's like. So cold and wet that you feel like you'll never be warm."

"Which I suppose makes all of this worse. I wasn't warm to start with. I've been in here at least a week or two."

"Much longer than that," he corrected her. He couldn't see her surprised look, but he must have somehow sensed it. "Time goes by differently when you're imprisoned, remember?"

She didn't ask him how he knew how long she'd been there, or how he knew she'd been there for long stretches before. He would tell her everything in his own time, she imagined. All she could do was go along for the ride until she decided it was no longer in her best interest.

"I should think you might want to give me your name. I ought to at least know the name of the man who has come to my rescue."

"Everyone calls me Ender."

"Ender? Why?"

"Because I put an end to things. You could say I'm really good at getting the last word."

She believed him.

They began to draw up to Suna, the water level dropping and allowing her to get back on her feet. He gripped Ambrea firmly by her backside and drew her away from himself and onto her feet. He thought nothing of it, whereas Ambrea could only squeak out a sound of surprise and shock. His hand was gone in a second, but the feel of its intimacy was the only warm spot on her body, and it lingered. His hand was so big that his fingers had reached all the way between her legs to her private places, albeit through the layers of her sodden clothes. So why did it feel as though those cold, wet clothes hadn't even existed? She was so shaken by that and everything else that she almost lost her footing again. But he made sure he kept hold of her elbow and set her steady in a second.

"We've been in the water much too long," he told them brusquely. "Hypothermia is already setting in. You're already losing control of your limbs and probably your reasoning. We've got to get out of here quickly. Besides, there's still a chance we're being pursued, although I find it highly unlikely."

"Well, where exactly are we supposed to go? It's not like I see an exit sign," Suna said with a sarcasm that even overreached what she was usually capable of.

"In lieu of that, will you accept this?"

He calmly pointed to a shadow in the upper curve of the tunnel. At this level the tunnels were untouched by man. They were purely part of the aqueduct system that nature had wrought. What he was pointing to looked like a hole, a smaller tunnel perhaps that had once fed water into the one they were in. The duct had since gone dry, or at least as dry as anything down there could get. As she looked up, Ambrea could feel heavy drops like rain falling onto her from the tunnel above them.

"And how are we supposed to get up there?" Suna wanted to know, her tone surly and tired all at once.

Ender didn't take it personally from what Ambrea could see. She watched as he closed his eyes again and tilted his head, as if he were listening to his own thoughts for a moment.

"Step back," he instructed Ambrea a moment later, laying a hand on her chest and guiding her gently back a few steps.

There was a sudden explosion of sparks, and then light from the tunnel. A heavy ladder made of rope unfurled and dropped into the water in front of the would-be empress of Allay.

CHAPTER
FOUR

Rush "Ender" Blakely handed the heir of Allay up to his commander, Bronse Chapel. He didn't let go of her until he was certain she was settled snugly in the belay harness they were going to use to pull her up and out of the long tunnel to the surface. He yanked the straps up tight, making sure they fit snugly to her backside and kept her fastened in at the crotch. Bronse worked from his position above to tighten a chest strap around her so she wouldn't turn or flip over once she was in the process of being hauled to the surface. There wasn't much room to move in there, and even a skinny little thing like Ambrea could become jammed if she didn't head up straight and steady.

They had used a sonic worm to bore a connecting tunnel from the surface, a campsite they had specifically chosen in the deep forested preserve that ran completely around the walls of Blossom City. Using geo sonar to map through the solid bedrock, they had found this unused aqueduct and tracked exactly how to connect from the deep tunnels to the surface and what it would take to make an exit route out of them. A fast exit at that. And a relatively hastily put together plan.

The sonic worm they'd used had been blessedly silent, devouring all the rock and silt and using the minerals found within to power itself as it dug a hole just wide enough to lower a large man down, or to pull a very important woman up.

Rush backtracked down the ladder and waited in the water with the other girl, the annoying one with the big mouth. Actually, he could appreciate her need to question everything, perhaps even more than the princess's lack of confrontation. But he made no snap judgments about the heiress of Allay. She had found herself in dire circumstances, even more dire than she had realized, he was sure, and after being locked down in the dark like this she was surely not functioning at her stellar best.

He was impressed with her calm, however. She had truly been stoic, no complaints and no shrill, squealing behaviors as he had anticipated from her before this mission had begun. Rush had had his doubts about being the one to go into the prison, but his commander, as usual, had been right. His size had made a good deal of difference in the operation. As had his heritage. Outside of the differences in his bone structure and the lighter touches of racial coloring that could be easily dismissed as being from anywhere here or there in the Three Worlds, the tribal tattoo on his arm had been easily recognizable for what it was. Which, he supposed, was the whole point of getting it in the first place. He wasn't ashamed to let everyone know he was from Tari. In fact, bring it on. And as Commander Chapel had anticipated, within five minutes of rolling up his sleeve in the Allay marketplace, Rush had had two city guards on his ass. Within ten minutes the count had tripled. By the time he'd reached the space dock, there'd been very obvious bait walking up to him. A woman trying to look like an average space shipper had played damsel in distress, using winning, flirtatious smiles to get herself onto his ship. Which, coincidentally, was exactly what they had wanted. When she'd snuck a peek at his illegal cargo, he had been swarmed and arrested.

The trick had been getting them to throw him in a cell on the same level as the princess, or somehow being able to quickly locate her even if they didn't. Commander Chapel had planned a tremendous distraction that would keep the exterior guards from entering again once they exited the catacombs, leaving Rush to deal with those left inside.

Fortune had also smiled on him. They'd actually tossed him in a cell across from his target. Frankly, he'd never had such a seat-of-the-pants mission go so smoothly. The only snafu had been when he'd almost lost the princess downriver. That would have sucked. Literally. The suction force of the current had almost yanked her into the aqueduct tunnel that the water was rushing into. He'd grabbed her in the nick of time. It had been a bitch fighting back against that current, though. She'd wiggled and slipped against him as if she didn't know how to hold on. He had taken it at face value and shown her how, and from then on it had been better.

Now all they had to do was complete the tricky part of the mission.

After Suna was aboveground, it was his turn to follow. He wasn't a great fan of dark, underground places, but his job seemed to take him into them a great deal lately. Still, he supposed it wasn't very different from living enclosed in a military spaceport for months at a time or even on an interplanetary flyer. Truth was, he hadn't spent much continuous time out of doors since his adolescence.

At first the lowest part of the naturally formed tunnel was plenty big enough for him to scale the walls using the crampons that Chapel had handed down to him, but the hole that the sonic borer had created was a different story. It was going to be an incredibly tight squeeze for a man his size. He trusted his team but it was unnerving to scrape so close to the walls. He envisioned himself getting stuck tightly at any moment like a cork being pushed the wrong way through the neck of a bottle.

Then he could hear the mechanical whine of the lift that they had suspended over the hole, heard it straining under his weight. They'd had to carry in equipment that broke down into camping gear, or what looked like it anyway, in order to get past the rangers at the park preserve without raising any eyebrows, and that meant the motor and braces had to be light. Light didn't translate into being recommended for his weight capacity. So they were stretching their equipment a little.

When Rush came over the lip of the hole, he wasted no time putting his hands on the edge and hoisting himself out. Good thing, too. He could smell ozone all around him, indicating that the motor of the overworked lift was burning out. He sat on the edge of the hole and looked up at his team. This part of it anyway.

He saw a mix of smiles and tension. He knew where to look, though, for a real read of the situation. That was at Chapel. The commander was tight and tense, his attention on the wooded park around them. It was true that the team and their royal prize wouldn't be safe until they were all a good long distance away. With the prison having been so obviously breached, whether or not the city guards believed them to have survived the tunnels, it wouldn't take long for the guards to start beating the bushes looking for either the princess or the group of strangers who had started the disturbance outside the guardhouse. Rush did a head count and saw that everyone who had dispatched to this stage of the mission was there. Commander Chapel; Captain Justice Muleterre, their resident pilot and a fellow Tarian; and Fallon, one of the very special Chosen Ones handpicked for this mission. Satisfied that none of them was worse for wear and there had been no casualties while he'd been off playing knight-errant, Rush stood up and wasted no time shucking off the lift harness and helping Justice and Fallon begin to break down the equipment.

As Rush threw the bits and pieces down the hole he'd just come up, he traded his attention between the forest surrounding them and the small tent tucked under the trees. He knew that was where his two charges had been brought so they could change quickly out of their sodden clothes and into something that would hopefully blend in to the Allayan mainstream. It was a minuscule help, he was sure, in the warming up that they needed, but it was the best they could do under the circumstances.

"Not too much trouble, was she?"

Rush looked over to Fallon when the notoriously silent Chosen One attempted small talk of a sort. Of all the Chosen Ones, a special group of young men and women from the wilds of Ebbany who had extraordinary powers, Fallon made him the most uncomfortable. Rush didn't like the idea that the boy could traipse around inside his thoughts at will. Rush usually did all he could to avoid him. But that had not been possible on this particular mission. It had been Fallon's powerful mind connected to his that had helped lead him through the tunnels below. Because Rush had been stripped of anything and everything that could have identified him as the soldier he was, he had been left without exterior communication and no way to find the bored-out hole they would escape through.

Except for Fallon. The young telepath, who normally despised the use of his own abilities, had proven just how valuable a team member he could be by making certain that Rush hadn't gotten lost with his charges. And now here they were, relatively safe and sound, and it hadn't been so bad after all.

"Easy enough," Rush replied gruffly. He eyed the young man with suspicion, unable to help himself. What exactly had Fallon come across while he'd been tiptoeing through his brain?

Fallon seemed to take the hint, a frown touching his lips as he moved away from Rush under the guise of busywork.

"Hey! Let's go! This isn't a fashion expo," Justice snapped out to the women in the changing tent. Clearly she didn't feel like going in there herself and preferred to harass them through the sheetlite walls. The featherlight fabric, which was dyed to match the strange blue-green foliage of the Allayan forest, weighed close to nothing and was dark enough for utter privacy from the outside world. It was also strong enough to withstand most wild animal attacks. Although it was a fabric, when an electrical current was run through it, the fabric became stiff and impenetrable. The frame supporting the sheetlite was Delran platinum, a highly conductive metal, and it was connected to a control panel that allowed just such a current to run safely through the sheetlite but not anyone who might touch it. Whether the walls were platinum hard or fabric soft, they could be heard through easily enough, and Justice's barking command had its desired effect. The imperial companion stumbled out first, followed less haphazardly by her mistress.

It amused Rush how, no matter what was thrown at her, she always seemed to radiate perfect decorum and grace. The trousers and wrapped shirt she wore were probably unlike anything she'd ever found herself in before, the clothing being the fashion of a commoner. Even imprisoned, she had been in a long, simple, elegant dress shot through with beautiful rays of Delran. Her bare feet had boasted delicately painted nails and foot jewelry, albeit they were a bit dirty from walking the unkempt floors of her catacomb cell.

He watched her struggle to tie back her hair within itself. He remembered that hair as a phenomenal, rich red when dry, with shining gold and copper penny high-lights streaked through the long, easy tendrils that reached nearly to her feet.

Shame, he thought.

Rush made his way over to her, watching her eyes go wide, like two big blue gems, as he loomed over her with his significant height. Then he reached out to grip hold of her heavy, wet hair at the midpoint and unsheathed the knife he'd brought with him. In a single stroke he ripped the blade through the mass, shearing it off. He ignored her shocked cry and walked away, tying the tail he'd retrieved into a knot and dumping it down the hole with the rest of the now-useless equipment.

"How dare you!" the one called Suna squawked, rush-ing up to him and having the audacity to smack him on the arm. He had no doubt she would have hit him in the face had she been tall enough. "How dare you lay violent hands on her most imperial majesty, you brutish pig! No one touches her without an express permission that I dare-say you will *never* earn! Do you have any idea what you've just done? You've assaulted her crowning glory! The one thing that outwardly marks her for who she is! No one in Allay may grow their hair longer than the princess!"

"It was in the way," he said with a shrug, the whole thing very obvious to him. "And if you hadn't noticed, the idea is to keep anyone from identifying her for who she is. For the time being anyway. One look at all that hair on her head and, like you said, everyone will know exactly who she is, and that she's alive. That she needs to be hunted down and gutted publicly so there will be no doubt that Ambrea Vas Allay is as dead as it gets."

The princess came around from behind her furious servant, again with all the pride and dignity she could muster settled on her long frame. Rush hadn't realized it in the press of their short acquaintance, but though the princess was a long, lean thing, she had quite the girlish curves that her court dress had done little to flatter. Come to think of it, it wasn't as though that dress had been the height of fashion. Allayan fashion was often the center of all fashion on the planet Ulrike. What the aristocracy wore in Allay set the tone for the entire world. Even over those who were famous or in power in the larger continent that Allay stood in the shadow of, also named Ulrike. But now that her majesty was in snug, comfortable, casual clothes, she looked far more the woman than she had before, in his opinion.

She looked up at him with those eyes, the ones he found to be far too big for her face and an uncanny sort of teal blue. He waited for her to throw a tantrum like Suna was doing, but instead she laid a hand on her companion's arm. It had an immediate calming effect, the servant clearly trained over many years to respond to even the smallest silent request.

"But majesty," Suna did protest quietly. But she turned her eyes down, lowering her head and making certain that her mistress knew it was an emotional protest and not a direct flouting of her mistress's command.

"Suna, he speaks the truth. This glory will pin a target on me. I have no majesty if I don't make it to my throne alive." She turned her attention back to him. "I have been fairly acquiescent so far, doing everything you've asked of me. Now you don't even ask? You just do? As if I am a creature of no intelligence, as if I can't be reasoned with or have logic wasted on me? Or is it just that you despise any authority and feel it necessary to literally cut it off at the knees to make yourself feel the better for it?"

Rush felt a chill of discomfort walk down his spine, the sensation alien and awkward for him, so he busied himself with sheathing his knife before he looked back into those extraordinarily big eyes.

"Not at all. I'm a soldier. Efficiency is only my nature."

"A soldier?" She turned to assess the group with sharp

eyes. "Is that what you all are? Soldiers? From what army?"

"The IM," Bronse spoke up, castigating Rush with a hard look. "Didn't he tell you anything about what's going on here?"

"Wasn't any time," Rush excused himself with a shrug.

Ambrea watched the big Tarian throw off the matter as easily as he was throwing debris from the camp down the hole they had come up. She had to admit, though, she was incredibly relieved to hear they were from the Interplanetary Militia. It changed the face of everything. Until now she had thought him some kind of mercenary for hire, someone engaged by a powerful Allayan noble, perhaps, who wished to fetch the power of the throne by using her.

"So you're with the IM," she said with a breathless sort of relief. "But I don't understand. What does the IM want with me?"

The Tarian named Ender's static answer seemed to be to simply shrug one of those big shoulders of his. But she did not mistake him for being as clueless as he would have her believe. For all that brawn, there was great intelligence beneath. But he wasn't interested in answering her question, so he blocked her focused attention on him by grabbing a shirt and working it over his head. The Skintex fabric was tight and clung comfortably to every contour of his chest. Somehow seeing him clothed accentuated all those muscular hills and valleys even better than seeing him barechested.

"I apologize," said the man whom Ambrea recognized as the group leader simply by his mannerisms and bearing. She recognized it in him because she had it within herself. He was tall, though still quite shy of the Tarian, and well built in his own right. The most unusual thing about him, though, was his eyes. They were a soft periwinkle color, too pretty by far to belong to a hardened military man. "I thought Lieutenant Blakely would have explained things to you a bit more. I'm sorry for the deficit in information. My name is Commander Bronse Chapel. This is Special Agent Fallon, and this is Captain Justice Muleterre," he said, pointing to the tough little Tarian female. "We're part of a Special Active team for the Interplanetary Militia. We're here to . . . well—"

"Stage a coup," Justice said with a grin of irreverence that lit up her entire face. "I love staging a coup."

"You love fucking up the works," Ender rejoined with a roll of his eyes.

"Anyway, as per our charter with the Three Worlds, we're here to see you take your rightful place as heir to the Allay throne," Commander Chapel said.

Ambrea should have known. She should have realized they were a military outfit the instant they surrounded her. Even everything about Ender's rescue had shouted a sharp, methodical efficiency that the military was famous for. But she had been thrown off by his savage Tarian act when she'd first seen him. Now, watching him gird himself to fit in with the normal Allay populace and also hide a significant number of arms on his person, she realized just how disciplined he really was. There was a quiet, deadly strength to him that was probably far more dangerous than any visual prejudice anyone could have about Tarian savagery.

That hard brunette was Tarian, too, Ambrea realized. It was in her facial structure and in her athletic shape. Certainly it was in the rolling depth of her accent. The two of them could try to dress the part of an Allayan civilian all they wanted, but their exotic looks and the strangeness in their eyes were as good as that blaring tribal tattoo on Ender's chest and arm. He may have since covered it up, but he may as well have not.

"I thank you for your rescue," Ambrea said softly. "But I'm afraid I can't oblige you."

That made the entire camp go quiet and still.

"Excuse me?" Ender barked the politesse at her, making it anything but polite. "Listen, sweetheart, I just risked my ass to get you out of that hole."

"And as I said, I thank you for your rescue," she bit back with firmness and as much strength as she could muster. "But if your coup means harming a single hair on my brother's head, I will not take part in it. I have sworn to myself and to the Great Being that I will abide by the law as it now stands and will recognize him as the true emperor of Allay. I will not now, or ever, start any would-be reign of mine with the bloodshed of any innocent of my line. In that way I will see myself different than all the Allay line before me."

She watched as he took this in, actually finding herself curious as to how he would react. She really was having a hard time getting a good read on him. One minute he played coarse and brutish, the next cocky and amused, the next quiet and reserved. He seemed to fluctuate between it all as if he didn't know what to settle on, which face to show.

She wasn't expecting his eyes to turn genuinely troubled.

"You don't know, do you? I would have thought that even in prison you'd hear things." He hesitated, looking to his leader for guidance. The commander nodded briefly and the Tarian squared his shoulders before meeting her gaze.

"Your brother is dead."

"Eirie!"

Balkin crashed into his rooms, startling the servants who were waiting on the lovely and calm creature in the center of the main salon. Eirie didn't so much as bat an eyelash, not even when he roared at the servants to be gone or he'd whip them to the bone. When one fell in his haste to make it to the door, Balkin couldn't seem to stop himself from planting his boot in his ribs in several rapid successive beats. There was something satisfying in the servant's squeals and pained coughs. Then Balkin picked him up and threw him into the hallway, slamming the door and sealing himself away with his treacherous little witch.

She was eating kio fruits, popping the round, juicy things into her mouth slowly, watching his actions dis-passionately. Her long, lush body was lounging out on a chaise, her day dress of lightly draped silk that glistened with platinum threading and a fair violet color that was no doubt going to be all the rage that week. Eirie was proud of her trendsetting ways, of being the one who was followed rather than emulating others. She would rather choke than be seen copying some lesser-ranked woman. Her bare feet were peeking out from the hem of the gown, sparkling platinum toe rings on all but her big toes and an exotic skin-tinting pattern freshly painted in a wreath around her ankle, a line down the length of the top of her foot, and a painstakingly executed tiny flow-ered pattern all around her toes.

"What have you done?" he demanded of her, march-ing across the room and flinging things off any table he passed. He was, perhaps, trying to vent his fury enough so that he wouldn't grab her around her delicate little throat and choke the bloody life out of her when he reached her.

"I'm sure I don't know what you mean," she said with a sigh.

"The boy is dead! A healthy, young boy! And mere weeks ago every other word out of your mouth was about poison. Give me good reason to think you didn't have anything to do with it!"

"I can hardly prove a negative," she noted with a

shrug. "How can I prove I *didn't* do something? And really, darling, must you treat the servants so ill? That one won't be able to stand for days now. And he does such a lovely cross braid." She touched her hairline where it had been cross-braided in tiny loops and twists.

"I could give a hair on the Great Being's ass about your cross braids, Eirie! Qua fell ill only two days ago, and he suffered terribly from the moment the 'illness' struck him. The doctors are baffled and everyone is looking to *me*. First the father, then the son so quickly? I am the only one with anything to gain. They will think I plotted this all along!"

"And so what if they think that? What can they do about it?" She leaned forward a little, her eyes flashing with a special sort of avarice. "You will be the only prince of the blood left, Balkin. The only heir to this throne. Benit destroyed all other contenders long, long ago, making the way clear and secure for his idiot child. Even if they could prove that you had a hand in this, there's nothing they can do. They would have to leave you to rule or else risk turning all of Allay on its ear and screaming for a new government. But," she said with a smile as she relaxed back again, "they can't prove any foul play, so it's no matter."

"You seem so cocksure about that! With today's technologies and forensics, no one can get away with something like murder. There is always a trail. Always someone who saw something who can be made to talk."

"I refuse to entertain all these supposed scenarios of doom and gloom and what may or may not happen." She stood up and gave a dismissive sniff, tossing back a long, curling lock of her hair. "I prefer to deal in cold, hard facts." She looked at him, snaring his gaze with hers. "And the fact is, you are the emperor of Allay."

She turned to face him and, in a rush of swishing silk, she knelt at his feet. She bowed until her forehead touched the toe of his boot, her graceful arms curling around his ankles. Balkin couldn't help the sudden racing of his heart and the clutch of excitement gripping at his soul. Just the same, he crouched down as she lifted her head, grabbed her by the chin, and gave her a mean little shake.

"And what about that little bitch in my jail? What do you propose I do with the empress of Allay? In truth I have nothing, my pretty love, as long as she is breathing!"

"Kill her. She is not your daughter, your mother, or your sister, and therefore not of your direct blood. There is no law against killing her to secure your throne."

He laughed coldly. "It's all so easy for you. You think you can simply discard the entire Allay line and there won't be repercussions? The IM—"

"The IM can interfere only if there's a crime against the laws of our country or some kind of mass brutality at your hands. An act of genocide or terrorism. An act of war against another country of Ulrike or any of the Three Worlds. An overthrow of the natural order of government in a given country. But this is the natural order of our government. You are the proper heir by blood and divine right. And as I said, there is no proof of any foul play. Nor will there be. Balkin suffered a massive stroke. His son's death was an unfortunate fluke. People die for unexplainable reasons all the time."

Balkin narrowed his eyes on her.

"Tell me. Did you do it? Did you kill the boy?"

She smiled. "If I did, I certainly would not tell you. You cannot be trusted, Balkin. If the IM did begin to investigate you and you felt you were in danger of their justice, you would feed me to them like a bone to a dog in order to escape them." She reached to stroke warm fingers over his cheek. "You are a strong man. A devious man. A man who knows when fortune is turning in his favor. I know you won't let this slip away from you."

"I wouldn't throw you away like you say," he said quietly. "I love you, you cunning little harlot. More today than ever before, I promise you. But there is one very large hiccup in all your puppeteering, my love."

"Oh?" She raised a silvery brow, clearly amused by the notion that she had not thought of every detail.

"The princess has escaped from the catacombs."

She went still, a hard coldness entering her eyes. "*What*?" she demanded. "No one has ever escaped from the catacombs."

"True. And at the moment we aren't sure she actually made it out alive. They're still sorting through the chaos. She never passed the outer portal, but instead went deeper into the tunnels. Odds are the little idiot drowned herself trying to make an escape. I would normally assume as much, except—"

"What is it?" she wanted to know, her impatience very out of character for her. Eirie did not like to show ruffled feathers. She was always seemingly calm and in control. At least in public.

"Except she had help. They came with explosives and a planned distraction to occupy the guards. Some Tarian brute. A mercenary no doubt. Hired perhaps by Prelate Kitsos or some other powermonger in this court."

She made an indelicate sound. "In that case I would hardly worry. It sounds as though it was a botched job all around." Her eyes lit and she smiled. "Actually, this could be very fortunate for us! If she died in an escape attempt, you can hardly be blamed. Oh, how clever. I wish I had thought of it myself. And if she is dead . . . oh, my great and glorious lord, you are well and truly emperor of all Allay."

CHAPTER
FIVE

"Dead!" Ambrea felt her entire chest closing in on itself. She had no idea how she was even able to force words and breath out of it. "I just saw him! He was well and healthy and . . . I just saw him!"

"Two days ago he fell suddenly ill. He was gone by dawn this morning."

"We suspect he was poisoned," the Tarian female said in her blunt way, clearly not considering that this was Ambrea's blood they were talking about. "But your uncle had him decimated. To hide the evidence no doubt. Nothing left to test after a decimation ceremony."

"My uncle has no claim to the throne as long as I—"

"Be assured, you were next on his list," Ender informed her dryly. "Lucky for you, the IM was already involved in Allayan affairs, investigating accusations made by some of the nobles that the succession had been made illegally. The fact is, your father's laws disinheriting you were unjust and illegal under the tenets of the monarchy laid down centuries ago. We had already come up with the plan to liberate you from the catacombs and see the matter fairly arbitrated in an IM court. Once we heard your brother was taken ill, we had to step up the plan. Your uncle is no doubt very hot to announce his ascendancy. The only thing he needed to do was tie up a loose end," Ender told her. "If you were still in that prison come dusk, I assure you he was going to cut your pretty head off and mount it on the palace gates so everyone would know there was no hope of the long lost princess ever coming to claim her rightful spot as empress."

"Even my uncle could not be so stupid. Such an act would provoke the IM into declaring martial law over Allay and trying him as a criminal against the rightful ascension."

"Only there is no one else in line for your throne, Blue Eyes." Ender gave her a grim smile. "Your father saw to that during his own reign so there wouldn't be any uprisings against him or his son. To be honest, I have no idea how you stayed alive this long. He was a paranoid son of a bitch."

"I am well aware of what my father was," she said sharply to him. "I am also aware that the IM took their bloody time about doing anything to put a stop to him."

"Your father always skirted IM involvement," Commander Chapel said. "He knew just how far he could push the envelope of the law. Infanticide would have been crossing the line. Your own tenets say that a ruler can do whatever is necessary to secure the safety of his monarchy, except the murder of direct blood. Meaning his or her own children, siblings, and parents."

"I didn't know that," Ambrea said softly. "All these years, I didn't know that." So, it had not been any lingering affection for her or sense of decency that had held Emperor Benit's hand against his firstborn child. It had been the law and his fear of the ramifications of breaking it. "Still, he could have seen me murdered in a hundred ways that could not be tracked back to him."

"There's always a link. Always proof. The IM is exceptionally good at finding proof like that."

"Are we going to sit here talking about this or are we going to get some distance between us and Balkin's guards?" Ender asked brusquely. "If we get caught, IM or no IM, it'll all be over before it begins. Right now it's all about your life, Blue Eyes. Your life is the only thing standing between your uncle and his direct ascendancy to the throne."

"What does it matter to the IM which of us ends up on that throne?" Ambrea asked quietly. "For all you know, I'm a monster just like my father."

"That doesn't matter," Ender said. "We're here to ensure that the rightful heir is safely put in her place." He gave her a soft sideways look. "But I'm going to take a wild stab and say you are nothing like your father. And Allay could use a bit of that."

"You have that right," Suna piped up. "My great lady is a kind and generous person. She would bring fairness and a gentle touch to a nation sorely in need of it."

"But like Ender said," Commander Chapel spoke up, "this is all going to be a moot point if Balkin's guards find her. Let's get going."

Ender and Justice hauled a huge fallen tree over the hole, making it invisible. In a few quick actions the campsite looked completely natural and unused. The group rapidly began to move out across the park preserve, all of them falling into a natural sort of protective circle around Ambrea.

"Explain something to me," Suna asked a while later when the sound of her own breathlessness got on her nerves. She was not cut out for all of this adventure and activity. She was more content to enjoy her mistress's company, to entertain her with wit and intellect, games and quieter hobbies. The lady Ambrea had never been one for sports, even those that were considered seemly for a woman of royal station, and that had been just fine with Suna. "Why all of this clandestine scrabbling about? Why doesn't the IM just come into Allay and force the regent to hand over the imperial seat to its rightful mistress?"

"There may come a time for that," Commander Chapel said.

"But it wouldn't do much good if the true heir was in his power, at the tip of his knife," Ender said dryly. "The moment the first soldier set foot in the Allayan presence chamber, the regent could have run into the wet rooms and cut Ambrea's throat. Then he would actually be the sole surviving and rightful heir to Allay. We had to secure your mistress before anything and everything else."

"Besides, Suna," Ambrea said quietly, "would you have all of Allay under martial law?"

"You mean *foreign* martial law," Suna scoffed. "Allay has been under martial law for decades. The emperor's troops are always everywhere. They call themselves a policing force, but what they really are is an army." Her eyes went wide as a terrible thought filled her head. "What if he won't abdicate his power? What if he decides to use that army to keep out the IM?"

"He wouldn't dare," Ambrea said, although it was clear she wasn't so sure. "That would make Allay the first country in the Three Worlds to break faith with the IM charter. Oh, Ephemeral Being, he would plunge Allay into a nightmare! War with the Three Worlds? Never mind the bloodshed; the socioeconomic ramifications would be crippling. There would be trade sanctions, the entire continent would be shut down from travel and tourism, and anything that Allay is dependent on from outside its borders would quickly be cut off and the people would suffer for it."

Like food. Allay was not nearly self-sufficient enough in its farming production to feed its entire population. They were quite dependent on food recombinant technologies. Then again, most places were these days. It was the raw materials and fuels to run those technologies that Allay imported heavily. If the IM imposed sanctions on Allay, those materials and fuels would be denied. They would make the population of Allay miserable, putting Balkin in the position of managing an unruly, angry country. It would force a revolution.

But lives could be lost that way. A great many Allayan lives. By starvation or in battle, people would die.

"I would not see the people of Allay suffer," Ambrea said softly. Ender scoffed under his breath, but she noted it. "What? You've something to say about it?" She didn't mean to be so rude to this man who had rescued her, but the obvious disapproval in the hard lines of his face rubbed her the wrong way.

"Princess, if you think you can make this omelet without breaking some eggs, you're in for a world of surprise."

"Spoken like a true soldier. You'd rather bash and smash and maim and kill your way from point A to point B," she snapped at him.

"Lady, you've got it so wrong," he bit off at her. "And that doesn't surprise me in the least. From what I hear, you've been raised in a bubble, ignorant of how these worlds really work, of how people really work. In my opinion, you—"

"Arms master," Chapel cut him off sharply. "We're not paid to have an opinion. We have a job to do. So let's do it."

"Yes, sir. Sorry, sir," Ender said with a firmness and sincerity that surprised Ambrea, because she got the feeling he wasn't at all happy about biting his tongue. But he did not behave sullenly or seem to stew. He accepted the order given and continued to march forward. It was so strange to see someone so big and clearly so capable of mastering a situation be so willingly subordinate. In a way she felt a peculiar respect for him. After all, had she not been subordinate all of her life to the wishes of others? She had done so, it could be said, with as much willingness as he was now exhibiting to his superior. In fact it was eerily parallel. She had different opinions, had strong desires contrary to those who controlled her, but she accepted that there was a natural order to things. That there was a price to pay for disrupting that natural order. She had never been willing to put anyone, not even herself, in any kind of danger in some wild bid for her throne.

But perhaps . . .

"Perhaps you're right," she said to him, engaging him despite his commander's wishes that he keep to himself. She suspected, though, that the order had been given for diplomatic reasons. The commander did not want his man to say anything that might offend the future empress of Allay. But Ambrea had always craved strong intellects and varying opinions. She had never sat above those around her thinking she was always in the right and that no one should gainsay her. "Perhaps I have been sheltered . . . and frightened. Afraid to move for fear of hurting someone. I always tried so hard to be the opposite of what my father was . . . what my uncle is. But I can see how neither extreme makes for good leadership."

"It's not a bad thing that you don't want to hurt anyone," Ender said rather gently. It made her smile, and she tilted her head and peered into his warm eyes. That brownish red color was just so peculiar, she thought. She'd never seen anything like it. Not that that was saying much. They were so exotic, dark golden lashes spiking away from their rims like the fanning tail of a durou bird. Again she saw a streak of strong beauty in what others might see as hardened and barbaric.

He was right to say she had been raised in a bubble. She'd been denied many things in her exile, things like a Universal Database connection, something every single person in the Three Worlds could have free access to if they wanted to buy the tech necessary to tap into it. Oh, how well educated she might have been had she been able to tap into the UD! Instead she'd been limited to what VidMags her ladies had access to or VidBooks in the server library at her house. Since the server library had been completely controlled by her father's aides, it had contained reams of florid propaganda about the emperor and the magnificence of Allay. Still, she had been able to pick out some truths and basics of things.

"But living my life in fear of that has allowed first my brother and now my uncle to usurp my rightful place," she continued. "To treat my people ill. It has been hard to know what to do, whom to throw in with. People have approached me over the years wanting to stage a coup, but I always felt it too risky, fearing that their motives were not necessarily pure."

"Very few of us have pure motives," he said.

But, Rush realized, *she* genuinely did. She was passionately dedicated to doing the right thing, according to her own intense moral code. He had noticed that the small paper book she had grabbed from her cell was in her hands, the pages wet all along the edges where the leather had not protected it from the dunking she had taken earlier. She was continually fanning out the pages, no doubt to dry them, as she walked. He realized that it was a devotional book. A prayer book that he often saw in the belongings of those, like Bronse, who followed the belief in the one Great Being. This was most prevalent on Ulrike, but ever since travel between the planets had begun, missionaries had spread the belief in the Great Being throughout the system.

Except for on the actual planet of Tari. Tarians believed in their many spirits, and it was likely never to change. The spirits and the people used one another to stay connected to the planet. To sever that connection would be to sever them from the world around them, the air they breathed, the food that nourished them, the animals that coexisted with them. There had been many things that had made it hard for Rush to leave Tari back when he had first joined the IM. Leaving his connection to the spirits had been one of the most difficult. Justice had been born on one of the platforms, so she had not been as imbued with that connection as those planetside Tarians were.

Rush found himself curious about Ambrea's connection to the book. Even in the heat of her escape, the first thing she had thought of, even at the risk of her own safety and the safety of Suna and himself, something she was clearly loath to put on the line, was that book.

"Are you very religious?" he asked, breaking another standing rule. Two things he didn't like to discuss were politics and religion. They tended to be hot, volatile topics, and he tried not to have any passionate thoughts on either. It kept him out of trouble, kept things relatively smooth and easy. It was best to be a soldier, obey orders from someone he trusted, use the skills he had in the way he knew best. Simple. Clean. Safe.

"I am," she said. "I try to be," she qualified after a moment. "I have faith in the Great Being. In the Being's plans for me. The lessons of the Followers are strong and beautiful. They help us to value one another, to value all life. Its simplicities, its complexities. Hardships in our lives create their own rewards later on. I firmly believe that." Then her voice was so soft he might not have heard her over the sound of their crunching through the forest bracken. "I need to believe that." She turned her head to narrow her pretty blue eyes on him. "What about you? Are you very religious?"

He didn't know how to answer that. Not just for her, but for himself. There had been a time when his connection to the spirits had meant everything. But he had left that all behind him. "I haven't communed with the spirits for a very long time."

"I didn't ask if you practiced your religion. No more than you did of me. I meant do you have faith in something more powerful, more comprehensive in the universe than yourself."

"I have faith in my fellow soldiers. Faith in my ability to kick some ass when it needs to be kicked, because the IM showed me how." He shrugged, knowing that someone like her, someone golden and privileged and serenely dedicated to her One Being, would frown on his more tangible beliefs. One Being or many spirits, whatever may or may not be out there, none of them had ever done anything to ease his way in this life. He had made his own mark, picked himself up, and driven himself to make a path. Gods had little to do with that. If there were gods out there, he was pretty sure they had forsaken him a long time ago.

"It must be exhausting to feel that way," she observed gently. "To feel that nothing keeps your head above water except you."

"I'm pretty damn strong. Pretty damn tough. I don't tire easily."

But looking at her, looking at how she seemed almost fragile in spite of being tall and long limbed, he could see why she would need to seek strength outside of herself. She wasn't physically strong like most women he knew. Then again, all the women he knew these days were soldiers like Justice. And although Justice ran a little shorter than the princess, it was clear she was in top shape, athletic and tough. He most certainly wouldn't want to meet up with a scrapper like the team's pilot in a dark corner somewhere. Tarian women were just as strong as the men, although they packed it into a more streamlined package. Just as strong as most Tarian men anyway. He wasn't exactly like most Tarian men.

Or any men, for that matter. He ran pretty big by all the standards of the Three Worlds. And honestly it seemed redundant. He had enough going for him. Size wasn't necessary.

Maybe it was because she was so pale. Deprived of sunlight for so long, she didn't have much color in her complexion. Perhaps that's why her eyes seemed so big, so brilliant. Her hair as well. Impractical as it had been, he'd actually hated to cut it off. It was the most glorious red, fiery and bright with streaks of glimmering gold. And soft. Despite all the hardship of living trapped in a cell, her hair had been as soft as if she had pampered it every day, dried it with Yojni silk, infused it with nourishing Ayalya spice, as many of the wealthier women in the Three Worlds were wont to do. He watched it now as the drying tendrils flew like tiny banners in the wind, one moment wrapping around her, the next trying to get away. It hung to the middle of her back now, still cumbersome, unbound as it was, but he found he couldn't be irritated by the inefficiency. The hair, the eyes, the woman as a whole was far too pretty and too sweet-natured to be an irritant. He liked the strong set of her shoulders, admired her for the things he'd learned about her in their mission briefing. Many people did not survive the type of imprisonment she had been made to suffer. No daylight. No movement outside of that same tiny space, hour after hour, day after day. That in itself was a torture. The only relief she had, he supposed, was the stimulation of the sharp-witted Suna.

But there had been no Suna that first time she'd been put into the wet rooms at the tender age of eleven. How had a child come through an entire year of incarceration like that? How had she managed to hold up in the face of a tyrannical adult accusing her of sedition, and power-hungry nobles all around her seeking to use her for exactly that?

"It must be a relief to be out in the open," he said, wondering why he continually felt the need to engage her in conversation. He wasn't known for being the talkative type. Quite the opposite. He kept quiet, pulled pins, blew shit up. Ate, slept, and then did it all again the next day. Simple. He liked simple.

"Aye, it is," she said passionately, taking in a very deep breath and turning her face to the sun. The sun burned a rosy gold in the sky, the day clear and crisp and almost eerily cloudless. The trees with their blue-green leaves creaked and groaned in the strong breeze, their massive height leaving the small group in shade more often than not. "I spend a great deal of time out of doors." She hedged. "When I'm able. I stitch and read outside all the time. We would take long walks, feed the stray bray-bray. It had gotten so they would eat straight out of my hand. I could feel their little forked tongues flickering against my palm."

"You're lucky you didn't feel their teeth," he said.

"If you're patient, approach them gently, and wait for them to come to you on their own terms, they will not bite you. People say the bray-bray are vicious through and through, but that's not true. They—"

"Shh!"

The soft hiss came from Chapel, and he raised a hand in a gesture indicating they should halt. Rush grabbed hold of the princess by her upper arm, drawing her close to the protection of his body yet giving himself room to move and access all his munitions if necessary. He felt her balk at being touched for a moment, but more from surprise at the sensation, he realized, than from some kind of privileged snobbery that Suna seemed to feel she should respond with. Ambrea had been the same way in the tunnels. She hadn't dissembled about being held and holding on; she just didn't have any experience with person-to-person contact.

Did that mean she had had no affection whatsoever growing up, he wondered. At least he'd had that much. His mother had loved him a great deal, had always showered him with attention and affection. She had always made certain he knew she thought he was a person of great value. That he was rich with the love of another. Her death when he was fifteen had devastated him. But at least he'd had her that long. How old had the princess been when her mother was executed? Four?

Rush shook off the trivial detail and focused on their situation. As soon as all of them were quiet, he could hear what had drawn Chapel's attention. Another group was moving through the woods. They were loud and even bawdy as their conversation echoed off the canopy above them.

"It's all over now," one man joked. "*Emperor* Balkin is the man of the hour, pretty concubines lining up on their knees to kiss his cock, ready to spread their legs to make him some heirs."

"Not if he has the same luck as Benit did," another snorted noisily. The unmistakable sound of a gun coming out of a holster made the hairs on the back of Rush's neck stand up. There was something very distinctive about the sound of metal escaping leather. The whine of the pistol being cocked and warmed up, the shuttle being checked, the power clip being removed and firmly reseated again—these were sounds that any soldier would recognize. The group must be Imperial Guards. The preserve's rangers didn't carry anything more powerful than a stunner. Rush's ears made the identification of an MX-240 by the power pitch and the snap in the shuttle. A 240 was made to kill. Painfully. It burned up a body from the inside out; the more powerful the setting, the more vicious the damage.

The weapon was outlawed in the Three Worlds for its barbarity. Clearly the emperor had not heeded that mandate any more than he had heeded others set down by the IM.

"Benit had three hundred concubines at any given moment, right?" the soldier continued. "How do you not make an army of royal brats with three hundred incubators lined up ready and waiting? They can't all have been the problem, right? The royal rocks were shooting blanks. I'll bet his kids aren't even his. Maybe some guard or some pit washer banged one of his bitches behind his back."

"Don't be stupid," another said as the heavy-footed contingent came closer and closer to the tree that Rush and his group were huddled behind. The trunk of the quoia tree was thick enough to conceal twenty men of Rush's size. With any luck the other group could keep walking and never see them. "As soon as the whelps are born, they test their DNA and prove their lineage. This isn't like the Third Age, when no one knew which bastard belonged to which bastard, 'cept by the woman's say-so."

"And we know how trustworthy a woman can be," a new voice piped up. The men laughed as a whole.

"I have to say, I'm surprised the princess finally got up the guts to try to escape. She's been meek as a mouse all these years in exile. Never so much as a peep out of her."

"Don't be an ass," the readily armed guard said. "She didn't try to escape. Balkin blistered her from the inside out, buried the body, and is making a show of it to satisfy the IM's suspicious eyes."

"So we're basically out here wasting our time," another said.

"Hey, I don't care. I get paid either way. It's not so bad as details go. Could be worse. We could be like those poor bastards who are searching through that brine at the bottom of the wet rooms."

And just like that, the soldier walked into sight, almost running into Rush.

Eirie swept silently through the rear halls of Blossom Palace, the Yojni silk of her dress fluttering behind her in the breeze of her own movement. She crept past the senior concubine quarters—the entire west wing of the palace that was dedicated to housing all of Emperor Benit's former concubines. Those who had family to return to had already been sent away with a retirement dowry to help them live in small comfort. Those who wanted their freedom had also been set adrift—with far too much of the treasury's monies, in Eirie's opinion. But tradition was tradition, and Balkin could not afford to upset the traditionalist public, which liked their royals to behave according to certain guidelines set down in the past. Eirie had respected Emperor Benit, though, for being a true man of power, for acting as he saw fit to use the law in his favor, or make new laws to suit. Those in the Noble Seat, the elected seats that supposedly represented the needs of the people from all over the continent and brought those needs to the emperor's ear, ideally had a say in which new laws were ratified, but all that really meant was who could and could not be swayed or bought to see things the emperor's way. The prelates and paxors were made fat and rich by giving the emperor his way. When they did not, they were considered thorns and personal enemies and had to struggle for survival amongst their contemporaries.

Balkin had a knack for buying his brother the majority vote. He also had a talent for punishing those who did not comply in creative ways. It wouldn't do to be obvious about it. So maybe a business would inexplicably suffer, or perhaps a cherished daughter would be chosen for a concubine. Under the guise of being bestowed a great honor, they would be forced to hand the girl over to the monster they knew could kill a concubine at whim. It was surprising, though, how many would eagerly send a girl into these opulent rooms, Eirie thought. They would always think, in their arrogance, that it would be their daughter to finally give the emperor the children he so desperately craved.

Idiots. The lot of them. There was only one true seat of power for any woman in Allay.

Empress.

That was why Eirie had written off Benit Tsu Allay a long time ago. With him, the best she could have hoped for was lead concubine. Benit would make no woman his wife, and no woman empress. He would not share his power. Ever. Except, perhaps, with his brother. It could be said that Benit had loved only two people in his lifetime. His brother and his son. Eirie did not count that contemptible concubine Junessa, because love was meant to be enduring, and Junessa had not lasted more than five years in Benit's affections. Damn fool of a woman. She had had him. Right in the palm of her hand. And she had let him slip through her fingers.

Junessa had made fatal mistakes. Eirie would not.

She pushed through the doors to the old chapel, the one that had been abandoned after the new one had been built directly off the concubines' main salon. The doors creaked, the hinges uncared for over time. She was immediately engulfed in the pervading dimness of the room, the smell of long-standing dust in the air, and the single window at the rear of the altar casting light onto the edges of the silvery cobwebs hanging in the rafters.

Eirie gathered up the train of her gown so it wouldn't trail in the dust, draping it over her forearm and continuing on her way through the chapel. She took care with her steps, lifting and placing each foot so she wouldn't kick up dust onto her handcrafted court slippers. At the rear of the chapel was the entrance to the rectory, what would normally be the priestess's private chambers. But unlike the chapel, these chambers were not in disrepair as Eirie let herself into them. They were soft and quaint, a simple sort of pretty that her grandmother's house had once been. They were far too simple for any priestess of the Great Being, although the walls were still made of beaten gold and platinum, as had been dictated by the previous tenant. There wasn't much that the current tenant could do about that. As it was, she wasn't even supposed to be in these rooms. Not officially anyway.

"Curta?"

Curta moved, startling Eirie, who had not seen her in the corner of the sitting room. As usual, the older woman was not sitting. She stood, wearing a classic peach-colored gown that was held on to her body by links of Delran platinum made into the most delicate of chains, one after another lying in gently sweeping loops against her dark skin. Skin so dark it was almost black. She was from the Farma continent, a place on the other side of the world where the people were sometimes only half as civilized as those in Allay and Ulrike. In contrast to her rich, near-ebony skin, the older woman's hair was golden, like threads of metal filament, only it was unmistakably soft as it rested in an array of whorls around her neck and down her back. It was hard to tell how old the Farma woman was. Her skin was smooth and without age. Her golden lashes seemed to glitter above her purple pupils and fair sky blue irises.

"You screwed up!" Eirie accused her sharply.

"I?" Curta raised a glittering brow, her expression completely unchanged by the flare of Eirie's temper. She moved out of the sitting room with even, graceful steps, the beads of the belt tied around her waist clacking together as the long ends bounced off her skirt at her knees. There were other things tied to her belt at various intervals. Strange things. Runes with old symbols carved into them, a small doll made of sticks with a wreath of tiny flowers around its head, something that looked like a dried-up finger. "The boy is dead and there is no trace of foul play that could lead to you or your lover. I call that perfection," said Curta.

She moved into her workroom, a lightless cell dominated by tables full of cups and bowls, beakers and flasks. One table held a soldering iron, wires of all sorts, and the cannibalized bits of any number of tech. A burner was lit beneath something on the far table, the dark liquid moving in a slow, rolling boil. The smell of it was everywhere, sickly sweet and yet tempting. Eirie could not help but sniff and sniff again, taking in the scent of it over and over. Her temper soothed inexplicably. She sighed.

"Yes, Grandmother Great. This is true. But what of the princess? She was supposed to be dead before the prince."

"I thought she was. Rumor is that she died in an attempt at escape," the older woman said with archness to her tone that made it clear she put little stock in palace rumor.

"Perhaps so. Perhaps not. There is no body. It was important that there be a body, visible proof. A thing for the commoners to walk past in mourning lines and stare at, shaking their heads at the misfortune of it all. Without a body there will be doubt. It will leave open for rumors that she yet lives. It will be a point of unrest. I want Balkin to be emperor free and clear. I want what you promised me!"

"I promised you nothing," Curta replied mildly. "I said only that I could craft the tools you could use and that they would work flawlessly. The boy clearly proves the potency of my tools. If the princess yet lives, it is because the tool has not yet been used."

Eirie paced the room impatiently, picking things up and inspecting them before putting them back down. "So we must hope that your tool is still within reach of the princess. That makes me very nervous. I don't like to be left unsure."

Curta reached to take from Eirie's hands the gourd that she had just picked up, placing it back very precisely on the table. "It is not wise for you to touch things on these tables. It would be most unfortunate if you were to make yourself ill when you are so close to attaining your victory. But," she smiled, "if you like I can consult the stones and see what fate has planned."

Eirie nodded, wiping her hands against the skirt of her dress. Unlike the priestesses of the Great Being, the Farma conjurer did not trust the uncertainty of prayer and did not blindly trust in leaving things to the Great Will. No more than Eirie would sit by and watch her youth fade as she waited for Balkin's tenure as emperor to begin. As it looked right now, that tenure was starting. But then perhaps not. It was impossible to know without knowing if the princess yet lived.

Curta moved to her casting table, sweeping her hands three times over the violet velveteen fabric that covered it before picking up the mother-of-pearl bowl at its edge and throwing the stones within it into the center circle that had been painted in platinum on the fabric. The round and oval stones scattered, some rolling completely off the table, some settling in the circle, some outside of it. Curta peered at the results for a long moment, toying absently with the shell bracelet on her wrist.

"It is true, the princess lives," she stated definitively.

"Cursed shit!" Eirie swore. "How does she do it? How does she skirt death at every turn?"

Curta held up a hand to silence the other woman.

"The stones say my tool is still close at hand. It lies like a viper, waiting to strike. So all is not lost." Curta's face then creased with puzzlement.

"What is it? What do you see?" Eirie demanded to know.

"There is . . . an uncertainty. This is so strange." She walked around the table slowly, peering at the stones from all directions. "She is near a danger that threatens to consume her. A viper not of my making. And yet the wall stone touches the heart stone, indicating a protector. A loyal protector."

"Wonderful," Eirie scoffed. "The beauty of her life thus far was that she lacked any and all protection, making her vulnerable. If someone has taken up her cause—"

"Worry not," Curta said dismissively. "Her protector is powerless against my tool. All it will take is a single instant and it will all be over."

"Do you promise me this? It is a certainty?"

"Tsk. You well know there are no certainties in the ways of fate. However, I have never seen such clarity in the stones before. Dangers consume the princess from all sides. She will not be able to survive them all. The stones say it clearly. Before three days have passed, the Princess of Allay will cease to be."

CHAPTER
SIX

Rush reacted without thinking. Or perhaps with more thought than he would like to admit. Present danger aside, the whole lot of them and their conversation, which was no doubt reflective of many conversations taking place all over Allay, just rubbed him the wrong way. Perhaps it had something to do with the raw flush of emotional color he'd seen creeping over the princess's face.

No matter. The guard took one look up at Rush before his attention jolted toward the princess. The muzzle of the gun came up, strands of her red-gold hair floating on the breeze wrapped around it and the guard's wrist, and the soldier's hand tightened on the trigger of his weapon. That brutal, deadly weapon. Rush grabbed the thing by the muzzle and slammed the entire gun up into the Imperial Guard's face, smashing his nose and teeth with a resounding crack. A second guard fired wildly, the 240 shot hitting his own man. The hapless Imperial Guard's shock vest defrayed some of the blast, but just the same the man screamed horrifically, the smell of flesh cooking filling the air. The guard spewed up blood and fell to his knees, exposing Rush to the pack of guards surging up behind him.

There was an explosive, searing sound, and Rush felt heat flashing through him. He was aware of the other guards falling on the rest of the team, but he immediately turned to protect the well-being of their precious cargo. He leapt past the dying soldier, punched the next nearest man square up under his chin, and then grabbed the stunned guard by the hair, jerking him around and shoving him into the next one who was right behind him. Gunfire erupted everywhere, and the princess cried out.

"Don't hurt them!" she exclaimed.

Don't hurt *them*? And what the hell was he supposed to do? Play gammon with them? Didn't she get it? Didn't she understand that sometimes it was kill or be killed?

Rush ignored her command. His orders didn't come from her. His orders were to protect her life at all costs. If he could keep his damage path to a minimum, so much the better, but her life superseded all these others. Even his own. That was his mission. That was what he had signed on for.

"Ender, get her out of here!"

Rush reacted to the order instantly, years of serving under Bronse Chapel making it a reflex. Rush toppled the oncoming guard with a flat-footed kick square in his breastbone, sending him flying back as if he'd been shot out of a cannon. Then he grabbed the girl, hauling her into his side protectively, and pulled a "sticker" off the munitions belt hiding under his jacket. He threw the sticker upward, a loud thunk telling him it had struck hard against the tree above them. He braced his feet hard apart.

One . . . two . . . three . . .

Boom.

The explosion was loud and percussive, jarring everyone off their feet except for him. Wood sprayed in a violent array above them, raining splinters down in raw yellow-white chunks. By then he was already running. Within two steps he'd swung Ambrea into his arms, clasping her to his chest and forcing her along for the ride. Not that she was kicking or screaming. He had to give her credit for that. She kept a cool head under some pretty wild circumstances. It was a mark of a good, strong leader. She may be unsure of herself, she may be green and a little hung up on her morals, but she showed strong signs of being what it would take to bring Allay under her control, to make Allay powerful without being brutal.

Not that it mattered to him, he reminded himself sternly. He wasn't interested in the political structure on any of the lands of the Three Worlds. Not even those on Tari. He was interested in the mission. And right now the mission was to save her ass.

The forest was in his favor. In mere steps he was around the next massive tree trunk, and a few strides later it was the next. Even with her added weight he ate up ground fast enough to put the team's track stars, Chapel and Lasher, to shame. Then again, he was motivated. The last thing he wanted was her pretty red head on his conscience. Granted, he'd failed a mission before, lost someone he was supposed to protect, seen casualties he felt he could have saved if only he'd been faster . . . stronger . . . smarter . . . or less of a coward. Those people had faded from his nightmares over time. But there was something about her—maybe it was knowing she had been betrayed by her own people at such a tender age, maybe it was the earnestness in her water-blue eyes. Regardless, instinct told him he wouldn't be able to shake it so easily if something were to happen to her while he was on watch.

"Stop! Please! I think you can stop!"

Rush would be the judge of that. Gunfire and explosions were loud. They attracted attention. Reinforcements could be coming from any quarter.

Which made it wise to stop. To hunker down and

quiet themselves. Bull-rushing through the bracken was only making them easier to follow. So he heeded her suggestion, swung them behind a quoia tree, and lowered them beneath the wide spade-shaped leaves of a copse of fan ferns. The ferns liked to grow in the shade of the quoias, feeding off the rich black earth around its thick, protruding roots. It made for perfect cover.

He set her down in the soil and leaves and motioned her into silence. She was quick to obey, curling her knees into her chest and pressing her face against them to conceal her hurried breathing. She had not been the one to exert herself, but her adrenaline must be running pretty damn high. That gun muzzle had come so close to her face just before he had grabbed it that he found himself double-checking to make sure she hadn't been accidentally hit. She was still all big blue eyes and slightly paler skin, but no worse for the event other than looking somewhat disheveled. Then again, she hadn't started out looking like some of those sculpted beauties from the VidMag society pages. He had to admit he found her simple, clean prettiness far more appealing than any of that high-maintenance bullshit. He preferred a girl who could get dirty and wouldn't squawk about it.

Not that he was thinking of her like that. She was a principal. He was assigned to protect her. It was as simple as that. Anything else made for undue complications, and he had no interest in complications.

Then, things got complicated.

"You've been shot!"

She was on him before he could react, grasping at the wide burn hole in his Skintex shirt near his lower left abdomen. He reacted, grabbing her hands an instant after he felt her fingertips sliding over his smooth, unblemished skin.

"B-but I heard the weapon go off. There's a burn in your shirt the size of my fist. Why . . . ?"

"Never mind," he said gruffly. "The gun must have misfired."

"MX's don't misfire," she said flatly. "But let's say I believe that, how does Skintex burn through, yet your skin isn't even so much as blistered? Not even reddened!"

"Will you hush?" he hissed at her. "Why don't you just jump up and down and start screaming 'Here we are!'?"

"Don't try to change the subject by yelling at me, thinking fear will shut me up!"

"I'm not changing the subject. I'm telling you there isn't any subject to discuss. And if we're not quiet, some other contingent of guards will find us. We got away because we had the whole team with us before. We're on our own for the time being, so maybe we won't be so lucky in another attack."

Ambrea wasn't fooled. He was still trying to deflect her interest in a wound that wasn't. She recalled him jerking the gun muzzle out of her face and pointing it toward his own body, and then hearing that loud perfunctory searing of the air that signified gunfire. He'd taken a shot directly in the gut, yet it hadn't touched him. Or so it seemed. She knew that soldiers wore Skintex to protect their skin, but it wasn't like a shock vest that could defray the power of a blaster strike. There was no way that Skintex was strong enough to account for what she *wasn't* seeing.

Still, she decided to keep quiet. It was true they were vulnerable, and chitchat wasn't wise. But she kept her eyes on him steadily, trying to see in his face some clue as to what was going on. His expression was implacable, however; just by the way he studiously ignored her focus, he was giving himself away.

"I—"

"Look, if you know what's good for you, you'll make

like none of this ever happened, like you never saw anything," he snapped suddenly, grabbing her face in his large hand and pushing himself nose to nose with her so she could feel the anger radiating off him and through his russet eyes. "And if I think you're going to whisper a single word of this to any of my friends, I'll cut your throat right here and now and your ass will never touch your precious throne of Allay. You got me, Princess?"

She blinked slowly and drew in a long, unsteady breath.

"I was just going to say I think we lost our pursuers," she said softly.

"Oh."

Ender slowly relaxed, the tension in his big shoulders releasing in tiny increments, his grip on her face becoming less cruel.

"Have you done that before?" she couldn't help but ask. "Killed someone to keep them quiet about . . . this?"

"I told you to drop it. Damn, woman, are you really this dense, or are you just bound and determined to test my resolve?"

"Oh, I believe you'll do what you say," she assured him. "I believe you'd plunge Allay into a lifetime of continued cruelty at the hands of my uncle by killing me just to . . . I guess to keep a secret. This . . . strange secret." She blinked. "But humor me a minute. I am forbidden to speak of it on pain of death, and it's likely you will kill me anyway. So why not tell me what it is I am bound to lose my life over?"

He growled under his breath, pushing her away. A nerve ticked in his jaw as he spent a moment checking his belt to make sure his munitions were pinned and secure before fastening an exterior communications device into his ear.

"You don't understand," he ground out. "I've been in

the IM for almost fifteen cycles, and never once . . . not once . . ." He made a sound of frustration, running a hand through the short, crisp ends of his hair. "So I'm a freak, all right?" he spat out. "Some kind of mutation or something. And people don't take kindly to freaks. They're afraid of them. Even friends, even family, even my team wouldn't understand."

"More like they'd feel hurt that you didn't trust them," she said quietly.

"There are things you can trust people with, and things you can't."

She tilted her head, studying the hard lines of tension in his face. There had been no mistaking the camaraderie amongst the IM teammates. There had been efficiency and professionalism, yes, but it had been clear as day that they were good friends as well. Especially the two Tarians in the group.

"So you . . . have really tough skin or something?" She couldn't help reaching out to touch the back of his hand. It was warm, smooth, and soft just like skin ought to be. The sparse hairs were slightly coarse and as blond as the hair on his head.

"Or something," he agreed. It didn't seem as though he was going to elaborate any further, but then he looked at her, his opposite hand gripping the trunk of the tree, bits of bark flaking off under his powerful fingers. "I just haven't spoken about it since before my mother died when I was fifteen. She told me never to speak of it. Never to show it. She said it was a curse, an aberration that would make people want to hurt me. I disobeyed her directive only once in my life, and I paid the price. People I grew up with, people who knew me and supposedly loved me, turned on me in an instant. I never made that mistake again. And now you—"

Ambrea could see that he was afraid. This tough, stalwart warrior who faced down weapons and danger and drowning without so much as a rise in blood pressure was very much afraid of being exposed for being—as he put it—a freak. And perhaps not because of what they might try to do to him, but because he feared being betrayed by those he trusted and cared about. He feared them rejecting him, casting him out of the position in life that he now maintained. That loss, to him, would be far more damaging than any physical wounds he might suffer should they try to hurt him.

"Do I look like I want to hurt you?" she asked quietly, lifting her gaze to his so he could see deeply into hers. "Do you think someone like me, someone who has been persecuted just because of the blood in her veins, could ever find it in herself to see another be hurt because of the blood in his?"

Seconds ticked past as their gazes held, his breath quick and noisy between them. Whether it was from running moments earlier or from that genuine fear, she couldn't tell. He reached up suddenly, swallowing the entire right side of her face in the span of his hand, holding her tightly in his fingers. She felt a strong flash of fear then, the understanding that he was so physically superior to her in strength, size, and skill. She sensed that he wasn't the sort of man who would harm an innocent for his own gain, but fear made people do things that they would not normally do. If his fear of exposure was truly that strong, there was no telling what he might be pushed to.

"You're being tolerant because you've seen only a little piece of it. If you saw it all—"

"Why are you so determined to frighten me?" she asked, drawing up all of her courage and going with her instincts. She had faith that he would not hurt her. "Why are you trying to provoke the very reaction you are dreading?"

He was so close to her, his heated breath cascading

over her face again and again, his thumb rubbing almost harshly at the corner of her lips. She could feel the energy of his need, his need to believe that maybe he was wrong to make a blanket judgment against her, just as others would be wrong to make a blanket judgment against him. She asked herself if this unknown power he harbored frightened her, honestly asked herself if it was wise to keep pushing like this. She imagined he was asking himself the very same thing.

"Perhaps if a stranger is willing to be accepting of you, then maybe you should have more faith in those who know you. I will not say you shouldn't be cautious. There is always danger. Those who are supposed to love you can and sometimes *will* turn on you, but I can't believe there is no one worthy of faith and trust in all of these Three Worlds."

"Knowing who you are, knowing what you've been through, I can't decide if you are really stupid for believing that, or really quite beautiful."

Ambrea felt a peculiar warmth infusing her face and neck, a tightening around her ribs. How strange it was for her to realize right then that she thought him to be quite attractive as well. At first she had been overwhelmed by his size, his roaring presence, the dramatic, sweeping ink on his skin, but when taken along with this more vulnerable aspect, the intensity of his brow and the glimmer of his fair hair . . . not to mention the depth of pain and emotion she could see in his eyes, she thought he was really quite beautiful too.

"Perhaps I am a little bit of both," she confessed. "I too find it very difficult to trust others. But we need to have faith in our long-standing relationships. Otherwise we will be forever on the outside looking in. I don't wish to be on the outside, in exile. I have been there all my life. It's time it came to an end."

He moved away from her a little, taking a moment to

look beyond their hiding spot, moving with an impressive silence for someone so big. Ambrea felt as though she were making too much noise just sitting there. But she felt safe just the same. Or perhaps it was more that she wasn't worried about dying anymore. She would live or she would die. The close call of minutes ago had made that very clear. She had stared down the barrel of that vicious gun, smelled the ozone of the power pack that charged it. It had been just that close. But if it was the "freak" part of Ender that had allowed him to move so fast in that moment, that had allowed him to take a violent hit in her stead, she couldn't see anything bad about it.

When he was settled down beside her again, she resumed her slow study of him. This time he smiled under her scrutiny.

"Didn't anyone ever tell you it's rude to stare?"

"Generally, not for me. The royalty are encouraged to inspect the details of those around them, to seek out strengths and flaws. If it makes you uncomfortable, however, I will stop."

"Not uncomfortable. Just not used to it. I prefer to blend in. Not be noticed."

She covered a short laugh with fingers against her lips.

"What?" he demanded with a frown.

"Yes, not noticed. That's why you carry around all those loud explosive things. So you won't be noticed."

That made him grin. "All right, you might have a point," he acceded. He touched the communication device in his ear. It was clear he was worried about the well-being of the rest of the team, but he didn't try to contact them. He was following some sort of protocol.

"What's your real name?" she asked him suddenly. "I know you prefer other soldiers to use this soldier's nickname you've been given, but if you don't mind, I'd like to know your real name. I am not a soldier, and a soldier is not all that you are."

He looked at her, clearly thinking about it for a second or two.

"Rush. My name is Rush."

"Will you mind if I call you Rush? I like it much better than Ender."

He shrugged as if it didn't matter to him one way or the other.

Ambrea let a full minute go by before she spoke up again.

"I'm sorry. I know I'm supposed to be quiet, but I confess I'm dying of curiosity. Just what is it that makes you so different? Are you impervious to injury? Or is it some things that can't hurt you as opposed to others?"

He sighed noisily, leaning back against the tree. He propped up a knee and rested his wrist on it. "You really aren't going to let this go, are you?"

She replied with a one-shouldered shrug and a little smile she couldn't seem to help.

"I asked, didn't I?"

He seemed to think hard about it for several beats. "This is a bad idea," he said aloud, more in a lecture to himself than to her, she supposed. "Truth is, I don't know the full extent of what I can do anymore. I just pretend it isn't there. Except to avoid accidental exposure like what happened with you. I've gotten so used to tamping down everything." He sighed with feeling. "When I was younger, it was connected hard to my emotions. When I got upset or angry, when I became excited . . ." The big man colored, and Ambrea hid a smile behind her fingers. It was obvious by the stilted manner of his speech that he wasn't used to talking about himself. She didn't want him to think she was laughing at him. In truth, she found it endearing.

"It?" she prompted.

"Yeah. It." He studied her for a moment and then seemed to make his choice. He lifted his hand and stared at his palm for a long, steady span of seconds.

Slowly, almost like a trick of her eyes, a wobbly effect bent the air around his hand, like what you might see when looking down a long, heat-baked road.

There was a startling popping sound and his hand burst into flames.

She squeaked in surprise, watching with wide eyes as he spread his fingers, showing her that they were all fully involved, golden orange flames curling and licking at them, the fire swirling over his skin as if it loved him, as if it had missed him and needed to embrace him any way it could. His response to seeing it was visceral as well. His eyes became hooded with a distinctive sense of pleasure. He drew the fire close as though to smell it, taking in a long, slow breath. She didn't think he even realized what he was doing. It was as if he had become instantly spellbound. Whatever he thought of his abilities, whatever the trauma he had suffered because of them, it was instantly clear to her that this was more than a natural part of him. It was a passionate part of him.

Ambrea was also fascinated. Thousands of questions filled her head. And like a child who didn't know better, who could appreciate fire just for the beauty of it and without the fearful respect she ought to have for it, she reached out to touch his fingers with hers. She wanted to know if the fire was real or just a visual effect. Was it hot? Would it burn? It wasn't burning him, but would it burn her?

Luckily he became aware of her movement and jerked his hand away, the action dousing the fire and leaving the tips of his fingers smoking in small, curling white tendrils. She reached to grab his hand, lacing her fingers through his. Before he had pulled away, she had felt the incredible concentrated heat of the flames and had known they were as real as could be. Now she gripped him and she felt how hot he was. She suddenly recalled how incredibly warm he had felt in that icy cold water, how he had not suffered from hypothermia at all. She also recalled the streak of light in the overwhelming darkness of the aqueduct water and realized that he had used his ability to generate light to find her, whether he realized it or not. Whether he wanted to admit to it or not. He may have distanced himself from it as much as he could distance himself from something that was in the very heart of him, but it would always be at the edge of his reflexes. Literally at the tips of his fingers.

"Oh, Rush," she breathed. "That was amazing. It was beautiful!" She took in a breath and could detect the odor of burnt wood. "Surely the Great Being has given you an astounding gift. How can you think this to be a curse?"

She exhaled, and smoke blew lightly out of her nostrils and between her lips. When she had breathed in, she had drawn it in from his smoking hand. Rush watched with an almost speechless fascination as she turned up his hand in both of hers, pulling his palm open and drawing it against her face. She nuzzled against its warmth like an eager, affection-starved kitten, drawing in another deeply pleasured breath. He sat frozen for a moment as she did this, stunned by her reaction and even more stunned by his own. Raw, unchecked delight flooded his big body, a sensation akin to sexual stimulation, but in no way that base. Yet he was very much aroused. The muscles in his body tightened in a clenching cascade, rather like when he was on the very edge of danger. And everything about this, he knew, was dangerous. He tried to pull free of her, but she held on. All he managed to do was jerk her onto his body, their chests colliding. Rush felt the weight of her, her warmth and softness wrapped up with her eagerness and vitality.

He balked at what she was saying with every inch of his psyche; his memory of that charred field, and a village of superstitious fools who would rather destroy themselves in a screaming conflagration than find it in themselves to understand a boy they professed to love as blood seeming so much more powerful with the passing of time than the traumatic moment it had happened. She hadn't heard the voices, voices that had once been warm and familiar to him, that had even idolized him, suddenly jeering and yelling for his head. She hadn't felt the caustic fever of the mob mentality that had quickly developed as they had staked him out in a field, nearly drowned him in fuel, then situated an explosive to set it all off.

"You just don't understand," he said quietly, unable to find the heart to be angry with her. After all, she was the first person to express some eagerness and a positive attitude as far as this thing was concerned. Perhaps, too, it had something to do with how close and warm she felt, how long and delicious her body was as it lay tangled onto his.

"I understand that something about a person can sometimes be perceived one way or another way depending on how the person himself feels about it."

Maybe there was some truth in that, but he wasn't willing to test the theory. Things had gone pretty well for him as long as he forced himself to keep this thing inside of him dormant. He didn't want to change the status quo.

And in the moment, the way she was making him feel was very much in danger of changing the status quo. In more ways than she could possibly realize. He had to get a better grip on himself, on the entire situation. When he lost control, things tended to spin into bad directions.

"Anyway, we have more important things to worry about for the moment," he told her. He reached up with his free hand, using two fingers to brush back some of that flyaway hair of hers. His initial intention was, of course, to dump her off of himself, put her at a safe distance, but instead he found himself noticing that before he had cut her hair, the sheer weight of it had kept it in place, made it an almost perfect sheet. Now that half of its weight was gone, it was clear there was body to it, that it was actually quite fine and soft. Rush had to confess to himself that because he didn't have much occasion in his lifestyle for soft and delicate things, he was significantly attracted to her. Perhaps just because of the novelty of it. Oh, he spent a lot of time with delicate, feminine women these days. The Chosen Ones.

The Chosen Ones.

Those priests and priestesses of a temple in the wilds of the planet Ebbany were gifted with extraordinary powers, from the ability to heal with a touch to the ability to see into the future. Abilities that no one in the Three Worlds had ever seen before. Abilities that Rush had never seen manifested in anyone other than himself. The Chosen Ones had since been forced to leave their wilderness temple and were now members of the Special Active team that had been created just to utilize their capabilities distinctive to each mission, as they had on this mission using Fallon to help psychically guide Rush through the aqueduct tunnels and to the point of extraction. The team was half Chosen Ones and half First Active soldiers, the elite of the IM's training and experience.

Rush had to confess that his experiences with meeting the Chosen Ones, training with them, and watching how everyone interacted with them and treated them had greatly softened his fears of ever being exposed to his team for what he was. He had been very reserved about the whole thing, watching quietly and pondering the results. But the problem still remained—his team would not look kindly on him having kept this secret from them all these years. There was also a huge difference between the Chosen Ones' abilities and the sheer destructive force that he was able to conjure up with just a moment's concentration. It was like the difference between a stunner and an MX-240. The Chosen Ones could stun and amaze; as such, they were a useful, benign tool, for the most part. He was a 240, savage and brutal, and could cook a person from the inside out and the outside in on a whim. The IM might feel that he was far too dangerous to be running loose and uncontrolled.

Then again, every last one of the former First Actives, now Special Actives, was a dangerous weapon. But they were completely controlled by the IM. As were the Chosen Ones. He had gone over this in his head time and again these past two cycles since they had been integrated into a team with the Chosen Ones. If ever there had been a time for him to come clean about who and what he really was, it had been two cycles ago when the Ebbanite priests and priestesses had first come on the scene. Now the window of opportunity had faded and was most likely gone.

No. He had made a choice and he was better off sticking to it.

It was via the female Chosen Ones that he had gotten more used to the delicate femininity that Ambrea represented. Still, he wasn't at all hands-on with any of those women, unlike Commander Chapel, who shared the bed of the head priestess, Ravenna. Truthfully, Rush shouldn't be hands-on with Ambrea either. Certainly not in this situation of high-intensity danger and pinpoint politics, and probably not under any circumstances. But she seemed so strangely compelling to him. All that strong, beautiful bone structure and pretty paleness, those enormous teal blue eyes. The counterpoint of her gold and red hair. Her golden lashes.

Most of all, she had seen his darkest, most dangerous secret and had not run screaming in fear, had not called him an abomination, a freak of nature. Quite the opposite, and nothing could have been more compelling to Rush's soul just then. He believed, then, that she would not betray his secret. That she did understand the fickle nature of people and that they could just as easily turn on you as not.

"What will we do now?" she asked softly, her lashes lowering halfway over her eyes.

"What we were going to do before. Make our way to the docking port that abuts the southwestern boundary of the preserve."

"But we'll never get past the guards—"

"I meant through the boundary itself. We'll cut through straight to where we have a ship ported on the tarmac."

"Won't a breach in the boundary set off an alarm?"

"Aye, it will. But we'll be airborne and at the outer rim before they even get to examine the breach. And the rest of the team will be waiting there for us. We have to start thinking about getting mobile again."

Although he was thinking about it, for some reason he wasn't feeling that he ought to be in such an all-fired hurry to push her off and away, to put distance between them either physically or personally. Rush had to admit that it was the closest he'd felt to a moment of true intimacy in as long as he could remember. There was something infinitely comforting about it. Welcoming in a way he wasn't used to. Sure, his friends were warm to him and welcoming, but there was always that distance between them, a distance created by the secret he harbored from them so zealously.

"We should go," he said quietly, his eyes fixating on the pale pink of her lips.

"Whenever you like," she said. "And Rush, I know you don't know me well or even have any cause to trust me, but I won't deliberately betray you. You don't need to threaten me or—"

"I know. I'm sorry I did that," he said with feeling, guilt tripping over itself inside of him. "I didn't . . . I wouldn't. Hurt you, I mean."

"You might," she countered, "if you were given good enough cause or if I threatened you and everything you hold dear. I can see that you are the sort of man to protect himself and what he loves at any cost. I see that because, perhaps, there is something similar inside of me."

Rush frowned. Yes, he would protect what he held dear, that much was very true. It was unnerving that he couldn't tell himself truthfully what he would do or what motivation would affect him the strongest. If he had to choose between saving himself or saving those he loved, he would sacrifice his life every single time, but if he had to choose between saving those he loved over exposing himself as a freak, he honestly couldn't say which would win out. There had been a time when the answer had been easy. He had chosen to save the life of a girl over a lifetime of silence. The result had been disastrous. Everyone, including that ungrateful girl, had turned on him like a nest of angry vipers. And every day he forced himself to remember that, to remember the easy changeability of people's natures.

"Come on, Princess," he said with a sigh, reaching to move her to the side so he could sit up.

Once again she resisted, staying his attempts at pushing her away. Funny thought, that. For all her long, lean stature, she was still hardly able to be any challenge to his size and strength. He could easily overpower her at any given moment. In any given way.

Ambrea didn't know why she insisted on clinging to him in such a way. She had never initiated such intimate contact before. And it really was intimate. She could feel all of his strength, all his hard muscle and coiled resistance, against every single point of her body where they connected. Yet for all that seeming rigidity, they seemed to fit together so snugly, so warmly. In the end, she thought that was a large part of what kept her clinging to him. He was so blessedly warm. She felt as though she had been miserably cold for so much of her lifetime, and here he was, heated and strong, vital and safe. How could an utter stranger feel so safe? If there was one thing she had learned in her lifetime, it was not to trust anyone, and yet he invaded her every cell with this overwhelming sense of security.

Perhaps it was because they both had something to lose now if they didn't trust each other. Perhaps it was all that steady strength she felt and saw in him. Or maybe it was just the gentle way he was touching her hair at the side of her face. He could bullishly threaten her all he liked, but he couldn't hide the gentleness of those callused fingertips as they toyed with her hair.

Ambrea didn't know why she did it, but she turned her head to the side and touched her lips to his hand in the merest brush of contact. She didn't mean to really kiss him, she told herself. But she just felt such a fervent need to make some kind of deeper contact with him. Some way, perhaps, of letting him know he wasn't as alone as he seemed to think he was. But at the same time it was so strange for her to want to express herself in such a way. A way she never had before.

Rush felt her lips press into the seat of his palm like a brief jolt of lightning. Nothing ever burned him, he couldn't really feel heat or electricity or shock the way he imagined others did, but this burned him. It seared him to the quick, racing up his arm and deeply into his bones. He drew in a sharp, startled breath, utterly fascinated with the sensation. His heart clenched tightly, began to race as if he were staring death in the face. Again, an unfamiliar sensation. As far as he knew, he was completely impervious to most modern weapons. The closest he'd ever come to death was when he'd almost drowned in Axiom fuel all those years ago.

Excitement hurried through his blood, and before he could check the response he had her head between both his hands and was dragging her mouth up to his. And there he held her, hovering, just a breath away. His chest hurt, his body was tight with the things it was feeling, the things it wanted to feel. Things he had wisely denied himself for fear . . .

It wasn't until that moment that the soldier realized just how much of his life was lived in fear. Fear of exposure. Fear of his own emotions. Fear of living.

Rush covered her mouth with his, probably just to fly in the face of that nauseating idea that he might be afraid of anything. But the moment he felt her gasp softly with surprise at the contact, he had to confess to himself that it was actually just a really good excuse to let himself taste a forbidden fruit that he knew by instinct would be utterly delicious. And she was. Warm and exotic, sweet and complex, her mouth under his was inexperienced and startled. It might have been enough to compel him to back off, to remember himself and their situation, but her surprise lasted only the span of a breath. Then she relaxed against him, her whole essence going liquid and receptive. Her lips parted under his, just to draw in an exquisite breath, but he couldn't help but exploit it for the advantage that it was. His tongue was seeking hers purely on instinct before she could even finish that breath.

He knew very well that he was not inclined to kiss a woman at whim, or even after a great deal of thought.

Like everything else, it was a terrible complication and a risk he couldn't afford. But none of that seemed to matter as he felt the heated flavor of her spreading over his senses. How strange it was that she should taste as sweet as he expected her to. How strange to realize he had already given it some thought. He couldn't believe the amount of pleasure attached to something so seemingly benign. But if anyone knew about the ability of something so seemingly simple to become so utterly explosive, it was him.

Ambrea couldn't claim to be surprised when he seized hold of her in that blisteringly hot kiss. It was more a feeling of unfamiliarity. But not awkwardness. Shouldn't she feel awkward? After all, she had never been kissed by a man before. Yet they seemed to mesh together as if they had done it thousands of times before, as if they made a regular habit of kissing each other.

She could sense the caution in him, just as she could sense the hunger in him. It was a peculiar combination. He wrestled with himself, it seemed, every single moment, and yet held her tighter, gripped her closer. There was a moment of suspense, as though he were on the cusp of recovering himself and pushing free, and then it all seemed to dissolve. Rush breathed hard against her, his hands swallowing her face and neck even as his mouth began to burn with desperation. He collapsed into his own need, into the kiss, as if something suddenly let go of him and sent him careening into it.

Ambrea's whole body lit up with fiery response. Her hands fumbled at his shoulders, needing to hold on as reality swung wildly around her, forced her to open herself to the sensations rushing through her. Because of her life, its restrictions, its precariousness, she had never even once entertained the idea of a simple kiss with a boy. But this was no boy. He was one hundred percent living, vital, overwhelming man. She felt how he tensed beneath her, how he seemed to grow restless against her body and against her lips. He tasted rich and smoky, like a delicious culinary char that enhanced a juicy entrée. Erotic hunger began to build inside of her and she shifted out of passivity. She took hold of him, spearing her eager fingers into his short, crisp hair, holding him to herself as she turned her head and attacked him at a whole new angle.

Rush never once forgot where he was, the danger they were in, and never once stopped thinking how crazy and irresponsible his behavior was. And yet it didn't seem to matter. She was lush and sweet and filling his hands as they slid down her back and burrowed under her shirt at the back of her waist. He gripped her curvy sides, his fingertips clutching at the center point of her spinal column. Blood was pounding in his ears, heat was burning through his body. He grew hard with his excitement, with the feel of her weight against him, her restlessness seemingly stroking the rapidly growing erection she was inspiring.

"Ow! *Ow!*" Ambrea yelped in sudden pain, her hands jolting down to his, yanking his touch free of her body. The kiss broke as she scrambled upright over him, straddling his thighs and pulling up her shirt in back as she wrenched around trying to see herself.

He knew instantly what had happened. It had happened before. It was why he didn't do things like this. Taking hold of her, he turned her so he could see her back. There was hardly a need to look. His touch on her clothing was making soft, crispy, sizzling sounds. And sure enough, on her back were the reddened imprints of his hands, of each individual finger, as if she had been branded.

"Shit!" he swore viciously. "Damn me!" Then more vehemently. "*Damn me!*"

"It's all right," she tried to assure him hastily.

But he was already dumping her off of himself and moving back so he wasn't touching her. Yet at the same time he was hovering over the injury on her back, guilt and sickly horror pervading every inch of his being.

Nothing had changed, he realized with disgust. The last time he'd tried to kiss a girl, back on Tari when he'd been just a youth, her skirt had caught fire. Luckily the fabric had been the only victim in that instance, a little bit of scorching because he'd been able to react quickly. He'd been able to convince her she'd caught a blowing ember from a nearby fire, and she'd believed him. But this woman knew exactly what had burned her. He could see it in her eyes. She realized that in his excitement he had lost control. And yet she reached for his hands again, took hold of his heated fingers, gripped them tightly.

"I'm all right," she said vehemently, forcing him to meet her reassuring teal gaze.

"I'm sorry . . . I can't . . . I told you . . ." He was choking on his own words, his own fury at himself for losing control, for allowing himself to forget.

"Rush, please. Look." She reached to scoop up her shirt and show him the angry red marks. "It's no worse than a burn from the sun, and I have had more than my share of those. I will be fine."

"Don't you see?" he gritted out. "It could have been worse! Much worse! I could have set you on *fire*!"

"But you didn't."

"I don't know what got into me. You shouldn't be touching me!" He yanked free of her grasp, but she immediately laid her hands on his chest. As upset as he was, some part of him just couldn't shake off the comfort she was trying to give.

And just like that an easy, calming intimacy settled over them. The feel of her hands on him soothed him somehow. Perhaps it was the idea that even though he had accidentally hurt her, she wasn't running away screaming. She didn't look at him as the freak he was even though she had more cause than ever to think so. As much as he hated himself for having hurt her, there was a part of him that was far too starved for intimacy to be able to shun it.

"Rush. It's all right. You didn't mean to do it. I know that. *You* know that."

"It won't happen again," he swore to her. "It won't . . . I had no right. We're in enough danger as it is. I have no idea what I was thinking."

He had been thinking how sweet she felt, how amazing she had tasted, how beautiful she was. He'd let himself run away from himself. He couldn't afford to do that. Not now, not ever. The only minuscule comfort he took was that she didn't hate him, wasn't afraid of him. He had a long way to go with her yet, needed her to trust him so he could properly protect her.

"I'm just as guilty," she said softly. "I have so many people counting on me, an entire country I owe responsibility to. The last thing I ought to be doing is . . ." She shrugged and looked away. "Never mind. We were both behaving . . . strangely." She met his eyes, licking her lips slowly, attracting his attention in spite of himself. Such a simple gesture and yet, somehow, he found it ridiculously arousing. Arousal put her in danger.

He shuttered himself away from the sensation, looked away from her, methodically checked his munitions belt, the rote behavior calming him. Comforting him.

"Then we're agreed," he said gruffly. "It won't happen again."

She didn't respond for a long beat, and he didn't look up to see the look on her face. He didn't think he could bear the relief in her eyes. Of course he didn't blame her for it at all, but just the same.

"I think that's best," she said softly. "We both have jobs to do, and it's best that we focus on that."

Rush nodded. Then he took her gingerly by her arms and set her alongside him so he could sit up. "Let's move. The sooner we go, the less chance of the Imperial Guard sending in reinforcements. With any luck, my team was able to silence the guards before they could report back anything about the trouble they ran into . . . about seeing you."

"Oh." He could tell by her troubled frown that she regretted whatever harm had come to the imperial soldiers, who she deemed to be hapless victims in a power war between her and her uncle. How quickly she seemed to have forgotten just how brutal some of those guards were. Her father had recruited very specific types of men into his armed forces. Rush was certain there wasn't a single one of them who could claim innocence and a pure moral compass. "Would you do me a favor, please?" she asked.

"I can try," he said awkwardly. He didn't know where she was going with this request. All he wanted was to put what had just happened behind them and move on. As she had said, they both had specific jobs they needed to focus on.

"Please call me Ambrea. I think at this point, after saving my life so many times, and . . . well, you have more than earned the right."

He gave her a wry smile. He didn't see how any of his behavior merited anything special. Still, the fact that she was asking, in spite of everything, meant far more to him than she might realize. "Well, like I said, I can try. I might lean more toward Blue Eyes, myself."

"Well, so long as you know I consider you a person of privilege and trust. That is a very important thing to be to the future empress of Allay. One day you may need a favor from me. I want you to know that you have more than earned that."

As she spoke the words, her mien and bearing were such that Rush no longer saw the helpless prisoner or powerless princess of exile. He saw exactly what she could and—if he had any say in the matter—would be. A queen. A true leader for people who truly needed her.

"Unfortunately, Prin—Ambrea," Rush caught himself, "we have a long way to go yet."

CHAPTER
SEVEN

"Crap." Justice spat as she shook guard guts off her left hand glove and the knife she'd been forced to pull. The idiot had tried to garrote her, catching her up from behind while she'd been in hand-to-hand with someone else. They were under strict no-kill orders, but both she and Ender had been forced to break the order. The forest was littered with the bodies of the squad that had come upon them, but most were just stunned to within an inch of their lives. Normally Ender would have had her back, protecting her from just this sort of situation, but he'd been given the strict duty of being personal protector to the little empress, so he'd been forced to ditch his companions in order to preserve her safety.

"You got any holes in you?" Bronse Chapel asked, eyeing the blood saturating her clothes from mid torso down.

"Nah," she rasped, her voice completely screwed up now that her windpipe had been crushed and bruised, nearly severed if the truth be told. She no doubt had a gash in her neck from one side to the other. That wire had been damn sharp, and the man behind it had been brutally strong. She coughed, sucking in air, trying to will her throat into not swelling closed. She'd be damned if she was going to become a liability on this mission.

Bad enough they were dragging around two pieces of deadweight.

"You sure? You look pretty raw, Justice." Commander Chapel touched her under her chin and made her lift it so he could inspect the damage. "Yeah, that's not good."

"Just slap a patch on me to keep the swelling down," she croaked. "I'll be singing solos again by sunset."

Bronse nodded, reaching into his pack for an aid kit. By now the rest of the group had realized she was injured and were surrounding her, concern written on all their features. The attention made her uncomfortable. If there was one thing Justice Muleterre was not, it was an object of pity. And now that they were essentially a man down, they couldn't afford for her to be weak or needy. Fallon was a good soldier, his talents as a telepath were astounding, but he was not a First Active soldier like Chapel, Justice, and Ender had once been. He was still something of a rookie as far as soldiering went.

She reached into the aid pack and grabbed the heal scal while the commander peeled off a patch and stuck it on her arm at the first piece of bare skin he could see. She was going to run the heal seal across her throat, but Bronse took it from her and gave her a scolding look. She set her lips together, grimly reminding herself not to be insubordinate, and lifted her chin so he could apply the seal. It was a medication stick about an inch across and four inches long. It was drawn across an open wound rather like lip balm was applied to lips, leaving a smeary sort of goo in its wake. The commander drew it over her wound slowly and with care to cover every bit of it. He did a far better job, no doubt, than she could have done since she was unable to actually see the wound.

"Did you contact Ender?"

The commander was pretty close to her, so she could

see clearly into his periwinkle eyes. In an instant, with just a look, she knew something wasn't right.

"Not yet," he said gruffly.

"What?" she asked. "What is it?"

He paused to glance surreptitiously at Suna checking to see how far away she was. Clearly he didn't want her overhearing what he wanted to say. That made Justice's chest clench with tightness. Suddenly it was hard for her to breathe. Thankfully Suna was at a significant distance, allowing the commander to speak softly and not be overheard.

"Be patient. I'm giving him time to shake anyone following him and to hunker down out of sight."

"What aren't you telling me?" she wanted to know.

He paused for a significant beat, presumably under the guise of touching up her wound. But Justice had been part of his team for too long not to know when he was hedging. Still, she had also been part of his team long enough to know that the commander would get to the point in his own way and in his own time. There was nothing she could do to rush him.

"I think he was hit," he said at last, so softly she hardly heard him over the rush of blood still pounding in her ears from fighting for her life moments ago.

"With a two-forty?" she asked just as softly.

"Seems like. Though I'm uncertain. I mean, if he'd been hit, even Ender would come to his knees on the badass end of a two-forty."

"Right." She took a great deal of relief in that understanding.

"He didn't so much as flinch from what I saw." But Bronse's brow was deeply furrowed, the commander clearly perplexed. "But I was a stride away. I could swear he was dead in sights when that two-forty went off."

"But you have to be wrong. I mean, he ran off at full steam, didn't he?"

"He did," Bronse agreed. "Then again I've seen Ender do some pretty amazing shit over our time together."

"Yeah, me too." And Justice had known Ender much longer than Bronse had. Justice and Ender had gone through initial training together. They'd been assigned to the same regiment after that. And they'd entered ETF training together. "So you think he took a hit, shook it off, and kept going?"

"I don't know what to think. I'm going to tell myself I was mistaken and he didn't take the hit. It's the only explanation."

However, Justice knew as well as Bronse did that he had as keen an eye as the rest of them. He was rarely mistaken about anything. Especially when it came to keeping track of what was happening in the heat of a moment. In the end, that's what being an ETF soldier was all about. You got to be on the Extreme Tactics Force only if you could keep your shit together in a fire-fight and perform above and beyond normal endurance to basically pull off miracles. Justice supposed that that explained things all around. The commander was right. Ender could shake off things that no one else would ever be able to.

But just because he could grit it out and shake it off didn't mean it wouldn't catch up with him later. Ender could be out there wounded, slowly dying, with nothing but some overprivileged twit to look out for him.

"No."

The commander said it firmly, stopping the words in Justice's throat before she had barely taken a breath to form them.

"I could recon out and be back before—"

"I could swear I heard myself say 'no,' Captain," he said implacably. He closed up the heal seal and put it back into the aid kit. "You're wounded. The last thing you need is to exert yourself out there alone and suddenly your throat swells shut. You'll do none of us any good if you're dead in the bushes, kiddo."

Justice had to bite down a flare of frustration and the half-dozen arguments she knew would only fall on deaf ears. Besides, he was right. There was no logic in taking that kind of risk, and the rest of the group certainly couldn't stay around the scene of their crimes waiting for backup to come to the Imperial Guards' assistance.

"Did these guys get a call out? Did they ID Miss Prim?"

Bronse raised a brow. "Miss Prim? I take it something about Princess Ambrea meets with your disapproval?"

Justice shrugged. "I don't have to like her. I just have to do my job."

"True. But you haven't known her long enough for her to get on your bad side."

"Eh. She lost my vote at mission briefing. What kind of a weakling lets people bully her around all her life? I mean, where's her backbone? She could have grown a spine and rebelled any number of times, escaped the planet maybe. Anything but sitting there meekly year after year." Justice shook off a shudder of disgust. She just didn't understand how someone could be so willing to let others push her around. How the princess wasn't already dead, Justice was at a loss to say.

Then again she'd never really understood these foreign courts. All of the manners and the ways they dressed. Jockeying for favor with a potentate or for a sound bite in the media. Give her the clear-cut rules of the Tari clans any day. As hateful as living on a space platform could be, at least it was easy to know where you stood, and the only thing that mattered was showing strength. The clan that was the strongest was the clan that ruled. And a clan ruled strongly because it was a family, each member covering the back of the next member. That attitude was also prevalent in the IM. Everyone was very much there for everyone else. That was why, among the clans, it was considered highly respectable to join the IM.

That was the one constant amongst the Tarians. Although those who lived on the platforms were merchants and dealt in and depended on high-end technologies, and those who lived planetside, like Ender, were far more primitive in their needs and lifestyles, the one thing they had in common was the clans. All the members of a clan lived as one family, whether or not they were blood kin. And although members of a clan might fight for dominance, once dominance was established it was respected, at least until unforgivable weakness was shown. You lived and died for your brothers and sisters in your clan. You could travel far and wide, even planet to planet, but you were always clan.

That was probably why Justice and Ender got on so well. They both understood what really mattered. Strength and loyalty. It wouldn't surprise her in the least if Ender had somehow managed to shake off a deadly 240 blast. She had never met anyone stronger. She was positive that, had he remained with his clan on Tari planet, he would be a chieftain by now. Still, she and Ender had both, for whatever reasons, been odd men out in their clans. He'd had to leave for his reasons, and she for hers.

Justice drew her thoughts to a halt right there. She wasn't in the mood to rehash her life choices and the reasons why things were the way they were. She really didn't like to waste her time. What she *did* know was that when things had gotten dicey in her life, she'd pulled herself into a new direction, forged ahead, and lived in a way she could find peace with. Frankly, she had no idea how the princess could stand her own company.

"As usual, Justice, you make no room for differences in culture, temperament, and laws. Princess Ambrea shows great respect for the laws of her land. She understands that there must be an order to things and if she doesn't show it homage then she can't expect others to do the same. She wants her place in this world to be earned fairly and cleanly. Otherwise she will be just as bad as those she seeks to replace. She waited for her time to come, and now it's here. Fairly and without plunging her entire country into civil war. I actually have a great deal of respect for her reserve and her wisdom."

Justice lifted a noncommittal shoulder. Realizing they weren't going to see eye to eye on the matter, the commander let the subject drop. He straightened up from inspecting her wound, seemingly satisfied that it had finally stopped bleeding.

"Can you breathe all right? It's still a bit of a trek before we reach the boundary."

"I'm fine," she insisted. "I'm going to sound like Jenri Hobar for a few days, so we best get me back on the station by starfall so I can take advantage of it with the boys." She gave him a mischievous grin and put her hand on her hip to vamp it up a second like the husky-voiced actress was known to do when the VidMags were taking her likeness. Chapel laughed and cuffed her playfully on the side of her head. She cuffed him right back, or tried to anyway, as he turned to gather their battle-shocked group together.

"Let's make distance away from here. The sooner we're off the planet and in the safety of the IM space station, the happier I'm going to be." He looked back at Justice as he pulled his weapon into his hand. They hadn't walked around armed before, hoping to blend in and act normal. Now with Justice covered in blood and both he and Fallon sporting scrapes and bruises of their own, it was unlikely they could pass without arousing suspicion, even without the flame-haired princess as a dead giveaway. It was better they be armed and at the ready rather than having to scramble for weapons the way they had this time. Justice sheathed her emergency knife back onto her hip and drew her weapon as well. She nodded to her commander and they headed out.

Rush pulled Ambrea up to the boundary and, as usual, situated her behind the bulk of the better part of his body. Still, he kept her slightly off center so he could keep a steady eye on her. This section of the boundary was tight up against a copse of trees, providing a good cover. Now all he had to do was wait for the rest of the group to show up and they could move as one entity through to the tarmac on the other side, backing up one another and making their insertion through the boundary in a smooth, single act of precision.

"Rush?"

"Mmm?"

He was shrugging out of his pack, pulling it around in front of himself. He didn't want to look up at her because, truth be told, he'd spent far too much time studying her ever since they had left their hiding spot after the attack. The soldier in him had wanted to find a cap or scarf of some kind to cover that brilliant hair of hers. It stuck out like a sore thumb, stood out in contrast to the blue-green leaves and gray-brown bark of the trees. Short or long, it was still her crowning glory, and it was a very distinctive trademark that told everyone exactly who she might be and, for those searching specifically for her, exactly who she was.

But it wasn't the soldier in him that preferred to leave it uncovered. He couldn't seem to help it, it fascinated him. A lot about her seemed to fascinate him. Tarians as a rule were either bright blond, as he was, or raven black, as Justice was. There were hardly any in betweens, although there was always the occasional genetic anomaly.

He chuckled noiselessly to himself at that. Occasional genetic anomaly indeed.

The black-haired Tarians seemed to be mostly concentrated on the space platforms. The blonds were planetside. It was hard to say what had happened between the planet and the platforms to create such a distinction. He imagined at some point they all must have lived mixed together on the planet. Or perhaps something about living in space had created the change. Anyway, he hadn't really given it much thought because he hadn't cared to think of his home planet much at all these past years.

But he had since seen his share of hair colors, from blue to violet to red, each more shocking than the last to a man born in a monochromatic society. Still, nothing compared to that golden red of Ambrea's hair, not to mention the way it seemed to reach out for everything with caressing fingers, the way it framed such a pretty face that was somehow strong and fragile all at once.

"You should do something about your shirt."

"Hmm?" He looked into her eyes. As much as he had tried to avoid engaging her again since they'd kissed and he'd hurt her so unwittingly, he felt the click of instant connection as easily as if he were a piece of a puzzle meant to interconnect with her. It was unnerving to him, even as it was strangely comforting. Rush had never before experienced anything like this sensation, and she was in such a ridiculous position for him to feel connected to her in any way, shape, or form. She was destined to be a queen for a single land. He was destined to be a soldier of many lands. When this assignment was over, it wasn't likely he would see the inside of the Allayan borders again for months. Perhaps even entire cycles. And anyway, what kind of friendship could a Tarian mutation ever expect to cultivate with the woman of station she was? They were, literally, worlds apart.

Now if only he could shake this instinct inside him that wanted to compel him to feel otherwise.

"Your shirt. Your teammates are sharp, clever people. They will see that burn hole and . . ." She trailed off, but there was no need for her to continue. She was right. He had been so absorbed in keeping them safe as he got them to this point in the mission that he hadn't remembered to cover any evidence of his mutation. He felt a strange, sick feeling at the realization, but then the even more important understanding that she was trying to protect him washed it away. He stripped off his shirt and balled it up in his hands for a moment.

"Thank you," he said. He hoped she could understand that his appreciation extended much further than the simple reminder to remove his shirt. He didn't really have the social skill needed to pretty it all up and make his gratitude known anywhere near the level she deserved. But when she reached out to brush fingers of comfort over his bare biceps, he knew she understood. She traced her thumb over the ink that had been painstakingly colored over his skin, her touch so soft in such a hard and harsh world. It was a strange thing, but he thought he could smell the warmth and beauty of her. In truth all he ought to be able to smell was the remnants of soil and leaf litter that had dirtied her clothes. And although he could recognize signs of the forest all over her, it was as though that outside influence couldn't compete with the natural sweetness that was just her. Without realizing it, he had turned toward her, his body leaning closer to her, the easy intimacy he felt with her all of a sudden coming back into play.

Damn, this was stupid of him, letting himself get distracted. Over what? A pretty face? That wild hair? She was just a woman. Just like any other woman. Just as untouchable as any other woman. She wasn't even the kind of woman he always thought he might take to. He liked them strong and sassy. Sexual and vivacious. Like Justice. He had always considered that if he were ever going to try to hook up with someone, it would be Justice, or someone like her. A Tarian, most likely. Tough, bold, and wild, and not so easily burned.

The princess was off-limits. Complicated. Breakable. Naïve as all get out.

Just the same, a breath later his fingertips were brushing her face along her hairline. His hands were thick, his fingers rough and covered with hard calluses that he'd earned and earned again over his lifetime. She was smooth as cream, soft as feathers. Regardless of the other dangers he presented to her, he could easily imagine himself touching her too harshly, breaking something on her by accident. The realization made him pull back, but she was quick and had hold of his hand in both of hers. She pulled open his fingers and drew the flat of his palm onto her cheek. Again she nuzzled against him for a long moment, the action slow and stimulating, the brush of her lashes along the inside of his thumb surprisingly intense. Her breath pooled in his palm, spinning warmly against his wrist.

Then she seemed to realize what she had done, and awkwardness flushed over her face. She dipped her head, drawing back a little.

"I'm sorry," she said. "I'm not used to . . . No one touches me. Everyone else who knows who I am would never think of touching me like this. Except for you. The sensation is so strange for me, and yet I find I am drawn to it."

"Why is it that no one can touch you?" He didn't point out the obvious, that he should be the last person she should allow to touch her. Those scorches on her back made that all too clear.

She sighed. "The idea is that I am royalty and too precious for the common touch. But I am also poisonous fruit, the daughter of a traitor and a whore. I am doubly cursed, then, to know no comfort."

"I am as common as it gets, Princess. And I don't really care who your parents were. They have no bearing on who you are as an individual. There is only so much you can blame your parents for. At some point you have to hold yourself responsible for your own actions."

"I couldn't agree more," she whispered. She studied his face, her gaze sharp and discerning.

Whatever else she was, he could tell she was intelligent. Perhaps not learned in worldly ways, but that would quickly change once she was out of her controlled exile. He could see that very clearly.

"I suppose you blamed your parents for what you are for quite some time," she speculated carefully.

He nodded shortly. He had treated his mother abysmally during his adolescence, his anger overtaking his love for her. He had hated what he was, and she had not made him feel any better about it, refusing to even discuss the matter. She wouldn't even tell him who his father was. No one else had known, either. It was a strange sort of thing in a tight-knit clan like theirs. Everyone always knew what was going on with whom, and who was in whose bed. But apparently his mother had been intensely discreet about her affair. She had never spoken a word of it, had never given him a clue as to whether she felt positively or negatively about the experience. He could only assume a negative. If she had loved his sire, wouldn't she have wanted to share that with him? Or perhaps what had once been love had turned to hate the moment she realized she had given birth to a freakish little child who one day could destroy everything she held dear if he didn't learn to control himself?

He had resented her for what he had determined to be a lack of love for him. A real mother, he had thought, would have loved him no matter what he was. If anyone should have loved him, it should have been his mother. So his behavior to her just before she died had been horrible. The lashing out of a confused boy under the pressure of becoming a man in a tribal system that worshipped personal strength above all else. After all, wasn't he the strongest and most powerful of them all? He could make a scathing mark in his clan, be the most powerful of men. It hadn't been until he had taken that brutal, life-changing step that he realized she had been right all along. That she had only been trying to protect him out of love for him, not trying to hold him back, as he had mistakenly accused her of in his heart.

"I learned it was wrong to blame my parents. They could no more control the manner of their genetic material than I could. Perhaps they ought not to have had children at all," he amended, "but for me to say that would be to say I believe that my life has no value. My life has had its trials, but it is because I am here that other lives have been spared. Not just one or two. Many."

"The lives of an entire nation, Rush," she reminded him quietly. "If not for you, countless people would suffer in Allay."

"Perhaps." He shrugged it off. "If it hadn't been me it would have been someone else. My team could have gotten you out of here just as well without me." He tried to repress a quick smile. "But I did it with far more style."

That made her laugh out loud, and he had to hush her with two fingers resting heavily over her lips. He regretted the need to do so. He felt that she probably didn't get the opportunity to laugh very often. It was a shame. She had a nice-sounding laugh. Not jolly or even raucous like Justice's could be, not even genteel like Ravenna's was. It was just . . . normal. Not what he would consider the laugh of an empress, but eminently suited to the woman before him.

"Ender?"

The sound of Bronse's voice in his ear made him jolt away from her guiltily. He straightened up and touched the comm piece in his ear. "Yes, sir?"

"We're two minutes out. You?"

"Sittin' and waitin'," he assured his commander.

There was a distinct beat before acknowledgment.

"Hang tight."

Rush's brow furrowed. In just a few words he heard things that no one else would have heard unless they were as tightly knit into their squad as he was. Chapel was notoriously sharp and efficient. It wasn't like him to hesitate in the least. In that small nuance, he knew there was something wrong, something left unsaid because he didn't want to share it over an open communications channel. Was someone injured? Had there been a casualty?

"Shit." He stuffed his shirt deep into his pack as tension ratcheted through his body. He had been under orders to protect their principal at all costs, but had his absence from the squad caused him to lose a good friend? Who hadn't he been there to protect? Fallon? Justice?

"What is it?" Ambrea asked him, worry etching lines into her face almost instantly.

"Nothing," he said, shrugging off her concern. Whatever it was, they were minutes away from finding out. He shouldn't have shown her his worries to start with. It had been thoughtless of him. Truth be told, he'd been off his mark, it seemed, for this entire mission. He would be grateful when it was finally over.

But there was still a long way to go. The mission would not end for him until the matter of her rights to her throne had been adjudicated and he had walked her into her palace and seen her take her rightful seat. As far as the IM was concerned, this was the most pressing matter in all of the Three Worlds at the moment. A great deal hinged on this single woman achieving her place in Allay. The economics alone could have far-reaching ramifications if all did not go as it should. As could Allay being plunged into civil war, or worse yet grasped in the grip of a dictator like Balkin Tsu Allay, who had orchestrated much of Benit Tsu Allay's iron-fisted imperial rule . . .

Balkin was far from being an unknown to the IM. It was Balkin's grasp of the laws of Allay and the laws of the Interplanetary Militia that had tied the militia's hands all these cycles. The IM had always lacked the solid proof it had needed that there were crimes against humanity being perpetrated in Allay, Balkin's brutal efficiency at seeing to it there were no witnesses, no evidence, and no one brave enough to raise a voice against the emperor. But when Benit died and the boy had inherited the throne, the nobles had finally found the backbone to speak up, seeing the opportunity for what it was . . . and seeing the writing on the wall if Balkin was allowed to control the boy absolutely.

It was unexpectedly ambitious and sloppy of Balkin to murder his nephew. The IM could only assume it was murder until evidence was found otherwise, but there was always the possibility that it had truly been a run of bad luck in the imperial family. After all, why would Balkin be so methodical for so long and then seemingly impulsive all of a sudden? And it was very strange that he hadn't seen to the princess's death first. He'd had her completely in his grasp in his prison. The only way he could claim the throne was if she were dead.

It didn't make sense.

Rush shrugged off the worry. It was none of his concern. His job was to protect Ambrea's life, not puzzle out the whys and wherefores of the politics around her. He was a grunt with a job to do and he was just going to do it.

The next sound he heard alerted him to the approach of a person, or group of persons. He cocked his head, listening sharply, automatically putting a powerful hand around the princess's upper arm, ready to pull her in whatever direction he needed her to go. Whoever it was knew how to walk with care and in near silence, in spite of all the noisy things littering the floor of the forest that made it nearly impossible to do so. He believed it was Chapel approaching at first, but then remembered something.

Suna.

Suna wasn't trained to walk a forest floor soundlessly. So he ought to be hearing her clumsy, crashing footsteps since she was with them.

He didn't know what made him throw up a guarding hand, but it allowed his forearm to block the sudden slice of a nasty double-edged blade. Rush stopped the thing from hitting his throat by a fraction, the metal so close that when he grabbed the offending arm on the other end of the blade, the metal scraped the underside of his jaw as if to shave him close and clean. He yanked the attacker out of the cover of the trees and threw him against the resonance boundary that cut them off from their escape. The contact made an impact wave shimmer through the energy of the resonance field. The sound was like the buckling of fatigued metal. The shock that burst into the attacker was meant to discourage animals from escaping onto the tarmac, or people from doing exactly what they were planning to do—escape the planet without going through proper channels. Unfortunately, since Rush had a tight grip on the man, the shock went straight into him as well, the power of the conduction rattling every nerve in his body. But like the stun guns, he could tolerate far more than the average person.

It immediately struck him as odd that the attacker, dressed in an imperial uniform, would take the risk of eliminating him with hand to hand. Rush was clearly superior in strength and size. Why not just shoot him from a safe distance if he knew he was there?

The question was answered when a streak of energy struck him hard in the side of his face. It felt as though he'd been smacked with a ball of acid, the sting fierce and burning. It was a shot from a 240, meant to painfully take him out of the picture.

All it did was piss him off.

He reached for his munitions belt with his off hand, his dominant hand crushing the first soldier into the resonance barrier. He realized that the first man was unconscious about the same time as multiple laser hits began to spray the air around him. He threw the spitter bomb he'd pulled from his belt, aiming directly for the first gunner. He let go of the knifer and grabbed for Ambrea, folding her into his arms and into the protective bend of his body. The spitter went off, spraying the area with bio-corrosive gel. Shouts and mayhem filled the air. The gel was meant to burn any living organism it touched, so any exposed skin, the trees, the brush—all of it sizzled as it corroded away like metal infested with virulent rust. He'd chosen the spitter because it was quieter than anything else he had, had a low radius of effect, and immediately incapacitated anything it touched. No one could tolerate the pain of the corrosive. It dropped them in their steps instantaneously.

* * *

Ambrea had gripped his arms, her breathing panicked and ragged. Her face was burrowed against his biceps. He reached up to touch her hair, stroking it gently for the briefest of moments but conveying the comfort she needed to get her to release her deathly grip on him. She silently nodded, moving free of him, realizing that he didn't have time to be dragged down by her.

"Get low. Stay here until I come back. I'll only be a second."

She crouched down into the fan ferns, trying not to look at the body of the soldier that lay crumpled on the ground mere inches away her. She had never seen anything like the jolting, clawing horror in that soldier's face as Rush had held him trapped in a place of excruciating pain. Ambrea knew that the power in the resonance boundary was incredible, a tremendous repelling force that was not meant to be used as anything other than a fierce repellent. It was not deadly as it repulsed whatever touched it, forcing it hard away. But Rush had used his incredible strength and that awesome mutation of his body to fight the repulse and keep the guard firmly against its power.

The power to create fire with a thought, the ability to withstand energy fire from the most savage of weapons, and now the strength necessary to endure the pulse of the resonance boundary. A skilled, trained warrior. An expert, clearly, in all sorts of munitions. Dogged and loyal.

That was when Ambrea Vas Allay knew she had to keep Rush "Ender" Blakely at her side at all costs.

CHAPTER
EIGHT

Eirie watched with intent eyes as Balkin paced the length of the private receiving room over and over again. She was silent, had been for the past half hour as he worked his mind around the issues he faced. So far there had been no reports that the princess was alive. But then again, there were no reports on who had tried to help her escape either. However, Eirie was not going to be fooled. Curta had been positive that the rightful heir of Allay yet lived. And although Curta's predictions were far from clear and perfect, she was rarely blatantly wrong. Still, Eirie had to act on the supposition that Ambrea was drowned and dead until she heard a report otherwise, just as Balkin was doing. Balkin was not a believer in the conjurer crafts. If he knew Eirie was motivated by them, he would dismiss her in disgust and would not listen to anything she had to say. But at the moment he wasn't aware of any predictions or magic at play, so she had to behave as if any advice she gave was based on the information at hand. Besides, Curta had been very specific. The Princess of Allay would no longer exist in three days' time.

"You must raise yourself to the emperor's seat," Eirie said at last. "You cannot show indecision. You must act with confidence and strength. Announce your coronation to all Allay. You are the rightful heir and you must not show that you have any doubts about it. You must not give them room to think about the whys and wherefores. Tell them what to think. Demand their obedience and acquiescence in this. Give them a powerful taste of the hand that will guide them until the day you die and, if the Being should grace us, pass your glorious seat on to our children and their children to come."

Balkin's pacing slowed as she spoke until finally he came to a complete halt. He was looking at her with no little wonder and surprise.

"Now you speak of children? You who, for all these years, denied me them because you were too vain a bitch to risk ruining your figure?"

She smiled, slowly getting to her feet, lifting her shoulders in a proud and perfect posture that she knew best displayed the charms of her body. Her silken gown breathed and swept against her curves as she moved with careful deliberation toward him. She knew that when she stood as close to him as she did that her perfume would wrap around his senses; the concoction was one of Curta's genius creations. It sought out a male's libido with purpose, aroused his senses and stimulated his hormones. Old or young, any man within her sphere would be aroused by her mere presence. She considered it a perfect enhancement to her already undeniable allure. The men of the court called her bewitching, the women seethed with jealousy as their supposedly loyal lovers were beckoned to her side and found themselves flirting with her. Some even put hands on her, cornered her, chased her down even though they knew that, should Balkin catch them touching her, they would forfeit their lives. Although Balkin took pleasure in watching other men covet her, and took power in the benefits that her flirtations could extract from the rich nobles, he was viciously jealous if he thought it was going too far.

"My love," she said softly as she raised her hands to

his chest and rubbed them over him with warmth and intimacy, absorbing the virile contours of the muscles beneath. Balkin was no weak bureaucrat. He was a man of vital strength who engaged in hard, violent sports that accentuated his prowess as a warrior. It was another reason why she had preferred to pursue his potential over that of his more indolent brother. "The face of the world has changed, and I must change with it. I was free to decide if I wished to give a man a child or not. But I am not free to decide if I should give a country desperately needed heirs. It is my duty to see to the continuation of your line."

"Orders. Duty. Demands. I become emperor and suddenly I have these powers over you and you say you will obey all of my wishes. All of my desires." He reached out to grasp her around both her upper arms, giving her a little shake. "I could not coax you to do it out of love for me, but now . . . now I can force you to my will. And you think this gives me pleasure? To know that as a mere man I could not win your obedience? That this mere man was not good enough for you?"

This was dangerous ground, but Eirie was not afraid.

"Don't be foolish," she whispered gently, lifting her fingers to touch his mouth. She knew even the smallest of her caresses drove him to distraction. "I have always loved you with all my heart, and I always will, whether you are emperor or the lowliest of peasants. I will be by your side every moment of every day for the rest of your life. You are everything to me, and you always have been. The only change is that I asked your indulgence before in my little vanities. My . . . preferences. But I no longer have the right to ask those indulgences of you. Nor should you continue to give them to me. You and I are going to bring Allay into a new era, a place of prosperity for this realm and order for its people. Together we are going to give birth to your dynasty. Allay will be ours forever. It will belong to our blood forever."

His lips curled into a sardonic smile.

"If I didn't know you for the avaricious, spoiled thing you are, I might believe your passionate, beautiful speeches, Eirie. You might love me now, but if I were that lowly peasant, you would have nothing to do with me."

"Untrue," she scolded him. Indeed, she would be by his side every moment of every day of his life. But she could guarantee that she would cut his throat in his sleep rather than allow herself to be dragged into the muck of mediocrity. Still, she had little fear of that happening now. "You wound me to think me so shallow. I freely admit to my vanities and even my ambition. After all, aren't these the things you love about me? But I have never given you any reason to doubt my loyalty to you, Balkin. Everything I have ever done has been to satisfy your needs. I have seduced potentates, hostessed massive pageants to display the wealth of Allay, and spied on the men of your court through my friendships with their women. Do I do this for my pleasure? No. It's all for you."

"And what if I decide to make you my concubine, Eirie," he threatened her in a low, taunting whisper that sent a chill of dread down her spine. Eirie was almost entirely certain of her power over him, but if life had taught her anything, it was that power could change anyone. Even though Balkin was not new to holding an exalted position, he had a cruel streak that could easily be fed by the idea of absolute supremacy. "You could be the first of many, you know. Potentates from all over the Three Worlds will want to give me their daughters for the fucking. They will readily and eagerly give me my dynasty. You will grow old and bored locked away in the House of Concubines."

"Then be prepared to never know the joys of my body again, Imperial Majesty, because I will cut your cock off at the root and wear it as a hair ornament if you try."

Balkin threw back his head and laughed. Then he forced a kiss on her, knowing it would infuriate her as her baited temper rose. He gripped her face in the power of a single hand, kissing her hard and long as she struggled to jerk free. He used his other hand to block the knee she tried to jam into his testicles. He pushed away from her, laughing again as she gathered her composure and shot venom at him with her eyes.

"There she is," he said with amusement. "My meek and obedient bride." He smiled at her, the expression turning him handsome in her eyes. Eirie had to admit, she was foolishly fond of the man. Especially when he could still surprise her like this and show her he had a dangerously strong backbone. Then again, none of this would be worth it if he were a simple conquest. She would have died of boredom long ago. She counted herself fortunate in many ways. Perhaps she would be a little sad if he ever did fall from grace and position. Luckily, that wasn't going to happen.

"Play the lord and emperor with any other person in your realm, my great lord," she said heatedly, "but I will be your equal in all things or I will be nothing to you. I promise you that."

He nodded slowly, making her heart stutter a beat. She felt everything just within her grasp, so very close, and knew he felt the exact same thing. The only burr was that missing girl. But she refused to let him equivocate over it any longer. It was time for decisive action all around. On his part and on hers. She was either all in or she was packing her bags and finding new game to hunt.

"I will announce the coronation and my acceptance of the imperial seat immediately. And you, my slippery bitch, will wed me the very instant the crown is against my brow."

"Gladly, my great lord," she said softly, bowing her head but never lowering her eyes from his. "A crowning followed by a great wedding ceremony. Such a spectacle has a way of making people forget things like missing heirs and dead boy kings."

"True. And you will plan it all?"

Eirie smiled.

"Nothing could possibly stop me."

"And a hearty hello to you, too," Bronse Chapel said dryly as he looked down on the collection of unconscious and incapacitated men. The men who were still conscious were delirious with pain, foaming at the mouth as they wished for the unconscious bliss their brother guards had found.

Rush had his hands clenched into fists as he stood over the carnage he had wrought. He looked up at the rest of his squad.

"I tried to keep it tight. I knew you were on your way into the fray. None of you got hit?"

There was no need to ask. If they had, they'd be in equally bad shape as the four suffering guards were. Five, counting the idiot who had thought he could distract him with a knife in his ribs. To tell the truth, if he hadn't been the impervious freak that he was, that energy blast to his face would have probably popped his head off from the inside out, like a kernel of kick corn in a pressure popper. And it was his own damn fault. He'd let himself get distracted with minutiae.

His gaze fell to immediately counting heads, and he was relieved to see everyone accounted for. But the relief lasted barely a second when he saw Justice. She looked as though someone had tried to cut her head off.

"Holy hell, Jus, what the fuck?"

"Eh, you should see the other guy," she said blithely. "Oh wait, here he is." She withdrew her dirty, bloodied blade, spinning the haft against her palm before putting it back in its sheath.

"Damn right," he said grimly with a nod. And that was all the fuss she would allow from any of them, so he accepted the fact that she was on her own two feet and under her own power. "Sir, we best get through this barrier and to the ship as soon as possible. Between the sounds of firefighting and me throwing one of these guys into the resonance field, we're bound to spark attention."

"Let's go. Is your principal still alive?"

"Last I checked. She's hunkered down on the other side of that quoia."

The group moved up to the boundary and Rush reached down to pull Ambrea out of hiding. She was starting to get that look in her eyes, something he often saw in battle-shocked people who weren't used to the violence of fighting or war and yet found themselves thrust in the middle of it. He felt compelled to hold her, to comfort her, but he knew he had to shake that feeling. Especially in front of the others. Just the same, he touched his thumb to the swell of her high cheekbone and briefly shaped it with a stroke.

"Still with me?" he asked.

"More than ever," she assured him cryptically.

Still, her visible regrouping made him smile a little.

"Good girl," he said. He grabbed his pack and retrieved the pair of aerosol cans strapped to the outside of it. He faced the resonance boundary—energy designed to repulse intruders combined with solid whey stone that was a good ten feet high. Dropping the pack onto the ground, he tossed the second can to his free hand and gave them both a good shaking to mix the contents. Then he aimed and sprayed with the left-hand canister. The contents were blue, leaving a vivid path as Rush painted an ovoid shape onto the wall. The droplets passed right through the resonance barrier, allowing him to easily tag the stone. That was a trick of the mixture. Normally the barrier would repel all liquids, just so vandals couldn't do what Rush was doing right then. Once he was satisfied with the first can, he quickly followed with the second, a brilliant pink paint that helped him track perfectly on top of the blue as the colors mixed into a vivid purple.

"Why aren't you people running away?" he asked dryly.

Bronse was already pulling the princess out of range, but he wasn't hurried. He knew, as did Rush, how much time it would take for the two mixtures to interact with each other.

As soon as he finished, Rush stuffed the cans into his pack and hurried after the retreating squad. He checked his timepiece and mentally calculated how much time there was before . . .

The explosion was fairly significant, sending a huge dispersal of debris everywhere. The squad ducked and dodged the hailstorm of shattered stone.

"All right, let's go!" Rush called as soon as most of the mess had settled. He didn't want to waste any more time in that forest. It was clear that the Imperial Guard knew they were there and also clear that they suspected what they were doing there. With so many enforcements in the area, there was no time to spare.

Rush swept an arm around Ambrea and hauled her over the brush and debris with a ground-devouring stride. The resonance field needed a solid surface to run continuously. By destroying the wall, Rush had disrupted the flow of the repulsor field. The hole he had created was perfect, and they could see straight through to the airfield. There were hundreds of ships parked on the tarmac, rows and rows of them stretching for miles, curving around an assortment of buildings and refueling stations. There was ground crew everywhere, and all of those nearby were scrambling for safety and hiding from the unknown source of destruction. It wouldn't be the first time a ship had blown up on the field for some reason or a fuel station blew up as it accidentally got caught in a low-flying ship's wash thanks to an inexperienced pilot.

Still, it wasn't so frequent an occurrence that they were able to quickly shake off their fear. The Special Active squad took advantage of that and raced onto the field with their precious cargo.

"Dead east!" Justice guided them.

They had purposely parked the ship so it was close to their planned extraction point. It was barely fifty feet away. Justice hit the auto start control strapped to her hip and they heard the distinctive sound of propulsion engines roaring to life. The short flyer came into view after the squad dodged a few smaller ships. The hatch door was already dropping as they ran up to it.

"In you go, Blue Eyes," Rush said as he hustled the princess up the gangway. He had one eye on the airfield behind them, watching for any incoming trouble. He felt better only when they were all in the belly of the ship and the hatch was closed tight behind them. Then Justice was flinging herself into the pilot's seat and inserting a comm earpiece into her ear.

"Flight command, SF-2-6-9-8 requesting permission to go outbound via transmitted vector." She punched in the vector rapidly, sending it to the command center.

"Vector received SF-2-6-9-8. All's clear."

Justice was already off the tarmac. She had every intention of going with or without permission. With permission would allow her to go without worrying that she was going to get shot down in the process of escap-

ing the atmosphere. They had hoped to get permission
and be outbound before the first reports of trouble even
began to filter into command. All the flights would be
suspended as safety protocol once reports of some kind
of mishap were received.

The trick had been to move faster than it took for
people to gather their wits about them and start reacting
according to their training in an emergency. Sure enough,
they were outbound at a fierce speed, pulling away from
Allay and all of Ulrike so fast that everyone in the ship
had to hang on to their seats because the inertia damp-
eners failed to compensate quickly enough. Justice had a
knack for that. Technology these days made for smooth
and easy flights into space, but it still couldn't seem to
keep up with Justice's way of yanking and banking
around the cosmos. But she got the job done faster and
better than any other pilot in the system. Rush had yet
to see anyone outmaneuver her in a firefight.

But luckily there was not going to be any firefight today.

They had escaped Allay with their prize alive and intact.

The first and most dangerous part of their mission
was complete.

Balkin had his fingers deep in his mistress's hair, the
chocolate and silver tresses tumbling over his hands as
he massaged her scalp, urged her onward in intense,
gripping squeezes. He was sprawled naked across her
bed, and she was prettily dressed in her very best court
clothes as they jointly worked his cock into and out
of her mouth. Whatever her emotional shortcomings,
whatever his doubts about the genuineness of her affections, Balkin couldn't fault her ability to floor him with
her skilled mouth and sexual intensity. Eirie had a tremendous appetite for sex, a seemingly endless hunger

for all things carnal. A perfect match for him. He sucked air in through his teeth, expelling it on a grunt of pleasure. So hot. She was so incredibly hot.

He didn't doubt that her voraciousness was directly attached to his very recent public address that he would be taking the crown of Allay for his own. He had not, however, announced his betrothal to her. Much to her well-contained fury. He knew she had expected the announcement, but for the first time in some time he had the pleasure of power over her, as she often held over him. But regardless of his games, she knew he was obsessed with her. And now she was wielding some of the reason why. She could have turned on him like a vicious little harpy, and it wouldn't have been the first time she had done so in their relationship. But she more often chose to win her way like this, with the power of her beauty and insatiable sexuality. It was why she never grew old to him, never trod across his tenuous nerves. Still, the fire of fighting with her was a pleasure all its own. He reveled in that just as well. And somehow she always seemed to know which side to show and when.

"By the Great Being, you have such a mouth!" he told her fiercely as he was flooded with the urge to climax. His rod and sac ached with the need of it. His heart pounded in his ears as the impulse crawled through his body over and over again. Yet he would resist as long as he could, forcing her to work for it, subjugating her as he could do only in moments like this.

The chime at the door was ill timed, to say the least. Balkin roared with irritation but ignored the interruption and refocused on Eirie. When the chime sounded a second time, she flicked a look of pure amusement up at him, the liner around her eyes making their color jump into stark relief. All of it—the expression, the precious rare perfection of their shape, and their exotic tilt fixed in the face of the woman he admittedly couldn't imagine living without—gripped him with such a combination of intense emotions that he had to will himself not to grip her so hard as to hurt her.

"If you do not leave off that chime you'll be dead, I swear it!"

There was a pause long enough to give him a sense of having made his point. He relaxed and was just beginning to refocus himself on Eirie when the chime sounded again. Balkin growled with fury even as Eirie laughed and rolled away from him. He lurched to his feet, storming to the door and touching the release. In his apartments, with the rooms and servants as open and available as they were, there was no privacy. There were no locked doors. He had to be available at every moment to anyone who might need him on matters of state. But these were Eirie's quarters. They were always kept ready for their mistress, who almost never had use of them anymore. The only reason they were there today was because they had not been able to wait until they reached his rooms.

The door shot open, revealing a gaggle of advisors, the usual tagalongs who fell all over themselves to be useful to the emperor of the day. They were mostly of his choosing, perhaps one or two holdovers from his brother's reign. It had taken painstaking work coaxing and convincing his nephew to appoint this one or that one, but not nearly as much of a struggle as it had been when he had tried to maneuver around Benit. Apparently, when he was officially crowned emperor, he was going to have to make a few more changes. He couldn't abide anyone who did not obey his every command.

He could see Prelate Jux with his hand hovering over the chime contact, and then the prelate jerking his hand back like a guilty child. Naked as he was, Balkin grabbed hold of Prelate Geraie's drape, yanked him close enough so he could pull the decorative dagger from its sheath at his waist, and then plunged the thing into Jux's chest. He grabbed the stunned prelate by the scruff and then stabbed him twice more, each thrust more violent and infuriated than the last. Then he shoved Jux into the shocked throng, who quickly jumped back and let their cohort fall dead to the floor.

Feeling infinitely better, Balkin threw down the blade and reached for Geraie. He was content to see the man flinch away in spite of the fact that Balkin was clearly unarmed now. He wiped his bloody hand on the man's drape slowly and deliberately.

"Now," he said calmly, "was there something you needed to tell me?"

The men were frozen in terror, clearly unable to process past their fear.

"Go on," he encouraged them. "Or have you interrupted me for no reason? Because that, you see, would make me quite angry." He heard Eirie giggle near his shoulder and realized she had come up behind him to watch him torment his advisors.

"My great lord," Paxor Freehold spoke up from the back of the pack, pushing his way forward yet keeping studiously out of Balkin's immediate grasp. "There has been a message from the IM central command."

The paxor held out the VidPad, which no doubt carried the message. The screen was locked with a bright chartreuse color, indicating that it was meant for imperial eyes only. Crown or no crown, Balkin was, for all intents and purposes, the acting imperial regent. He took the pad and glanced up at them. He was no fool. They had to know what was in the message or they wouldn't have been so urgent to disturb him, especially in the face of his angry warnings. Their pale faces and the way they all, as a single entity, seemed to back away from him told him that he was not going to like what he was about to see.

He entered his private code and the message cued up. He could feel Eirie leaning into his side, eager to see what was about to play.

The admiral who resolved onto the screen was quick to begin.

"Acting Regent Balkin Tsu Allay, you are hereby recalled to the judiciary court of the Interplanetary Militia to answer for arguments that you are not the rightful heir to the throne of Allay. This court has been petitioned by Ambrea Vas Allay to represent her interests as the rightful heir and empress of Allay. Proceedings will begin at skyrise Allayan time. All arguments will be heard in a fair and impartial IM court. All case law should be presented at that time. Any failure to present yourself will be considered an act of defiance and all rights will presumptively default to the claimant. Martial law will be declared and the IM will be sent in force to your doorstep. Your compliance would be"—he paused and, it seemed, smiled a little—"wise."

As shocked as she was, Eirie very wisely took a step back. She leaned against the wall and out of the way as her lover exploded. His fury was nuclear and his advisors tried to scatter, but the blood of their previously abused compatriot was under their feet and they began to slip and fall in a tangle of desperate bodies. She watched with some consternation as Balkin dragged one of them into the room by his hair, the two of them tracking blood over her carpeting. Balkin knelt on a single knee and began smashing the advisor's head against the ground, all the while roaring profanities.

"Fucking bitch! Bitch! Spawn of a conjuring whore!"

Eirie waited until he had spent the better part of his initial rage. After all, if she interrupted him too soon, he might turn his anger on her. He would regret it eventually, but she had no desire to negotiate the pain that would come into play in the meantime. She watched as he was kneeling over his unconscious victim, panting for breath, his naked body looking so primal in its blood-spattered state. Oh yes. He was a true warrior. But she didn't want a warrior. Not just a warrior. She wanted an emperor.

She moved forward and crouched before him, careful to keep her dress from getting soiled in the mess he had made.

"Really, darling, this was my favorite rug," she scolded gently. The acidic look he shot her told her to tread carefully. But she knew him well. "Don't be so easily vexed, my lord," she said softly, her voice as gentle and coaxing as if she were speaking to an easily spooked forest creature. She knew this creature was just as wild, just as much a slave to its instincts. For all of his education and refined upbringing, the volatility of Balkin's temper had always damaged his political power. Ruling with an iron fist was one thing, ruling with terrorism quite another. Terrorism could lead to revolts and revolutions. It could lead to the interference of the IM. If anyone could appreciate how crucial it was to keep up perfect appearances, it was Balkin, but the stress and pressure of these past few days had left him raw and uncontrolled. "You have committed no crime," she reminded him, "in the eyes of the IM. You did not know that she yet lived. You were only doing what you were required to do, what you had the right to do, on the premise that she had died in her escape attempt. You were the next logical heir to the throne of Allay."

"I didn't even want any of this," he seethed darkly, "until you told me it was possible! I was content to rule in tandem with my brother! I did not want his death!"

"Of course not," she agreed, glancing through the open door to ensure that everyone else was long gone and they were essentially alone. No doubt there were those lurking down the hall, unable to help themselves as they witnessed the new turn in the court and craved to be the very first to impart crucial gossip. "No one dares accuse you of that. And anyway, that is not the issue at hand. Think clearly and think gently. You are thwarted for the moment, it is true, but only for the moment. Don't forget that you are still at the greatest advantage. This . . . this *girl* has spent her entire life suffocated and insulated from this court. She has not a single clue how to rule this land. She will be out of her element, floundering and helpless. Honestly, this escape of hers doesn't seem like her at all. I am willing to bet she is nothing more than a pawn for someone else's political agenda. She certainly never showed any backbone of her own before this."

Balkin's brow furrowed, but Eirie could see that he was calming down and beginning to think more deeply, more clearly.

"She could just as easily be your pawn as another's," she continued.

"It is unlikely she will want anything to do with me," he said, shaking his head. "She sees me as the instrument of all her suffering. I was the one who imprisoned her. I am the one who interrogated her."

"All in the past and all in the name of your loyalty to the emperor. All you have to do is win her trust. You will easily be able to do so because, like it or not, you are in control of all the key elements of this empire. She will have no choice but to turn to you for teaching. Make amends simply, but do not grovel. You are a strong man with strong opinions. She will not believe you to be meek and acquiescent all of a sudden."

"I'd rather cut my own throat in any event. I will not kowtow to that . . . that—"

"You will be respectful," Eirie reminded him firmly. "You will act as any loyal subject would be expected to act, Balkin. You will wait until things grow quiet and easy. Then, later, who knows what will happen? Misfortunes happen all the time."

His laugh was sardonic.

"And you think you could get away with that? First the boy and then her? Without setting the IM dogs on us?"

"The IM can come all they like, my lord, but they will not be able to prove anything any more than they could prove foul play in the boy."

Balkin stood up to his full height and she followed suit. She watched him run a bloodied hand back through his hair as he worked his mind around the altering situation he found himself in. She knew how he was feeling. She was feeling the same way. To have the ultimate prize so close, just within their grasp, and then have it slip between their fingers was the ultimate frustration. But they were both veterans of this government and this court. The girl was a fish out of water, whatever her blood rights might be. Blood may dictate position, but it didn't guarantee she'd have the first idea what to do with herself.

"Don't fret, my lord," she soothed him, reaching to run her hands over his broad shoulders. "We will yet win the day from her. Just think of it as a new game. And the prize will be all the sweeter this time."

Balkin's dark eyes fixed on hers and the corner of his hard lips lifted in a small smile.

"Indeed. It's only a shame she will be such a lacking opponent."

CHAPTER
NINE

Rush toyed with the VidPad on the conference table, flipping the handheld piece of technology over and over again very slowly and methodically, steadily watching it as it fell over, turned, fell over again. Bronse stood in the doorway of the conference room watching his munitions expert, fascinated by this brooding side of him. Ender was not known for emotional preoccupations. The soldier was two-dimensional when it came down to it. He liked to work, liked to blow things up, liked to sleep, and liked to eat. The most emotional he ever seemed to get was in his unwavering loyalty to the squad. So, Bronse had to assume that Ender's disturbance was connected to the latter issue.

"Justice is fine, you know," he spoke up, assuming that Ender was guilting himself about her injuries. "Jet tidied her up. She's already in the training hall yelling at Kith."

"That's good," he said quietly.

Now Bronse was doubly intrigued. If it wasn't Justice, what was eating at the big Tarian? More important, how would the Special Active team leader get him to open up about it? Should he bother or should he leave Rush to his own devices?

The thing was, when you worked on a team as specialized and as high-intensity dangerous as theirs was, one member's problems became the entire team's problem. Bronse had never been the type of leader who stuck his head in the sand and left his team members to their own devices, or the whole of their well-being to the professional circuit of psyche services and doctors they had at their fingertips. There was always a need for those doctors in a posttraumatic venue, and they were good at what they did, but Ender wasn't suffering from trauma or a mental breakdown. He was just moody. And he had been ever since they'd landed in the bay of the IM station.

"Mind if I ask you something?" Bronse said, moving into the room more fully and grabbing the chair across the table from Ender. He turned it backward and straddled it, crossing his arms over the back as he trained a steady gaze on his man.

Ender's response was rote. The rise and fall of one big shoulder.

"How the hell did you manage to avoid getting seared by that two-forty shot? I could swear you took it right in the gut."

Ender's fingers went still, the VidPad balancing for a moment. The hesitation lasted a fraction of an instant, but it grabbed all of Bronse's attention. *Curious.*

"Guess I'm faster than I look," the arms master said with another shrug. "It was close, though. I felt the heat."

"I'm sure you did. Rush, I read your report. I know you've been debriefed, but I can't help feeling there's something you aren't disclosing."

Ender sat up straighter, turning so his body directly faced Bronse's. It was as much of a defensive stance as Bronse had ever seen from a man who was still sitting down.

"I don't know what you mean. I've told you everything there is to know." The VidPad began to tap rapidly against the tabletop. "I'm just a little . . . I'm going over things in my head, trying to figure out what I should have done, could have done differently."

Rush did not disclose to his boss that he was talking about that damned kiss. He was utterly baffled by his own behavior. He'd shut himself off from those kinds of needs, from anything resembling desire. He knew well enough the danger it would pose to anyone who might be the object of that desire. There was so much about this power of his that could easily slip out of his control if he wasn't careful. What had happened with Ambrea was full proof of that. Sure, she was fine. But he knew she had avoided the physician when she'd come on board so he wouldn't see the burn on her back that very clearly looked like two handprints. She didn't want to be put in the position of having to explain it, so she was letting herself heal the old-fashioned way. The harder way. The more uncomfortable way. Just to protect him.

That kind of chapped his ass. The whole stupid thing chapped his ass. If only he could figure out what the hell had gotten into him, then maybe he could figure out how to avoid it in the future.

"Rush, you're being too hard on yourself," Bronse said. "And I don't know why, to be honest. Regardless of what happened or didn't, what could have been avoided or not, you did what you usually do. You won the day. Tomorrow the princess will regain the throne of Allay and we will move on to the next mission. And on that mission you will do what you usually do. You will win the day."

And therein lay the next thing on his mind. Tomorrow they were going to put Ambrea on top of her country, like an ornament meant to swing and sparkle for all to see, as if that would mean anything. But the cold, hard fact remained that she had no idea what she was doing, that she was being let loose in a box full of Hutha lions.

One day in that court and she'd be easily torn to shreds. And no matter how much he told himself it wasn't his problem, he couldn't ignore the overwhelming sick feeling that had taken hold of his gut. It was as though every instinct in his body was screaming at him to protect her. But why?

"It's not my job to protect her," he muttered aloud.

He realized he'd spoken into the room only when Commander Chapel suddenly sat up straight.

"Justice can take care of herself," Bronse fished carefully.

Rush flicked a wry gaze at his commanding officer.

"I think we both know I'm not worried about Justice. Jus could kick my ass coming and going if she was pressed to it."

The commander lifted a brow in agreement, his periwinkle eyes shining with amusement and no small amount of pride. Bronse took great satisfaction in the capability of his crew, be they straight soldiers or Chosen Ones. He was well versed in their strengths and their shortcomings.

"So we're talking about the princess."

"But it's not my problem, right? She'll have some kind of personal guard or something. And she's managed to survive this long."

"I think the empress of Allay chooses her personal guard for herself. Usually from the Imperial Guard."

"Those corrupt little fuckers?" Rush ejected, his entire body going tight and tense. "And they were all probably handpicked by her uncle, or officers raised up by her uncle. She can't trust any of them!"

Bronse watched as Rush pushed away from the table and out of his seat. He began to pace in his agitation, rubbing his fingertips over the shimmering blond spikes of his hair.

"Get under your skin, did she?" Bronse asked his arms master archly.

"No! I just—" He looked over at Bronse and threw away his denial with a nod. "A little bit. She has . . . strong convictions. I guess it'd be nice to see one of the good people win for a change. Your Great Being knows these worlds could use it."

"Very true. But like you said, we have our own roles in seeing to that. We can't be responsible for what happens outside of the job of the moment. Not if we are going to be effective soldiers. We just have to have faith that we're helping to design the bigger picture. We threw our lot in with the IM because we know they are a worthy organization with a worthy agenda. But in the end we soldiers are only workers in a larger hive of activity. We have to move on. There are perhaps other princes of other countries in need of our talents."

"I know that." Rush nodded firmly, as if making up his mind on the matter. "You're right. We're both right."

Rush reached to sweep up the VidPad and gave Bronse a resolute smile.

But Bronse had a feeling that Ender was not quite as convinced of his own directives as he would like to be.

Ravenna sighed softly, turning around in the arms of her lover. She opened her eyes, smiling before she even saw Bronse's face. But instead of the warmth of periwinkle and his sweet devotion, she found herself staring into the cold, dark eyes of a stranger. His hands shot out and wrapped around her long throat, and he flung himself over her body, throwing all of his significant weight onto her chest, pinning her beneath his powerful frame.

The head priestess of the Chosen Ones tried to gasp for breath, tried to scream. But he was throttling her with a vehemence bordering on mania. The fury in his eyes and the shuddering throughout his body were punctuated by the savage growl of rage he emitted.

"You stupid, stupid bitch! I'm going to choke you until your eyes explode in your head! Once and for all, I'm going to teach you not to cross me!"

Ravenna reached up for him, clawing at him in panic, desperately trying to figure out who he was, where he had come from. Where was Bronse? What had this maniac done with him? But all that faded away as tendons in her neck popped under the strain of his attack. The small delicate bones in her throat cracked even as she tried to gouge at his eyes.

Suddenly he yanked her up closer to his face, showing her the details of his otherwise handsome features, the marks of his age, the clean and kempt cut of his beard and hair. Reflected in his eyes, she could see herself.

Ravenna woke with a ragged, choking gasp, the violence of it nearly toppling her out of her bed. Her distress woke Bronse in an instant and he grabbed for her, pulling her around to look at him, his warm, loving hands coming to cradle her face.

"What? What is it?"

They had been together for two cycles now. More than long enough for him to know the difference between her waking from a bad dream and waking from a vision. For one, her face was tracked with the tears of her struggle with the attacker. Also, she was inadvertently clawing at her throat, trying to remove hands that were no longer there . . . That had never actually been there. Still, her visions were as real to her as the beautiful man holding her was.

"It's all right, baby. Just breathe. You're here and you're safe," he reminded her over and over again until it actually began to sink in. Eventually her hands left her throat and went to clutch at his bare skin. The warmth of him was even more grounding. Slowly the familiar smell of him surrounded her.

She began to realize she was breathing. Easily.

"Bronse," she rasped.

"Right here. Waiting for you," he assured her.

"I need to see your last mission file," she said, trying not to sound panicked. She knew her mate very well. If he thought she was acting or reacting too emotionally, he would make her pause, make her wait until she had calmed down. But the desperation racing through her blood told her that she didn't have time to waste. Or at least she didn't think she did. Regardless of how imminent the danger might be, there was danger and she had to figure out what it was.

The gods knew she didn't want to keep reliving that particular vision over and over again while she stumbled around in mystery. They were persistent like that. If the forces that guided her abilities thought she was being dense, they'd beat her over the head until she was near dead with it.

His brows lifted at the request. She hadn't been part of the mission and so had not been briefed on it. Usually an IM soldier not assigned to a mission wouldn't be briefed, and shouldn't be. And even though the Chosen Ones had particularly high clearance, it was an odd demand, one that was potentially rife with questions of ethics and protocol.

But that brief moment was all the time Bronse Chapel gave to those potential questions. Ravenna would never ask him about his missions without cause. He reached above the bed, fumbling with one hand for the secured VidPad he kept on the shelf there. His other hand never left her face, his fingers keeping a solid hold on her to reassure her that he was what was real, that he was there for her. No matter what. There was only one thing that could supersede Bronse's love for the IM and his squad, and she would never doubt that she was that one thing. Moments like this, small details like that hand on her face, reminded her of that far more than the words he whispered to her so fervently when they made love.

He pulled down the VidPad.

"Lights up," he commanded. The low, heavily muted lighting they slept to raised up by half. Not quite full strength, but still bright enough to make her flinch. "Great Being, Ravenna," he swore, his hand sliding to her throat where she had unwittingly raked at her own skin in the throes of the vision. All the while he was thumbing over the VidPad screen, leafing through files as rapidly as he could. "What do you need, baby?"

"Pictures. All the principals surrounding the princess of Allay." She had known that much about the mission. That he had been sent to retrieve Allay's rightful heir. She knew this because almost the entire Special Active team had gone with him, and things were talked about easily among the Chosen Ones. In fact, she had been the only one to remain behind.

Ravenna lowered her hand to her belly, anxiously rubbing at the unnoticeable reason why she had come up with an excuse not to be part of that mission. She couldn't be but six weeks into her gestation, but it was enough to raise a flag on medical equipment if she were scanned or in need of some kind of repair after an injury. That, and ever since she'd realized she was carrying Bronse's baby she'd been inexplicably terrified of letting it come to some kind of harm. The general rule of thumb in the IM was that they allowed pregnant soldiers to decide for themselves when they wanted to call it quits for active status. With differing species and differing races, and with gestations that followed all kinds of rules and no norms, they couldn't set a specific guideline.

But the Special Active team was nothing average when

it came to the IM and its rules. They took on the highest-risk jobs, used abilities that no others had, and, for the most part, had no idea what kind of physical strain their job might put on their bodies. No two Chosen Ones were ever the same, it seemed, and even if they had been, Ravenna and her Chosen Ones had been routed out of their temple in the dead of night, making a hasty escape without any opportunity to bring any historical scrolls of written histories with them. All they had to go on, in fact, was whatever she as High Priestess could remember from her studies and readings.

"Are you all right?" Bronse asked, sliding his hand down her arm to cover hers.

"I'm fine. Just . . . it was a very violent vision, Bronse. Your princess . . ." Bronse turned the VidPad toward her and she grabbed for it, thumbing rapidly through the mission file's photos. "Here." She turned it back to him, her hands shaking visibly as she showed him the face of her attacker. "But it wasn't me he was attacking. When he brought me close enough, I saw my reflection in his eyes. It was your Princess of Allay."

"This is her uncle," Bronse told her grimly. "The would-be emperor of Allay. Far be it from me to doubt one of your visions, Ravenna, but you know very well that what you see is not always what you get."

"Well, I hope not, or otherwise he is going to wrap his hands around her neck and throttle her to death," she snapped irritably. He lifted a brow at her tone and she sighed. "I'm sorry. It's just that I have never felt such virulent hatred before, Bronse. Such all-consuming rage. That man is dangerous. Deadly."

"And proven to be both," he agreed with her. "It's not that he isn't capable of doing harm to Ambrea, Rave. It's that it would be political suicide if he did. If he wants this throne, he has to be more than a bully to get it. And

Balkin has proven himself very wise when it comes to walking the line between what is legal and what is not."

"Sometimes it's not a matter of what is right or what is wrong, what is logical and what is illogical. Sometimes it boils down to an evil temperament finally snapping, finally losing all control. Doesn't it follow that these circumstances might produce just that sort of environment for someone so violent?"

Bronse frowned. "True, love. But the fact remains, we're the IM. Whether Balkin Tsu Allay follows the rules or not, we have to. And we cannot interfere in the ruling of a government on any of the Three Worlds, unless—"

"Unless the ruler of that government asks you or the government has fallen into chaos. Yes, I know." She gave him a wry little smile, reaching out to rub warm fingers over the well-shaped curve of his pectoral muscle. "Lucky for us, tomorrow the empress of Allay is going to ask you for that help."

"She is?" He tossed the VidPad down to the foot of the bed and moved closer to her. "Did I ever tell you I think you're sexy when you make my job easier?"

She snorted out a laugh. "I must have missed it between you yelling at me for letting Kith get away with murder or for not letting Devan come on mission with you." She pulled back a little when he went to kiss her. "Or perhaps it was a few days ago when you were ordering me not to accompany you on this last mission because I'm pregnant."

Bronse had the grace to wince.

"I panicked," he said with a shrug. "And anyway, you weren't exactly chasing me down demanding otherwise. You were just as stunned as I was, just as afraid of something happening to you."

"Regardless, you shouldn't have been so bossy."

"I'm your commanding officer," he reminded her

dryly. "It's kind of in my job description. And by the way"—he leaned in to kiss her gently, and she didn't move back from him this time—"you do let Kith get away with murder."

She wrinkled up her nose, but they both knew that her empathic brother was a pain in the ass, only marginally improved over the years as the structure and discipline of the IM shaped him into a pretty decent soldier.

"I am, perhaps, a bit too tender with him. But he is my brother, after all. I don't think I am any more or less so with my sister."

"Hmph. Your sister, Ophelia, is a damn angel. Far too sweet for this kind of work, but stronger than Kith is in many ways. And I don't just mean in the sheer power of her healing ability."

"I know you don't. But why is it that every time we argue, it has something to do with Kith or one of the other Chosen Ones?"

"Because that's work and we each have a vested interest in goals that are naturally counter to each other. Your job is to protect the Chosen Ones; mine is to put them in harm's way. Outside of work, we're perfect. You're perfect."

Bronse quit playing her game of doling out sparse little affections. He wrapped an arm around her and hauled her up against his body, rolling her beneath him while he seared her with a demanding kiss. Once she was suitably breathless and quieted, he took a moment to inspect the damage she had done to her throat.

"It's nothing," she breathed softly, not wanting him to be deterred from the promise of that fiery kiss of a second ago.

"Damn woman, must you contradict me before I even say anything?"

"I thought I was perfect," she said with a laugh.

"A perfect pain in my—"

She didn't think the remark was worth finishing so she cut him off with a kiss of her own.

Ambrea looked at herself in the mirror and felt as though a stranger was staring back at her. After living such an austere and simple life in her exile, and then surviving with even less while incarcerated by her uncle, the extravagance and luxury of the gown she now wore, the jewels that Suna had carefully dressed into her hair, and the soft perfumes and cosmetics that had been made available to her were like a layer of alien things all over her body. It wasn't that she didn't look pretty. Quite the contrary. She had never realized she could look so beautiful. Her hair was upswept, weaving in and around itself, long coils then falling loosely from the crown of her head and onto the nape of her neck. It shone with a cleanliness it had long been denied in prison. Suna had chosen jewels from the array offered to them—the many shades of green, from the purest to the near-blue of her own eyes, were perfectly displayed against her red-gold hair. Ambrea had been unaware that Suna knew how to create such an intricate look. Her companion had always seemed to have such simple skills. Now Ambrea realized that Suna had adapted to the simplicity of their imposed lifestyle.

Suna had insisted on placing a simple Delran platinum wire tiara at the crest of her curls. Ambrea knew it was her companion's way of making it very clear to all who saw her that she was an empress. Born. Bred. Destined.

The woman looking back at Ambrea from the mirror certainly looked the part of an empress. Without the crown and the imperial jewels, of course. Those awaited her on Allay. But first there was something else that must be done.

She must stake her claim.

Every time she thought of the confrontation to come

her heart began to thunder in her chest. It wasn't that she feared her uncle any longer, was it? After all, she was in the position of dominance now, her claim legal and powerful, backed by the indomitable power of the IM. Her uncle would be a fool if he took a stand against her. Not only would the IM not tolerate it, she was certain that the beleaguered people of Allay would not stand for it either. She felt badly for her people. A constantly shifting seat of government made people feel insecure, exposed, and confused. It probably mattered little to them who had what rights to the throne. It mattered more to them where their daily bread was coming from, whether the free flow of trade would continue, and whether their borders would remain safe and controlled. True, the IM kept watch over part of that, but if the government fell apart, the country would fall under IM control until it could restructure the government. Times like that almost always made for hardship on the common man, confused the natural order of things. The military had a very different way of doing things, and difference meant trouble.

But worse than all of that would be a woman taking power who had no idea what to do with it. Oh, she had seen enough to know what she didn't want done, what she wouldn't do to others. She had faith in her moral beliefs and the religious tenets that she used as a guide in her daily life. But there was so much more to being a good sovereign than good intentions.

"Perhaps, though, it is a good start," Suna said comfortingly, making Ambrea realize she must have spoken her final thought aloud. Ambrea bit her lip even as she squared her posture. She would not let anyone see her fear, her insecurities. All she could do was her best. She would learn as she went.

"Madam, the judiciary awaits your—"

Rush came to an abrupt halt, all that massive male

energy going amazingly still as Ambrea turned away from her mirror and slowly rose to her full height. He was staring at her with blatant surprise in his russet eyes.

"Holy shit," he said with genuine intensity. It made her smile, a warmth spreading throughout her entire body as she understood his stark appreciation for what it was. She could easily return the sentiment. There was something to be said for Rush in full dress uniform. The sharp black jacket, the gold and crimson epaulets, the high shine of black jackboots, and the smooth sheen of the dress breeches that clung to every last contour of his powerful thighs—it all made for an official and impressively powerful-looking figure. It was as though the bare-chested, tattooed Tarian had utterly disappeared. She could understand his sense of shock. She was feeling it herself, both looking at him and when looking at herself. "I mean . . ." He tried to recoup, but floundered as he continued to stare at her.

"I'm sure I don't look much like the helpless prisoner of the past two days," she said quietly.

"Hell no." He moved a little closer to her and she felt her breath catch when he reached toward her. She found she craved his touch, wherever it might land, however simple it might be. She supposed she ought to be afraid of it in light of the burns she had suffered, but his repetitive flouting of propriety had spoiled her. Instead of touching her, though, all he did was catch up one of her curls between two of his fingers, rubbing the texture of it slowly.

"Rush, I need to ask a favor of you," she said suddenly. For an entire day, all throughout her debriefing with the IM, and an entire night when she should have been sleeping and recovering the strength and rest she had been long in desperate need of, she had been trying to figure out how to ask him this favor.

His gaze flicked away from its apparent fascination with her hair and met with hers. The instant intimacy that had been stirring between them came into play, and she felt as if everything outside their immediate sphere simply melted away.

"Ask," he said quietly.

"I need you with me," she said with quick heat. "I need your strength and protection. Especially these first weeks. I am not a fool. I know there is danger around me still. Making this claim will make me tremendous enemies in a court designed for the comfort of my father and uncle. A court that thought they would be serving my prodigal brother and not the dirty-blooded castoff they have shunned for almost all the cycles of my life."

She saw his expression darken and, thinking he was going to dismiss her out of hand, she hurried onward. "I have already made a formal request with your superiors and they have given clearance. They are willing to detach you from the Special Active squad for as long as I might need while I stabilize my government around me. But . . . I don't want you to be ordered to my side, Rush. I want it to be your choice. Your desire. I can see that the Special Actives are what you love, that they are where you belong. But . . ." She looked down and away from him, twisting one hand within the other. "I honestly believe I won't survive a week without your protection. And I know of no one else. No one impartial or trustworthy. I will have no friends around me other than Suna. I need, at the very least, someone who I can depend on to watch my back and defend me."

The bald truth of it was, Rush thought, Ambrea could have forced him into her service one way or another. She could have demanded it of his superiors, and they, wanting to cultivate good faith and relations with the imminent ruler of Allay, would have quickly ordered him to comply. Or she could have blackmailed him into it, used what she knew about him to force him to her side. But Rush realized that none of that would ever even occur to her. As ruthless as others had been to her, she was unwilling to be so in kind.

It was going to be her downfall, he was sure of it. Ambrea was too gentle a soul to navigate the cutthroat world she was about to enter. She did, indeed, need his protection. Not that spending months cooped up in a single assignment really appealed to his adventurous nature, but he had done it before. Anyway, it would be only a couple of months. Just until she got her feet under her.

He reached to touch a finger under her chin, pulling her head up and making her look him dead in the eyes.

"From now on, Empress of Allay, when you make a request or a demand of those around you, you will use that steady, penetrating stare of yours and make them see it for unwavering strength and sharpness. When you look away like that, you make them think you are unsure and weak. I know you *are* unsure," he acknowledged softly, "but there is no reason why others should know it." He held that teal gaze a moment longer. "And you are not in any way weak. Your survival all these cycles has proven that."

Rush watched her draw a deep breath, saw her visibly gather her strength and stoicism around her. Again, in his mind, he uttered *holy shit*. It was like looking at a completely different person, and yet there was no mistaking that it was the same woman he had rescued from the catacombs. He would have thought that all this polish would make her look as plastic as he thought it made other high-society women look, but she wore it in a way that was more earthy than elite. She was no doubt reeking of refinement and royalty. It wasn't as if that were lacking. Nor had it ever been. But despite all of these accoutrements, she still reflected that wholesomeness he had found so appealing from the start. He wondered if she would be able to hold on to that or if, with the weight of years of governing, she would lose that quality.

The idea of it saddened him, made him feel almost desperate to stand in the way of it. But he couldn't possibly do that. Not for the rest of her life. And why would he want to? The political scene was not his natural habitat. Far from it. But he most certainly could watch her back while she got her feet wet. Then he would find someone trustworthy to assume the duty so he could leave her to her rule and go back to the Special Active team that would be waiting for him. He felt a twinge of doubt about leaving his friends, however. Yes, they were strong and capable and could surely make do without him for a little while, but in the wake of Justice being injured, nearly killed, it was hard for him to think of leaving them unprotected. If something should happen to one of them while he was away, he might never be able to forgive himself.

And then there was that other issue . . .

"And you don't have to worry that I'll . . . this will be strictly professional. I mean, I will be strictly professional." He said it as firmly as he could. "It was wrong of me to kiss you. I was on the job, for starters, and also I knew that I could hurt you. I just was off my mark." Rush cleared his throat. "I have no excuse really."

"I wasn't looking for an explanation for that," she said quietly. "And clearly we both have bigger issues to deal with at the moment." She smoothed her hands down over the skirt of her dress, looking away from him as she fussed with the way it fell around her feet. "I have huge responsibilities to my country. Of course I can't spend my energies . . . elsewhere."

That made sense, but Rush couldn't help but think it was a very polite way of telling him she'd rather eat dirt than let him touch her again. Which was what he wanted, right? Then why did he feel gripped with a furious sense of rejection? It stung to feel her withdraw like that. Perhaps because until that moment she had been the first person who knew all of what he was who didn't pull back with fear.

She looked up at him with those big eyes of hers. He must have been wearing his feelings on his face because she immediately drew a soft breath and reached to touch him, her hand running up over his pectoral muscle and gripping his shoulder.

"No," she breathed anxiously. "No, I didn't mean that the way you think. It isn't an excuse or a rejection of you." Her eyes shifted to Suna, who was busily rearranging things on the vanity counter that didn't need rearranging. "It is simply a truth, Rush. I need to put all of my energy into my reign. If things were different . . ."

"I would still be who and what I am," he said bitterly. "And I accepted my limitations long ago."

To his surprise she moved closer to him, so close he could feel her body warmth through his clothes. Her hand lifted from his shoulder, and gentle, graceful fingers brushed through his hair, drew a curved stroke around his ear. The sensation, the proximity and intimacy were things he was very unused to, and there was a sense of immediate pleasure and satisfaction attached to the easy way she seemed to come toward him all the time. He couldn't resist the urge to touch her in kind. It was just his fingertips at her throat, and so light he was barely making contact, but it was like closing an electrical circuit. The comfortable intimacy between them became something stronger, something more intense. It was all the things he ought to be avoiding but couldn't bear the idea of turning it away.

"I think that, given a chance, given freedom from this lifetime of repression your ability has been subjected to, you might be surprised by the things that could be accomplished," she said softly.

He might have argued the point with anyone else, but he had to admit that she had a distinctive perspective on such things. And he couldn't find it in himself just then to tell her that things were what they were and would never likely change. After all, hadn't he told her that she was capable of this venture she was about to embark on? How could he argue against himself without calling himself a liar?

"I'll come with you," he told her quietly then. "But only until you get a grip on things. I'll keep the vipers off your back for a while."

She exhaled mightily, and he could see the relief washing through her. He chuckled.

"You're going to make a terrible politician if you don't become better at hiding your every emotion."

"Trust me, I'm better at it when I need to be. But right now I'm among those I trust."

She reached to enfold his hand in both of hers and pressed her lips firmly against the curve of his knuckles. He normally would have been uncomfortable under the expression of such gratitude, but instead he found himself fascinated with the warm feel of her mouth on his skin. He had the strongest urge to grab her by those silky smooth red curls of hers and yank her up under another kiss, but he knew that path would be disastrous. Hadn't he just said as much? But she meant her affection so genuinely, so innocently, that he couldn't bring himself to pull away either. So he forced himself to tamp down the inappropriate impulse. And even though he knew what terrible consequences could come from doing otherwise, it was harder than he might have expected. Maybe it was all that spit and polish she had used to enhance the pretty that she already was, or maybe not. Regardless, it was ten thousand kinds of unacceptable.

She was putting a great deal of trust in him. A great deal of faith. It made him feel good. He was used to the faith and trust of his teammates—he had earned it and returned it hundreds of times. And he supposed he had earned it from her as well. But he wasn't used to it coming from someone who knew all about him, knew his mutation for what it was and had seen it in action. Part of him was completely baffled to realize she wasn't trying to shake him off her boots as quickly as she could, as one would do the moment they realized they had stepped in shit. Instead she was pulling him closer. Insisting on his presence.

It felt odd.

Perhaps even good.

"We better get going," he said. "I have to stop by my quarters and change."

"Oh, really? Why?"

He wondered if she realized how utterly disappointed she sounded. He tried not to smile and probably did a lousy job of it. Her transparency was something they would have to work on. "If I'm going to be by your side for the next little while, I'd rather not do it in uniform. I think I'd like to keep your enemies ignorant as to who I am. I think their behavior might shine a little truer in front of a big savage Tarian as opposed to a representative of the IM."

It was unfortunately very true. Knowing how her people felt about Tarians to begin with would make his reception hostile, and surely coming in at her side would not help his case. She wished it didn't have to be this way, but she had no illusions that she would walk into the court of Allay, the court of her father, uncle, and brother, and find herself a warm welcome.

CHAPTER
TEN

Ambrea paused outside the arbitration hall, taking a deep breath and squaring her shoulders. She had been dreading this moment with every fiber of her being, the moment when she would come face-to-face with her uncle once again. She felt she presented a strong face; indeed, it went deeper than that for her. Perhaps it was the relief of knowing she had Rush's power at her back. His mere presence made her feel that she had an advantage she would not otherwise have. The truth was, ever since he had appeared in her life, she had found a new vantage point in the way she was able to approach all things. Be it the reclamation of her throne or facing down the quick blade of a would-be assassin, she had a power now that she had not had before. She had an armor, a shield. Finally she had gained a position of advantage, and finally she could do something for the people of Allay. Something that ought to have been done a long time ago.

She touched the access panel and the doors glided open. She moved forward and faced the raised dais where the IM judges sat. There were five of them, an odd number purposely chosen so that their decisions would always have a majority rule. Each wore the same dress uniform that Rush had been wearing earlier, only they were more highly decorated, a distinct sign that they were significantly tenured in the IM, all of very high and trusted rank. These judges often decided the fates of entire countries, of worlds. They were experts in the laws of the IM charters and well versed in the individual laws of the many countries of the Three Worlds. In this case it was their expertise in the succession laws of Allay that would come into play.

Then she saw her uncle. He was seated with a small entourage of assistants and advisors, all of whom began to whisper things to him the moment she entered the room. Her uncle, however, was staring directly at her, his attention cold and unwavering. Knowing him as she did from those brief snippets of harassment he'd subjected her to, she could imagine he was seething underneath that calm. She remembered his threats. And now that she was snatching the total power of Allay out from under him, she could only imagine how magnified his rage toward her must be.

She didn't realize she had hesitated until she felt Rush's hand at her back, his fingers moving to curve into the bend of her waist, then squeezing gently. It was meant as a gesture of silent support, and she felt it through her entire body and spirit. He helped to cover her pause by leaning in to whisper to her, as if he were the one holding her back and not her own transparent fears.

"You are the Empress of Allay," he said softly against her ear.

It was all she needed. The reminder poured strength into her body, steeled her in the face of her tyrannical uncle. Rush was telling her she couldn't show her fear, and she knew how right that was. Even more, he was telling her she should not be the one in fear. She was the one with all the power. She had to remember that.

She moved quickly to her place across from the judges and opposite her uncle. She remained standing, however. She was the queen of all Allay, and she would not sit until all others in the room had been seated first. The idea was that her head must always remain above others around her. Of course the height of the dais and the fact that she was not taller than most of the men around her prevented a literal truth, but it was the principle of the thing, she supposed. She stood with her chin raised as Suna took her seat behind her and Rush threw himself into the chair at her side. He flung both feet onto the table, stretching back casually and crossing his feet at his ankles, playing up the mannerless Tarian he wished to portray. Ambrea could see her uncle's attention shift to her protector and his subsequent whisper to an aide. No doubt that aide's next duty would be to find out who the Tarian at her side was and what he was doing there.

"This court is called to presence, both parties of the arbitration now being accounted for and in attendance," the lead judge announced.

Now that everyone was seated, Ambrea could take her seat. However, she felt the extraordinary need to stand, to command the presence of the room and dominance over her uncle. It would prove to be a keen instinct, as her uncle immediately got to his feet.

"Arbitors, may I speak? I believe we can clear up this matter very quickly and without a protracted hearing."

Ambrea felt Rush tense up tightly, his nearness to her hip making it easy to sense his reactions. That and the fact that it was growing decidedly warmer where they were. Rush was expecting the worst from Balkin. Frankly, so was she. Nothing good had ever come out of that man's mouth as far as Ambrea was concerned. He was up to something. Luckily she didn't have to wait long to find out what it was.

"You may speak briefly, but then we will continue," the lead judge said with a dour look, a warning to Balkin to keep his grandstanding to a minimum. The IM judiciary would not tolerate any of his tricks.

"I would like to announce to this court and to my niece that I willingly abdicate any previous claim I had made on the throne of Allay. Allayan law is very clear. The Princess of Allay is the rightful heir to the throne and I would never try to circumvent that right. I made my claim only because I was assured she was dead. Had this been true, I would have been fully in my rights to make the claim I did. I never have wished to cheat my niece of her blood-born rights. I graciously bow to my empress and the queen of all Allay."

Balkin turned to face her. With a surprising elegance for a man she had always deemed as being hard and rough, he bowed to her. Not just a quick, resentful acknowledgment but a sincere lowering of his head as he dropped to a single knee. He kept his head lowered and did not move. Allayan court manners demanded he not move until the ruling hand dismissed him.

All of Balkin's aides suddenly made haste to emulate their master. The entire right side of the room lowered themselves into acknowledging bows.

Ambrea moved around Rush, her spine straight, her shoulders level and proud. She stood over her uncle, looking down on him as her mind raced with a lifetime of images. All the times he had threatened her. All the times he had tried to crush her under the heel of his power. Now she was in the position to do the same. Now she held his life and his comfort in the palm of her hand. Now, if she wanted to, she could banish him to the wet rooms. Perhaps that one room in particular where the familiar rivulet of water ran down the wall.

"Uncle," she spoke, her voice strong and steady in spite of the emotions roiling through her. "You show great wisdom and a keen respect for the well-being of your homeland. It would pain me greatly if we were to be at war with each other, dragging all of Allay along with us."

"I have no desire to be at war with you, my niece. I hope you understand that everything I have ever done has been in pursuit of what I or your father felt was best for the well-being of Allay. I hope you can forgive me for any injuries or pains you may have suffered in the name of that pursuit."

He looked up at her then, his dark eyes filled with an unnerving level of sincerity. She had never seen him like this. Quiet, sincere, and respectful. Of course she had to suspect him of ulterior motives—she wasn't a fool—but she also had to be fair. What he said was true. She couldn't judge him solely on the acts he had committed while working under others in power. Her father had been deranged. When he made a demand, no one gainsaid him. Perhaps not even his most trusted brother.

"The survival and perfection of Allay is all I want, Uncle," she said softly. She looked up at the judges. "I accept his gracious abdication. I cannot see why you will not do the same."

"It seems our work is done then," the lead judge said with a grin. "I wish all of these arbitrations were this easy. Allay is henceforth in the hands of its proper heir, the Empress Ambrea Vas Allay."

"Long live our gracious lady queen," the aides spoke up in unison.

Ambrea turned to her uncle once more and reached to touch him on the shoulder, the epaulet of golden ribbon and metal charms reminding her of the dress uniform that Rush had been wearing only a little while ago. Only these were of royal design, marking her uncle clearly as a male of the royal bloodlines and a potential future heir. It reminded Ambrea that no matter what she did, Balkin Tsu Allay was direct heir to her throne and there was nothing she could do to change that. If anything should happen to her, he would be emperor.

More than ever, she was grateful that Rush had accepted her plea for protection. She had a feeling that he would be the only thing to stand in the way of any underhanded attempt that Balkin might yet make to gain the throne. Only if she were to bear a child could she thwart him forever . . .

She *could* bear a child.

Her entire chest tightened at the thought. A child. A life. A freedom she had never thought to taste. She had been convinced she would die never knowing the touch of a lover. Of a man. Of anyone.

She looked over at Rush, unable to help herself. His was the first and only touch she could remember other than that of her mother. His was the first and only kiss. Just thinking about it made her entire body flush with receptive warmth. She pulled her hand away from her uncle, his proximity feeling strangely obscene as she remembered something so sweet and pure. Something Balkin had made certain she was denied in her exile as he controlled every single detail of her life. But she was free of him now.

She didn't give her uncle leave to rise. Instead, she left him kneeling and then moved to leave the room.

Rush watched Ambrea's uncle very carefully as she left him like that, silently exerting her command and power over him, silently demanding his respect. Rush stood up and followed Ambrea, making sure everyone understood that he was going to be by her side every moment. He saw Balkin's eyes tracking him.

Rush would have bet good money that the man was seething with venom on the inside. He didn't need to hear Ravenna's report of her vision to understand that of all the dangers in the Allay court, Balkin Tsu Allay would be the most deadly. He might be acquiescent now, but this was not a man who easily bent his head to others. No more than Rush would. If he was doing so, then he was doing so for a reason.

Rush was going to make sure that that reason did not result in any harm to Ambrea.

Balkin kept his teeth clenched tightly as she left him kneeling there like a kowtowing servant. It made his gut turn sour to think of himself handing his power over to her, but he consoled himself with thoughts of the future. Whether it was by his hand or by his clever Eirie's, the princess—the *empress*—was not long for this world.

The only unexpected thing was this brute at her back. As Balkin was forced to kneel until she fully left the room, he used his vantage point to make a study of the big blond Tarian. Everything about him seemed to scream land-born Tarian. His body was heavily conditioned, clearly a man who used his muscle for a living. It was strange. You didn't see very many land-born Tarians outside their own world and their own clan. There were a few, of course. But practically none who wanted anything to do with Allay. Mainly because Allay made it clear that it wanted nothing to do with them. So how did a land-born Tarian come to be at the back of the Allayan empress?

As soon as Ambrea and the brute were out of the room, Balkin surged up to his full height, shrugging his shoulders into his usual powerful stance. He shot a cold look at the other men slowly climbing to their own proper heights.

"Find out who that Tarian is. I want his name, his age, the names of who he runs with."

"You're thinking he's some kind of gangster? Or mercenary?" Paxor Ricks asked as he dusted off his knee.

"I'd lean toward mercenary," Balkin mused. "He reeks of being a hired gun. But who hired him? My little twit of a niece isn't known for being so forward thinking. It has to be whoever orchestrated her escape from prison."

"There was a report that a Tarian had been thrown in gaol right before the break. Possibly the same one?" Ricks queried.

Balkin's eyes narrowed. "I'd say that would be a hell of a coincidence otherwise. So he liberates her from the wet rooms and brings her to the IM to claim her throne. But what's in it for him?"

"Is he her lover?"

Balkin snorted. "I'm having a hard time imagining my milky niece being attractive to a man like that in any way, except perhaps as a means to an end. We'll have to watch them. But if they're lovers, my niece is going to be in for a very big shock when commoners realize there's a Tarian in the royal bed. Especially a land-born beast like that. At least the space-born ones are somewhat civilized. The common people will be lying awake nights horrified at the idea of her dirty blood mixing with his savagery. In just a few weeks they'll be crying for me to take the throne."

But in the meantime, he was going to torture the hell out of his upstart niece. He was going to shove her monarchy down her fucking throat.

"She has no idea what it means to be queen. I'm going to take great pleasure in helping her find out."

Ambrea walked briskly down the palace corridors, the very same path she had last taken when she thought it was her father who had called her there. She had thought she was anxious then, but there was nothing about that previous walk that measured up to this one. Now she was entering Blossom Palace as the duly recognized Empress of Allay. It was the lead story in all the Allayan media, in all of Ulrike's news sources. When she had left the IM space station, it had been with Rush by her side and the reassuring presence of a team of four Special Active members. Rush's commander, Bronse; the dark-haired Tarian, Justice; a smaller, younger female who looked more like a girl than a woman, named Devan; and the young communications officer they called Trick. They were visibly unarmed, of course, just a show of the IM's strength and support of her position. But their duty and presence would end the moment she officially took the throne for the first time. Yet even with them there, even with Rush so close to her back, and even with the phalanx of reporters and videographers they had acquired since landing on Allayan soil, she still couldn't escape the feeling of aloneness that had stalked her every step, just as it had the last time she'd navigated these corridors.

As she gripped her prayer book between her hands and forced herself once again to keep her head held high and her posture perfectly straight, the questions reeling through her mind were eerily similar.

What did they want from her?

What did this mean for her future?

Was this the end of life as she knew it? Of course it was. But there was something to be said for that quiet little life of exile, a life that moved relatively peacefully as long as she kept her head down. This had to be the ultimate in sticking her neck out.

Ambrea shrugged off that thought. There was no sense wishing for what could never be again. And she had made her choice the moment she settled her hand into Rush's and let him lead her out of her prison cell. It was all for the best. The best for her, the best for Allay. And she didn't mind being petty enough to think it would do her uncle a bit of good, too, to get a huge lesson in humility and what it felt like to have others wielding power over his fate. The thing that kept her from being just like her uncle, however, was that she knew she would never terrorize him just for the pleasure of the game and for seeing someone else tremble in her shadow.

The huge doors to the receiving room came into sight as the growing entourage rounded a bend in the corridor, the pressed and sculpted Delran platinum doors gleaming under the directed lighting. Unlike her last travels down this stretch, this time the corridors were lined with people who were eagerly shifting to get a look at her, to take in the unlikely sight of the first female ruler that Allay had seen in over a century, a female they had thought long dead or too dirty-blooded to ever rule. Some of them probably didn't even know what they thought of her anymore.

Rush reached out to her, his arm crossing in front of her like a restraining belt and his big hand grasping the curve of her waist to make certain she came to a stop. This set up a speculative murmur down both sides of the hallway. It was considered a very familiar way for a male to touch the Empress of Allay, though Rush probably didn't realize that. Or perhaps he did. It was hard for her to tell just how deeply clever his intentions could be from one moment to the next. She had certainly learned not to underestimate him. He had proven himself to have far more depth and layers than the great Tarian brute he might like to be mistaken for.

She came to a stop and waited as his keen, brooding eyes traveled quickly over both sides of the hallway. He glanced back at the other IM soldiers, just the merest of glances, and they moved up to flank her, two on either side and Rush moving to step protectively in front of her. But this time it was her hand against his chest that did the staying, to keep him from blocking everyone's view of her.

"Rush," she said softly, "be the protective shadow over me, not one that overshadows me."

He frowned, looked as though he wanted to argue with her, but after a moment gave her a curt nod. He reached to touch a firm finger against her chin.

"Just so you know, anyone who so much as sneezes is likely to get his head ripped off," he breathed softly into her ear.

"You don't strike me as being so undiscerning when choosing someone to attack," she whispered back to him. "If it were all about creating a path of victims for you, you wouldn't have taken the time to move those gaolers out of the way of the explosions you created in the lower wet rooms."

"Well, I was under orders to create a near zero body count," he said with a shrug and an irreverent sort of grin that turned up half his mouth.

"Well, you're working for me now, but you can consider yourself under those same orders. Do nothing unless you absolutely have no choice." Ambrea could see that that didn't sit perfectly well with him. He was no doubt chafing at the directive more because he was worried for her safety than he was eager to do others harm. "But feel free to scare the piss out of anyone you deem deserves it."

That made him laugh out loud, the jolly sound echoing up and down the corridor. He countermanded any irreverence it might have projected by giving her a deep, respectful bow, or as respectful as he could manage without taking his eyes off hers. Those who were hard core about court etiquette would have a difficult time swallowing the Tarian's presence, which was exactly what Rush wanted. To stir things up, put them all off their mark, make them question his role. What he didn't want was for them to be looking at her with any more question than they already were. No Allayan would have any doubt that he was full of reverence for Ambrea, that she had tamed a savage to her side, that there was something about her that had earned his respect. And watching what she'd had to face down at the arbitration and what she was facing now, on top of what she had gone through to get to this point, she had certainly earned enough of his respect to make it a truth.

It was difficult for Ambrea to resist her sudden urge to reach out and touch him. She might have even settled for a touch on his arm in lieu of his handsome face, which was what truly beckoned her, but she had to be careful not to do anything that could be misconstrued as a flirtation. It was one thing to put a Tarian protector at her back and quite another to lead the people scrutinizing her to speculate in even the slightest way that she was flirting with him, possibly even bringing him into the court as her lover. She had a strong image, it was reported, as a devout and virginal princess. A woman who had been kept in a protective tower of exile, the victim of her father's petty jealousies. She hadn't even realized that the people of Allay had any opinion of her at all. She had thought her absence from the public eye had removed her from their thoughts and speculations. Apparently, Suna reported, she was fairly far off the mark in that thinking.

Out here in the hallway was mostly palace staff. They were not allowed in the receiving room, where the nobles and the influential wealthy were given preferred audience. At least, not unless the staff members behaved in a servile capacity. In truth, had the palace guards been doing their duty, there ought not to have been this crowd around her. But Ambrea had no doubt that the master of the Imperial Guard, also known as her uncle, had seen to it that she would have to run an unprotected gauntlet into her own throne room. He had no doubt wanted her to feel alone, vulnerable, and afraid.

He was going to be sorely disappointed.

Ambrea held out her hands as Rush moved into place at her back, so close she could feel his overwhelming warmth. Her extended reach forced the IM soldiers to take a few steps back as well, exposing her a bit more on either side in front, and allowing her to reach for the hands of the first woman she saw on her right side. The woman looked shocked, to say the least, to feel the touch of royal fingers against her own. Ambrea could feel the startling difference in the texture of their skin. Whereas the empress's hands were not as soft and spoiled as those of most women of her rank, she was still clearly not as hard worked as this woman was.

The servant dropped to her knees, not willing to insult her queen by yanking her hands free and not willing to presume she could touch royalty, as her lax but trembling hands attested to. She lowered her head between her upraised arms, hoping that by maneuvering herself as close to the ground as possible she could prevent herself from being offensive in any way, even though she had not been the one to initiate the touch. There was a loud sound of movement as everyone else followed suit, dropping to their knees in respect and reverence. Their experience was that any failure to kowtow to their leader with perfection could mean attracting a negative sort of attention.

Ambrea's first instinct was to raise the woman from her groveling position and demand that the others also stand, but this was her first visit to court, her first day as ruler, and it was important that she be paid homage and expect others to show their respect, that courtly etiquette would be followed. If she flouted those sorts of traditional understandings, she was inviting insolence or perhaps criticism from those among her nobles who were conservative and traditionalist. But neither would she let them think they were dealing with royal blood of the same mien as her father, brother, and uncle. She was not spoiled, was not full of herself, and was not best pleased when others were placed lower than her boot heel.

Slowly she bent her knees, crouching before the prostrate woman, folding the woman's hand between both of hers and pressing against the chill of her fingertips.

"And what do you think of your new mistress, divine worker?" she asked softly, reaching to touch the servant's chin and raising her eyes up to hers. "Does it even matter to you? You think that all rulers are the same, none of us able to understand how hard you work to provide for your family? Your ever-hungry children?"

"No, great lady, I would not presume to know your mind. We know so little about you."

"That will change. Hopefully for the better."

Ambrea rose up to her full, graceful height again. Rush was overwhelmed with a curious sense of pride in her. He didn't know why it should matter to him one way or the other, but it seemed to. Just as it seemed to matter that she continued to reach for people along either side of the corridor. She spoke to each person she touched, giving them small reassurances, knowing they were mostly too awestruck or baffled to speak anything of value to her this time around. But if she made a habit of this, she would soon be inviting commentary, remarks, and even arguments. Eventually she would begin to hear those whom she didn't want to hear, perhaps some who would hurt her. Rush was eaten up with curiosity about how she would react to that.

But at the moment she was bowing her beautiful head near the head of a young woman. Her gleaming golden-red hair was lovely with its simple circlet of Delran platinum and a small clip of gems shaped into a flit-flyer holding it back and keeping it from fluttering hither and yon, as it had done in the forest. She had not bound it or braided it in any other way, and Rush realized that there was something significant to this, some kind of symbolism. He recalled Suna's volatile reaction to his having cut her hair. Now, as his eyes drifted from one side of the hall to the other and caught sight of women self-consciously and hastily trying to tie up their hair, he realized they were worried about their hair being longer than the empress's. The understanding crystallized when one of the Imperial Guards suddenly grabbed a woman along the wall who was too distracted by her new mistress's actions to be more aware of her lacking etiquette. He jerked a dagger out of his belt, one of the many decorative pieces Rush saw at the waists of all the guards and all the nobles.

The guard threw the woman down at his feet, yanked her by the long chestnut sheaf that was her hair, and brought the blade into play. If Rush understood the rules, all that she was guilty of was wearing her hair longer than her queen, a perceived affront. Correction might require the guard to shear off only about a foot at the end. But instead he placed the blade against her scalp and began to saw at the blameless tresses.

"You will hold!"

Rush reacted when he saw Ambrea leap toward the violent guard. Decorative it may be, but the blade was clearly very sharp, evidenced by the blood that began to run down the exposed length of the common woman's neck from the harsh tactics of the careless guard.

Rush leapt for the guard over Ambrea's head, grabbing for his hand and the blade within it, yanking it up so hard that the pop of the man's shoulder socket echoed in the suddenly silent hall. Rush disarmed the man just as he began to scream out with pain. But the Tarian would not be satisfied until the guard was pinned to the floor with his neck under Rush's boot and his twisted arm pulled back tautly.

Ambrea reached for the sobbing woman, using her bare hand to staunch the flow of blood from the mean cut on her scalp. The empress hushed and soothed her subject, hugging her tightly as she blinked back obvious tears.

"You will hear me now," she ground out in a loud, angry voice, a sudden terribleness entering her eyes and steel etched in the frown of distaste marring her lips. For the first time, Rush could see the determined blood of her father shimmering to the surface. "The next soldier to lay a hand on a woman—on *any* subject of my realm in such a way—will answer to me with their lives. This is the end to all senseless brutality in this realm! Between noble and commoner, between subject and empress, between one person and another. I swear to you, I will not have it!" She turned an angry eye toward the Imperial Guards standing outside the palace receiving room. "Fear for your jobs, gentlemen, for you are in no way assured of them! You all as well!" She was shouting toward the nobles awaiting her in the inner room. "There will be new elections, elections where the people will have their true desires met, not the desires of my father, my brother, or my uncle appeased! Those of you who are honest, who are an honest representation of the desires of this land, will have nothing to fear, but believe me when I tell you that the desires of this country are much, much altered now. My Tarian will take control of my Imperial Forces and will clean house there as well. He will set very high standards, and you will meet them or find yourselves begging at the interim offices for assistance in feeding yourselves and your families. But until such time as these things can be put into motion, you will question your every act and impulse. You will wonder what might please or displease me hard enough to stay your hand against such senseless brutalities!"

"But the law—!" The soldier squeaked in protest for only a second before Rush pulled his wrist up tighter, forcing enough pain into him to choke off any further argument.

"The law, as I understand it, states that no woman

may wear her hair longer than the highest-ranking female in the royal family. It also is quite clear that there
is a forgiveness period of one week if that ranking female suddenly changes her style or length. Punishment,"
she said in hard, cold disgust, "is a fine and a warning,
then a public shearing if that fine and warning go un-
paid and unheeded. You didn't even think to verbally
warn her! And a shearing is done with a laser trimmer,
not a sharpened blade! You will not play fast and loose
with my laws so that you can be a bully and a brute!"
She leaned forward toward the man, whose face was
pinned hard to the floor. "I have a bigger bully and a
meaner brute, as you see."

"Yes, great lady," he gritted out.

"You are relieved of your duties, soldier," she told
him.

Rush let go of the man, his numb and dislocated arm
falling hard on the floor. The young man fumbled to get
to his knees, flopping around like a fallen hoofed beast,
a long line of spittle dripping from his lips and onto the
floor.

Ambrea watched him with a careful gaze as he struggled to keep from puking in his pain. Rush knew even
before it happened that compassion would overcome
her anger. He couldn't suppress the strange, full feeling
that blossomed in his chest as her eyes warmed and softened. He wanted to jump between her and the proven-
violent man as she leaned toward him, reaching out a
hand to touch her bloodied palm to his stubbled cheek.
As far as Rush was concerned, it was akin to painting
herself with honey and dangling herself in front of a
wild kabrea. Utter insanity. But he had also come far
enough with her to know when he was needed and when
he would be interfering.

"Perhaps, my Tarian bully," she said to him in a loud

voice, "this is a flaw of his trainers and not the man himself?"

"I doubt it, madam," he said with a dark frown. "All these soldiers were trained in the same manner, and none of them took a blade to an innocent woman. None of them created the opportunity for themselves."

"True." She pushed the soldier's chin up, forcing his eyes to hers, searching his gaze for . . . who knew what she was looking for. Rush wouldn't presume to know her mind at this point. She was always and infinitely surprising to him. And more and more beautiful, it seemed, with every passing moment. There was something ethereal and angelic to her as he watched her bend close to the head of the suffering and undeserving soldier. "What say you, misguided boy? Is it nature or nurture that makes you what you are?"

She was able to glean her answer only from the eyes she was gazing into. He was unable or unwilling to answer her. Most likely he was afraid at his own unsure footing, unable to guess what he could do or say to please this new and strange sovereign who would be so different from those most recently come before her.

"It's my experience, madam, that this particular kind of initiative is a mark of a bad nature," Rush said darkly.

"So would many of my people say about you," she countered with a small smile as she flicked mischievous bright eyes up at him.

"Not that they'd be wrong," he remarked with a grin.

"No indeed. But I have faith in you, my lord. I have faith that you can train a better nature into this young man."

She looked back at the soldier. "But first," she said softly to him, "you must make amends for your brutality. You will be servant to this woman, once you are well, until she is satisfied." She indicated the injured fe-

male, who immediately looked fearful. But Ambrea
soothed her fear. "If he so much as touches you, or even
speaks to you in insolence, he will forfeit his life. For as
long as you feel is necessary, you will hold this power
over him. When you come to me and release him, he will
go into retraining with my Tarian friend here. Between
us both we will teach him to respect others because one
never knows when power between two individuals
might shift. Perhaps from there he will progress to learning that one must always treat others as one would wish
to be treated themselves. And then, perhaps if my hope
is fulfilled, we will teach him true empathy, and true
wrong versus right. Perhaps then he will never want to
be so brutal to another again simply because he has
learned how wrong it is."

She then handed the guard and his victim off to the
imperial medics who had arrived. Rush held a hand
down to her and helped her back to her feet. A quick-
thinking servant had appeared at his elbow with a tray
bearing a bowl of fresh water and a clean cloth. Rush
guided her hands to the bowl, where she could rinse
them. But instead of handing her the cloth, he took on
the task of drying her hands himself, slowly moving the
absorbent, slippery silk over her every single finger until
all traces of blood and moisture had been blotted away.

He didn't realize the reverence he was using to do this
until he looked down into her upturned face and saw
the bemused little smile touching her lips. He suddenly
became aware of the utter silence in the hallway and
that all eyes were on him. Including the eyes of his teammates. Rush became uncomfortably aware of the realization that he was supposed to be playing a part, though
the definition of that part was being made on the fly.
However, he knew very well that the way he was touching her could potentially be misconstrued as something

far more intimate than would be healthy for her young reign. In truth he hadn't meant to.

But the real truth, he admitted to himself, was that he did find her far more attractive, far more compelling than was healthy for either of them.

CHAPTER
ELEVEN

Rush stood in an attentive stance beside Ambrea's throne as she sat in the royal receiving room and was introduced to what seemed like a never-ending flow of nobles. They all groveled in one way or another, many falling to kiss the hem of her dress or touch their foreheads to her feet. Rush hated when they came that close to her. He most certainly didn't like them touching her in any way, and he didn't like them getting within what he called "dagger's distance" of her. But he realized he had little choice in the matter. Everyone wanted to see the new empress; everyone wanted to touch their beautiful new queen. And to be honest it was beneficial to her to have them in awe of her, to have them praising her pale beauty and her regal demeanor. If the nobles and the people developed an infatuation with her, it would make her transition far easier.

What he was even more aware of was that the real danger to her was standing a respectful distance away. Balkin was in full court regalia, making certain that everyone knew he was still in play, still ready to gain power should the opportunity arise. Yet he was keeping a proper distance from her, keeping his head down, so to speak. Rush actually had to admire the man's ability to keep his feelings to himself. All reports had said he was very hot tempered, especially when his desires were thwarted. So either he had suddenly acquired a new level of patience, or he truly was not upset about the power shift going on around him.

Not that that made much sense either. Balkin had to know that his days of power might be numbered as his niece phased him out of her reign. Perhaps that was his game, Rush mused. Perhaps he was trying to avoid being phased out, as if keeping his head down might allow her to overlook all the injustices she had suffered under his boot.

"So, *my great lady*," spoke up the nobleman who stood before her now, his respectful address full of a rather snide tone, "you think you can rule this country and all of us?"

Ambrea smiled slightly in the face of the man's rudeness. The room, which had been buzzing with conversation, suddenly quieted. All eyes were trained on the exchange. Rush tensed beside her, but before he could step forward and cuff the little prick, she laid a calming hand over Rush's wrist, staying him. Still, the request didn't mean he couldn't glare at the obnoxious man. He did so with all the pent-up energy he could muster.

"I will do my best," she replied. "But I know I have much to learn."

"Your first lesson ought to be that not all of us will fall at your feet, kissing your hem. In truth, some of us think you are a waste of our time."

Ambrea had to squeeze her fingers closed around Rush's wrist when she heard a sinister growl roll out of him. She realized he was playing a part, but sometimes she wondered if he wasn't serious. He had her completely convinced that he could and would rip out any throat necessary just on a whim. But she wasn't intent on ruling by dictatorial fear as her father and uncle had done. Although Rush's display would let everyone know that she was personally protected, it was up to her to show her strength in other matters.

"And you are . . . ?" she asked the thin-framed man whose court robes seemed to ride his frame a bit haphazardly. There was something about it that reminded her of her unfortunate young brother and the only time she had ever met him in person. How sad it was that he never had a chance to find his own footing. Perhaps he might have surprised them all and become far more worthy than she had given him credit for.

"I am Prelate Landrea, prelate over Cirqine province, the largest of your provinces, madam. The paxors of Cirqine answer to my voice and act in unison with me. Together we speak many voices on your council."

The inference was clear in his tone and haughty bearing that her power was only as good as the council votes she managed to draw into her favor. Rush despised men like him. They existed everywhere, in all political structures, doing their best to make themselves feel more powerful by making others feel less so. They were so often more interested in throwing their power around that they forgot that their job was meant to be a voice for others.

"Prelate, I am delighted to have you here," Ambrea said with ambitious warmth as she rose to her full height and stepped slowly down the steps of the dais, moving toward him as her hand and fingers slid away from Rush's. He felt her leave him like a strange, bewitching sort of caress. There was an encompassing feeling of regret when she went, something oddly like deprivation. Rush tried to tell himself that it was his need to protect her and the fact that she was moving out of his range that caused it, but a deeper voice, one that was more truthful with him and a bit quieter, told him that that simply wasn't the case.

"I trust more a voice that is bravely willing to speak against me than one that kisses at my feet and oozes false charms." She reached to place both her hands on his shoulders, framing him with her presence. Her receptiveness seemed to baffle him for a moment, and he looked at her as though she was an idiot child. Then he recovered himself and with a rather rude turn of his shoulders he shrugged her off and stepped back out of her reach. The only more rude thing he could have done would have also broken with court etiquette, and that would be to have slapped her away. Although he was willing to be disrespectful to the very limit of the line, he was apparently not willing to cross the line into raw flouting of her authority and imperial blood. A good thing, too, Rush noted to himself as he seethed with a hot desire to bitch-slap the ingrate. Didn't the man appreciate at all how different politics could be under the reign of this extraordinary woman?

"Madam," he rejoined coldly, "you would do well to remember that royal blood is always easy to come by. Figureheads will come and go, but in the end it is we politicians who manage Allay."

"Was that a threat?" Rush snarled suddenly, knowing full well that was exactly what it was. He surged forward, but yet again she stayed him, her hand hitting him squarely in the center of his chest and holding him at bay while she kept her gaze steadily trained on her political adversary.

"Sir," she said, dropping the address just as coldly as he had dropped hers, if not with an added chill of tempered Delran running through it. "You would do well to remember that the entirety of the council exists at my leisure and for my pleasure. The council was created by a long-ago emperor and can be dissolved by a present one, should she understand that it is not serving its purpose in this world. Instead of casting threats about and feeling your cock to see how big it is compared to mine, perhaps you can take your energies and direct them toward bringing forth the needs of the *people* to the ear of their ruler. Isn't that, after all, the essence of your job? And if I believe for all of an instant that you are failing to do your job, Prelate, I will cut you off from all this power you seem to think you have and replace you with one of the no-doubt very hungry paxors who are currently sitting so tamely at your heels but will, given the moment's opportunity, turn and bite you on your ass and gleefully drag you down to sit tamely at theirs."

The nobles and politicians in the room collectively gasped at her crude speech, all of them staring in silent awe as they saw the blood of her family line pulse powerfully through her. But instead of using that power for selfish gains and vanities, she was turning it into something else. Something that would, perhaps, be stronger in the long run. Rush smiled crookedly to see the shock on all those faces and the way they looked at her. They didn't know what to make of her. Every time they thought they were able to pigeonhole her into some kind of neat package, she changed things on them. But in spite of her ability to hand the prelate his ass on a platter, Rush was infuriated by her constantly cutting him off from doing what he deemed as his job. How could he protect her if she wouldn't give him a chance?

He reached out to curl a slow, powerful hand around her upper arm and pull her close so he could speak to her ear alone.

"Madam, a moment in private, if you will?"

"Now, nobles," she spoke aloud to the crowded room before her, "I am told I am needed elsewhere. Please. You will join me tonight at the inaugural ball." She straightened up, and all save Rush lowered themselves in respect. Rush merely raised his hand to her and took a moment of odd pleasure in the way she slid her fingers against his. It was the closest thing to a caress they would likely ever share again.

As he led her away, he tried to understand why that thought made him so irritable. He walked her through the private receiving room behind the public one and with a sharp gesture ordered back the small entourage of servants and retainers she seemed to be gathering at her train. *They* irritated him too. He had not yet vetted any of them, except for Suna, and didn't know what their purposes were supposed to be or even if they could be trusted to do so much as hand her a glass of water. The rest of the IM had fallen back once she had reached her throne safely, occupying the rear of the room as discreetly as they could, and allowing the Imperial Guard to stand watch over her, and Rush to watch over the Imperial Guard. He realized very clearly that they could not be trusted any more than anyone else in this damn place. He had a hell of a lot of work to do, just as she did, and there honestly was no protecting her. If her uncle decided to stage a coup right there in the palace, ordering the guards who were loyal to him to cut off her head, Rush would be the only thing to stand between them, and demented mutation or no, he couldn't see how he could stand between Ambrea and an entire country and somehow manage to keep her alive.

This was what he was thinking as he let the door shut them away from the rest of the palace, his thoughts feeding his already tested temper. He wasn't exactly known for being hotheaded. Quite the opposite, he'd say. He had learned long ago to keep control of his emotions for fear of what his hidden freakishness might set up on display. But there was something about Ambrea that put him on a knife's point.

"Can I ask you what the hell I'm here for?" he growled at her the moment they were securely alone. He had spun her about, seizing her between his two hands, giving her a little bit of a shake even though his actual urge was to shake the head off her shoulders.

She blinked at him with those big blue eyes of hers, the action so slow and deliberate that he was instantly torn between the anger he was feeling and the peculiar sensation that he was about to make a total ass of himself. He had never realized just how much power Ambrea could pack into a single look. After spending a day watching her make powerful eye contact with her subjects, though, he was seeing much more of her depth with every passing instant. And on top of everything else, she was wearing this beautiful gown made of a gauzy, shimmering material in soft pastel lavender that seemed to accentuate all of the things he found so enchanting about her physically. That golden red hair running down her back in natural crimped waves, that ever-so-pale skin and its milky perfection, and her tall, statuesque figure that would make other women seek out surgeons in order to achieve it. Perhaps he had thought she was a bit bony early on, but now that he was seeing her in flattering clothes and a neckline that tortured him as it hovered on the precipice of demure and daring, he was ready to admit he had been wrong.

"I'm sure you know the answer to that. I need you for my protection. I'm dancing among vipers out there," she said, a delicate shiver running through her. It was the first sign she had given, in all of the hours gone by so far, that she was in any way intimidated by her surroundings. Rush knew that was the way it had to be. If she showed even an instant of weakness in front of them, they would fall on her like rabid beasts. He was the one who had pressed that understanding on her.

"Then why do you constantly push me back?" he demanded through tight teeth. "Let me smack a few of the insolent bastards around, teach them—"

"Teach them what?" she cut in with a hot demand.

"That I'm just like my father? That I will knock out the teeth of anyone who speaks against me? That I will be a tyrant and a bully?"

"No!" He growled in a long sound of frustration, his hands tightening on her, pulling her up closer. "You can't let them treat you like that! There is such a thing as a healthy fear. Respect! You must demand their respect!"

"I must *earn* their respect!" she countered fervently. "Setting you loose on them is not the way!"

She was breathing quickly as she challenged him with her strong gaze and her raised chin. Rush couldn't resist the urge he had to reach up and thread his big fingers through her soft, fine hair, the delicacy of it in his grip seeming almost obscene to him, as though he was some kind of uncouth, unwashed thing daring to touch a goddess.

"You are too naïve," he accused her in a low voice. "You wish to see things in these people that are simply not going to be there. You have to learn to expect the worst and then protect yourself from that worst."

"I do not have to learn that," she said fiercely. "Perhaps you do, perhaps all of my guards who will be protecting me do, but I do not. I'm going to give each one of these people the benefit of the doubt for as long as it is reasonable to do so. It's your job to catch them with the knife in their hand as they're trying to stab me in the back. Then you will bring them—and the evidence—to me and I will be cold and terrible and consign them to the wet rooms or worse."

He was so close to her that he saw the instant her eyes went wet, the moment they filled, and he felt when she began to shake. That was when he realized she would never lightly cast a sentence like that on anyone. She would always remember what it had felt like to live in those rooms, always wondering how those who had sent her there could consign her to such a life so unfairly and still manage to sleep so effortlessly. She would rather die in her efforts to treat others fairly than for one instant find herself casting down an unfair or false sentence.

Rush was overwhelmed by the sudden and painfully needy impulse that rode down through his body and caused him to pull her mouth under his. He knew all the reasons why he shouldn't do this, all the things that were dangerous about it, and all the ways it made her vulnerable to what he was, but he had looked all of his life for so pure a place of acceptance and fairness in the universe. It felt as though it would be such an essential crime to his soul to make himself walk away from her right then, to deny himself what he had longed for. He simply was not strong enough to do that.

Her lips were sweet and soft, as untried as they had been the first time he had kissed her. The realization that he was the first and only man to know her this intimately warmed him from the inside out, livened the nerves all along his skin. That sensation made him very aware of what could happen next, and almost as soon as he had seized her he was jolting away from her, pulling his hands free of her and holding them up and out of reach so he couldn't hurt her, burn her, set her on fire.

His frustration rushed out of him in an infuriated roar through clenched teeth. But she suddenly was stepping up close to him, wrapping his face between her soft hands and gripping the whole of his head between them as she forced him to look down into her eyes. She was flush up against the front of his body, feeling so achingly warm and perfect. He could feel the weight of her breasts against his chest, and even as he feared the heat flushing through his body he deeply craved all the most sinful intimate knowledge of her. He wondered what she would feel like, if only they could meet naked skin to naked skin, if only he could lose himself blindly and deeply within her.

Her large blue eyes searched his for a moment, no doubt seeing the hot desire within him. Rush wished he could show her remorse. What kind of man did it make him if he knew he could hurt her, possibly kill her, and yet showed no shame for losing control of himself like that?

But she must have cared very little for all of that, very little for her personal safety, because she pulled his head down to hers, pulled his mouth onto hers, covering his lips with the sweetness of her own. Rush was not strong enough to step away a second time. He wanted her too badly, and freely admitted it to himself. The truth of the matter was that he knew just as little about the touch of a woman as she knew about the touch of a man. He could never allow himself even the most blunted of experiences, his arousal so intrinsically connected to his emotions, and his emotions so dangerously connected to his mutation.

He hungrily devoured her mouth, craving a sense of depth that could be achieved only by holding on to her. But he kept his hands raised and held away from her. Luckily she held on to him, and standing on the tips of her toes she sought for just the depth he was yearning for. She was painfully inexperienced and she was clearly being held back by her own awareness of that. She was afraid she was doing something wrong, afraid she somehow wouldn't measure up. Gods and spirits, didn't she understand? Hundreds of women could have come before her and still she would have, on her very worst day, outstripped them all in his mind and in his eyes.

She broke away from him, her mouth only an instant's distance away from his, her breath washing fast and hot over his wet lips. Insecure she may be, but the blatant hunger he saw in her eyes just then made him rock hard. The instant erection was like no other sensation he could compare it to. Perhaps he had experienced it in the past, but whatever may have caused it in his distant youth had certainly never compared to such a volatile moment and such volatile emotions as were connected to the way he was feeling about this intricate and gorgeous woman.

Rush couldn't remember the last time he had purposely toyed with sexual need and all of the things that came with it. His few encounters with it in his youth had made him realize how deadly it could be, how dangerous it was for any woman to come anywhere close to him. So he had simply shut it all down, turned his back on it just as he had turned his back on the freakishness that sometimes begged to be set free.

"I can't touch you." He ejected a primal sound of frustration even as he lowered his face against hers, let himself breathe in the scent of her hair. "I don't want to hurt you."

"Is it just me? Or is it every woman you've ever tried to touch?" she asked him breathlessly as her fingers brushed down the length of his neck. He swallowed, felt her tracing the movement of the action as he shifted under her fingers.

He pulled back so he could look deep into her eyes, seeing her curiosity and that she was teetering on the verge of understanding him a little bit better.

"Every woman. Always. Although I have to tell you, none of them made me feel so desperately out of control. With them I could pull back, shut down, walk away. With you, I just can't seem to do that." He curbed an impulse to brush back some of her hair where it was loosened and falling feather soft against her jaw. It was only one of a hundred other impulses he'd had to reach out and touch her. "Why can't I do that with you, above all others, when I should do anything to protect what is most worthy of protecting in my eyes?"

She dipped her head briefly, hiding the emotion that his words triggered in her gaze, but unable to hide the soft, vivid coloring along her cheekbones and down her fair neck.

"Rush, did it ever occur to you that all of this repression, all of this denial you subject yourself to, is only making matters worse for you?"

"How so?"

She looked up at him. "It's like any skill, Rush. Swordplay, marksmanship, or even the intricacies of learning to set the yield and focus of your munitions. None of that is an innately perfected skill. None of us was born knowing how to walk. We first started with a crawl, then learned to stand, then stagger and stumble our way into steps, then strides, then running and more. You've never allowed yourself to crawl. How do you think you will ever learn to run smoothly and powerfully and with all of your body under your control?"

She reached up to take his hand, forcefully threading her fingers through his when he tried to pull away. Granted, if he had really wanted to, he could have avoided her, but the one thing he wanted to do most right then was touch her. Somehow. Anyhow. Maybe that was why he was seeing logic in what she was saying. Because he wanted to so badly.

She drew him forward into the large patrician rooms they had entered, the private residence of the ruler of Allay. He guessed that she disliked the look of them almost as much as he did. They revealed a contrived opulence, an almost crude display of wealth, and a definite masculine hardness that in no way reflected the gentility and refinement of their new mistress. The open floor plan allowed an easy view of one room from the next, something he appreciated from a security perspective because it would allow him to keep his eyes on her at almost every moment. Of course that advantage could easily work as a disadvantage. Although these rooms with their large windows and streams of sunlight faced nothing but a dropoff of a cliff, exposing an enormous view of Blossom City from an eagle's nest view, it didn't rule out a clever assassin using a short-flyer or similar ship and then using those same exposing windows as a vantage point to finding her anywhere within her rooms and taking her out before any of the guards realized they were even there. It would likely take out half the palace as well to use the kind of firepower necessary to get through the defensive glass, but no doubt an assassin wouldn't care about collateral damage.

Rush had let himself be distracted by these thoughts in hopes that it would cool his overfired libido and lessen the risk to her as she held his hand. They had not had time to scope out these private quarters, having gone straight to the throne room on arrival, but she seemed to know exactly where she was going as she led him around a corner and into the only completely private room in the royal quarters. As they crossed the threshold, the lights blazed on and the entire rear wall came alive in a sudden rush of water over a lipped outcropping that was a mere foot lower than the ceiling and extended three feet out from the wall. It ran the entire length of the room, forming a waterfall about sixteen feet in length that poured down into a deep tub that would come to his hip should he stand in it.

And apparently standing in it was exactly what she had in mind. She pulled him toward the steps leading down into all that rushing water. He dug his feet in and resisted, making her turn back to him. She looked surprised. She tacked on a smile full of mischief, just to make him feel even more awkward he suspected, with no little sense of petulance.

"Madam, I don't see the point in all of this. We would do better to walk off and remember all of our own limitations and leave it at that," he said firmly. Obstinately.

"I see," she said, turning back to face him and promptly staring him down with those searching, soul-stripping eyes of hers. "So my big, bad soldier is afraid of something after all," she noted.

The supposition instantly burned his biscuits. Probably because it was true. Damn her and her uncanny way of seeing into people. It was his own fault, he supposed. He had shown her more of himself than he had ever shown anyone else. She had a right to think she knew him better than any other person might. She could make that claim even over his IM family.

"I'm afraid of hurting you. I've made no secret of that," he said gruffly, once again resisting her when she went to pull him forward. "I truly would be a monster if I weren't afraid."

"I think it goes a little further than such an altruistic ideal," she countered. "I think you are far more afraid of the unknown than the known, just as I am." She reached up with her free hand and stripped off the regal tiara she wore. It pulled all the other pins and combs free as it went, sending them onto the stone floor with various little pings and clinks of sound as she shook back that glorious sheet of hair.

Then she stepped closer to him and reached for the fabric of his shirt where it clung tight to his strong, firm belly.

CHAPTER
TWELVE

Ambrea tried not to jump out of her own skin as his free hand smacked tight around hers, seizing her in an almost painful grip. But if there was one thing she had become an expert at over the cycles of her lifetime, it was in not giving away her fear to those she least wanted to see it. The truth was, she was terrified and incredibly out of her depth. But there had been a clear understanding a few moments ago that had made her so suddenly willing to be so bold and brave where she might never have been before.

Rush Blakely was just as much of an untried virgin as she was.

That understanding had just about broken her heart. There was something about how this man had lived his life on the tipping point of life and death, flinging himself into every danger that the Three Worlds could throw at him, almost as if he were hunting down the one danger that would finally be able to beat his unusual genetics right in its tracks. And yet for all of that, he had not lived his life in the ways that truly counted any more than she had. But where she had been held back by others, he had been held back only by himself and his own fears. Just the same, she could see more similarities between them than differences. However, the one difference between them now was that she had been set free.

From her father, her uncle, and more than anything, from herself. She was finally in charge of her own destiny, in charge of the way she chose to live her life. And she honestly couldn't spin free and leave him chained behind her. There was no one else she would ever want to take with her. No one else had made her feel so much with just the look in his eyes or the smile quirking at the edges of his lips. No one had ever come so close to setting her on fire. Figuratively speaking. Literally as well, but for some reason she wasn't afraid of that. She would never be able to touch him again if they both were afraid of that.

And that simply would not do.

She needed him. Needed his hands on her skin. Needed to feel him let loose, to feel him set free, to be within reach of his every impulse the minute he realized he was able to indulge in them.

She stepped forward into him, closing all distance between them, pushing her reaching hand up against his belly in spite of his attempts to stay her. She took a deep breath, the rugged, rich smell of him invading her nostrils. It was a combination of so many things, a deep story of who he was. She could smell a harsh solvent of some sort, blending with the softer, more mechanical smell of weapons lubricant. But once she got past those hints of his career, there were the more personal aromas that were strictly Rush. Sweat left behind from working at a high intensity level of awareness and alertness from the moment they had landed. Leather from the clothing he had chosen to wear to keep him from being identified as an IM soldier. Musk from the brief moments of arousal he had allowed himself to indulge in when he kissed her. All of these things combined to make the scent she had come to recognize as strictly his. Ambrea realized that even if she were struck blind, she would always be able to pick him out of a crowd of men. He smelled incredible, he smelled delicious. Dozens of men could cross her path, she was certain, and no other would affect her this way by the sheer power of his smell.

And that was only the beginning.

She gripped hold of his shirt successfully this time, pulling the Skintex free from the wall of muscle it clung to. He still wore a jacket and a lazily left open shock vest, as if he didn't care enough to link it properly closed across his chest. It wasn't military grade. Even her father had worn a military-grade shock vest under his court clothing. And she could swear she'd caught a peek of one under her uncle's clothing as well at the tribunal. Many high-end mercenaries managed to get their hands on IM-grade equipment, or close to it. She supposed that Rush was trying to come across as less than high end.

Ambrea didn't see how that was possible. To her, everything about him was high end. She unlaced her fingers from his and shoved her hand under the vest and jacket, pushing both back off his shoulder as she worked the Skintex free of his pants.

"You can't do this," he said in a hot fall of words where his lips had fallen against her forehead. "Bad enough you're in here alone with me now. You don't want them thinking I'm your lover, Ambrea. They don't even know if they want to accept you versus your uncle. But if they think you're making love with a savage like me—"

"Right now what 'they' think is not my first concern," she told him.

"It should be!" he snapped, trying to pull her under some sort of control and failing so miserably that she realized he wasn't trying all that hard.

"I have spent so much time denying myself everything there is in life to be lived. What I did not deny myself, my father saw to it that I was denied it. If all Allay is going to turn on me in these next few moments simply because I was alone too long with my Tarian protector, then let it be. I won't live afraid of them. Not when I'm just learning to live unafraid of everything else. I won't ever give anyone that kind of power over me again. And neither should you."

His jacket and vest fell at his heels with a hard thud, telling her just how heavily armed he was in just those two iniquitous pieces of clothing. How he managed to make it all so invisible to the outside eye she would never know, but just the same she smiled at the sound of it. Because it made her feel more protected? Because it was so essentially Rush? She couldn't say.

"What I am afraid of has nothing to do with something so shallow as my concerns of what someone else might think of me," he said tightly as both her hands went to the task of peeling up the Skintex. He might have been trying to fight her a moment ago, but in this particular moment he raised his arms and helped her skin the thing off him. He did shrug her off immediately afterward, though, stepping back and holding up a hand between them in an effort to stay her. "I won't do anything that could hurt you!"

"And do you think I want to be hurt?" she asked him with an admonishing click of her tongue. "Now that would just be silly." She reached up and took hold of his hand where it was trying to hold guard between them. "Kick off your boots."

"But I . . ." He floundered for what to say, for how to argue with her. She supposed he wouldn't be having such a hard time if he hadn't wanted this so badly. The realization made her skin go warm from head to toe.

"It's either that or come under the water fully dressed, Rush. If you leave here just as you entered, my courtiers can only guess at what we've been doing. If you leave here wearing wet clothes, I imagine that would remove all doubt."

Her logic flustered him. He didn't know how to fight her reasoning and his own blatant desires at the same time. It was also keeping him from comprehending the totality of what she had planned. Regardless, she got her way. He kicked off his boots. Then he reached down to unfasten the knife sheath he had strapped to his calf. After that, he reached up between his shoulder blades and pulled free the suction sheath attached to his skin there, the strong technology of the sheath designed to keep the weapon strapped to skin no matter how much the wearer moved or sweated. This particular sheath held some sort of small munitions that she couldn't even begin to guess the nature of after all the many things she had seen him use. The strap contained only three bombs, each visibly different from the others. She didn't doubt that he knew what each one did and where each one was located precisely in the sheath so he could quickly grab and use them.

Ambrea stepped in to take his belt under her nimble fingers. When he caught her hands in his to stop her, it was the first time she could recall him feeling cold to the touch. She looked up at him, saw him swallow hard.

"What if—" he tried to say.

"Yes, but what if?" she countered.

That was a powerful "what if," a compelling one. A tempting one. She knew that, and very likely so did he. His hands fell away from hers, a clear surrender. But still he took no active part in what she was doing. He remained as passive as possible, his breath coming in difficult spurts, his gaze shifting all around the room as if the little details he was focusing on could keep him from thinking too much in one direction or the other. Anything, she realized, except looking at her and touching her. And just by that singular lack of focus on her, she felt the erotic fullness of his entire attention. She felt it in a way that she would never have responded to the full-force flirtations of any other man. So she unfastened his pants and boldly pushed them down over his flexed hips and taut buttocks, down thighs locked into a rigid stance, and then knelt to help him step free of them as a servant might do for her.

When she looked up from her kneeling position before him, she caught him quickly looking away, looking toward the wall, then the ceiling, anywhere but down at her. His hands curled into fists so tight and powerful that they looked as though they could destroy empires with a single blow. But more impressive was the growing size of his penis. Despite his best efforts, a single glance in her direction had resulted in the very response he was working so hard to avoid. It lengthened and thickened, rose away from his body like some kind of deadly and powerful arrow.

It was the first time she had seen an erect penis in person. Pictures, she realized, had done the magnificence of it a terrible injustice. PhotoVids had added a clinical crudeness to something that simply could not be captured, she believed. Or maybe such poetic thoughts occurred to all inexperienced girls. Strangely, though, she was convinced that, had it been anyone else but Rush, she might have been scared to death. She wondered if it was the first time he had been naked in front of a woman, then realized that it wasn't likely to be the case since he was a soldier and there were many women soldiers out there in rough countries on hard assignments that provided very little privacy between the sexes.

Ambrea rose to her full height and resisted the incredible urge she had to reach out and touch him. She wanted to know how he felt. Was he soft or hard? Warm? Hot? Hotter still?

She met his eyes, and something very much like panic appeared there.

"This is a bad idea," he croaked as he suddenly bent, reaching for his clothes.

She threw her body against him instinctively in order to stop him, but she realized very quickly that it wasn't the wisest of moves. He was so hot that she pulled quickly away in order to avoid being burned. But she grasped at his hand and ignored the scorching of her skin for as long as it took her to hurriedly yank him down the steps and under the warm fall of water in the bath. The instant it hit him, there was a hiss and sizzle sound followed by steam, much like the reaction of water against a superhot skittle. Ambrea had to lean back to avoid the steam, but she still didn't let go of his hand, instead allowing their palms to part and letting the water cool the space between them.

The instant all the steam ceased, she stepped against him, sealing her body to his, reaching with her free hand for his and turning his palm toward her as she pressed it to her face. It was a total leap of faith. There was no guarantee that the water was enough to constantly cool the fierce heat he could generate. Especially at its mildly warm temperature. Perhaps she should command the computer regulating its temperature to go icy cold, providing even more of a buffer, but she refused to show a moment's doubt. She knew that if she did, he would turn tail and run back to his place of denial and would continue to let his fear reign over him. Between the two of them, someone had to have faith.

She *needed* to have faith. She longed so much for him, burned in a way that no waterfall could possibly cool. This had to work.

Please, let this work.

She stared up hard into his eyes, waiting with him for several long moments, waiting for him to burn her in spite of the cooling effect of the water, waiting to see if there was any hope to be found in her mad methods. His heart was thundering in his chest so hard that she could feel it as it pulsed against her. His fingers opened and closed around her head, one moment feeling as though he was going to push her away, the next feeling as though he would never let her go. The longer the time stretched between them, the harder his breath seemed to come. A slow, virulent heat began to burn in his eyes, the expression far hotter than the hand she had held to pull him under the water.

In the next instant his mouth was crashing against hers, devouring everything about her as quickly as he could possibly manage. His hands came alive and climbed over her everywhere at once. His stroke was dominant and possessive as it raced over her sodden clothing. Her beautiful gown, its delicate fabrics utterly ruined, meant nothing to either of them. She had never felt the power of such encompassing desire, never known someone could want her so much. Need her so blatantly. She had been such an unwanted creature for so long that this was utter nirvana.

He tangled his tongue with hers, tasting her again and again, his breath mixing with hers and water washing wildly between their lips. She became aware of him abruptly laughing into her mouth, sharp disbelieving bursts of deep male laughter that suddenly filled the room as he threw back his head and let the water crash directly into his face.

"Sweet merciful spirits," he ejected as he looked back at her, wrapping her face between his hands. "Such a simple idea, and never once did it occur to me."

"A simple beginning," she warned him, purposefully raining on his delight.

"Good enough for now," he told her as he grabbed for

her backside with both hands and hauled her up tightly into his body. "Aye, more than enough for now."

That much she was willing to give him. After so many years of denial, he had earned himself a few precious minutes of letting loose. Of indulgence. And by the Being, he took full advantage, she thought as his hands moved wildly over her body. At first he kept the heavy, wet silk of her dress between his hands and her skin, one last prophylaxis to keep her safe as his touch moved in staccato strokes up her back, over her belly and hips, up over her heavy breasts. He left almost no area of her body untouched, now that he felt free to do so. Issues as to whether it was wise or not because of who she was and who he was never even came into play. Not in the face of the other obstacles that had been surmounted. For the moment, in any event.

But she didn't let herself think about that. Ambrea was too busy feeling. Like him, it was all for the first time, and she reacted to it as though a floodgate had been thrown open. She wanted him to touch her skin and refused to let his fear interfere with that. She reached for the closure of the dress and pulled it open, dragging the now-heavy material down over her shoulders. She peeled it off her body, peeled it away from between them, allowing them to come in skin to skin contact. They seemed to gasp in unison as they did so, each of them reveling in the fiery sensation that was all passion and no actual fire. That he was hot was understandable, but it was a bearable heat, the kind of heat that she could safely devour as she plastered herself to him. Her arms wrapped around his neck as she taught herself again and again all the new and delightful ways she could touch and hold another person. She reveled in how he felt, in the strength of every part of his body as he came up hard against her and she molded softly against him.

Now his hands went over her again, this time closer, slower, so much more intimately, and the sensation of it all made her moan against his lips. That was when she realized he was kissing her again. It felt like an entirely different experience now that she was naked against him. It was crazy. In the grand scheme of things, they must have skipped about a thousand steps in proper courting rituals, those rituals that she had always been trained to believe were so important to maintaining her status as a lady. But it wasn't the first time she had flown in the face of what they had tried to train into her, and she doubted it would be the last. Besides, if she had obeyed every rule of etiquette expected of her in court, she would have signed away all of her rights to being empress a very, very long time ago. Now she reaped the ultimate reward for defying that rule and defying her father. Here again was another ultimate reward. His strong fingers dragging against her skin, sending electrical delight over all her nerve endings was worth any and all fallout she might suffer for taking this beautifully wild Tarian to her bed.

"Sweet taunting spirits," he breathed against her skin as his mouth moved to taste the curve of her jaw, the rise of her cheek, the long, graceful length of her neck, "I never knew a woman could taste this sweet. I never knew you would feel so soft. It's beyond any imaginings."

"You imagined touching me?" she asked breathlessly as he lifted her breast to the quick approach of his mouth.

"Aye. Once I kissed you, it seemed I could think of nothing else. As futile as it was, I couldn't make myself stop. I knew you'd be warm and soft, Blue Eyes, but I never thought you'd feel so hot. Nothing ever feels hot to me. I've always had to pretend something was hot to the touch, a frying pan or such." His tongue came out to flick teasingly at her rigid, sensitive nipple. Ambrea sucked in a breath of surprise at the sensation it elicited, at the way her insides seemed to swirl with intensity. In spite of all the water already spilling all around her, she felt herself growing wet between her legs. And with that wetness came an incredible craving, a sensation of being void and empty and a craving for being filled.

"But now, the first time I am touching you, I can feel your heat." His fascination was put aside for the moment as a new one came to the forefront of his attention. He tongued over her nipple again and again, rubbing his thumb over her in his tongue's wake each time, feeling the changes in the rigidity of it. She was squirming in his hold so blindly, her head having fallen back as she abandoned herself to the sensations he was subjecting her to. She wasn't even aware of when she parted her thighs around one of his, or when she started to ride herself in slow undulations against him in an effort to alleviate the incredible aching emptiness he was tormenting her with. She felt him go still for an instant, his teeth on the point of her nipple, his mouth on the verge of devouring her.

But he forgot all about sucking on her there as the fiery wetness between her legs smeared over his thigh, burning him in a way that nothing had ever before been able to do. It was like a fine and beautiful acid, hot and burning, yet instead of hurting him it had the power to beckon all sorts of desires from him. Those desires crashed over him as wildly as the waterfall, one tumbling over the next, things he had only ever read or dreamed about. Things he had been a voyeur to on one or two occasions before he'd been forced to take himself away or else risk putting others in danger.

But there was no danger now. Not as long as the water ran over him and cooled him of the heat he knew he was generating. There was no guarantee that this was foolproof, no guarantee that the water could compensate as he grew more and more aroused, but he couldn't bring himself to behave with fear when all he wanted was to act with passion. She was there, she was beautiful, and she was willing to risk so much just to be with him. When had anyone, any woman especially, been willing to stick her neck out to be seen by his side? To be held in his hands? To revel in his touch?

Rush dropped to his knees, uncaring of the stone that bit into his skin, no doubt cutting him. What did he care for any of that when there was a gorgeous feast awaiting his senses? His hands raked down the back of her body. He felt her fingers fumbling to grip at his hair as he pulled one of her legs up over his shoulder. The action spread her open to him, allowing him to see the smoothness of her, the plump thrust of her clit from between her outer lips, and the pretty pink of her moist, intimate flesh. He reached out to touch her, going directly for what fascinated him most and forgetting there might be a more clever way to go about it.

She felt his fingers against her clit. An outrageous sensation, or so she thought until one of those fingers slid immediately inside of her, seeking for the tight feel of her. Feeling overwheled Ambrea tensed up tightly, pushed against him in sudden confusion even as her body devoured the sensations and reacted to them in its own way. He tore his eyes from the sight of her when he felt her lock up in resistance. He looked up at her. Ambrea had never before seen such an open, fascinated expression on his face. Always he had been so guarded and so shuttered, so filled with his mistrust of others and his conviction that, given half a chance, they would betray him. But the way he was looking at her just then it could only be described as innocence. Pure and unadulterated, the last thing she had ever expected to see on him.

"Am I hurting you?" was the first thing he wanted to

know. It was always the first thing he wanted to know. Was she okay? Was she safe? And she knew he didn't do it just because it was his job.

"No," she said breathlessly. "I'm just not . . . it feels . . . I've never felt . . ."

He nodded even though she was unable to complete a single thought. Perhaps that was because he didn't remove his touch in the slightest.

"Just let me know if I hurt you. Or if you don't like something. You'll do that, right? You'll tell me?"

"I don't think you have to worry about that," she said as pleasure shuddered violently through her. The sensation was so keen that it made her eyes fill with tears.

"But you'll tell me," he demanded of her.

"Yes. Of course," she gasped as he worked his thick finger even deeper inside of her.

"Good," he muttered as his attention refocused on where his touch met her body. Rush felt hot wetness oozing down over his probing finger, and he let loose an appreciative growl. He gripped her between her legs and pulled her forward onto his mouth. Now it was his tongue stroking boldly over her stimulated clit, followed quickly by the entirety of his mouth. He was oblivious to the water sluicing down her skin. It was not even a factor in what he was seeing, feeling, and tasting. It most certainly wasn't a factor in the incredible way she smelled—alluring and sweet, and here it was all in concentrate, like a liquid ambrosia that was purely and intensely Ambrea.

He lapped his tongue over her again and again, devouring the delicate taste of her even as he breathed in the smell of her. It was all Ambrea, Ambrea in resoundingly full dimension. The impact of it sent fiery heat down the length of his already distended phallus. He believed that were it not for the water rushing over his body, he would have burst into flame. He didn't know how much of that was truth and how much of that was a perception of passion, but he was overwhelmed with the feeling.

More than anything, he wanted to lose himself inside her, to thrust into that tight place that housed and wetted his probing tongue. But he became keenly aware that to thrust into her body would be to seal himself away from the cooling protection of the water. Without the run of water over his skin, how would she be protected from being burned?

Rush suddenly sat down hard away from her, pulled back completely in the rising bathwater. He lifted his knees, propped his elbows on them, and settled his head between his hands after running them through his hair and sending a shower of water droplets bouncing off their ends. Disoriented for a moment, Ambrea had to catch her breath and draw her wits back into place. She looked down at him as she stood over him, saw how his hands were shaking and through the crystal clear water could see that he was rapidly loosing all interest in anything sexual.

It was hard for a moment not to take it personally, not to feel a horrible flush of embarrassment run over her face and move down through her body. Her first instinct was to think she had done something wrong, that there was something about her he didn't like. Perhaps she was far too green even for him. To wait so long to be able to express desire and then be disappointed by the experience?

"I-I'm s-sorry," she heard herself uttering awkwardly as she turned first left, and then, remembering where the steps were, turned right in an attempt to escape the moment. But he reached out and snagged her by the wrist, locking his fingers so tightly around it that she couldn't possibly have broken free.

"For what?" he demanded. "For being perfect? For

being normal? For being just as fragile as every other woman in the Three Worlds? I'm not rejecting you, Ambrea," he said softly then, seeming to suddenly realize what she must be thinking in that moment. "Spirits curse me, is that what you think? That I'm rejecting you for some reason?"

After that reaction, she wasn't thinking it any longer. She lowered herself to her knees between his legs, the water coming to just above her breasts. The beating of the water falling behind her created a tidal effect, making her body waver back and forth toward him no matter how hard she tried to steady herself. She reached out to touch his rugged face, her fingers smoothing over the length of the whiskers he had allowed to grow these past two days. They were soft to the touch, thickly blond, and gleaming like gold as the sunlight bounced off the bathwater and shimmered across his face.

"The only thing that keeps me from you is the same thing that has ever held me in check," he said to her vehemently. "Were I given a choice, I would be buried deep inside of you right now. But clever as you are, as incredibly wet as you are," he said as he brought her fingers against his lips, "you cannot bring your clever waterfall inside your body. When I think of the pain you would feel—"

"Shh," she hushed him softly as she reached to hug him, drawing his head to hers, kissing his cooled cheek with a slow touch of her lips. "This was never meant to be a complete answer, Rush," she told him softly against his ear. "Just a training ground. You can hand a man a sword and he can hack and slash at things and maybe do a little damage, but skill and finesse come with the building of strength and control, with lessons learned and mastered. Come, let's make a lesson." She stood up and held her hands down to him. His brows were drawn down tight in the center of his forehead, but he took her hands and let her help him to his feet. "But I will make a disclaimer right now, Rush. I expect to be burned. I know you will not mean to. I know you will not want to, but because we are doing this blindly without the guidance of someone who knows any better than we do, I expect we will make mistakes."

"That is unacceptable to me," he ground out, pulling his hands free of hers.

"What is unacceptable," she said in that hard voice he had come to know as inarguable, "is you living half a life. You are prisoner to yourself just as surely as I ever was to others, Rush." She held out her hand to him. "One day you are going to have to cross the line," she said quietly. "You're going to have to take action to get what you want. To claim what is rightfully yours. Why not take that action today?"

That made him smile a bit wryly, and he chuckled softly as he shook his head at her. "Ah. That's a low blow, Princess."

"That's 'Empress,' " she corrected him, forcing him to meet her eyes. "Empress because I threw in my lot with a stranger who seemed as crazy as the day was long. I'm asking you to do so with a friend who is far wiser than that and just as brave."

He smirked. "Brat." He sat there for a long minute just looking at her, then with a noisy, capitulating sigh he put his hand in hers and together they rose to full height. "But if you get hurt . . ." he tried to threaten her sternly.

"I will use a burn salve and it will be gone in hours. Please. Must we go through this again? Hush and stand outside the fall of water." She maneuvered him outside the stream of water, but he was still standing almost thigh deep in it in the tub. "Now create fire in the palm of a single hand."

"While in the water?"

"If you are able to do it, then you are right, it is possible you will be able to burn me. But if you can't do it, then perhaps you have nothing to worry about." She gave him a provocative smile, her hand falling onto his chest and drawing a brief caressing shape over it. "If you need inspiration, I could very much help with that."

"But I wouldn't be able to concentrate on bringing fire to a single hand," he said with an appreciative little growl. "Now stand clear." He pushed her back a bit, the distance a little too overprotective. He'd never burned her while not touching her.

Ambrea watched him concentrate, watched him try to create fire in a single hand. She carefully kept an eye on the water and the air around him, looking for steam or that telltale ripple in the air that said it was heating up.

There was nothing.

"So," she said softly after watching him try with all his will. "It seems we've discovered your weakness, Rush. You can't create fire while part of you is immersed in water."

"It would seem so." He shot a sudden look at her that seared and burned far more than any fire might have done. "But let's give it a wee bit of a testing, shall we?"

And just like that she was swept into his arms and under the crush of his mouth. Just as easily as he had shut everything down earlier, he threw a switch and turned it all back on again. And Ambrea was very okay with that. She did notice that he took the added precaution of moving them back under the fall of the water.

"Ah, that's better," he rumbled, his voice deep and rough as his hands slid fast and hot all over her skin. "Watching you stand there naked, these pretty breasts of yours so proud and so damn tempting. If that couldn't inspire heat in my hands and body, then nothing can."

"I think you're mostly right. But I've seen the power inside you, Rush. I believe with a little practice and a little control you can make anything happen, or *not* happen. At your will."

"Perhaps. Right now, Empress, my will is to create a bit of fire inside you. Let's start with that, shall we now?"

She was too breathless to speak, so she merely nodded her head.

CHAPTER
THIRTEEN

Balkin had carefully followed in the wake of the empress's departure. After all, he did not want his curiosity to be blatant. He couldn't imagine where else she would need to be. He had instructed everyone to keep court business away from her. At least, for today. Tomorrow, however, was another story. Tomorrow he wanted them to overwhelm her, to flood her with all their business as they would never otherwise have dared to do. So far, she had shown a surprising bit of strength and backbone, but a few insults thrown at her by one of the more imprudent prelates was nothing compared to the clamor of what it took to manage the state of Allay.

Balkin lived in the royal wing, mere doors down from the royal quarters, so he had a right to walk these particular halls, whether by the outer approach or by following the receding procession through the private receiving rooms and council chambers. He came up on the small crowd of milling servants who seemed at a loss as to what to do with themselves. They'd all been locked away and out, denied access to the royal person. Yet the definition of their jobs demanded they be ready to serve the empress at a moment's notice. So essentially they couldn't leave.

Most of them anyway. The entirety of the picture became clear to him when he realized that there was one

royal servant missing. The Tarian. Balkin had been trying to make heads or tails of the brute since first laying
eyes on him. He'd decided that he was a mercenary hire,
a bit of muscle she had acquired to help make her feel
safe as she took her place in decidedly hostile territory.
Truly, it was a wise choice. He begrudgingly had to give
her some credit for it. But unless the Tarian was going to
taste every bit of her food and sleep guard beside her
bed . . .

But here now he was entertaining another idea. What
if the Tarian was going to be sleeping *in* her bed? It was
a major breach in court etiquette if he was locked away
with her behind closed doors. It allowed for the specula-
tion that they were lovers. Some wild savage like the
Tarian male was proving to be was, however, far from
an acceptable choice as a bedmate for the Empress of
Allay. The nobles would not stand for it, and neither
would the Tari-hating commoners. Indeed, it surprised
him that she would make so unwise a move in her opening salvo to win the favor of the court and the country.

"Why stand you all here?" Balkin demanded of them
loudly and gruffly, watching the servants jump in their
own skin at the surprise of his strident voice. "Why do
you not attend your mistress?"

The only one who had not jumped at his voice turned
to meet him eye to eye, a notable action because commoners had never been allowed to meet the eyes of royals under the rule of his brother. But he knew this
woman. She had been in exile with the princess. She
would not be used to the sound of his voice or the fear
it ought to instill in her.

"You. Are you not companion to the empress?"

"I am, great lord." She gave him what he would consider a begrudging bow. But still she did not look away
from his eyes. It ought to have enraged him under any
other circumstances, but for some reason her backbone

stimulated him. That she had a pretty face and a fine set of tits didn't hurt either.

He let his appreciation show as he stepped up to her, broke into the safety of her personal space. At last she wavered and her gaze flew from his. She wanted to step back but was torn, he could tell. She was confident in the strength of her mistress, but not as yet confident in her own place amongst the court. She was a pretty fish out of water. He could use her against Ambrea if he played her right.

"Your mistress should never be left alone with anyone whom others might perceive as below her regard," he reminded her. "It is your job as her most trusted servant to protect your mistress from unseemly behaviors. What is your name?"

"Suna," she answered, clearly trying to find her footing against him. She bravely raised her chin and met his eyes. "I have been companion to my mistress for many years, great lord," she said, clearing her throat a minute before becoming a bit more strident. "Her protection has always been my ultimate goal. I can assure you, she is very well protected with her Tarian by her side. And if she wishes to confer with him in private about matters, it is innocently meant and essential to her safety and protection." She squared her shoulders then, and Balkin got an instant erection at the sight of her proud stance. "And anyone who thinks otherwise is a lascivious prig. My mistress is innocent of men, as she has always been. She is also pious and sweet and would not ride just any stallion that trotted across her path."

"I never said she would. I only mentioned that perception is everything, and here we have a corridor full of servants with opinions of their own who do not know your mistress as well as you do."

"Opinions are rather like assholes," she countered

crudely. "Everyone has one and they are all usually full of shit."

Balkin chuckled, giving her what he deemed his most charming smile. "Truer words were never spoken, Lady Suna. But where would we be without the rules of etiquette and genteel behaviors? Such chaos creates fear among those little assholes. And before you know it, they are crapping all over your sweet mistress."

He turned to the milling peons in the hall. "Be gone, all the rest of you! The only ones who ought to be here are the empress's personal guard and the Lady Suna. She will fetch any of you who are needed when you are needed."

They began to hastily clear out under his order, and turning back to Suna he smiled again. Though she remained strongly raised against him, he saw her flush darkly over the rise of her cheekbones. He reached out to brush back a loose curl where it rested on her collarbone, the length respectfully and obviously shorter than that of her royal mistress. He suspected she was a very loyal girl and she would report all of his actions to her mistress, so he remained well behaved and did nothing untoward, although that didn't mean he wouldn't remember her in the future. But it would be fun to toy with the little fish.

For the moment he would use her to report good things about him to her mistress. She would tell Ambrea that he was kind, concerned, and fair. That perhaps he was a good source of information, a good place to turn when she needed guidance. In a very lowered voice he spoke to her.

"Whether your mistress's behavior is pure and innocent or more tawdry, that is her private business. It is your responsibility, Lady Suna, to keep opinionated witnesses to the ultimate minimum. You are loyal to the empress, and that is good. You must protect her and her image at all costs. It is one thing for there to be rumors, quite another for someone to say, 'It's true. I was there standing outside her private rooms when they were locked away together.' You understand?"

Suna nodded, her expression turning contrite and a bit lost. Clearly she was angry with herself for not acting more definitively.

"I will do better, great lord," she said, that stubborn chin rising up again.

"I know you will," he assured her, touching a gentle fingertip under her chin. "And if you have any questions or need any help, I could guide you to someone of the court who can help train you in its etiquettes. She can help empower you with the servants. After all, you must remember you are now the right hand to the most powerful woman of all Allay, and, as her right hand, you must act just as powerfully."

"I can do just fine on my own," she said stubbornly. "I merely forgot . . ." She paused for a few beats and he waited patiently. His patience of late had been surprising even to himself. "But perhaps . . . if you point someone out . . ."

He took her by her elbow and guided her back down the passages and to the entrance of the court hall, where nobles still milled about in heavy numbers.

"Let's see," he mused as he made a big show of thinking about things. "There is Paxor Brigitte. She is a bit rigid at times as far as protocol and proper behavior are concerned, but you will find no better walking rule book." He continued to scan about. "And then there's Mistress Holbiert. She is wed to one of our paxors and has been a friend to many of the greater ladies of the court, although she has been known to be quite crushing to anyone she feels has crossed her. A great friend to have, but beware if you make an enemy of her."

"Perhaps it is best she remain on the periphery altogether," Suna said dismissively.

"Perhaps you are right. Well, my only other choice would be the Lady Eirie. She is young and wise. The wealthy widow of a man long respected in court circles. She has been at court since a very young age and knows all of its ins and outs quite well. She understands all the finest points of etiquette and has an impeccable reputation for it; however, I think you would find her to be more flexible and understanding of your mistress's inexperience and youthful needs."

Balkin had given her a choice, and she could easily choose in a less favorable direction, but he didn't think she would. Still it was important that she feel in charge of the decision. It would help her to form a quicker bond of trust with her selection if she felt she had had full power when making it.

"I think perhaps the Lady Eirie is the best choice," she said.

Balkin didn't even feel relief. He had been that confident.

"Are you certain? There is something to be said for older wisdom."

"My lady is not known for her rigidity and cold adherence to the rules. I think someone of youth who knows the rules but is more easily able to flex is the better choice."

"Perhaps you are correct," he said with a noncommittal shrug. "Come with me and I will introduce you to her. Then you ought to hurry back to your mistress in case she comes out of her conference and needs you."

It was as though all the last chains holding Rush had finally slipped away. Earlier he had been hasty and still unsure of the wisdom of his actions, but after trying so hard to create even the smallest amount of heat and being so thoroughly thwarted by the water he stood in, he was utterly convinced that he would not hurt her. Knowing that was like swallowing a strange and powerful aphrodisiac, like empowering himself on a visceral level.

Ambrea moaned softly against his lips as he kissed her until they were both breathless and their mouths tender from his constant devouring hunger for her. He couldn't explain why she was so damn enticing, so incredibly delightful to him. But then again, why wouldn't she be? He had never met anyone like her. She was such a compilation of bravery and strength, yet full of gentility and fairness. He was very aware of the power she was now wielding, of what it could do to her, of what he had seen power do to others in many other countries of the Three Worlds. But he didn't question her. He felt a faith in her that he had not felt in anyone else in his life. Not even Bronse, a leader he trusted with his life and followed faithfully. Even after all his years under Bronse's guidance and all the scrapes they had been through together, he still couldn't bring himself to trust the commander with the secret he held on to so vehemently.

But Rush trusted Ambrea, now more than ever, he realized as he pulled her body tightly to his, gripping her slender thighs and dragging them up around his waist. She eagerly clung to him, her mouth just as impassioned against his as his was against hers.

Rush let his eyes close as his entire spirit breathed an emotional sigh of relief. It seemed as though he had craved her from the moment of his birth. Even his mother had not wanted to accept him in his entirety. From the moment he had first accidentally burned her, she had not been comfortable touching him. She had tried to cover it up, had made every effort to make up for it in other ways, but he had easily sensed his mother's fear of him.

Rush had known in that moment that not just anyone

would have done for him. Ambrea was not a convenient body, close at hand when he realized it was safe for him to touch a woman. He didn't want anyone else. No one else would feel so precious and good, no one else could make him so hard with lust and need because no one else would have earned the trust necessary for him to feel free to indulge in those feelings.

He pulled away from her mouth and dragged his lips down her throat, his tongue tasting her creamy skin, his hands exploring the stretching length of her back. What he wouldn't give right then to have her sprawled out before him in a bed, those long, pale limbs reaching for him, spreading to welcome him.

"Ah, it's never enough, is it?" he breathed against the crest of her collarbone. "We're never content to have what we have. We're always seeking more."

"What more are you looking for?" she asked him, her voice light with the speed of her breathing. "Tell me what I can give to you, Rush."

"You've given me more than enough already," he told her hotly, his hands gripping her hard where he held her. "I only want you. More of you. Everything about you. All I crave now are the things about you that stand out of my momentary reach. But I will have them all, Blue Eyes. I will find a way to have them all."

"And you are welcome to them," she promised him as she pressed her lips against the corner of his eye. "What we don't have now we will find a way to have later. Your limitations are only what your own mind holds up in your way. I firmly believe that."

"And you are making a believing scholar out of me, Ambrea." He drew back to meet her eyes with his, unaware of the emotion that his amber gaze betrayed along with the fiery heat of need. "You've done nothing but teach me new things and reteach me what I thought I knew. Ah, how fitting it is," he exhaled, "that we both learn this together."

She nodded. "I always thought I would be afraid of this. I always thought I would be awkward and inept because"—she swallowed but did not look away from his intense regard—"I'm so old and so ridiculously inexperienced."

He laughed at that, pushing back the wet fall of her cinnamon dark hair.

"And what does that make me, eh?"

That made her giggle, and he was happy that his own lack of experience could put her at ease. For himself, he wasn't going to let it stand in his way. This wasn't going to be about an expertise he could not magically acquire in the next few minutes. It was just about her and the incredible gift she was giving him, the incredible craving for her he could not deny.

Rush ran his hands down her back, curving them around the fullness of her backside and gripping her there for a moment before pulling her up higher against himself. Her weight was nothing to his strength, yet it felt so good as she rewrapped her legs around his ribs. Her hands dove into his hair, clasping him around his head as he nosed against her breast. As wet as she was, he could smell the sweetness of her, the aroma that was so unique to her and so arousing to his senses. He opened his mouth against her and drew her distended nipple between his lips. It seemed so strange that this place on her body would be any more or less arousing than any of the others, but it was very much the case. Her nipple was a fair and pretty pink, the tip of it thrusting hard against his laving tongue. And when he sucked on her strongly, she let out a cry that made him ache with wildly increasing need. She clutched him to her and even forced him to relinquish one breast in order to attend to the other, which he gladly did. By the time he was sated enough with this particular discovery, he could feel her tempting pussy rubbing hot and wet against his chest. She was squirming against him, stimulating herself. The way she was moaning and panting was driving him insane. He dropped an arm down, prying it under her leg and forcing her to relinquish the vise grip of her thighs around his ribs. She was all long limbs as he lowered her back onto the tub ledge and the floor that ran up to its edge. Her hands grasped for his shoulders until he drew fully out of her reach and she was forced to settle for locking her fingers around his hair or dragging them up and down the length of his arms. She reacted to the cold tile floor at her back, her body arching and creating a beautiful plateau of curves and feminine flesh, unlike anything he had ever seen before.

Rush took a long moment to simply absorb everything. As hasty as the rest of him was clamoring to be, he wouldn't rush this. He wouldn't cheat himself of a single thing, and he most certainly wouldn't cheat her.

It would be a much harder ideal than he realized as her hands strove to stroke over him anywhere she could reach. He closed his eyes for a moment, simply feeling the caress of her hands over all the tautly distended muscles of his arms, shoulders, chest, and belly. He had settled his stance against the side of the tub, directly between her smooth thighs. He seized her around her hips and dragged her right to the lip of the tub and right into secure contact with him, his hot and hard sex to her hot and soft one. The connection made her breath hitch in her throat, made her hands dig into his forearms where they were settled at that moment.

Rush smiled, not realizing just how supremely wicked the expression was. He let himself lay nestled in the channel of her sex's outer lips, but only for a moment. He immediately had to give in to the urge to rub himself against her, over and over again, wetting himself in the precious fluid of her aroused body. His intention at first had been perhaps to touch her with his hands, explore her slowly like that, familiarize himself with her wet and sensitive tissues, but that plan quickly went out the window and this particular contact grabbed deeply at him, held him prisoner and a slave to the open heat of her body.

It most certainly didn't help when she reached down and feathered curious fingers over his painfully tight erection. He gripped hold of her thigh when she maneuvered her hand fully around him and, without much seeming patience herself, guided him straight to the cusp of her body's entrance.

"Ah damn," he breathed as they both worked with sudden haste to readjust and better align their bodies. "I suppose there's time later for the little things."

"Yes. Later," she agreed urgently.

He chuckled at that, but was hardly even giving any attention to his humor. What held his entire focus was the way she felt as he pressed for entrance into her body. She was tight and resistant, yet the wet of her was everything welcoming that it could be. It took only a moment's persistence for him to start intruding into all that fierce heat and snugness.

And just like that, in a blinding flash, the urge to thrust was gripping at him violently. He couldn't control it, it came on him so suddenly and in such a driving, instinctual way. In all his years of knowing just how to pace himself, of knowing when to toss out ordnance so he had just enough time to get free of a blast radius, or to wait until just the right moment so his team was protected as best they could be . . .

But all that skill and patience abandoned him. As the burn of need settled around his brain, he tried to remind himself that she was no doubt going to be scared, or perhaps it might even hurt her if he didn't keep command of himself. Yet none of that held him back from thrusting hard into her, trying to arrow into her tempting but tight little channel. Before he knew it, he was halfway into her, listening to her gasp and pant for breath, feeling her legs gripping him like a vise as she held him tensely. He wasn't sure if she was waiting for him to continue or waiting for the moment she would kick him away, and he was willing to bet she wasn't sure either. He was aware that it shouldn't be a question, that he shouldn't have come this far without making sure she was as relaxed and as ready as she needed to be. However, even if he wanted to, he couldn't go back and fix what may or may not even be a problem. That wasn't what he wanted. What he wanted was to take away her residual fear and insecurities the same way he wanted to take away his own. The same way he had always pushed through them. Straight ahead. Firmly forward.

When he thrust deeper into her, she gasped and cried out all at once. Her nails suddenly gripped his flesh, a reflection of the pain she was feeling. It was enough to give him a moment's pause, to remind him to have better care with her, to slow down his selfish pace.

"Easy," he said softly to her, bending over her to look down into her eyes as they grew wet with the light touch of tears. "Am I hurting you, Blue Eyes?"

"No," she exhaled quickly. "It's just . . . it feels . . . I never thought I would ever get to feel like this."

"This is barely the start of it," he said. When she lifted a brow, he had to chuckle sheepishly. "Or so I'm told."

That made her smile up at him, and Rush felt his chest tighten and felt his entire body wormed through with a feverish heat. Though her reactions had been enough to give him pause, he had needed to fight for every second of that pause. Whether they were ready for it or not, their bodies most certainly felt otherwise. And the liquidity of her grasp around his throbbing cock made him feel very certain that he could speak for her as well as for himself. He reached to brush his hand over her face, his fingertips burrowing into her wet hair, his opposite hand pinning her at the hip as he shifted and thrust fully forward once more. Now he was firmly and fully seated inside her, somehow her smaller body accepting his bigger one with hardly a complaint. It seemed impossible for something as soft and elegant as she was to be so easily able to accept something as hard and uncouth as he was, but there it was, the perfect meshing of two bodies, and an uprising wall of need and heat in its wake demanding even more. He scooped her up at the shoulders, sitting her into his embrace, hugging her tightly to his chest as he took a moment to burrow his face against her neck and ear. She was panting in quick, heated breaths that just about drove him out of his mind, her hands flitting like a confused flit-flyer around his shoulders, his chest, and through his hair.

Rush felt a heart-stinging emotion that was too intense to comprehend, to mentally dissect. For a moment he couldn't even breathe as it washed over him. All he could do was hold on to her, take deep breaths full of her, feel each of her laboring breaths shuddering through her and squeezing around him. His throat went so tight that it almost strangled him, and his feelings were so overwhelming just then that he knew he couldn't speak even if his life had depended on it. Even if she looked into his eyes, as she was doing just then, and saw all of his soul laid bare and exposed, he could do nothing to shade himself, protect himself from revealing too much to her, revealing more than even he had realized.

So instead of acknowledging his vulnerability, he simply held her close and pulled slightly free of her so he could thrust deeply in return. Ambrea clenched around him, from the inside of her body to the clutching of her arms and legs, her breath a sensual-sounding hitch close to his ear. When she shivered in his hands, her lips brushing against his whiskered cheek, he held her closer and repeated the movement, only this time drawing it out longer, more slowly, a deeper, more intense return. And somehow this time it felt even more intimate than it had the first time. She may as well have just crawled beneath his skin and wrapped herself around his heart, because the feeling was the same.

Easy, Rush, he told himself. *Don't let the newness of it all carry you away.*

But as much as he would like to blame it on that, Rush knew it went much further than that. He also knew it was a damned inconvenient muck of emotions that he couldn't afford to get wrapped up in. Still, when he closed his eyes and felt her heat burning him, he couldn't make himself close off any part from her in that moment.

Ambrea was making every effort not to cry. Her entire body was on fire, though there were no visible flames. Her skin practically vibrated with sensation. And that was speaking nothing of the overwhelming feel of him as he invaded her innermost core, writhed around inside her, pulled her closer and closer and clearly had no desire to let her go. She had never felt so thoroughly connected to another human being. She had never been touched so well and so deeply. That he aroused her was the purest of understatements in that moment, and as she watched the passion and indefinable emotion flowering in his rich red-brown eyes, she could only be overwhelmed by her own feelings. He would never understand what this felt like for her. He would never comprehend how deeply even the simplest of his touches affected her, never mind a touch as intimate as this one. But she suspected that the surest way to make him leave her, to make him want to put distance between them and to guard himself, would be to show him the intensity of the emotions she was feeling.

So she fought it back, closed her eyes so she could protect them both from her rampant, girlish feelings, and instead focused on the pure carnality of the moment. Her breasts weighed heavily with her arousal, their tips thrusting into sensitive, hard points that screamed sensation back at her every time she brushed up against him. Her hands moved over him again and again, shaping around the contours of his well-developed muscle and the way it all came strapped together beneath his skin and making up this powerful body that now moved against her . . . moved deeply inside of her. She held back the sudden urge to scream out by biting into his shoulder. It was a strong bite, though not enough to break his skin. It was just strong enough to help her keep her sanity.

He soon discarded the excruciatingly slow way he was moving into her, reaching instead for a more instinctual need, a deeper rhythm. Ambrea was stretched to her limits every time he sank into her, and every time he withdrew she felt devastated, as if she had been abandoned. But soon he was moving too quickly for her to distinguish between the two states of being. She felt simply as though she were along for a ride that she had no power over, no way to maintain focus on, no way to gain any semblance of control. Before long her teeth relinquished their hold on him and she began to cry out in uncontrollable bursts. She couldn't help herself. It was the only way she could withstand the fierce sensations bolting through her body. It was like having a storm build, only to have it break fiercely and suddenly. But feeling the storm break was a false sense of relief, because in fact the break was only the beginning. It rapidly whipped itself into another fury, shuddering along her nerves, weakening her muscles until she was upright only because of the strength in his hands and the ferocity he used to hold on to her.

Suddenly lightning seared through her, and she threw back her head and screamed. She wasn't even aware of his hand fumbling to cover her mouth until she found herself with his fingers between her teeth. And just when she thought the feeling might finally release her, might finally send her crashing down, she heard him grind out a savage cry of his own. She was somehow more aware of his orgasm being what it was than she was able to label her own. Perhaps it was because of the way he flexed into a being of tightly tense muscle, the hardness of his whole body like holding on to a man made of stone. Or perhaps it was because he suddenly pulled free of her and sent hot stripes of ejaculate shooting across her stomach and thighs.

They clung to each other as the briskness of their physical sensations slowly regulated to something manageable and coherent. Ambrea felt him huffing hard for breath in the crook where her neck met her shoulder. Her legs had gone lax, her calves dangling into the water that should have felt cold in contrast to the heat of her body, but was instead superheated. The realization sank into her pleasure-addled brain slowly but impressionably just the same. She peeked around at the water and was aware of the steam rising off it. Not until that moment did she remember that Rush had, indeed, used his power in the water once before. When she'd nearly drowned, there had been a sudden streak of light.

Did he remember that? Had he done it on purpose, or had it been something instinctual? Did he even remember doing it?

Regardless, if he looked around himself and took note of the heated water, he might well lose all sense of calm and control. True, it was after the fact, and, as far as she could tell, she had come through it unscathed and unburned. But she knew by now the way Rush's mind worked. He would call an immediate halt to any further contact between them.

And that simply would not do.

The fact was, there were thousands of reasons why they shouldn't be lovers. Some of them were crucial to the future of her empire, some were crucial to the safety of her simple woman's heart. But none of it mattered to Ambrea. None of it mattered to her any more in that moment than it had ten moments earlier. She had made more than enough sacrifices in her life because of the blood she had been born with, and so had Rush. It was time they started making choices that took care of their hearts and their souls and let their blood flow in its own directions.

It would be only a matter of minutes before the waterfall and cycling water would refresh itself, regulating its temperature back to what it had initially been. Ambrea took advantage of those minutes by holding his head close against hers. When he lifted away from her, she turned his attention back in her direction with the swift, gentle employment of her mouth against his.

Rush felt her kisses like the sweet, stunning rush of a narcotic, the dazing strength of it so erotically overwhelming. He lost himself in her kisses, savoring the incredible flavor of her mouth, using it to draw out the heart-pounding pleasure that his body had just experienced. He had never before comprehended how utterly different orgasm would be when taken inside the body of a woman. Even taking it by his own hand had been a rare occurrence, something more frequent in his youth and even then not often at all because of the uncontrollable nature of his mutation.

But where it had been easy to deny himself and his sexuality before, he was struck with the inalienable understanding that he would never be able to do so again.

How could he? How could he know something so exquisite and think it would be within his power to return once more to the state of denial he was used to?

He separated from her lips so he could look at her face. He couldn't believe how easily he was able to read her, even though they had really known each other for a very short time. But in that short time he had come to know she was not very good at concealing her emotions. And although the lazy, sated expression in her eyes was easy to decipher, he was also aware of a shaded caution within them.

He immediately began to rewind their hastily orchestrated coupling in his mind, seeking something that he had done wrong or, worse, neglected to do for her. Had he hurt her after all? Been too selfish? Too crass?

"What is it?" He blurted out the words before he could check himself. He'd apparently grown too accustomed to being forthcoming with her and now couldn't make himself hold his own tongue, not even to spare his own male ego. "What did I do? Are you hurt?"

She giggled like a young girl, quickly covering her mouth when she heard the sound escape her own lips. She tried to lift her posture into something resembling the regal creature she was supposed to be, but failed miserably as she remained brazenly entangled with him, her floating legs wound gently around the backs of his while her fingers toyed with his hair. She certainly wasn't otherwise acting the part of a woman who'd been cheated of a special first experience. That was the only thing that kept him from shrilly repeating his demands.

"You did nothing wrong. Everything was perfect," she insisted, her sultry lips popping over the word perfect in a way that sent an arousing vibration down the length of his spent cock.

"Perfect?" he echoed. "Then what is that reservation

I see in your eyes? And don't try to deny it. You might perhaps convince someone else, but you won't convince me."

"Mmm." She smiled and reached to press a slow kiss to his chin, his jaw, and then his cheek. "Perhaps not perfect," she agreed. "Perhaps it might be improved only had you not pulled away at the last moment."

Silence and breathing ticked between them for a long minute as their gazes locked, each trying to read through layers of things about the other they had yet to learn. It was Ambrea who abruptly decided she didn't want to hear whatever harsh truth there was behind his actions.

"But I thank you for it," she said quietly as she looked away. "The Empress of Allay cannot turn up pregnant under these conditions. Nor would it be wise for me to bring forth a child into such a risky climate around me. If you would like, I can see my personal medic about contraception, so it will not be an issue any longer."

She didn't wait for him to reply. She unwound herself from him and, sliding past him on the right, she entered the water and stepped beneath the flow of the waterfall.

Rush ran a hand back through his hair, searching for something to say. The truth was she had spared him the need for saying anything. He would be much better off to leave it at that. With a nod of his head, he decided to do exactly that. After all, what she was saying made perfect sense, though he had to admit that her perspective had not entered his mind for even an instant. He had more than enough of his own reasons for seeing to it that she didn't get pregnant.

"You don't have to do that," he said as he watched her wash her body clean of all traces of their lovemaking.

"Oh?" She cocked a brow.

"The IM has much more efficient methods of contraception than those of Allay."

"Oh." She sighed, closed her eyes, and turned her face up to the stream of water.

"Besides, you know how quickly gossip will fly. And we don't know if you can trust your medics yet, even if it's just to keep their mouths shut."

"True."

She wasn't looking at him at all, seemingly completely preoccupied with her bathing. Truth be told, he was finding her bathing a bit preoccupying as well. There was something wholly distracting about watching her run her hands over her own skin that had his spent body instantly stirring back to life. But her lack of engagement as she spoke to him raised a red flag in his head. He was all too aware of how she now purposely sought out direct eye contact with others when she spoke with them.

He opened his mouth to speak, not really knowing what he was going to say, wondering why he was determined to challenge her when it was a matter best left exactly the way it was. But before he could get out a single word, she said, "There was a guard in the wet rooms. Durbin Cara I think was his name. He was very good to me. And clearly he was very loyal to me. He did whatever he could to see to my comfort, even sometimes risking his job or perhaps a reprimand in order to do so. I think he would be a good man to bring up closer to me."

Words died in his throat, but still his mouth remained open as if poised for speaking. He watched as she walked to the steps and exited the tub.

"You should get dressed. Dry your hair," she instructed him. "We shouldn't be alone together for too long. As it is, our being cloistered together is considered an unseemly act. It leaves us open to just the sort of gossip you are hoping to avoid."

"*We,*" he bit out sharply. "You are hoping to avoid them thinking you have a Tarian beast in your bed."

She turned to look at him, the glance she shot him that cold, concise look she had used to cut down the paxor earlier.

"Think what you will. Anything I say to the contrary will no doubt be ignored or disbelieved as usual."

"As usual?" he ground out. He immediately moved to leap out of the water, hoisting himself onto the ledge and pushing up into his full height within seconds. He marched up to her, his wet feet slapping across the tile as she dismissively stepped beneath a dryer and engaged the cycle. The machine's hum was distinct but low enough for him to be heard over without raising his voice too much. His pricked temper more readily demanded a raise in his voice. "You say that like I'm the one who comes from a country full of bigots who'd just as soon wipe their asses with you than give you the time of day. It's your precious reputation we're needing to protect, Princess, not mine. You and I both know what just about the whole damn galaxy thinks of Tarians."

"Just about," she countered quietly as the dryer cycle spun down softly. She stepped out of the marked ring on the floor, her hair now perfectly dry and running in crimped waves down her back. Her smooth skin was soft and dry but was no longer unblemished. She was bruised and scraped in places, places where he'd grabbed hold of her a bit too hard. He hadn't even realized he'd done that. But nowhere did he see a burn on her. It was an almost delightful sort of normalcy to see her like that.

Normal except for what they were talking about. There was no mistaking what she meant by that contrary little "just about." She meant that she had never once seen him for anything other than who he was. Not the bias of his being Tarian. Not the fear of his being a freakish mutant. She had never reacted the way others did. But she knew as well as he did that most of her people were not going to be as open-minded as she was, and she had to be careful. Especially with Balkin lurking in the background. The very instant public opinion turned against her, he would seize the opportunity to win back their fickle attentions. And the only way he could seize an opportunity would be over her dead body.

Rush stepped under the dryer and let it cycle on, but his finger had barely left the button before hers appeared and punched it off again. He looked at her quizzically.

"Rush, you don't need to use a dryer. You have one built into your own body."

"Yeah, if you want me to leave telltale scorch marks all over your fancy tile," he sniped sarcastically.

"Really? Are you that convinced that you are too weak to exert even just a little control over this?" she wanted to know.

That statement royally irked him, as, he had no doubt, she had intended it to. Rush knew she was playing him by dangling some sort of ego-bruising psychology in front of him, but knowing that didn't make it any less effective a tool in her arsenal. The truth was, he had always despised the idea of this thing being stronger than he was. The only way he'd ever been able to exert power over it was by keeping it shut off altogether. He'd been able to do that since he was a boy. What she was talking about was a true act of control. The power of his will containing the wild conflagration always itching for freedom inside him. The most he'd ever been able to do was let just a little bit eke out to light up his hand and arm. That was it. And even that wasn't what he could call control. He couldn't call it control if it didn't feel controlled.

"Step back," he warned her.

She looked as though she was going to argue with him, but she did step back. She also looked as though she was ready to jump on his back if he even thought about going for the dryer switch again. He was instantly nervous the moment he decided to try this little act of insanity. His palms would have gone wet with perspiration if they weren't already wet from the bath. He remained inside the circle marked on the tiles for the dryer. If worse came to worst, he supposed they could blame any scorching on a faulty dryer mechanism.

"Think of it like not letting out flame, but just an increase in your natural body temperature," she said suddenly. "You're always so warm. Just a few degrees more and you'll steam all the water off your body."

It wasn't a half-bad concept. But conceptualizing and actualizing were a huge distance from each other as far as he was concerned. He'd never tried anything like this, and every time he'd ever let loose there had always been flame involved. How did he know whether what she was asking for was even possible?

At first he tried to close his eyes and focus, but he heard her step closer and it made him open his eyes so he could watch her warily. He didn't want her to get too close.

"You've done it before," she said softly.

"I have not!" he argued tightly.

"If you had produced flame at the time, you would have set my shirt on fire when you burned me. You've done this before—grown hot without growing flame."

She was right, he realized with surprise. When he experienced arousal. But that reaction was completely out of his control. Still, it meant he was capable of doing it. He simply had to figure out how to do it without the wild stimulus of sexual need and with total reign over the response.

"Warmer," she said softly.

He thought about becoming warmer. It felt surreal when he'd spent so many years doing the opposite. Stranger still, looking into her eyes was like holding on to an anchor. It helped steady him. It made him feel strong in a strange metaphysical way. After so many years as a soldier, a grunt who lived by the power and development of his body and the percussive, persuasive force of his explosives, he'd never considered himself much of a high-thinking man. His connection to the spirits of his people had been broken the day his people had betrayed him. How could he have faith in those gods when the ways of those spirits had been taught to him by such hypocrites?

"Rush!"

Thinking of his home world was such an emotional trigger for him, and the wrong place to go right then, that his hands had erupted in flame. Quickly he dismissed all that emotional flotsam. He took several deep breaths to withdraw the flame from his fingertips and palms. It disappeared. But he tried to make the heat remain, tried to let it ripple all down his body. The air around him seemed to bend and waver. He realized it was water molecules evaporating into the air all around him. He reached to touch his hair and felt it was nearly dry. A second longer and it was completely so. Now the trick would be to tamp it down again. To his surprise, it was quite simple. After only a few beats, the air became normal around him.

"I think I'm dry."

Ambrea reached out with tentative fingers to touch the hair on his forearm. She smiled brilliantly and then wrapped her hand around his wrist, proving to him that she wasn't being burned.

"One day," she said, "I believe you will be able to do

that while I'm holding your hand and you will exhibit enough control to keep from burning me."

For the very first time, Rush believed it too.

Suddenly their conversation about the prejudices against him harbored by the worlds around them no longer held any import. This breakthrough with the guidance of the one woman he knew would never hold his heritage against him triumphed over anything that anyone else might think of him.

CHAPTER
FOURTEEN

"My, my. You do seem cozy with the Lady Suna."

Eirie sniffed at the elegance of title given to such a girl as that. Really, a fifth daughter of a very wealthy merchant? How had she risen enough to become companion to even a disgraced and disowned princess? There was no nobility to her. But still, the wealth of her father must have been a powerful motivator. Benit must have needed him for some reason or other and had paid the merchant back with the strange favor of exiling his daughter with the princess. The Lady Suna had even been imprisoned twice with Ambrea.

But how clever it turned out to be, because now that fallen princess was empress. Perhaps the Lady Suna's father had outfoxed Benit Tsu Allay in the long run.

"Suna is a simpleton. She is trained just enough in court etiquette to get by as the companion of an exiled princess, but here she is a lost little fish floundering among the sharks. I doubt she would last the week without me. Now her mistress—that's a bit of a puzzle."

Balkin's only response was a contemptuous growl low in his throat.

"Suit yourself," Eirie said dismissively. "Personally, an adversary is not worth tussling with if she's going to be light prey."

"With your methods of defeat, they are all light prey," Balkin grumbled.

"True." She shrugged a graceful shoulder, drawing Balkin's attention to the bareness of it, to the way her flowing gown tipped off to the sides of each one and the way it pulled tight over her breasts, plumping them over her neckline. The gown was fiery orange, a color that no other woman seemed able to pull off, in Balkin's opinion, or certainly not with such perfection. He had managed to catch her alone in an alcove of a distant corridor for the first time in an entire day. She was always occupied, it seemed, with either guiding the Lady Suna and working her way into the empress's inner circle, as they had planned, or she was being buzzed over by other men who saw her move out of Balkin's quarters and back into her own as a waving flag of opportunity. The entire court thought he was done with her at last. Or perhaps more of them thought she was done with him in the face of his failure to claim the throne for himself.

That was what Balkin and Eirie had wanted them to think.

However, it didn't suit his jealous temperament to know that her seeming independence was just a charade. This was the first opportunity he had had to come close to her, and he wanted to discuss further plans. But she smelled incredibly good, and Balkin found himself more distracted by what he had been denied these past hours than what he had been denied politically.

In the grand scheme, however, it seemed that all of these deprivations he was suffering were squarely the fault of that usurping little bitch.

"So now that she is contentedly settled and has received all of her fickle accolades," he said as he reached to fondle one of those prettily exposed shoulders, "it's time to hit our new queen with a barrage of reality. I have arranged for there to be a grievance session."

Eirie raised a brow and chuckled. "Truly, Balkin, that's too cruel." But her smirk said that she was delighted by any such act he could muster.

"And after the official grievance session, we will subject her to a private council meeting. And tomorrow she will attend a public council session."

"She'll be exhausted. And all this haste and business will make it hard for her Tarian watchdog to dig his feet in and protect her. It will be quite a long time before she will be able to find anyone worth trusting. Anyone worthy of protecting her, be it socially, politically, or physically. She is exposed and in danger and will remain so."

"And what of her Tarian brute? What do you make of him?" Balkin wanted to know. "What has Suna said about him?"

"Nothing of note. My feeling is he is a hired mercenary. Hired loyalty. She must be paying him a lot because he is quite watchful and loyal so far."

"If he is bought, then he can be bought again," Balkin mused. "All it will take is a higher price. But I am not in haste to make such an offer. They were alone together for some time the other day. I am not so certain they aren't lovers."

Eirie had to laugh at that idea. Something so mousy and mushy as the princess being adequate enough for a beast like that? The idea was absurd. And when they were in public, they even seemed to flirt. The Tarian seemed the type to be too hot-blooded to keep his hands to himself, and Tarians were not known for their self-discipline. But she would continue to hold the idea in reserve. Her spies told her that the empress didn't use contraception, so it would seem she was as much the pasty little virgin as she appeared to be. Of course it was possible she didn't care what seed took root in her womb. Or perhaps she was sterile! Oh what a glorious thing that would be! Perhaps it would be wise in the near future for Eirie to marry Balkin and breed many babies, proving him to be the more prolific heir to the empire. The more the people's sympathies were turned against the usurper witch, the more likely Eirie would one day be empress.

Eirie tilted her head, giving Balkin easier access to her neck, where he was nibbling at her with increasingly hungry kisses. She would stop him soon, deny him her charms. She would not risk their intrigue failing because the wrong pair of eyes caught them trysting in a corner.

Damn that Curta anyway. The conjurer had been tauntingly right when she had said that the princess would no longer exist in three days' time. Within those three days the princess had been discarded and the empress had been born. Eirie had been terribly infuriated over that tricky little portent, but unlike Balkin she had not raged and screamed like a child in a tantrum. No. She had turned her disappointment into the strongest determination she had ever felt. She would conquer that tricky little bitch if it was the last thing she ever did. Did Ambrea really think herself so clever? She was so far out of her depth, it was laughable.

"Come now, I need to get back. If you are going to assault her with all of this political nonsense, then I need to be in position for Suna to lean on me, and perhaps Her Eminence herself." Eirie pushed him firmly away, which he didn't like at all by the look on his face. "Remember, keep your eye on the bigger picture. Or do you like being dirt beneath her heel?"

Eirie knew that his relegation to sudden nothingness in the court where he had ruled with ironfisted power beside his brother was chafing Balkin terribly, but on the other hand he thrived on the field of political machinations. Perhaps he had grown bored with the usual grind at Benit's side and had hardly been aware of it. He most certainly had come alive since his brother's death in a way she wasn't sure he even realized. But she saw it very clearly. The challenge was titillating him just as all her maneuverings to sit at his right hand had titillated her. Granted, she was growing a little impatient waiting for the ultimate prize when it had seemed so close.

"You need to watch how you word things," he threatened her in a dangerous voice that sent an excited shiver down the length of her back.

"A mere temporary truth, my love," she assured him, leaning toward him to brush her lips against his jawline and let him get one last lungful of the pheremones emanating from her skin. "But hold the picture of her defeat in your heart and it will be less of a pill to swallow."

"I am holding on to it with all my will," he told her. "How do you think I have managed to show her such amicability and such even temper so far? Otherwise I might have ripped her heart out with my bare hands before now."

"If you could get past her Tarian. But never fear. He is next on my list of things to tackle after I have begun to win the princess's trust."

With that remark and a controlled toss of her exotically coifed hair, she turned and left him standing there in the hallway.

Bronse, Ravenna, Trick, and Justice were slated to attend the court of the new empress throughout the next few days, their presence meant to be a subtle reminder that the IM would support Ambrea's rightful heritage with everything it had should someone decide to think differently and with force. Unfortunately it meant they would be doing a lot of standing around trying not to be bored. They couldn't actively engage in the political scene, couldn't even help Ambrea get her Imperial Guard under control and under the proper guidance it needed. Rush could because technically he wasn't acting as an IM officer and, so far, no one even knew he was one.

But the one thing Rush wasn't, Bronse could see, was bored. The munitions expert never once left his charge's side, never once stopped watching her with careful attentiveness. Even when he lounged beside her throne with seeming carelessness and boredom, his mates knew well enough that it was all a show. His casualness was bait, meant to be seen as inattentiveness or a weakness, meant to lure out anyone with ill intentions toward the empress.

But for Bronse's part and for the part of his teammates, they were left with the dubious pleasure of mingling and socializing with Ambrea's courtiers. Everyone appeared to be on his or her best behavior, but even with appearances there was a venomous little undertow that could be felt amongst those who feared for the stability of their positions, their wealth, and their small pleasure of power. And why wouldn't they be afraid? Ambrea had made it very clear that she would remove anyone who didn't perform to her specifications, whatever those were. They couldn't figure out how to satisfy her. They didn't know how to please someone who wasn't looking for a bribe, a favor, or some sort of kickback. They couldn't figure out how to buy her pleasure.

"How are we feeling today?" Bronse asked softly as Ravenna went to move past him in the process of circulating from one discussion to the next. She paused to smile at him, turning her body toward him in an act of overt flirtation, something she normally didn't do when they were in uniform and in mixed company. She reached out to touch a seeking fingertip to his forehead, drawing it slowly from the right side to the left in a peculiar sort of caress. Bemused, he smiled at her.

"We are feeling fine," she replied softly. "But I missed waking up to you this morning. The baby and I have decided we don't like your new workout schedule. We don't like to be left sleeping only to wake to an empty bed."

Then she actually pouted at him.

He chuckled. "It's only while we're planetside. I run the palace grounds in a circuit that, as you well know, has more to do with security checks than it does exercise."

"Just the same." That pout again. "The baby and I miss you in the morning." She leaned against him, fitting to him with that sense of perfection they had had since the first moment they met. "I think I miss you more. Your warmth, your smell . . ." She nuzzled him along the side of his neck and took a deep breath.

"All right!" Bronse suddenly put her away from him, clearing his throat and adjusting his dress uniform jacket to make sure it was hiding the instant erection that her flirtatious come-on had inspired. "By the Being, Rave, what's gotten into you?" He looked around the room quickly to see who, if anyone, was watching them. It certainly was not acceptable behavior to snuggle with another soldier when working in an official capacity, even if that other soldier was his wife.

"I don't know," she whispered hotly as her hands came up to rub at her neck and shoulders. It was such a provocative gesture that he half expected her to begin fondling her breasts right there in the middle of the crowded room. And as delightful an idea as watching her do that might be under other circumstances, this was beyond an inappropriate time and place. Bronse reached out to take hold of her hands, bringing them down firmly between their facing bodies and holding tightly even when she struggled with him for a moment.

"Soldier, are you fit for duty?" he demanded of her in a fierce whisper.

She looked straight at him, her eyes a little glazed, as if she were on some kind of drug. Considering the environment they were in, he wouldn't put aside the possibility. But what purpose would it serve to poison a random IM soldier?

The word "poison" floating through his mind made his entire body clench with fear. Though there was no proof, they fully believed that the recent young emperor had been poisoned. It had been cruel, whatever it was, making him suffer for days before taking him at last to the Great Beyond.

Ravenna wasn't answering him. She seemed dazed and a bit preoccupied with her own thoughts and the fact that his hold on her hands kept her from satisfying her clear need to be tactile. Bronse looked around the room with sharp eyes, catching Justice's attention and calling her over with a sharp jerk of his head. Justice hurried to them with a snap in her stride that made people back away from her as she went. Jus could be very intimidating when she got that cold, no-nonsense look in her eye. Not to mention the striking figure she cut in the highly respected dress uniform of an elite IM soldier.

"What's up, boss?" she asked without preamble.

"Something's wrong with Ravenna," Bronse said. Speaking the words aloud had an overwhelming impact on him that the simple knowledge of it had not. For as many death-defying and life-threatening situations as he had been in, he could honestly say he had never felt more fear than he did in that moment. The trick then, as it was now, was to not let the fear win control over him. Bronse could tell that this wasn't going to be as easy for him as it usually was. It never would be when Ravenna was in danger. Especially a danger he couldn't get out in front of. Otherwise he could protect her against anything, he believed.

Almost anything.

But as he swept his bride into his arms, gripped her to his pounding heart, he knew what an arrogant and foolish man he was for ever thinking that way. Unless he was willing to suffocate her, taste everything she ate, take every step for her before she took it, he couldn't possibly protect her from everything and everyone. And considering their chosen profession, it wouldn't make for any kind of sanity. Right then, though, he had a strong appreciation for how women in his past must have felt as he left them behind to do what it was he did.

"What's wrong?" Jus demanded, keeping her voice low as she hastened to follow him out of the room.

"Unknown. But she's behaving strangely."

"Let's make love," Ravenna whispered loudly against his ear as her hands began to touch his face and fondle the crisp ends of his hair.

"Seems pretty normal to me," Justice quipped, giving him a snarky little smile.

"Shut up," he snapped, half commanding, half embarrassed. The truth was he'd had a hard time separating work and his passion for Ravenna from the very beginning. His team loved to give him endless amounts of shit for that. But as good-natured as it was intended, he wasn't in the mood. Not when he was afraid that the lives of his wife and child might be dangling in the balance.

He glanced at Justice as she pushed a path for them through the milling courtiers. She was well aware that Ravenna was circumspect when it came to showing Bronse affection because it could endanger their ability to be on the same team together. The IM would reassign them if they felt they couldn't comport themselves in the manner of proper soldiers. Especially on an assignment as crucial to the balance of power on Ulrike as this was.

Justice led them out of the room and immediately went to charge ahead to make sure his path was clear all the way to the IM base that they were working out of.

"No, Justice, you need to stay here."

That drew her up short, and she gave him what bordered on being a dirty look. She wanted to rebel against his command, something she didn't do all that often, so it surprised him. But he had noticed that Justice was chafing at the bit a lot lately as they stood in the back of the room unable to act, whereas Rush stood in the line of fire at the side of a woman to whom he held no loyalty yet acted as though he did.

"But—" Jus began.

"It occurs to me that if she has been poisoned, this is a good way of clearing out the IM presence in the room," he said to her quietly.

Justice took a deep breath, cursing to herself at how obvious and simple a ploy it was and how easily she would have been taken in by it. She supposed that was why Bronse was in command and she was not. Granted, she had no aspirations at the moment of leading her own team because she was happy where she was and finally content to trust the team around her, but that could change. Life always changed. People did unexpected things. Loved ones left.

She watched Bronse's back for a long minute as he hurried down the corridor with Ravenna in his arms. Justice wasn't terribly worried though. Ophelia was planetside, though at the Allay base rather than in the Allay court with them. The delicate little Chosen One could heal with her touch just about anything that came her way. With her own eyes, Justice had seen Ophelia do some pretty incredible things. Jus was certain there was nothing Ophelia couldn't heal, except perhaps death.

And maybe insanity.

Justice turned to look back into the receiving room, her gaze quickly tracking to the newly seated empress and the Tarian male at her side. As far as Justice was concerned, Rush had lost his mind. It wasn't as though he had been *assigned* to watch over her as they had been doing. Distinctly not. He had shed his uniform so he could act outside the rules of the IM. But why? For the life of her, Justice couldn't figure it out. And part of why she couldn't figure it out was because Ender hadn't taken so much as a second to explain his thinking to her.

That kind of bruised her a bit. They had shared a special sort of bond from the first day they had been assigned together into the First Active squad. She had thought they were best friends, or at least as much as anyone could be with Ender. As close as they were, as smoothly as they acted when working together, the one other thing they shared was what they *didn't* share. They both had that closed-off place inside them, that hard nut of history from their place of heritage. Planet-side born or station born, it was simply a bitch growing up on Tari. She had shared a little of it with Ender, but he had proven more than just recalcitrant about his own upbringing. And that was okay with her. To be his friend she didn't need him to get all touchy-feely with his past emotions.

But she did expect other things. She expected him to be simple in his logic. She expected him to be content just blowing up shit. She expected a casual irreverence from him and his uncomplicated way of going through life. He was a grunt and happy to be one.

So what was with the hero and savior gig he suddenly had going on? She was pretty sure he couldn't care less about the political structure of Allay. She was definitely sure he had no opportunity to blow up stuff, and from across the room she could tell he wasn't carrying any kind of explosive ordnance. That made sense in crowded venues such as this, but it honestly made no sense that Ender would want to purposely cut himself off from the thing he did best.

True, Rush had armed himself in other ways. Most of it was hidden, and only other First Actives or well-trained eyes could spot what he was carrying and where. But it wasn't an extension of what he seemed to be born to do. Everything about it seemed contrary to everything she knew about him. She wished she could contrive a reason for pulling him aside, for asking him what the hell he was thinking, but anything she did like that could blow his cover. It irritated her that she hadn't had the opportunity to speak to him before they had gone planetside.

Okay, maybe it even hurt a little that he hadn't even sought her out for her counsel or just to keep her up to date. Not even to toss back a few drinks as a farewell before he separated from the Actives for what could be a significant amount of time.

It all seemed a big mess. Rush was trying to do a job on his own that he really needed an army for. He had no backup, no protection, and no way to fall back. And if Empress Ambrea's enemies were now trying to eliminate the IM soldiers in the room, it could mean they were gearing up for something.

She lightly brushed her fingertips against the side of her neck, activating the communications chip embedded in her head.

"Command, we're going to need some backup. Two replacement soldiers ASAP."

There was a click before Kith's voice vibrated into her head. "Dispatching Fallon and Domino to your location. Is there a problem?"

"Ravenna is ill. Bronse is bringing her in."

"Copy that. I'll have Ophelia and Jet ready and waiting." He paused a bit. "Is this a suspicious circumstance?"

"We'll let Ophelia and Jet determine that."

* * *

Rush had watched with carefully detatched attention as Bronse scooped up Ravenna and hustled her out of the room, leaving Justice pretty much on her own and standing coolly attentive at the rear of the room. He knew she was concerned just by the effort she made to look completely unconcerned. He also knew that she was calling for reinforcements. He had been leaning rather lazily against the back of the throne of Allay, watching as its mistress was being pulled back and forth between a crowd of people demanding her attention and her arbitration in what seemed like an endless number of ridiculous arguments and a waste of her time as a higher ruler.

Why weren't there lesser magistrates to handle things like:

"Those fish in that lake belong to me and my family," one noble argued. "We were the ones who took the trouble to farm them, cultivate them, and seed them into the lake. And this . . . this *thief* thinks he can reap our hard work for his own profit!"

"I hardly call letting my vassals fish the lake to feed their families thievery or profiteering! And that lake sits as much on my property as it does onto yours!" the opposing noble argued.

"Your vassals sell those fish at the noonday market!"

"You've overbred them anyway, and the lake is so crowded—"

"Well, it won't be, once we reap them!"

"Then what are you waiting for? For them to have to take turns finding a spot to swim in?"

"Oh for the love of the spirits," Rush interjected unexpectedly. "Seriously, madam, are you going to let them pick and peck at you with this drivel?"

Silence fell over the entire court with such speed that Rush was almost amused by it. However, he had not meant to speak aloud, knowing how much his opinion was worth in this particular venue. Who was he, really, to complain about how things were traditionally done in Allay? But he did see that Ambrea's father had liked to personally arbitrate these disputes because it gave him control right down to the smallest of issues. When it came to his realm, Benit had not trusted others to work on his behalf, except for his brother.

Balkin was standing close to the dais, trying to appear the part of a mentor, imparting a word of guidance and advice here and there to his niece as long as he felt it would be tolerated. And tolerate it she did because she had quickly come to realize that she had no one else to train her in the way things were done in matters of the Allayan state.

Ambrea looked up at Rush, her expression open but her thoughts unreadable. He was concerned, always, even when advising her in private, that he was overstepping himself. But so far she had listened to him with equanimity. However, he was a much-distrusted Tarian with seemingly no respect for Allayan traditions. It could do her injury if she took something he advised to heart out in the open in front of everybody. The last thing she needed was for her people to think she didn't have a strong mind of her own, that a Tarian barbarian was secretly holding the reins of the government.

After a long moment of silence, the entire room heard her draw a breath to speak.

"It seems to me that the fish are free to stay on your side of the pond, Sir Grenar, if they so choose. However, since they are rude enough to trespass on my kind Sir Harrum's side of the lake, I fully believe that his only recourse is to snag the little lack-laws and give them a good broiling. Perhaps the other fish will learn by that example and keep to your side of the lake from now on."

It was a ridiculous response to a ridiculous complaint,

and it was brilliant. Rush looked at the way she kept her expression kind and smiling, obviously thoughtful and in no way patronizing, and watched with amazement as the soft chuckles of the court made both complaining men smile a bit sheepishly. They bowed low to her, indicating their acceptance of her wisdom and decision.

In that moment Rush felt a very dangerous wash of emotion wrapping around his gut and his heart. Dangerous because it had nowhere to go. It had no logic and no wisdom. He tried to shake it off, tried not to continue to stare at her, at the way the sunlight crept over her face and highlighted the apple of her cheek in just such a way that he was overwhelmed with the urge to reach out and touch her. She turned to look up at him and he felt his heart clench tight with amazement over just how beautiful she really was. It was an encompassing beauty, with a depth and an outer diameter that glowed a halo of light all around her even as it shone from inside her. It spoke of her intellect, her compassion, her patience, and her unwavering ability to accept. Simply accept. Him. Them. All of it. All of it on its own terms.

And it was amazing.

"And you are very correct, my wise Tarian friend," she said then, reaching out to cover his hand with hers the way she might Suna or any other Allayan equal. "This country is in dire need of growth and advancement, and that can't happen if its empress is mired down by every small detail. It is long past time that we appointed a series of magistrates to broker these sorts of decisions." She turned and spoke loudly to the room. "I will accept candidates to fill forty-five positions, three for each of the fifteen Allayan territories. In this way, no one person can abuse his power without answering to the others, and there will always be a way to break a tie in the event that two of the magistrates see things firmly from opposite ends of an argument. Magistrates will answer directly to me for the lawful or lawless condition of each of their provinces. Credentials will be accepted for my review until the end of Great Peace day."

She stood up and smiled at the complainants lined up still awaiting her ear.

"Surely all of your business can wait for the magistrates to take office," she said. "If you feel your matter is of life-and-death urgency, then bring it to my Lady Suna's attention and she will decide whether to bring it to me."

Suna looked absolutely stunned as Ambrea handed off to her what was considered the responsibility of the empress's personal secretary, a coveted position of much power and respect. Ambrea stepped down from the dais, moving past her uncle, who quickly fell into step at her side.

"If you will hear my counsel," he dissembled.

"I will hear it. But it does not follow that I will heed it."

Rush was a step behind her, so he could see the flash of rage that suddenly whipped across the man's features. But Balkin schooled himself quickly, presenting a serene nod to the empress.

"Too much change all at once will make the people feel insecure. It will confuse them. Perhaps you might think of stepping more slowly before changing a system that has worked well throughout time."

She stopped her progress through the public room to turn and look him full in the face. "You'll forgive me if I strongly disagree, Uncle. The methods you and my father used to rule this country are rickety, corrupt, and well beyond flawed. They are long past due for an overhaul."

This time her uncle's fury kept hold of him. He was loud enough to be heard throughout the room when he said, "So you'll take advice from a Tarian beast but not from a true son of Allay?"

Quiet dropped over the room again like the sudden cover of a blanket. Rush realized it happened so frequently because they were hanging on her every decision, none of them knowing what to expect from her. But he realized *he* knew what to expect from her. He knew it well enough to feel pride crawling up through him even before she spoke.

"This Tarian beast, as you call him, saved my life from the wet room hell that you, true son of Allay, consigned me to. I think Allay has had enough of her true sons to choke on. A true daughter of Allay is what is called for now, and if she wishes to take the words of a Tarian under advisement, then she will. I would rather heed his advice than ever heed any of yours."

She turned her back on him. Rush could see that this was going to be the breaking act. Balkin absolutely couldn't swallow being insulted and then dismissed as though he were beneath trivial. Ambrea's uncle reached out and grabbed her arm, jerking her to a halt and forcing her back around to face him. To face his overwhelming rage.

All of Ambrea's courage washed away in that single act of aggression. She reeled back in time to those endless cycles spent under his boot heel, facing down his rage, her life hanging in the balance. Rush saw it all in her face in that instant. But as quickly as Balkin had pulled at her, Rush was seizing him around his throat, hard up under his jaw and yanking him several inches upward. Balkin released Ambrea even as Rush used his own body to move her away and out of any further reach. Balkin was startled to feel someone lay hands on him, but he didn't waste time pulling a weapon—a short knife that Rush realized had been far too close to Ambrea just moments ago. The knife slashed at Rush's face, and he had to let go of Balkin to block him and keep the sharp blade from gouging a path through his throat.

Ambrea fell back at Rush's body check, Suna's quick presence at her back keeping her from spilling onto the floor. She watched as Balkin spent no time regrouping. He lunged for Rush with a vicious roar of fury, the man a great wall of muscle and darkness that suddenly seemed on par with Rush's towering strength. Ambrea felt her heart leap into her throat as Balkin's blade and fist slammed into Rush's chest. Only the Tarian's last-minute turn of his body and the swift catch of his hand forced the blade to glance aside rather than sink deep into his flesh. But the power of Balkin's strike still set Rush back a step, still kept him on the defensive. He was armed, Ambrea knew, in several places. She had seen as much as he had stripped before her, peeling away all those layers of pure soldier and still leaving behind an extraordinary warrior even in his naked skin.

But Balkin was in a rage, savagely attacking, yet with the deadly grace of a skill honed sharply over the many cycles of his life. He was a good twenty cycles older than Rush, but it didn't show. Except perhaps in his hand-to-hand skill and the relentless way he tried to sink his blade into Rush's skin.

Then it happened. He got under Rush's guard and metal sank into flesh, the blade finding a home in Rush's left shoulder. When Balkin pulled back with a victorious shout, a brilliant crimson shower of blood arced off the blade, the momentum of it splattering across Ambrea's face. Shocked and afraid, she reached up to touch the wet warmth of it.

"Suna! Get your mistress clear!" Rush roared out the command even as he lunged for Balkin, tackling him down to the ground so hard that they both skidded over the smooth tile flooring until they reached the bamboo runner leading up to Ambrea's throne. The runner protected the beautiful carpet beneath from the wear and tear of court traffic.

Suna was pulling on Ambrea, saying something to her, but she shrugged off her companion, unable to allow herself to leave when Rush was fighting for his life and for hers. Ambrea was aware of growing shouts from her so-called respectable nobles and courtiers.

"Kill him!"

"It's about time someone did something about him!"

The bloodthirsty commands were everywhere at once, or so it seemed to her. She couldn't tell whom they were rooting for or whom they were against. But she did notice that the Imperial Guard stood where they were, making no move to help either man.

She realized it was because this was the real tipping point. Blood-born heirs and official rights meant nothing to them. In the end it came down to who was going to be stronger in a down-and-dirty dogfight. In the end it was going to be about who had the real power in that room, the dictatorial Allayan who had held his country in fearful bondage for so long, or the strangely altruistic Allayan princess and her Tarian champion.

"Come, my lady queen, you must get to safety," a soft voice suddenly urged her, a gentle hand touching her arm. Ambrea looked dazedly into the eyes of the Lady Eirie, a kind noblewoman who had been lately steadily guiding Ambrea and Suna in the finer points of courtly etiquettes and royal expectations.

"Yes, please," Suna spoke up as well. "If Balkin should try and turn on you—"

"I have no fear of that," Ambrea said quietly, the understanding putting renewed strength into her backbone. "Rush will never let him touch me again."

"But your man is wounded already," Lady Eirie said. "As he bleeds he weakens. Balkin is mad with rage. Madam, I fear for you!"

"I do not," Ambrea said with sudden and decisive strength. "And I will not leave this room and let them think this savagery is acceptable in my court. I will not leave Rush to win this battle alone."

But just as Ambrea was opening her mouth to command the Imperial Guard into action, the whine and percussive force of laser fire sent a bolt across the room, the shot coming close enough to singe the hair of her uncle's eyebrows. There was the sound of the gun's shuttle recocking as Justice stepped into sight and aimed the pistol in her hand right at Balkin's head.

"I hate it when I miss like that," she ground out between tight teeth.

Balkin was heaving for breath, his face florid with his rage and his exertions in the fight, but he had come to a decisive stop. His blade was clutched in a bloody hand, poised to strike again, frozen in a tableau of unrealized violence.

"Drop the blade," Justice commanded with a sharpened emphasis on each word.

Now that an outsider had intervened, suddenly everyone seemed to remember protocol and laws and responsibilities to act. The Imperial Guard stepped up to seize the two combatants, dragging them to their feet and then cuffing them before presenting them forward to the empress whom they had mightily offended by acting with unsanctioned violence in her presence. Or that was how the law saw it. And the law was unbiased. It would find Rush equally as responsible for the offense as it would find Balkin because Rush was not an Imperial Guard, and technically only the Imperial Guard could act in physical defense of the empress.

Technically.

And her uncle, being of royal blood and family, was freer than most to put his hands on her. The worst he had done was grab hold of her arm, up to that point.

She had no doubt, as Rush had clearly had no doubt, that he would have gone further. It had been in his expression, in his words, and in every ounce of his aura. But supposition was not fact.

And then if she were to free Rush, a distrusted alien, from all punishment but condemn her uncle, a member of the royal family, it could invite negative public opinion. And public opinion meant everything to her fledgling reign. She would make no progress and get nothing done if her people turned against her. It was bad enough that she had so recently seemed to make a wide-sweeping political decision based on the advice of someone whom so many of them deemed untrustworthy.

Suddenly what had seemed like an impulsive act of violence on her uncle's part began to feel far more clever and sinister. He had seen an opportunity to force her into a position that he knew she didn't want to be in, into a position that could very well require her to send them equally to prison, or perhaps send Rush to prison and grant her uncle the special consideration that would be expected when it came to a member of the royal family. Balkin had known he was far more protected, that he could claim he acted in self-defense because no commoner, least of all some Tarian beast, had the right to touch a member of the imperial family without permission. In a single act, her uncle had put her into a position to send away the only thing standing in protection of her, the only person who cared whether she lived or died. All of the Allayan people, all of her soldiers, were numb from the political machinations of these past months. As far as they were concerned, they wouldn't believe her power and stability until they saw it for themselves.

And yet all she could see, all she could feel right then, was the blood running down Rush's arm. He was wearing a short-sleeved Skintex shirt, the black material molded to his body tightly beneath the heavier bulk of the lazily draped shock vest. Now that the Skintex material was saturated, blood ran in a series of crisscrossing rivulets down his arm, some stopping at his elbow before dripping onto the floor, some continuing to meander down to his bound wrist and fingers before dropping into a puddle of their own. Rush was breathing hard, his russet eyes full of fury as they stared at her. He knew as much as she did what was on the line as she stood there presented with an impossible choice. Ambrea had no doubt that the fury she was seeing was self-directed and perhaps a much-thwarted desire to slit her uncle's throat. Rush was no doubt wishing he'd done exactly that while the opportunity had presented itself, but she was glad he had shown restraint.

Restraint. That was why he had been injured, she suddenly realized. She had never once seen him come so close to being critically wounded, and the only reason she was seeing it now was because he had become aware long before she had what the consequences might be if he drew blood from her uncle. Without his IM uniform to protect him, he would have been executed.

Could have been executed.

But this was not her father's realm any longer, and she would not continue to live by her father's rules. She might have to bend a little against her desires and instincts because of traditions and public expectations, but she would not be ruled when it was she who should be ruling instead.

She made a noisy tsk with her tongue, pacing a few short steps across the paths of her uncle and her lover. She was aware of the press of the room behind the two detained men, aware that all eyes were steadily trained on her and waiting for what move she would make next. Would she prove herself a pushover or a tyrant? Was she indeed under the thrall of her Tarian so much that law and respectful tradition would mean nothing? Was she too weak to stand up to her bully of an uncle? Was she as savage as the rest of her blood who would think nothing of unfairly tormenting or murdering those who crossed her, be they of royal blood or not?

It was enough to paralyze her, and it might have done so if she'd had the time and luxury of indecision.

"Gentlemen, you have behaved very badly," she scolded them, rather like they were scrapping boys in a schoolyard rather than great offenders of her crown. "This is perhaps why it is long past time for a woman's touch in this empire. Men are much too hotheaded and bloodthirsty."

Chuckles jumped through the waiting crowd, popping up here and there in light touches.

"Uncle," she said standing before him. "This is clearly my fault. I have been remiss in explaining myself to you. So let me make myself resoundingly clear." She stepped closer to him. "You are never to touch me again. Unless I hold my hand out to you to kiss it or extend my foot to you to hold it, your skin is never again to touch mine, your physical body is never to contact mine. If it does, it will be seen by me and those who protect me as an act of treason. It is only by my large ability to forgive your trespasses against me, and my keen understanding that no one knows the workings of this realm better than you, that I have tolerated your existence in my sphere. Rest assured, however, that once your usefulness to me is ended, you and all who side with you will find themselves banished to the coldest, darkest province in Allay where no one but the Great Being will ever have to set eyes on you again. The last thing my people need is the poison you have readily injected into their lives all of these cycles. And so the farther away you are from any sort of position of power that could potentially hurt them, the happier they and I will be."

Then she turned to the Tarian before her, her eyes moving slowly over him from head to toe, carefully assessing him for any potential need for immediate care. He looked as powerful as ever, perhaps more so because he was riled up and frustrated. His muscles were bunched around his shoulders and down his arms, tense with his temper and, no doubt, with pain.

"My Tarian friend," she said strongly, making certain that all of the court heard her, heard the respect with which she addressed him. A respect she would always use toward him. He had brought her so far in so many ways. "I thank you for your quick actions in protecting me. I only regret that I did not make it clearer to all of my people that, regardless of your lack of proper uniform, I have appointed you as Regal General, head of my Imperial Forces."

Therefore making it perfectly legal for him to act in her defense.

"Forgive me for allowing the misunderstanding. Guards, you will please uncuff him. My uncle as well. But I suggest you remove my uncle from my sight for the remainder of the day."

Then she turned and walked toward the rear exit of the room.

"General, follow me so my medic can attend your wound," she said needlessly. It was unlikely that he would let her go anywhere without him.

The travel time to the Allay IM planetside depot was relatively short by most standards, but for Bronse the time it took was interminable. He held Ravenna close as the transport driver whisked them along. With the driver's attention focused forward, they were as good as alone. And it was a good thing too. Whatever Ravenna had ingested or been affected by was acting like a powerful aphrodisiac. She couldn't keep her hands in neutral quarters, and her words were twice as volatile.

"I want to make you hard for me," she breathed against his cheek. "I want you to hunger for me the way I am hungering for you."

It would have been a knee-jerk reaction for him to be aroused by her words and actions. It had always been so easy for her to turn him on. But the understanding that she was in danger left him cold inside. What was more, his concern was split in two. He was worried about Justice being alone in the Allay court. He should have waited for relief to arrive before leaving, but if this was poison, he knew that every second would count. And it wasn't just Ravenna's life on the line.

"How fares our child?" he asked her softly.

For the first time she stilled, stopped squirming against him, stopped stroking her hands over him. She had straddled his lap at some point and now looked him straight in the face. She tilted her head as if thinking about it for a moment. As a Chosen One with the ability to see the future in short but powerfully clear snippets, she also seemed to have an inner connection to their baby. Or perhaps this was true of all Chosen women. There was no way of knowing because all of their history had been lost in the Nomaadic raid they had fled from. All except the history in the remaining Chosen Ones' memories.

"She is fine. Sleepy. Resting."

"Or do you mean lethargic?" he pushed before Rave could get it in her head to resume her torturous touches.

Again that introspective cocking of her head. She closed her eyes, making certain to be careful, it seemed, as she took her time.

"Sleepy," she reiterated with an assured nod. It was comforting to know that she was able to break her sexual fixation and that the well-being of their child still took precedence in her attentions.

Their daughter.

It was the first time she had given the baby a definitive sex. Whether she had realized it earlier or not, whether she had even intended to disclose the sex to him at all, it was like being hit with a stun gun, only nothing so painful and everything weakening to the point that he was glad he was sitting down. A daughter. He was going to be father to a little girl. He was suddenly overwhelmed by the idea, trying to figure out how he was going to be a proper role model for a girl. He'd been an only child, and the only women he knew were his mother, his wife, and several dozen hard-assed soldiers. Ravenna was the closest thing he'd ever come to what was feminine and delicate.

"I want you to fuck me hard enough to split me in two," Ravenna murmured against his ear.

Well, on a good day, he thought wryly. And there was nothing wrong with raising a daughter who could kick a little ass, he told himself. Her mother might not be as physically powerful as Justice, but Ravenna had remarkable power in other ways. At the moment that meant pushing past his firm attempts to stay her groping hands. Bronse breathed a sigh of relief when the transport pulled up to the depot. He gathered Ravenna up close and the hatch hissed opened, revealing Jet and Ophelia standing there in their simple red and black work uniforms, which indicated they were IM medical personnel.

"What's going on?" Jet asked.

"I have no idea. She suddenly—"

"Oh, this isn't good," Rave interrupted noisily, almost as if she were drunk on something, her head lolling back against Bronse's shoulder. "We can't have sex in front of my little sister."

Bronse rolled his eyes and looked askance at Ophelia. Ravenna's young sister hardly looked old enough or big enough to be wearing an IM uniform, and truthfully she wasn't either, but she had proven stronger and more determined than any of them had expected when they had assimilated the Chosen Ones into the Special Active team. What she was, what she had always been from even the youngest age, was an extremely competent healer.

Ophelia stepped up and touched her fey fingers to her sister's warm cheek for all of a moment.

"Let's bring her inside. And Bronse, don't worry, she'll be just fine."

Now that Rave was in Ophelia's care, he had no doubts about that. He had seen the girl do miraculous things with just the power of her touch. Ophelia had once healed him away from the brink of death after a savage attack by a Hutha lion back on her homeworld. She was, in a word, amazing.

But since she was too young to pass for a real IM doctor, and since she was not supposed to reveal her powers, she worked in tandem with Jet, a skilled physician, and they "hid" her abilities as a working team, with Ophelia currently playing the part of a medical intern. Also, Ophelia would exhaust herself if she were allowed to, so Jet had become something of a monitor. He forced her to do the majority of her healing through conventional medical means and save her Chosen power for instances when convention wasn't quite enough or simply didn't have the necessary answers.

The truth was, Ophelia was learning a great deal from Jet and the other IM doctors who surrounded her. The healing she had learned in the temple of the Chosen Ones in her backward little village on Ebbany had been nothing compared to what she was learning here. She was so grateful for the opportunity and was glad that her sister, as head priestess of the Chosen Ones, had made the life-altering decision to bring them to the attention of the IM.

As Bronse brought his mate into the sick bay and set her down on the diagnosis bed, Ophelia smiled at him reassuringly. There was no need for the worry and fear she saw clutching at his expression. But he loved her sister deeply. It showed every day and in every way. He was going to worry until she explained why he shouldn't.

"Bronse," she said, reaching to cover his hand with hers, "why haven't you told anyone she's with child?"

Bronse shrugged, unsurprised that Ophelia knew of it with just that one touch. "We weren't ready yet."

"Well, Ravenna ought to have known better. There are things about a Chosen woman's pregnancy that are very different from that of other women. For instance, the baby will sometimes emit a raw dump of hormones into the bloodstream of the mother, which will act as an aphrodisiac. Or sometimes it's like an emotional bender. She'll seem like she's gone crazy, but I assure you it's normal for her expectant state. However, it can also be counteracted if need be."

"If need be?" Bronse was incredulous. "She's practically tried to rape me several times already!"

"Bronse, the baby creates these dumps as part of its growth process. The hormones flood the mother, the mother's body reacts, and that reaction fosters growth in the fetus. If we interfere too much or in the wrong way, we endanger the baby's growth process."

"So you're telling me this has nothing to do with the Allayan court? She has not been poisoned?" he demanded.

"Nothing at all like that. Just poor timing. But Jet and I can help her. We'll at least be able to tone down her behavior and perhaps quicken the process." She paused for a beat before looking her brother-by-law dead in the eye and saying, "I must be blunt, though. You have to consider that . . . umm . . . she very likely needs what she is asking you for."

Bronse remained frowning for a beat, but then a single brow lifted over one of his periwinkle eyes. "Did you just tell me . . . are you prescribing sex for my wife?"

Ophelia lifted a shoulder in a light shrug and smiled.

"It's rather like when we crave certain foods suddenly because our body reacts to a deficiency."

"I assure you, Ravenna is in no way deficient of a healthy sex life," Bronse said, having lowered his voice.

"A normal healthy sex life. The pregnancy makes things a bit abnormal, Bronse."

"What could she possibly get out of sex that would benefit a growing fetus?" he demanded in a hot whisper. He really didn't want to be discussing this with his wife's baby sister, but he didn't see how he had much choice in the matter.

"Hormone spikes mainly. Endorphins. Orgasm releases massive floods of pleasurable endorphins. This can provide energy and strength for your baby that—"

"All right." He cut her off with a motion of his hand, shooting a glaring look at Jet, who was trying to make himself look busy while hanging on the discourse with the unquenchable fascination of a die-hard doctor faced with the opportunity to learn. But Jet was also a Special Active soldier, just as tough and ready as any of the other Special Actives, so Bronse's attempt at intimidation was met with a shrug. "So, what do I . . . ?"

Ophelia suppressed the urge to giggle. It wasn't often that Bronse Chapel was at a loss for words or actions.

"Let us look her over, work on her a bit. Then I think it best you take her back to your rooms and, well, let nature take its course."

"Let nature . . ." Bronse huffed in frustration. "We're

on assignment! Justice needs backup! We can't just ditch work and . . . and—"

"Fornicate?" Jet said helpfully.

"Fuck you," Bronse snapped irritably.

"Actually—" Jet began leadingly.

"Say it and you're a dead man."

Jet shrugged and chuckled. "Bronse, you and Ravenna aren't the only soldiers in the IM. I'm sure we'll survive."

Bronse turned to a chair and sat down with a sigh. "Yeah."

CHAPTER
FIFTEEN

It was the end of the day and Ambrea was utterly wiped out. The suns had faded away long ago and there was nothing but darkness and city lights outside her windows. She stood looking out at Blossom City with drooping eyelids as Suna and another young woman helped her out of her intricate court dress and jewelry. They had barely begun when the outer door opened, admitting Rush into the room.

"She's exhausted," she heard Suna murmur to him under her breath after taking a few steps away to greet him.

Ambrea felt fingers at her throat and opened her eyes to look into an increasingly familiar face.

"Lady Eirie," she greeted the noblewoman softly.

"Great Lady," the woman said in return with an inclination of her head. Ambrea smiled softly. Eirie was such a pretty girl. Her warm, chocolaty hair was brilliantly streaked with sparkling silver much in the way her own red hair was accented with gold. She must be close to her own age, Ambrea mused, but it was clear she was a bit younger.

"How does someone so young manage to float so easily in that sea of sharks?" Ambrea couldn't help but ask her. "And how is it you are so independent and so court-wise?"

"I have been at court since I was an adolescent," said Eirie. "When I was sixteen cycles my parents were killed, leaving me their titles and the independence of wealth. I suppose that's all the more reason I might be gobbled up by your sharks, madam," she said with a smile, "but I was fortunate to find a kind protector or two."

"You mean lover," Ambrea corrected the young woman, knowing very well how things really worked for women in the court of her father. "You were very lucky my father did not tap you for his harem."

"Yes, Great Lady," she agreed. "But my fortune and independent status thwarted any desires he might have had in that regard."

Yes. Benit could prey on the daughters of his nobles, but not the nobles themselves. Those he would have to treat more like equals, more like lovers. Although, had Benit wanted her, he could have made Eirie's life very difficult. He could have found ways to attack the wealth that kept her safe. She had indeed needed protectors.

"But this court is not always about the machinations you are inundated with at the moment," Eirie assured her. "This is just typical of any change in regime."

"Balkin would have my seat for himself," Ambrea sighed. "And everyone knows it. Everyone is waiting to see if I fall under his heels as he tramples over me."

"Perhaps. But I suspect you know they act more in fear than anything. Many of them are just sheep looking for a herder to hustle them along."

"I do not like having a court full of sharks on one side and sheep on the other. Though perhaps they will merely devour one another and leave me in peace."

Eirie smiled, her soft eyes lighting with humor.

"Ambrea."

Rush stepped up behind her, his presence falling over her like a warm, heavy blanket. She never truly felt safe unless she felt him there, at her back, watching over her in his careful way. As she held her arm up for Eirie, who was disconnecting her intricate, decorative series of ringed Delran platinum bracelets, she turned to look at him. Her eyes immediately went to his shoulder, seeking any visible evidence of the wound he had suffered.

"You behaved rashly today, General," she scolded him gently and equally praised him by giving him the incredibly honorable title she had bestowed on him.

"I . . ." He paused and she wondered what it was he was trying not to say because they weren't alone. Then he shrugged his uninjured shoulder. "I couldn't stand to see him put his hands on you like that."

She smiled. That was the Tarian warrior she knew best. The one who didn't much care what anyone thought of him. Yet in contradiction he did care very deeply. It was why he hid himself within himself.

"You denied me the pleasure of smacking him for myself," she informed him. "I would have been well within my rights. And perhaps I would have provoked him to take that extra step that would have given you the right to rip his head off once and for all."

"What extra step would that have been? Backhanding you? Wrapping your throat between his hands?" His words were coming hard, telling her that the very idea of it enraged him. She reached out a hand and laid it over his steadily throbbing heart. He seemed to take the gesture of comfort strongly. He reached up and took hold of her hand where it lay against him, his earth and fire eyes locking gazes with her. His free hand came up to brush back a few stray strands of her hair.

"You shouldn't have . . ." He hesitated, then flicked a finger at the cuff of his new office around his wrist. He might have been in uniform already, she supposed, if they had had one to fit him. He knew as well as she did that it was important he visually represent his position in order to command the authority he deserved. Still, it seemed more suited to the role he was playing that he didn't step in line as neatly as he was supposed to. She preferred he keep the cuff and have nothing else change. He probably preferred that as well since his true loyalties were to a very different uniform.

"There was no other choice. And when I say that, I mean I would have chosen no other for the spot—not that you forced my back to a wall. I could have found other ways of dealing with my uncle. I am much smarter than he appears to give me credit for."

"Be careful you don't make the same mistake in return. Balkin planned that little outburst on a moment's notice, taking advantage of quickly presented conditions. He set a trap, one I neatly walked into I might add." His frown told her how furious he was with himself for that.

"Be easy on yourself, my fine Tarian brute. In an instant you find yourself elevated in a way that no alien before you has ever achieved here in Allay."

"Only because, as you say, you are smarter than your uncle." He smirked at her and she laughed. She had to switch hands so the Lady Eirie could continue to remove her complex adornments.

Ambrea reached to run gentle fingertips over the ridge of his shoulder. "Are you all right?" They had not had an opportunity to speak since the incident. She had not been free to show her concern. Perhaps she was being reckless doing so even now while there were others in the room, but she fully trusted Suna and wasn't worried about Lady Eirie. The lady had seemed very protective of her during the earlier scuffle and had proven herself valuable these past couple of days when it came to courtly advice from a woman's perspective. Besides, Ambrea needed at least one place to be free and to be herself. If not her private quarters, then where?

Rush must have agreed with her assessment because

he enclosed her hand in his and lifted it to the brief, almost invisible brush of his lips. Anyone who had blinked would have missed the caress. But for Ambrea, the way it sent skips of energy up her arm made certain she would never have missed anything about it.

"The medics did what they could with it in the brief time I allowed them. I wasn't about to leave you alone and exposed while they poked and fussed at me. I wasn't going to take the chance that it was exactly the opportunity Balkin was looking for."

"You need to find someone you trust in the Imperial Guard, Rush. You can't watch over me every second. Surely you sleep?"

Ambrea had been so overwhelmed with her new duties and with dancing over the hot coals of her court that she hadn't even thought about her exposure during sleeping hours.

"He sleeps at the foot of your door," Suna tattled on him, her lips turning up with amusement when Rush gave her a dirty look.

"Rush!"

"What do you want me to do?" he demanded when she tried to scold him. "Leave you in trust with those fools who stood around today trying to figure out which direction they ought to go? I like that one guard well enough, the one from the wet rooms you had me promote. I've put him on night duty. But still."

"But still you watch me yourself because you really can't trust anybody."

"Do you trust anybody?"

"I trust *you*," she said.

"And I," he said as he touched the tip of his finger under her chin, "am only trying to be worthy of that trust you are putting in me."

"You already have done so," she assured him.

She watched as his eyes shot quickly to the other

women in the room, then he let his eyes drift over her face in such a way as she could almost feel the touch of his hand against her skin.

"We need to discuss where we go from here," he said, his voice suddenly deeper, more intent. "I have ideas for the retraining of your guard. What happened today was unforgivable and can't ever be repeated. They ought to have been between you and your uncle instantly. And if it was an offense for me to put my hands on royal blood, they ought to have at least come between me and Balkin. But at least I showed the restraint not to draw a weapon. Your uncle was not so circumspect."

Ambrea gave him a whimsical little smile as she realized he was couching other desires in the guise of official business. She could tell he was more reluctant than ever to expose the physical relationship between them. Rush was always afraid of what the Allayan public would think of her if it became wide knowledge that they were lovers. But the fact was, it was impossible to hide in such a public court and a life under so much scrutiny. Still, if it was what he wanted, then she would oblige him.

"Lady Eirie, I thank you for your service. Will you attend me in the morning? There are many questions I still have, and you have been a great resource."

"Of course, madam. I am at your service in all things," the beautiful young woman said with a deep and graceful bow. "But if you will permit me before I am dismissed. I made you this tonic. It will help you cleanse your mind, body, and soul and help you to relax and sleep tonight. You will awaken refreshed in the morning." Eirie turned to retrieve a Delran platinum serving cup, holding it in both hands and offering it to Ambrea.

"Later perhaps," Ambrea said, waving away the offer.

Eirie bowed again and put the cup aside on an ornate

little table. Then she and Suna made their respectful exits, leaving Ambrea alone with Rush.

The moment they were gone, it was as if a barrier between Rush and her had been thrown aside. She moved forward and suddenly his hands were there catching hold of her. She expected him to pull her close and tight, but instead he reached to touch his fingers to her face, caressing the shape of it slowly even as he breathed heavily and looked into her eyes with a fierce craving that could not be mistaken. At first Ambrea didn't understand, but then she stopped trying to assess his actions, closed her eyes, and simply reveled in the tenderness of the touch. But there wasn't just innocence and purity to his needs, she quickly understood as his opposite hand fit into the curve of her waist and slowly slid down over her hip. His fingers fanned out wide, sliding over her backside and gripping hold of her as he finally drew her in tight to his body and locked her against him. She had always felt so gangly and full of sharp, bony angles while she had grown through her adolescence and deep into womanhood. But in his arms she became everything light and feminine, everything graceful and soft. The perception took such solid hold because he looked at her as though she were all of those sweet and gentle things. He looked at her as though he were completely convinced of her preciousness. And because he was convinced, she became just as certain of it.

His fingertips caressed her lips slowly, provoking her to catch the pads of his fingers individually between her teeth in light nips, her lips cradling them erotically in tongue-touched kisses. Rush took a deep breath, exhaling slowly, never once letting his gaze fall away from hers.

"I can feel my blood heating up already," he breathed. "Soon my touch will burn you."

"I believe you can keep that from happening even without the aid of water," she said to him, her hand coming up to touch his wounded shoulder, trying to seek information through the snug Skintex fabric. But if there was a flaw, she couldn't find it. It had killed her to see him hurt, especially while defending her from the venom of her uncle. He would never know what it had taken for her to keep from falling against him with worry and concern, from tending to him herself. Did he know that at all? Did he understand just how much he had come to mean to her in such a short while?

"You're always so sure," he marveled. "Never a moment of doubt. Never any hesitation—not since the first time you paused before taking my hand in the wet rooms."

"I can't afford it any longer. I have hesitated and prevaricated all my life. Now I refuse to do so. And I believe, with all my heart, that all your hesitations should also come to an end."

"And what if you're wrong, Blue Eyes? Then you will be burned."

"And if I hesitate for even a moment now, I could lose my life and all of Allay. What if I had taken too long to think today, when faced with you in cuffs and an act of high treason dangling over your head?"

"But you didn't," he said softly, almost sensually as he bent to brush warm, dry lips over the rise of her cheek. "Your mind works with such lightning brilliance, sees paths and solutions so damn quickly that I can't ever hope to keep up."

"Then don't try to keep up," she urged him breathlessly. "Simply trust me. Simply believe in me. And believe in yourself."

"I have never lacked faith in myself."

"Except when it comes to this one thing. Except when it comes to the fire inside you. In all other things you have command and control, you see your way perfectly clear. I believe you can do the same with your fire."

"If it means I can touch you freely without being drenched in water, then I want to believe it too," he said with vehemence. "I want to make love to you in a bed, to have that one act of normalcy. If only for a moment. And I want to do it safely. But you can't ask me to use you as *heprap* might be used in a laboratory. You aren't an animal to be callously tested on."

"I think we have gone well beyond that," she pointed out to him. "Everything we have done has been testing, daring, and taking risks. To the outside eye anyway. But I believe that it's your will that controls your burn, my fine Tarian brute. If you do not wish to hurt me, then you won't."

"I already have," he reminded her softly.

"Only because you were taken by surprise. But we are familiar lovers now," she whispered against those still-stroking fingertips. "And now you are very aware of what you're doing. But do let's take things very, very slowly if you are that worried." She drew out each word like a sultry invitation, tempting him as she finally closed her lips around his thumb and took it into her mouth, letting her tongue stroke over it slowly. When she released it, she felt it wet against her lips. She smiled at the way he was breathing, as though he had run some sort of endurance race. "See?" she tempted him. "See how aroused you are, and yet I remain unscorched?"

"Give it time," he growled in a low rumble of words as his hands came up suddenly to cradle her face. There was a heightened awareness, both of them knowing that any one of his touches could be the one to burn her, but Ambrea refused to let it paralyze her. Instead she was determined to seek it out, determined to see how far she could push him before it became too much for him to control.

She literally wanted to play with fire.

Ambrea knew it could all backfire on her at any moment, that it was a supreme test of faith, a test of what she was willing to put on the line. She reached up for his hands and, holding each one firmly in hers, began to slowly draw his touch down over her body. Her outer court dress had been removed, leaving the thin under dress, the silken material alleviating all friction as she guided his large palms and widespread fingers. She drew him over her neck, against her upper chest and shoulders, then down over the fullness of her breasts. She didn't have to move any farther than that before he came alive all on his own, his fingers and palms turning to mold and massage the weight of her over and over again. The heat that instantly burned through her body had nothing to do with any fire inside him other than the fire of passion playing against the sensitive nerves of her quickly distending nipples.

Rush ran his thumbs roughly over her, holding nothing in reserve, although he should have been doing just that. It was almost as though he wanted to prove her wrong, to shake this crazy faith she seemed to have in him. Perhaps if he burned her again, then she would want to put distance between them, and it would help him to rein in the wild, headlong feelings he was swimming in. Perhaps . . . perhaps he could force her to control what he could clearly not control in himself. Every time he told himself to put a healthy distance between them, every time he felt that they were going places he simply could not, should not go, he failed miserably and seemed to fall even faster into the headlong rush of it all.

But as much as his burgeoning feelings for her intimidated him, he could not truly use that to justify hurting her, even in the slightest way. And in spite of the push-me pull-me emotions swirling through him, there was still a clarity at his core that he had never known. At least not while testing the strength of his ability to suppress the fire within him while toying with the fire of his desire.

Rush lowered his head, rubbing his face against the rise of her chest, breathing deeply of the exotic perfume she wore and of the simpler, more natural scent of her body that teased him and told him she was aroused.

"You should be with anybody but me," he told her in a powerful exhalation of breath.

Her fingers sliding into the crispness of his hair and holding on tightly told him that she disagreed. She rose up on tiptoe, in effect burying his face right between the softness and warmth of her breasts.

"I don't want anybody but you," she told him as she shrugged off her under dress. As the thin straps slid down her upper arms, the top of her dress dropped down, boldly baring her breasts and nipples. It was a temptation that would truly test his ability to keep from burning her. But he didn't see how he could possibly relax and enjoy her and yet remain in rigid control of himself at the same time. But the sound of her words in his ears had a fixating effect. Again there was that sensation of focus even as he rubbed his hungry lips over her breast and seized one of her nipples with his mouth.

Ambrea's fingernails dragged down through his hair, over his temples, and onto his face, scraping over his cheeks where he'd let himself become haphazardly unshaven. His whiskers crackled under her nails as the suction against her breast grew stronger and tighter. Heat swirled down through her like a lazy sort of cyclone, creating havoc with her senses, sending her equilibrium spinning. Then she felt him grab hold of her dress and pull hard at it. When he couldn't strip it free of her easily, she felt him pause for a beat, and then watched him lift his head from her body to allow her the space to look down at his hands. As she watched, the fabric of her dress began to smolder, although there were no flames. He was careful that none of the fabric touched her, but in an instant it fell away from her body and fluttered in pieces to the floor.

In the next instant his hands were back on her body and felt no warmer than they should. She looked at his face and realized he was so focused on gaining better access to her that he didn't even seem to notice what he had done, the control he had just exhibited. He had used the ability like a second nature, a stunning advancement for him when he had done nothing but learn how to suppress that nature. It was like the light in the water. Ambrea was beginning to wonder if the nature inside him had found its own way of climbing free of his regimented control.

And yet control remained, she thought, as his warm hands curved over her bare skin. A different kind of control. The instinctual one she had told him she believed was there. It was, she realized, a part of the fire he suppressed. And because he had fought so hard to suppress all that part of himself, he had unwittingly suppressed the safety mechanism inside himself that kept him from unintentionally hurting others as well.

"Rush!" She reached for his wrists, her fingers trying to wrap around the thickness of them, trying to pull his determined, focused hands to a halt. "Rush, look what you did!"

Rush stilled, blinked his eyes and looked, seeing for the first time the ashes that had once been her pretty little under dress.

"Oh, no," he whispered in immediate horror, "no, no, no!"

"Yes! Rush don't you see? Look at me. Look!" She had to pull his horrified gaze away from the remnants of the dress down around her feet and made him look at her unblemished body. "You did it without burning me. And then you touched me right afterward. Don't you understand? It means you already have the control you are looking for! It's as deeply bred inside you as the fire itself. It means I was right. If you simply let it come to the surface, stop forcing it down, it will regulate itself. Most probably with very little effort on your part."

"It was never like that when I was—"

"Younger?" she interrupted. "A child? An adolescent? Show me any child or adolescent in balance with themselves with all the constant changes of growth and maturation. You can't use your childhood as a barometer for what you can do now as a mature, disciplined man. Anyone who can keep all of this volatility under such tight control must surely have the natural strength it must take to safely manipulate the gift you have. And yes, I said gift," she spoke over him when he went to say something. "Just as sure as your natural ability to touch me in all the right ways without any training and teaching is a gift." Ambrea took his hands and put them back on her bare skin.

Whatever argument he had been gearing up for seemed to ease out of him the instant her warmth infused the tips of his fingers. And that was when Rush realized that he could actually feel the nuances of her heat. As a being impervious to fire and unable to be burned, he had also been unable to feel even the most extreme heat. But maybe this was part of what she was saying. He had forced himself to suppress his every natural and seemingly unnatural ability when it came to this mutation. Perhaps in the process of all that, he had numbed and dulled his own ability to feel things. Even these soft, exquisite things.

"How is it you can know me even better than I know myself?" he asked her as he watched his fingers trail over the smooth perfection of her fair skin. "How is it you can take command of a country after a lifetime in exile and do it so brilliantly? How is it . . ." *How is it*

*you are so deeply entrenched in a man's heart when he
barely even knows what his heart is?*

"You were born to make fire, Rush, either with your
bare hands or the explosives you juggle so well. Perhaps
those things you mention are the things *I* was born to
do."

His gaze jolted up to hers. She had not heard his
thoughts, couldn't have known what he was thinking,
yet the truth rang no less clear in his head.

Rush pushed away from her, stumbling back in his
haste as confusion played havoc with his equilibrium.
His heart was crashing around inside his chest as he
tried to look anywhere but at her, at how beautiful she
was, at how confused she was by his withdrawal just
then. Then she tried to rally her courage, and he was
forced to realize that though she made every appearance
of being steady and sure, she was still just as delicate
and vulnerable as she had been the day they met. The
only difference was, now she pushed past her doubts
and fears and forced herself to continue onward. She
had learned that lesson while in his hands.

"Rush—"

"No. I—I believe you," he said, holding out a staying
hand, keeping her at arm's length while he tried to clear
his head. "I believe you," he repeated more softly.

Ambrea no longer knew what to say or do. For the
first time in days, she felt at a complete loss for action or
even thought. She was tangled up in the confusion of a
body in need and a man even more so. But he said he
believed her.

That was when she realized there was nothing she
could do for him. She couldn't push him over a line that
he was clearly unwilling to cross. She couldn't give him
a faith that he needed to find for himself. She would
need to mean far more to him than she did in order to
do those things. He had very steadily made it clear to

her that she was a brief stop in his life, that all his devotion was to the IM and the family he had made for himself there. And in truth she had never expected anything more from him.

Had she?

Of course not. It was impossible and they both knew it. A Tarian as lover to the queen of Allay? Bad enough she was looking to him for protection. And whoever became the empress's consort would be expected to provide future heirs for Allay. Ambrea was no fool. She had known the very first time they made love that his withdrawal from her had been much less about protecting her interests and much more about his personal dislike of the idea of procreating. And frankly it didn't surprise her. Why would he ever want to pass on the very genes he swore to be the bane of his existence? Why would he ever take the chance of subjecting a child to all the pain and rejection he himself had suffered?

Not that she was thinking . . .

Ambrea hastily turned away from him, reaching to grab the robe that one of the women had left handy for her. Her unsteady hands craved occupation, so as soon as she had tied the robe shut she reached for the platinum goblet that Eirie had left behind. The tonic was still cold, a thin mist wetting the outside of the metal cup and getting lost in the sudden dampness of her palms. She raised the cup to her lips, but before she could touch it to them his hand covered the mouth of it, urged her to replace it on the table. He turned her toward him gently, a finger touching under her chin and raising her gaze to his.

"I'm sorry. I know I'm a mess," he said, forcing himself to give her a half-smile. "Can't seem to make up my mind, can I? One moment I'm indulging in everything about you that makes me feel so much, and then the next I'm—"

"It's all right," she said softly. "I understand. I overstep myself. I take advantage of the intimacy you've been forced into because I know your secret."

"Forced intimacy?" He frowned so deeply and darkly that she felt a frisson of fear touch her spine.

"I meant you were forced to me, not that I was forced to you," she hastily made sure to clarify.

"I know what you meant," he snapped. "Is that what you think? That I'm using you for the sake of convenience?"

"Not so much using as taking advantage of an opportunity. And after all, isn't that what all love affairs are?" She tried to turn away but he held tight, refusing to let her.

But Rush didn't know why he wouldn't let go. What she was saying made sense. It was the perfect escape clause. It freed him from everything. It kept their relationship on the logical ground it belonged on.

So why did he want to shake the hell out of her? Yell at her? And what would he demand from her? Nothing. He could ask for nothing because he knew he could give nothing she needed in return.

"Rush, you're too close," she said suddenly, refocusing his attention on her face. She was perspiring, he realized. In his temper he must have been generating too much heat. And yet she wasn't pushing his hands away, wasn't being burned by his touch on her face. Maybe she was right. Maybe he could control this thing even when his emotions were out of his control. Maybe that came more naturally to him than he was giving himself credit for.

Still, he was generating too much heat for her, so he stepped back because he didn't know how not to without dumping a bucket of water over his head.

Ambrea fanned herself with her hand, trying to cool

herself as she pulled at the collar of her robe. And that was when he saw the red flush of her skin. Not on her face and neck, but from the collar of the robe downward, over her shoulder and chest. No sooner did he notice it than she gasped, pulled on the material some more, and looked at him in confusion.

"You're burning me!"

And for the first time in his life, Rush was absolutely positive he was under complete and easy control of himself. He was in no way burning her. But he also became aware of something in his senses clicking to attention, becoming aware of the rising heat of her body. But all of it was taking place from her neck downward. Clarity and understanding came the very instant she started to scream.

Ambrea was on fire. There were no flames she could see, but she was burning as savagely as if she were. She screamed as sudden pain ripped through her, the burn coming everywhere at once. She began to frantically rip at her robe, trying to see the source of the fire on her skin. In her panic she couldn't seem to act. Her hands were numb and clumsy. Nothing she did was helping. She ripped away from the man she thought was the cause and stumbled blindly for the only source of relief she could think of.

Water.

"No! No!"

He locked his hands onto her, holding her as she screamed from the pain blistering all over her skin. She fought him madly, not even realizing he was grabbing for the tie to her robe, trying to unknot it. Finally with a curse of frustration he burned through it, the softer, plusher fabric much more dangerous to do that with because he could indeed end up setting her on fire. But there was no time to think about it, no time to worry about *his* fire because something *else* entirely had a scorching hold on her.

He stripped her robe off just as the outer doors to her chamber were flung open. The guard she had hand-picked to help Rush protect her came barreling in and saw her fighting him off, saw her screaming as he locked an arm around her waist and yanked her close to his body, forcibly keeping her away from the water she was seeking.

"Release her!" the guard demanded, not caring that Rush was nearly twice his size and for all purposes his highest superior next to her. Ambrea's screams were climbing over one another. Rush didn't have time to explain himself. He was positive that Ambrea was on the verge of death, and as he watched her skin blister and bubble right before his eyes, he thought he was watching her die.

He didn't think. He couldn't think. The years of training he'd had keeping a cool head as all hell broke out around him seemed to evaporate. None of it helped him. None of it could.

The woman he had fallen in love with needed him. Needed something more than the steel-spined soldier in him.

Rush closed his eyes and exhaled.

Durbin Cara, the guard who had burst into the room, was about to open fire on the Tarian man when suddenly the force of an explosion struck the room, the epicenter of it the place where his empress had been held imprisoned in his general's arms only an instant ago. Fire roiled out toward him in a mushrooming cloud, and he hit the deck in an effort to avoid it. As it blanketed mere inches above his head, it also dissipated and then almost as fast as it began it disappeared. When Durbin dared to peer up again, the entire room was black with soot, except for the spot on the floor where he had been lying, he noted as he got to his feet.

The general and the empress were gone.

Eirie ducked around the corner of the hallway, her heart racing with joy. The pandemonium taking place in the royal quarters was all she had needed to see to know that her well-laid plans had finally come to fruition. Curta's poisons never failed, although this one was far more obvious than the others had been. But Suna had laid that robe in the empress's path, as Eirie was very willing to testify. And it would be the truth of the matter. Blame and suspicion would fall squarely on Suna's head. Perhaps Eirie would enrich the accusations to come by mentioning Suna's discontent and jealousy. That part would be a lie, of course, but who was there to say otherwise? In the face of such evidence, the death of the Empress of Allay would be unsurprising and such a tragedy, but would in no way cloud Balkin's immediate rise to power.

Eirie laughed and moved quickly down the hall to seek out Curta and thank her. Perhaps when Eirie became empress, she would elevate the witch to the status of her personal advisor.

It was the very least she could do.

Otherwise she would have to kill her because she knew far too much.

CHAPTER
SIXTEEN

Bronse was pacing the open areas of the medical bay, not doing a very good job of waiting while Jet and Ophelia took their time balancing Ravenna's hormones. Their success was measured by the occasional plaintive cries of his wife from the diagnosis bed asking him to—well, the host of ideas and choices was far too revealing of their sex life in mixed company. He was rather grateful that Jet and Rave's little sister pretended that they weren't hearing a single word of it.

Then, suddenly, there was a percussive explosion. After he slid down the wall he was thrown off his feet and into a nearby wall. Everything that wasn't fastened down went flying, crashing and breaking and becoming dangerous projectiles. He managed to crouch, making himself as small as possible as a matter of instinct, and instantly looked for Rave. All three of the occupants of her care bay had been thrown aside like paper dolls. He would have run to her side, but the explosion wasn't over. The power of it continued to press against him, on and on in a way he couldn't understand. This was like no explosion he had ever experienced.

Then there was a huge fireball, about the size of half the open area. Had it come a moment sooner, Bronse would have burned to ashes. It first appeared as a sphere, as though a live comet had struck the room, and then it swirled into a cylinder. Only a second later it belched toward the ceiling and dissipated.

There, in its place, stood Ender and the Empress of Allay.

Violently bruised and battered, Bronse got to his feet. His ears were ringing, so he didn't hear the screaming at first. He realized very quickly that Ambrea was suffering, in terrible agony, her naked body covered in burns and blisters, her skin peeling away and just about cooking before his eyes.

"Ophelia!" Ender roared, stumbling as he turned to look for her. Bronse could see the absolute panic on the arms master's face. Rush was pulling Ambrea's unburnt cheek against his. "It's all right, honey. I'll make it all right!"

"Rush! Help me!" she croaked, her voice giving out, her whole body shuddering in his hold. Then shock finally set in and she went suddenly limp in his arms.

Bronse acted, running over to the bay that Rave and the others were in, pulling toppled furniture off the stunned trio and snagging Ophelia's hand.

"Are you hurt?" he demanded.

She gave him a look.

Satisfied she was all right, he yanked her to her feet and hurried her over to Rush's side.

"All right," she said in a soothing voice as she touched Ender's hand. "I'm here," she said softly to him.

It was all her teammate needed. They had worked together long enough to know how to trust each other. The moment it registered on Rush's face that Ophelia was there, he fell to his knees and gently laid his burden at the young woman's feet.

"It's . . . it's a chemical burn," he rasped, his big hands shaking as he smoothed aside Ambrea's gleaming red-gold hair, carefully pulling it away from her skin. "They put it in her clothes. Some sort of alkali I think."

"Go wash your hands with the chemical wash," Ophelia instructed him as she knelt beside her new patient.

"I'm fine. It won't burn me."

Bronse found that remark very interesting. The whole thing was pretty damn enlightening, but he was too busy lifting his wife out of the rubble and checking her for damage to dwell too much on Ender.

Rush grabbed for Ophelia's hand and tried to pull her into contact with Ambrea. When the girl resisted, he felt himself explode with frustration and fear. "Help her, damn you! She's dying! Do . . . do what it is that you do! What the hell good is it being a freak like we are if you aren't going to use your power when it matters most?"

But Ophelia remained calm in the face of his tirade, as she almost always did. She met his eyes, continuing to pull away from his efforts to make her touch Ambrea.

"We have to wash away the chemical first or she will continue to burn while I heal her. It will only serve to exhaust me before I can heal her all the way. Isn't that what you want? For her to be healed?"

"Yes! Heal her. Please," he begged her in the barest of whispers.

"Then bring me all the bottles of chemical wash you can find, Rush."

Finally faced with something he could do to actually help her, Rush looked up and around the room. The clinic was a disaster. He could see Bronse, Ravenna, and Jet picking themselves up out of the mess. Then he realized he had no idea what chemical wash looked like or even of the most likely place in the room to find it.

"I've got it," Jet said suddenly.

Relief flooded through Rush so fast that he felt completely weak, the weakest he had ever felt in his life. The whole experience was like being invaded by some kind of disease, some kind of alien thing he didn't know how to cope with or fend off. All he could make himself do was hover protectively over Ambrea's head, his fingers touching her pale, pale cheeks as gently as he had ever touched anything.

Bottles of chemical wash began to appear and Ophelia tore off the seals. She and Jet dumped the wash onto Ambrea, coating her twice with the stuff before rolling her over and repeating the act. Once she was on her back again, her hair and body were in a puddle of the blue gel. It had soaked into the knees of Rush's pants even as it made its way slowly toward the drain in the floor. Ophelia gingerly examined the damage so brutally done to Ambrea's skin. Rush knew that those puckish touches were not Ophelia's healing touch, and it took everything in him to keep from roaring at her in fury, to beg her once more to do something.

The frustration of it burned tears into his eyes. In just a moment they were spilling free, dropping onto Ambrea's face, settling into the wells of her eyes. Those startlingly beautiful blue eyes that he realized he might never see again if Ophelia failed him.

"Please, don't fail me, Phee," he said aloud to Ophelia without even realizing he was speaking.

"I won't," she promised him softly.

Then she reached out and laid her full hand on the only other unburned place on Ambrea's body—her lower calf, where the robe had not reached to touch her. When she did so, a feeling crashed through Rush as though he had been holding his breath and had suddenly let it go.

"Thank you. Thank you so much, Phee," he rasped.

Then he looked up into the bright, steady regard of his commander's eyes. Rush had worked under the man long enough to know what that look meant. It said that when the crisis of the moment was over, Rush was going to have a lot to answer to. He hoped his commander could read his expression equally well, because it said he really didn't give a shit.

No. Everything he gave a damn about was lying on the floor covered in blue gunk and hovering on the brink of death.

No, he had no idea how it had come to this. Yes, he was pretty damn sure he was signing himself up for nothing but trouble and disappointment because no matter how he sliced it, there was no future for a Tarian barbarian from the IM and an empress from Allay. But none of that would even matter if Ophelia couldn't make good on the promise of her mutation. Rush lowered his gaze and stared at the only thing that mattered— the blistered and bloodied flesh of the woman he loved.

"I'm such a damn fool," he spoke softly to her, bending to press a gentle kiss to her forehead, uncaring that the gel wash chilled his lips. Then he realized she was shivering. Hard. Between being in shock and lying doused in chilled chemical wash, it was no wonder. He looked up at Ophelia. "Phee, can I warm her?"

"Blankets would be cruel on her skin. Even though she is unconscious, she will still feel it, and we need to let the wash chill the burn for a little—" She broke off and met his eyes. "Or did you mean something else?"

There it was. The first moment he would speak of it aloud to the family he had never trusted enough after the betrayal of the first family he'd had. Oh, they had already witnessed an incredible feat of his making, but speaking it somehow gave it life. Somehow made it real and undeniable.

"With my touch. I can warm the core of her without warming her skin."

How peculiar that he spoke of it as if he had done it a thousand times, as if he really knew if he could do it. But he had never before tried to control it in such a direct way.

But then again, he had never before traveled through space as a fireball either. And he had done so without burning a hair on Ambrea's head. It was exactly as she had said. By relaxing and letting what was instinctive have free rein, it had come with a natural reflex of protection that had kept her safe. He was counting on that now. After all, it wasn't as though he could burn her any worse than she already was.

Ophelia looked absolutely fascinated. She nodded to him almost eagerly and then watched him very fixedly as he gently rubbed his knuckles over the rise of Ambrea's cheek. He spoke to her softly, things he himself could not hear or understand. All of his focus was on the horrible shivers wracking her body almost like a seizure. He knew that shock could kill her long before the actual damage from the burns could. It was very important that he succeed. The more he could do to help Ophelia along, the better Ambrea would heal.

And then, slowly, he became aware of Ambrea's body settling, of her shivers softening. Afraid it was a negative development, he sought Ophelia's guidance. She was smiling at him with such wonder and strength. Such acceptance. It was the expression he had first seen on Ambrea's face. Always she had accepted him. As a Tarian. As a mutation. As a soldier. As a man. Always.

He should never have doubted her. If she had told him he could belch fire like a dragon, he ought to have believed her. Believed in her.

Loved her.

"So I take it those burns on her had nothing to do with your rather pyrotechnic entrance?"

Rush smiled grimly and didn't bother to look up at his commander.

"Unless you mean they prompted me to make said entrance, then no."

Bronse let it go from there. For the time being. He

pulled Ravenna close and kept her hands prisoner in one of his, pressing them to his chest to keep them from absently wandering over his body.

Slowly, as everyone watched, Ophelia's Chosen power did what it did best. Ambrea's damaged, dead skin fell away, revealing beneath it something raw and pink and healing. It took the better part of twenty minutes, but eventually there wasn't an inch of blistered skin left on her body. She wasn't perfectly healed; her whole body was still raw and pink with advanced healing and the promise of scar-free perfection in the future. Ophelia didn't take her all the way to that perfection, though, and when she saw Rush ready to protest her sitting back with her task seemingly undone, she held up a hand.

"Jet and I, with modern medicine and Ambrea's own healing abilities, can do the rest, Ender. Sometimes it's best to let nature have a part in the way things are done. When we try to fight it or do an end run around it, the result is not always positive."

Rush knew that better than anyone, he supposed. All these years of fighting what he was had only made things worse for him. Now it seemed that relaxing and letting this thing inside him work itself out was the best answer.

"Fair enough," he said.

"Come. Bring her to the bath. We'll clean all this off her, bandage her up, and give her something for her remaining pain so she can rest."

"So let's have this conversation," Bronse said softly as he stepped into Ambrea's recovery bay. Rush was sitting beside her bed, his chair turned to face the empress, his eyes trained on her, watching every breath she took, making sure there was no sign of pain, and hoping for the moment when she would finally open her eyes again.

Rush didn't need to prevaricate any more than Bronse did, so he shrugged.

"I'm a mutated freak from Tari planet who can erupt into a ball of fire at will. What's to discuss?"

They both knew it wouldn't be that easy, but Rush needed to be blasé about it. He couldn't even make himself look at Bronse as they talked. Part of him dreaded the censure and horror that could follow; part of him knew he should feel guilty for not being forthcoming about all of this when he'd had a chance.

"Why didn't you come out about this when the Chosen Ones showed up?" Bronse wanted to know. "Surely then you could see we would handle it well."

"Yeah. You probably would have. Maybe even the IM would have in spite of the fact that, for all I know, I could be a weapon of mass destruction." Now he looked at Bronse, wanting to see how that understanding registered on his commander. The other man didn't even blink. "Look," said Rush, "the last time I showed someone what I could do, they gathered a mob, tied me to a stake, dumped an industrial amount of jet fuel on me, and torched it." He shrugged again. "They were so busy stabbing me in the back in spite of a lifetime of knowing me that it never occurred to them that setting me on fire was a stupid way to go about it."

"Not a shining example of intelligence, no. So what *does* douse you? Water?"

Rush knew Bronse was asking him that probably because he couldn't help himself. As a soldier he always wanted to know how to defeat everything in the room with him, just in case. But as the corner of Bronse's lips lifted in a mysterious little smile, Rush realized it was more than that. Bronse wanted to know if Rush would trust him enough to give him the information.

"Seems like. Maybe the equivalent of four or five stun guns. But that's more of a 'get my attention' rather than a defeat."

"You know, I feel sorry for you," Bronse said quietly, his attention briefly turning to the bed.

"Why?" Rush demanded, everything in him bristling at the idea of his commander taking pity on him because he was a warped-out mutation. That might be even worse than betraying him.

"Because Justice is going to kill you when she finds out. All these years? Man, she's going to kill you."

Rush grimaced as he relaxed again. He had to stop doing that. He had to stop expecting the worst from the friends of today because of the actions of the friends of yesterday.

"Let me worry about Jus and my life expectancy. I just want to know where I stand in the IM."

Bronse chuckled softly and tried to cover it with a cough when Rush shot him a dirty look. Then, as always, Commander Chapel was blunt with him.

"Ender, I have a feeling that your days in the IM are numbered. Or am I mistaken in thinking your heart lies in the heart of Allay?" He nodded his head at Ambrea.

"I . . ." It was one thing to realize it for himself and quite another to say anything that might put things irrevocably in motion. "What I feel could very well be irrelevant in this case, Commander. She is the sweetheart empress of a country that despises everything I am. More so once reports of what I've done begin to circulate. Bad enough a Tarian, but a Tarian freak? And she'll want children one day. Heirs. Her people won't want my backwater blood in them, and I won't want to pass on this crazy curse of mine."

"I think her people will have to accept anything she wants them to accept. Especially when their only other option is the brother of the worst tyrant in the history of the planet Ulrike. And nothing says this is a dominant gene. Even if it were, it could be a handy tool to have when trying to run a country." Bronse suddenly shrugged off the notion. "But perhaps you ought to worry about other things first. Like who just tried to kill your empress."

"Someone needs to fetch that robe and have it tested. I want to know exactly what it was," Rush said darkly.

"Justice is on her way here with it as we speak. Jet can start to run tests immediately."

"Did you—?"

"Not my place," Bronse said with a shrug. "It has always been your place. And I don't hold it against you for keeping quiet. I just wish you'd been able to trust your team a little more."

Rush nodded solemnly. "Yeah. So do I."

Justice burst into the bay with her impeccable sense of timing. She was out of breath, having run all the way up from the landing bay. She carried a bag in one hand, which was protected by her black uniform glove.

"What in the name of the great gorked-up spirits just happened over there?" she demanded breathlessly. "The whole place is up in arms saying the empress is dead and that Ender blew her all the way to Ebbany! Do you have any idea how hard it was to get hold of this thing?" She shook the bag, which no doubt held the remains of the robe. "Her uncle declared the place a crime scene and is putting the country under martial law as we speak! That means the IM is no longer welcome, since the heir we were protecting is—hey, that's her, isn't it?" she said, ending her rush of words with the softly surprised question and a finger pointing at Ambrea.

"Yeah, that's her," Rush affirmed.

"Oh. Well, then, why are they saying she's dead? I mean—sure, she doesn't look so hot, but—"

"Jus," Rush began with a sigh, "I think you might want to pull up a chair."

CHAPTER
SEVENTEEN

"I want to know how you did it," Balkin said with a chuckle. "Even I believed that Tarian was loyal to her. And he never struck me as the suicide bomber type. What did you pay him? What did you promise him?" Balkin's smile faded as he began to think about it. "What did you give him, Eirie?"

"Oh, please," she laughed at him, "I don't flatter myself to think my pussy would tempt a man into throwing his life away for me. Not with his full knowledge, in any event. And anyway, I had nothing to do with the Tarian or the bomb that went off. My methods are somewhat more subtle." She drifted across the room to him, her smile sweetly seductive as she touched him for what felt like the first time in ages. "This time I can honestly swear to you I had nothing to do with it. In fact, I had thought it rang more of your way of dealing with things." She leaned against him. "Violent. Bloody. Deliciously definitive." She kissed his lips with each word, the last one snapping his control of himself and forcing him to grab hold of her and kiss her until she was wildly breathless. It was nice to see her impassioned. Nice to see her stirred and rustled up out of her constant placidity.

"I wish I could take the credit. Especially since it seems to make you so fiery. But I can't. It was probably some wild unknown faction we know nothing about.

Perhaps someone didn't take too kindly to her rapidly sweeping changes and the idea of their ruler taking advice from a savage. Whatever the reason," he practically purred against her mouth, "she's dead and this time she won't magically reappear with the IM at her back. And do you know what that means, my pretty love?"

"That I am going to be empress!"

"Indeed you are!" He laughed when she cried out with glee, shaking away her constantly coolly dignified veneer for a moment of dancing with delight in his arms, her light body spinning between his hands. "And screw a proper mourning. They hardly knew the bitch. I say it's crowns for us both by week's end."

That made her stop her spinning dance, her body smoothing up against his seductively, her hands running deep into his hair.

"Say it clearly, Balkin Tsu Allay. You will wed me before the week is out?"

"Before the day is done tomorrow, Eirie Vas Allay."

"Eirie Vas Allay," she repeated softly. "Vas Allay!" She threw back her head and laughed with pure exultation. "*Eirie Vas Allay!*"

Ambrea opened her eyes with a sudden blink. She coughed, her dry throat catching when she drew in a painful breath. Then Rush was there, cradling her close, pressing a cup to her lips, already knowing what she needed before she could even work up a way to give it voice. She swallowed the cool, creamy liquid, Rush forcing her to take it slow by tipping the cup in increments. He waited until she reached to push the cup away, indicating she had had her fill for the moment.

"It's biotinate," he explained of the beverage as he put the cup aside. "Jet says you should drink as much as possible. It helps in cell regeneration."

Shock had robbed her memory of a lot of the particulars, but she recalled instantly what had happened.

"It wasn't you," she said to him, her first desire to make it clear to him she knew he hadn't been the one to burn her. "I couldn't understand . . . it didn't make sense. I'm sorry I accused you."

"Don't be ridiculous," he said sharply. "Whatever slight you imagine I might be feeling, you're wrong. And the only thing you ought to be worried about here is yourself, your health, and how to recover from this."

She sat up in the diagnosis bed, pushing against him when he blocked her from moving further.

"Rush, you're wrong," she insisted as she resisted him. "I have all of Allay to worry about." She saw the expression that crossed his features and latched on to it instantly. "What? What is it?"

"Apparently they think you're dead," he said quietly, his knuckles reaching up to sweep her hair back against her temple. "We weren't sure we should announce otherwise while you were still vulnerable. But it's just me, you, Jet, and Ophelia here. Lasher and Justice are standing guard. Everything you eat, drink, and touch will go through us first. Your robe was poisoned, but I guess you figured that out. It was dusted with some kind of alkali. If you'd gone underwater, you would have set off a chemical reaction and probably destroyed your flesh completely. Only the inside of the robe was treated, so it was very clear that it was meant to burn only the wearer. I was trying to remember who brought it to you."

"Suna," she said softly. Her eyes widened. "Oh, Rush, no. A thousand other people maybe, but not Suna."

"I have to question her just the same," he warned her.

"Fairly," she demanded of him. "No wild, unfounded accusations. You will bring me proof it was her doing or I won't hear anything against her." Then, suddenly, she deflated, going weak in his arms, all of her weight falling against his chest. "If it was Suna, I don't think I could bear it."

"You can," he said softly into her hair. "I've never seen anyone with your strength. Whatever the outcome, whatever your enemies throw in your path, you will survive. And soon others will see that too. But between now and then lies a great deal of time and danger. And I . . . well, you should rest. There's time later to talk."

"On the contrary," she said, tears welling in her eyes and using the quick touch of her fingertips to sweep away evidence of her weaker emotions. She let determination stiffen her spine once again. "Time is at a halt and I cannot afford to rest." She pushed him away and threw her legs over the side of the bed. She seemed to falter as she did so, clearly overwhelmed by the pain and trauma of what her body had endured.

"Madam," he said sternly, "you aren't fit to move around."

"And you've never continued to work in spite of an injury?" She knew as well as he did that they had both seen him do exactly that only a short time ago.

"This is significantly different," he insisted, automatically helping to steady her as she slid off the edge of the diagnosis bed and tried to gain her feet. Ambrea couldn't help but smile. He was more than strong enough to bully her back into bed if he wanted to. But despite his genuinely worried protests, he was as aware as she that every second she spent outside the court of Allay was hard-earned ground she would lose.

More important, she would lose crucial evidence. Although they had the robe to identify and track the chemicals that had been used, it was witnesses and the trail of people invariably left behind that would really lead to the identification of her betrayers.

Yet, without a single shred of evidence, Ambrea knew without a doubt where this was going to lead. There was only one person who stood to gain with any significance from her death.

"Can I take these off?" she asked impatiently as she tugged at her bandages. She was bound like a mummy from wrists to knees. It made it difficult to move and each movement tugged on the material and made it hurt.

"Ophelia!" Rush bellowed, startling her. She blinked at him in confusion for a moment, but when a delicate-featured girl in a medical uniform popped around the open corner of the bay, she realized that this was the person he had been calling for. She looked barely old enough to be in uniform at all, never mind that of a trained, skilled medic, so Ambrea's expression was dubious as the young woman approached her.

"You need to be at rest," the girl named Ophelia said sternly as she walked up to Ambrea with a frown marring her very pretty features. She was as blond as Rush was, only her hair hung in hundreds of thin braids, each woven with fragile ceramic beads that looked hand-painted. Ambrea found herself wondering where she got so many of them. Everything seemed to be done via technology these days, and simple arts like this were long lost in favor of technological precision.

"I need to run my country," Ambrea argued once she realized that the girl would be a hindrance rather than a help. Ambrea wished she had time to tease Rush for calling in the small girl to act the bully he couldn't seem to bring himself to play—big bad soldier that he was. "Either help me or I will cut these things off myself."

"No." Ophelia sighed and rolled her eyes. "No need to do that." She reached into a nearby drawer and searched for a tool of some sort, all the while muttering to herself about "type A" personalities and if she wanted to practice "real" medicine she would have to find another job. Ophelia found what she was looking for and turned back to Ambrea. She looked sternly at the empress, effectively making Ambrea feel like an unruly child, although she was certain she had never been any such thing. "I'm only taking away what is necessary to allow you to move freely. The rest must stay in place to prevent any troublesome infections. It is imperative"— here she looked hard at Rush—"*absolutely* imperative that there is no further trauma. If there is you must return to me immediately. But I promise you, if you show up here again, I will tie your ass to the bed until I think it's reasonably safe to leave you to your own devices. I would be doing so now, except apparently it would cause some kind of interstellar incident."

"Thanks, Phee," Rush said with a grin as he bent to buss her roughly against her temple and pat her heavily on the head, as if she were his ten-year-old kid sister instead of a well-trained colleague. Ophelia elbowed him off, but she was grinning widely.

Ambrea leaned back against the bed and blinked a bit dumbly at the sight of him interacting with the young woman. She had seen only a marginalized version of Rush, she realized then. Despite all of his secrets and his unwillingness to trust anyone with them, it became clear to her that it hadn't interfered with his ability to make warm connections with others around him. Taken as a whole, he was very much connected to his IM world, and as more than just a skilled soldier. These people were his real family. Sisters and brothers, mother and father figures—everything he had always wanted or needed, albeit on his terms.

How naïve of her to think she had something to offer him that he couldn't find anywhere else. The only thing she had been able to give him was nothing he had freely or willingly given back. Had he not been shot at, accidentally revealing his deepest secret to her, their acquaintance would have ended the moment she had stepped onto IM territory. And outside of that secret and all the threads between them that connected back to it, what else did they really share?

As soon as Ophelia cut away the last restriction to her movement, Ambrea quickly pushed away from them, moving across the bay and trying to give herself a moment to regain control of a wildly unexplainable surge of emotion. She blinked in rapid succession, fighting the sting of tears in her eyes. Why did this upset her so much? She had known from the beginning that she was merely borrowing him from his world so he could help her in hers. And she clearly had far more complex things to worry about. Her future was nothing to be envied, nothing to tempt a man of action. Sure, there was danger now, but that would eventually ease and then all there would be was the tedium of political life. For her that was fine; for her it was a matter of destiny and responsibility. It would be everything she could ever want.

Almost.

But Rush was a man of action and danger. He lived on the edge of his own spiking adrenaline. Court life would promise him nothing but the prickliness of the occasionally perturbed politico or noble. And he had said it himself: she was thriving in that venue. Finding her own strength and footing. She could and would learn to handle them all herself.

So she really wouldn't need him at all.

Ambrea squared her shoulders, fighting back the scream of dismay moving reflexively through her soul. She pressed brief, angry fingers into her eyes, took a breath, and then turned to face the other two people in the room.

"I think I might require some clothing," she said steadily. "Something non-Allayan in fashion." Allayan fashion meant bare shoulders and arms, a deep neckline and a low back. She wasn't going to walk into that nest of treachery showing off her wounds. "What are the chances I can find something with long sleeves and a bit of elegance around an IM depot?"

Ophelia smiled.

"I think my sister is about your height. I'll bet she can find you something."

CHAPTER
EIGHTEEN

The queen of Allay stormed back into her court with hard, snapping steps, her unbound hair flying behind her like a streak of whipping flames, the long sweeping panels of her gown fluttering with the speed of her movement. People barely had a moment to register their shock before they were forced to sketch hasty bows of respect. The entire room suddenly dropped low in honor of her, exposing her to the man lounging unsuspectingly in her throne.

Had she been in a better place mentally, Ambrea might have taken a moment to enjoy the stuttering shock that smashed into her uncle as he stumbled hastily to his feet, his eyes growing wide as he took in her, her Tarian protector, and the IM guard at her back who was meant to ensure her safe return to her quickly commandeered political position.

"This is a trick! You're dead!" Balkin blurted out, his well-established temper gripping hold of him as, once again, she was reborn.

"Oh, how you wish it were so," she spat at him as she showed equal temper, marching up the dais so he would not be looking down on her. "But you see it is not. And so make your obedience to me, Uncle, or others here might think you do not love your empress!"

Balkin lurched toward her, his face mottling with rage

as she thrust at the pride that was his weakness. Rush was there in a heartbeat, a powerful hand planted hard in the Allayan heir's chest, and his kinetic strength forcing Balkin back at a stagger. Balkin turned his rage to Rush, the only place he could think of to safely vent it without cutting off his own head.

"You dare touch me, barbarian?" he nearly screeched. He went for the blade at his waist, but Rush was too quick for him this time. He grabbed the man by his wrist, forcing the blade back into its sheath.

"That's *General* barbarian to you, dickhead," he took pleasure in saying loudly and firmly.

It was a deflating reminder to the would-be heir of Allay that his empress had elevated Rush to the one and only position in all of Allay that would give him the right to beat him to a pulp, if necessary, or assassinate him, if desired.

Desired by the living, breathing queen standing nearby.

"Your days in this court are over, Balkin Tsu Allay," she said coldly to him as she rounded the men to make sure she could see into her uncle's eyes. "You are hereby exiled from the country of your birth. We are done giving you service and loyalty. You are no longer one of her sons, Balkin." She didn't have to make him sign away his name to extricate him from her life. "I am giving you a gift. Leave under your own power before the end of this day. Live free. Make something else of yourself. Or stay, push your rights if you dare, and give me time to trace evidence back to you of this attempt on my life. If you are caught in this country when I find it, and I think we both know that I will, then your life is forfeit. No wet rooms, no prevaricating. Not for me, Uncle. Without ceremony my general will seek you out and cut the head from your shoulders. Then I will show that the blood of my family runs in my veins and I will mount your head on a spike in Blossom Square so that no one can ever doubt that the traitor Balkin, formerly of Allay, has been dealt with and will not be making a miraculous return. Am I making myself resoundingly clear to you?"

She reached to place a hand on Rush, pressing him back. Only she was aware of the moment of resistance he gave, feeling it in the bunching muscles of his chest and arm. But he did step back, although not before disarming Balkin of his most readily available weapon. Ambrea moved to stand toe to toe with her uncle, meeting his eyes squarely and for the first time in her life truly feeling no fear of him.

"The Great Being has touched me, don't you think, Uncle? Time and again you have tried to erase me from my destined path in life, and time and again I have come back. Can't you see divine intervention for what it is? To take on the mortal flesh of your niece is one thing, but to be so arrogant as to think you can fly in the face of the obvious desires of our godliest guider, that is not only blasphemy but absolutely the densest example of arrogance I have ever seen. Go," she breathed in his face. "Live. Choose life. Take what mobile wealth you have and live in comfortable retirement. Once you are gone from these borders, I will not hunt you with whatever proof of crime I find. But return to the land that spawned you and I promise you a view of Blossom Square like no other."

It seemed all of Allay was holding their breath, waiting—all except Balkin, who was breathing hard enough to give birth. Ambrea could see that he was thinking, tapping his lifetime's experience with the law, seeking a loophole, some way to stop what she was doing. But she too had experienced a lifetime of imperial law. She too had studied, hoping to find a way around imperial decree. It was quite empowering to be on the other side of that equation. Perhaps more so because it was in the face of her tormenter.

Balkin blinked. His head lowered and he bowed as deeply as she had ever seen him do.

"I accept your generous offer, madam," he said quietly.

And for the very first time, Ambrea believed him. When he looked up at her, she saw the resignation in his eyes. The relief that washed through her was twice as powerful because she had honestly thought she would have to fight her uncle to the death.

She held her hand out to him, took his hand in hers, and raised him up to full height.

"Go," she encouraged him softy. "You're a man of strength and fortitude. There are worlds of challenges out there waiting for you."

Balkin nodded and sketched a last bow to her. Then he walked down the runner and, presumably, out of her life forever.

"Letting him live is a mistake," Rush said grimly as they watched him disappear out the door.

"But it's my mistake to make. And I'd rather make the mistake than have to keep my promise and behead the fool. I am not my father."

"Aye," Rush said, shooting her a grin, "you're something far better and a bit more dangerous I think." He touched her under the chin with a finger and then herded her out of the throne room and into her private quarters so she could get some much-needed rest.

Eirie was reeling. She ducked out the rear of the court and into the corridor, pressing her back to the cold marble wall as she sucked for breath and fought off nausea.

How? How could she be alive?

Eirie hastened for Balkin's quarters. She swept in probably right on his heels and ordered the servants out immediately.

"Don't start with me, Eirie. This is over. I'm done. I never sought this. Clearly she cannot be defeated, and even if she dropped dead at my feet this instant I would not take the throne for fear she would resurrect before my eyes."

Eirie gaped at him, watching as he went straight to his security hold, unlocked it, and began to withdraw the wealth he had stored inside it. It was one of ten such holds that she knew of, and always she had seen him open them to place things carefully within, never to extract. There was cash, platinum, jewels, and hard data chips with account information on them. Balkin reached for a satchel to put them in, unlocked it, and hastily tossed things inside.

"If you leave you'll be throwing everything away! The way she pants after that Tarian she'll be spawning half-bred heirs in no time and everything we've worked for will disappear!" She was being shrill, she could hear it in her voice, but she couldn't seem to control herself. Her entire future was circling the drain when moments ago it had been illustrious and secured.

How had Ambrea done it? How had she survived?

"I'm leaving and there's the end of it," Balkin barked. "I'm lucky she hasn't already had me tossed in some dark, wet cell. I'll not live out the rest of my days like she has lived most of hers. And if I stay, my days will end very shortly on the end of that Tarian's blade, make no mistake about it. I'm going to live long and free a very wealthy man with some other fate." He turned sharply to her. "Face facts, Eirie, and go pack your things. After all, you are in the worst of the danger. They'll figure out it was you who had that robe dusted and sent to her. It's only a matter of moments before they realize that you and I are actually connected. Court gossip will catch up with us."

"Leave?" She laughed, aghast. "And go where? Do what?"

"We'll find a nice country manse somewhere. Or perhaps live in the city in Ulrike. Between my money and yours, we could get a shoe into the social strata there, if you like to hobnob so much. The point is we'll be living. Together."

This time, when she laughed, it drew all of Balkin's attention. The laugh was a most perfect sound of derision, and he had never been on the receiving end of such before. The feeling it created inside him was not pleasant.

"Do you really," she said slowly with a smile of contempt shaping her lips, "think that I would go anywhere with such a weak fool? You are a breath away from being the second most powerful man on the planet of Ulrike and look at you! Look at you so eager to throw it away because you're afraid of some stupid little girl!"

Heat seared through Balkin, a streaming torch on his temper as he looked into that ridiculously beautiful face and saw what every man dreaded seeing, watched the movement of her lush lips and heard what every man dreaded hearing—the loss of his woman's respect, love, and everything he wanted to be in her eyes.

"I am the same man I have always been," he said through his teeth. "A man wise enough to know when he should make a tactical retreat. And what are you? Just a vain, manipulative bitch who is using me to become the second most powerful woman on all of Ulrike. Do you think I am really so stupid that I don't know exactly what you are? Exactly what you have done? But damn your gorgeous eyes, I love you all the more for it, Eirie. Your ambition, your strength—all of it can be put to other uses! Together we could burn other paths of power, move in social circles as an exiled prince and his bride. People eat that shit up. Everyone will want to know us. My wealth and yours will open any door you want. Simply name it and you will have it!"

"I want to be Empress of Allay!" she screamed at him.

"That will never happen. Unless she drops dead in the next half hour, I will be gone and won't look back," he informed her coldly. "So unless you have a miracle at hand, I suggest you kiss that desire good-bye and learn to make the most of it. Or you can stay and circulate amongst all those powerless politicians who have wanted to creep inside your ass for years now. You can fuck your way through a long line of weaklings, learning the true meaning of the word, and know that none of your wiles or ways will bring you any closer to the throne than I could."

And there it was, the real and frustrating truth of the matter. Panic began to swim through Eirie, sinking its claws deeply into her and crawling around inside her. She could never, after so many years of grooming herself and grooming Balkin for their true destiny, be satisfied with anything less than a crown.

"Fine," she hissed at him. "If you'll do nothing, as usual, it's up to me to provide that miracle you need!"

She turned to leave and he lunged for her, grabbing her arm and swinging her back around to face him.

"Eirie, if you murder the Empress of Allay and are caught, you will be executed for treason."

"A risk I've taken before and will take again because, apparently, I am the only one with the spine to do so!" she spat contemptuously. She yanked free of him and flew out the door, this time running down the corridors heading for Curta's hidden dwelling.

She burst into the conjurer's rooms and found her standing there, patiently waiting for her.

"All is lost for you," Curta said softly and with pity.

"Shut up, witch," Eirie hissed. "If I am lost, then so are you! You provided those poisons. Those weak, ineffectual poisons!"

"Effective enough to kill a boy king," Curta reminded her with a shrug. "The poisoned robe was meant to be worn by an unprotected girl hidden away in exile. Not an empress with a hero to protect her. A very special hero. You would be wise to make your escape with Balkin," the conjurer advised quietly, "lest the queen's hero consume you like redemptive fire. For that is what he is. The fire of redemption."

"I've heard enough from weak, sniveling idiots for one day. Can you give me a weapon to kill the empress?"

Curta shrugged a shoulder and turned to pack a few more things into an open bag. That was when Eirie realized that Curta, too, had every intention of abandoning Blossom Palace. She had a mobile trunk already packed so full that it looked as though it might burst. The shoulder bag she was currently packing looked just as overburdened.

"No! You cannot leave until you give me one last chance! Ambrea trusts me enough to let me get close to her. The opportunity to strike is on me at this moment. It will be gone soon if I don't act!"

"Resolve yourself to a different future, Eirie," Curta said quietly. "Fate has walked its steps around you. Don't make it whip back and eye you too closely."

Eirie stepped into the other woman's personal space, her face pushed into hers. "Fuck you and your backward mysticisms. You've been wrong too often to suit my tastes, woman. Give me what I'm asking for!"

Curta straightened away from the noblewoman and reached into her pocket with two fingers. She pulled out a small aerosol container and dangled it in front of Eirie.

"A single spray into her face and she will breathe it in and, within seconds, will never breathe again. It paralyzes the diaphragm and lungs. She will suffocate slowly and painfully. But she won't be able to speak to accuse you. Only take care not to breathe it in yourself once it is airborne. Hold your breath for at least ten seconds, and then it will dissipate and be gone. And now I am gone. You'll never see me again. I have seen my future and you are never in it again, nor will I die in the land of

Allay. Perhaps you should consider a like future for yourself."

Curta sealed her bags shut, grabbed hold of both of them, and made her way around Eirie, whose full fascination and attention was on the little aerosol canister.

It was just small enough to fit down the cleavage of her dress and easily concealed in the palm of her hand.

"Perfect," she breathed.

Rush settled Ambrea into bed, touching her damp forehead with gentle fingertips.

"You're in pain," he noted. It wasn't a question. He knew it as naturally as he knew how to breathe. He believed he would know everything about her that easily from now on.

She didn't deny it. She closed her eyes and exhaled. Her pain, no doubt, was countered by her uncle's acceptance of defeat. But Rush wouldn't be happy until the bastard was off getting drunk in some hole somewhere accepting the fact that the better person had won. Right now he wasn't even sure that Balkin had that kind of conciliatory behavior in his makeup.

"Rush, how long will you stay?"

"Until you fall asleep," he said.

Her eyes flew open and in a wild streak of emotion he saw her panic.

"So soon? But just because my uncle is put in his place doesn't mean my throne is by any means secure! You promised to help me at least be that safe."

Rush blinked, and then his expression softened, his hands gently framing her face. "I meant for the moment, sweetheart. I'll still be here when you wake."

"Oh."

It was probably because she was in pain and so exhausted by her ordeal, but she couldn't catch the telling sob that erupted from her. And before she knew it, she was crying, an open mess of emotions she didn't want to show, weakness and neediness all rising to the surface. And the more he touched her, the more he tried to soothe her, the worse it seemed to become.

"Hey now. Shh. It's all going to be all right," he said softly and surely, pulling her head under his chin and holding her against the warmth and strength of his chest.

"No, it won't," she argued in a rush before she could catch her own tongue. "Because one day you'll leave me and I know how fast it will come. But I won't want you to go. Not because I will be afraid to lead by myself, but because—"

"Because?" he prompted her softly, a steady, intense expression in his eyes as he made her look into them.

"Because it will hardly mean anything without you, Rush. I know I'm going to seem foolish and weak to you. An inexperienced girl forming imagined attachments to her first lover. How common I am. How ridiculous."

She burst into harder tears.

"It's only been days. How can anyone feel anything real for someone they've known only for days? And you have all that family waiting for you in the IM. People you've known and loved for years."

Rush could hardly follow what she was saying. It was all coming at him in such an emotional tide. But what his logical brain couldn't comprehend, his heart heard loud and clear. A riptide of elation swirled through him as she gave him this first indication that she felt something for him. Something other than the desire she had shown him as his lover. She had always rolled so easily with everything, had always seemed so untouched. He had been convinced he was going to be a fool for her, lingering for years in her court at her side, serving her needs however she would let him just so long as he could be close to her, keeping her safe and protected.

"Oh, you idiot," he whispered against her forehead.

He realized he had spoken aloud when she sucked in a hard breath and struggled to hold back her next sob. He saw her wounded eyes and he wanted to smack himself.

"I meant me," he told her quickly. "I am an idiot because I forgot that underneath all this coolness and steadiness beats the heart of a passionately emotional woman. You are so fair and sweet, so accepting and generous to everyone that whenever you were any of those things to me I just put it down to your nature. I never once thought I could actually be special in your eyes."

Ambrea's weeping dropped into quietly stunned little hiccups.

"But Rush, everything about you is special. And it ought not be just in my eyes. And I really doubt that it is. I saw how Ophelia acted with you. She cares so much for you, I can tell. All of your IM companions do, and I . . ." She looked down at her hands in her lap, her fingers tugging at one another anxiously. "What am I but another task to you? The only bond we formed was because of a secret you never wished to share with me in the first place."

"A secret that was outed the moment you were in danger. A power that showed its true strength and true control the instant I thought you were being taken away from me. I don't know what it was or how I even knew I could do it, but I closed my eyes and one moment I was here, the next I was in the clinic, leaving explosions before and after me."

Her eyes widened.

"You were able to do that?"

"Yes. And there were plenty of witnesses. Including my boss, and one of your guards."

"Oh my. We ought to debrief him," she said distractedly.

"I plan to once you are asleep and resting peacefully.

But first I need you to tell me—are you asking me to stay here?" He turned awkward and unsure before her eyes, and it was so endearing that she couldn't help but smile. "I mean, I'm a Tarian, you know."

"Yes, I know."

"Allayans despise Tarians."

"Not this Allayan," she said softly. "And after all, isn't that the only one that should matter?"

"Not if it makes things harder for you," he said with a dark frown. "And you need a bloodline to secure the future of your throne, and I'm not sure I want to . . . I have this thing inside me I can barely control. Bad enough to pass my heritage on, but this mutation as well?"

"I am aware that is how you feel. At the moment."

That surprised him.

"You are?" Again the frown. "And this moment may last forever. I may never change my mind. I don't want to subject any other living being to the things I suffered."

"I know," she said softly, her hands gently cupping his face. "But can you imagine there would ever be anything inside a child of mine that I would not be able to love and accept? Unless we breed a psychopath," she said dryly. "And that would come from my genes. So perhaps I should make you reconsider any ideas of breeding with *me*."

Rush chuckled, looking deeply into her warm, smiling eyes, the wash of fresh tears making them sparkle like gems. "I hadn't considered that. You've got something of a point there."

"Mmm. So let's agree to focus on other things first," she suggested. "Like, how will I ever keep a man like you sufficiently excited and entertained in my boring political world?"

"Boring?" he exclaimed. He laughed heartily. "I think you might still be in shock. There is nothing in the least bit boring about your world. Is it going out and blowing up shit? No, not immediately. But I imagine that as general of your armies, I will have more than my fair share of excitement. Or are you going to renege on my appointment now that you know I am considering taking it on permanently?"

"Hardly," she sniffed, reaching to poke him hard in the chest. "But you must promise me not to be stabbed too often. It rather upsets me."

"As long as you promise not to be assassinated too often because it rather upsets me," he countered.

"Hmm. What a conundrum this whole thing promises to be," she noted.

"Yes," he agreed. "Very perplexing on all fronts." He swept a tender thumb under the well of her eye. "I think I must advise you that it's all very unwise."

"I think I must advise you the same," she said just as gravely.

"Well, frankly my alternatives suck. The IM is going to find out about what I've been hiding once Bronse makes his report. They will not be happy."

"Oh, you know they're going to want you more than ever," she huffed at him. "I won't buy this 'poor disenfranchised orphan' routine. Your friends haven't tried to string you up recently, in spite of them discovering your mutation. So you must assume you've been wrong all these years not to trust them."

"Yes. Very wrong," he agreed, suddenly overwhelmed with the urge to kiss the breath right out of her body. So he pulled her mouth under his and did exactly that. She responded intensely, and like the pounding force of an explosion against him, she left him equally breathless and stunned. *Was this really happening?* Was she really choosing him over any other man? She was the empress of a powerful country. She had realized her power in so many ways, surely she realized she could have anyone she wanted.

And as if she had read his mind, she pulled away from his lips, hovering a breath away as her hands drew warmly over his face, mapping his features with unmistakable hunger. "There will never be anyone better in my eyes, my fine Tarian brute," she whispered to him.

Rush felt his heart beat harder, as though it wanted to take flight out of his chest. He had never once in his life been in love, but how amazing it was that he knew the sensation as well as he would know an old friend.

"I think I've loved you since the moment you tried to touch the flames on my hand, full of a faith that I wouldn't hurt you that you had no sane reason to have. And you pursued me even after I did hurt you. How could I not love someone so clearly insane? We're so much the same, Blue Eyes, but so much in our own ways." He reached to catch her hands when they promised to wander his body aggressively. "And you're too injured for lovemaking. Ophelia would have my hide if anything happened to yours."

That she relented so easily told him more about her pain level than she would have preferred to give away. She lay back in her bed, the plush comfort of it not nearly gentle enough to keep from hurting her. He could imagine that her skin felt as though it were still on fire, as it remained raw beneath the bandages.

"But you will promise to make love with me as soon as possible?" she extracted from him. "We have yet to see if we can manage it out of the water."

"Perhaps someone's faith has infected me, but I believe we will be able to manage that," he said as he continued to touch gentle strokes to her face. He had to marvel at how every contour seemed to be so sweet to him. He found it hard to believe there had been a time when he had not been amazed by her beauty. Perhaps it was because every time he looked at her he was awash with the strength that was inside her.

Little did Rush know that she was thinking the very same thing. As her fingertips toyed over the rugged handsomeness of his face, she only wanted to devour him with her memory. Life did not turn out well for her like this. Not usually. So she felt the need to make the most of every moment. To appreciate every single blessing that came her way.

"A handsome warrior came to rescue me one day," she breathed softly. "He has been my protector ever since. The Great Being sent him to me, I know. But who could have guessed he would rescue and protect my very heart as well?"

"Give me that job for the rest of my life and I think I will always be satisfied," he said before pressing light kisses to her cheeks. "But as your protector, madam, I insist you rest. Ophelia sent something for your pain." He reached for one of the pain patches he had left in a little pile on a nearby table.

"Let me do that, sir."

Graceful fingers intercepted him, reaching for the patch. He looked up in surprise, forgetting that their lives would never be private. The Lady Eirie as well as Suna and several other female servants were always moving quietly in and out of their sphere unless ordered away. He had yet to question Suna or Eirie about the poisoned robe, so he resisted the idea of her coming close to Ambrea, although she had not seemed to be in any way responsible. Still, what could she do while he was sitting right there? He looked her over quickly for any kind of weapon and saw only a jeweled knife hanging sheathed from a decoratively linked and bejeweled waist chain.

"I would prefer it if you no longer wear decorative weaponry in the presence of your empress," he said with a frown.

She seemed genuinely surprised, almost as if she had

forgotten it was there. She quickly reached to open the catch and handed the entire chain, including the knife, to him.

"I certainly don't blame you, General, and I ought to have thought of it myself."

"Where is the Lady Suna?" he asked her.

"She's being held pending questioning," Eirie replied. "I'm sorry, madam," she said to Ambrea, bowing her head sadly. "I saw Suna lay out that robe for you. I was told it was poisoned. It's just too horrible." She reached for the pain patch, peeled off its backing, and gingerly applied it to Ambrea's neck. Now that she was in the privacy of her rooms, Ambrea had shed all of her clothing, the weight of it too intense for her. She lay in bed under a light cover wrapped well with bandages except for the ones Ophelia had removed to facilitate movement. It would be immediately obvious to those serving her that she was weakened and injured, although if Ambrea could have her way she would never show weakness to any of her subjects. But she would have to settle for keeping it hidden in public and let speculations fly as they may.

Rush didn't know why the movement Eirie made next struck him as odd, but instinct made his hand snap out to grab hers. He felt and saw the small spray container in her hand.

"It's only perfume, General," she said. "To freshen the bed."

"They do it all the time," Ambrea said with amusement as she rested a calming hand over his.

"Would you care to smell it?" Eirie asked.

The Tarian let go of her hand. Eirie extended her arm, held it out practically under his nose, then sprayed the contents of the vial onto her wrist.

But just before she did it, he heard her take in her breath and hold it.

It was the very opposite thing a person would do when about to spray a fragrance. But before it could all register, she had sprayed the entire space between himself and Ambrea with the mist. His reaction was fully reflexive and completely subconscious, he would later realize. Fire burst out of him on the exhalation of his breath. He literally breathed it out into the air, setting the mist on fire as its flammable properties ignited. The Lady Eirie screeched in surprise, falling back away from them as her hair and gown caught fire. But it seemed as though the fire were selective, because even though it roiled over Ambrea's face, it did not burn her, and it did not set her on fire. The fire inside of Rush was like a living, sentient thing. It knew what it wanted to destroy, even if the man it lived inside of didn't fully comprehend why.

The canister that Eirie had held fell to the floor, rolling away, while Rush surged to his feet and grabbed for the burning woman. He threw her down to the floor, covering her body, using the sweep of his hands to extinguish the flames.

There was an eeriness to the sound in the room. It was silent in the wake of Eirie's horrible screams, but it was far from quiet. The young woman lay curled in the fetal position beneath Rush, the sounds of pain and shock bursting out of her. Most of her hair was burned away, her dress, that fine silk, had burned like flash paper all around her and was sticking to her skin, which in turn had begun to burn and blister. Her face was raw and red, and she no longer had any lashes or brows. There was no sign of the beauty that had taken her so far in life. Too far.

"What was that?" Rush demanded, feeling no pity for her. She cowered in fear of him, and it was no wonder. He was a fire-breathing monster to her. "What were you trying to do?"

She whined and shook her head.

"Mercy" was all she could croak out.

Rush had not realized it, but Ambrea had risen from the bed. She now leaned over the unfortunate woman on the floor.

"It seems you really will protect me to all extremes, my fine Tarian brute," she said softly. "Whether you realize you are doing so or not." Then she turned toward Eirie. "If it was you who put that vile burning robe in my path, then I hope now you can appreciate the enormity of what you did. Perhaps now you know the pain you have caused." She straightened up slowly, her movements a little off because the narcotics of the pain patch were entering her bloodstream. "Take her to the nearest Allayan trauma center. She can hope Allayan medicine will help. If she survives, put her in the wet rooms and question her thoroughly. If she survives that process and is found guilty of treason . . ." Ambrea smiled. "After the crown takes away her lands, her wealth, and her status, perhaps it will be too cruel to let her live, her beauty damaged, her position in life destroyed. I would not wish to be thought of as cruel."

"No, madam," Rush agreed. "You are above such petty cruelties." He leaned close to the suffering girl. "Aren't you fortunate that none of those vicious Allayan males rule this place?"

All Eirie could do was whimper.

EPILOGUE

"My goodness, she's really quite pregnant."

Rush turned his head to look, seeing Ravenna enter the enormous catering hall of Blossom Palace. He had not seen her in many months, so she did, indeed, look very much more pregnant than she had at his last visit with her. The knowledge made him frown a little. He had expected he would drift away from his IM family a little as their lives took them in opposing directions, but seeing it so starkly represented in the size of Ravenna's belly made him more than a little sad.

"I've been neglecting them," he said quietly.

"Perhaps. A little," Ambrea agreed. "You've been somewhat preoccupied of late. But things are getting better now," she reminded him. "You've reformed nearly the entire Imperial Guard, my personal aides and assistants are all trustworthy, and we've routed out I'd say sixty-five percent of the poisonous prelates and paxors."

Rush smiled and glanced at her from the corner of his eyes. "I bet you can't say that three times fast," he mused.

"Hush," she scolded him in a fierce little whisper. "And you aren't supposed to look at me."

"A ridiculous custom," he insisted for the hundredth time. But he turned his gaze forward again to the catering room and waited with her until the room had been wholly settled, all their most distinguished guests having been marched past them in a respectful procession line.

Once everyone was seated, Rush gave a slight nod to Suna, who then hurried to touch the shoulder of the hall manager. At his direction the window shutters were dramatically lifted, rising to expose thirty-foot-tall sheets of crystal clear therma glass and the brilliant sunny day beyond them.

As well as the tremendous crowd of commoners that had been allowed onto the grounds of Blossom Palace, all pressed as close to the therma glass as they could possibly get in order to see the spectacle within the catering hall.

"I feel like a flit-flyer trapped in a jar," Rush muttered, his gloved finger touching the snug collar of his uniform.

"Shh," Ambrea soothed him softly, breaking protocol in order to take hold of his hand, threading her gloved fingers between his.

"This is ridiculous. Any number of those people can try to attack you and your guests through the glass—"

"*Our* guests. And you had the glass replaced and reinforced, did you not?"

"And I don't like them running loose on the grounds—"

"The lower grounds. Our private areas and residences are perfectly guarded. You saw to that. Or don't you trust your people?"

"I do." He nodded his head then, exhaling strongly in an act of moderate relaxation. "Yes, I do. They're good men. Better than I had hoped for."

"Distinguished guests," the hall manager suddenly announced in a strident, booming voice that echoed into every corner. "Welcome to Blossom Palace. You honor us with your presence. Now, if you will, allow me to introduce to you our most benevolent and beauteous mistress, the Empress Ambrea Vas Allay, and her betrothed, General Rush Blakely!"

The room erupted in cheers and applause, the effect radiating like a wave through the vast windows and into the excited crowd beyond. Ambrea broke protocol yet again and turned her head to look at Rush, leaning close to him so their shoulders touched.

"Now tell me, my fine Tarian brute," she whispered to him, "does that sound like a country that hates you?"

Ambrea had known that it was fear that had been causing him to be a bundle of nerves and testy temperament the past few days leading up to this, their official betrothal event. This despite the fact that they had been working so publicly hand in hand for months, that she had visibly taken his guidance and advice on a nonstop basis, and that the people had long ago come to understand that the Tarian was much more to their empress than a glorified bodyguard.

Perhaps it was because her people were high from the dramatic, life-improving changes that her regime had been instilling seemingly nonstop since her coronation, or perhaps it was because the common people weren't quite as prejudiced against Tarians as her father and his brutal military sect had been, or more likely it was because they had come to respect this particular Tarian as they realized he was good at what he did, fair in his actions, and quietly intelligent as he thought things out. Whatever the reason or combination of reasons, they had looked very favorably on Rush. And therefore much more favorably than expected on this, their sanctioned betrothal ceremony, and the impending wedding to follow sometime within the next cycle.

"It doesn't hurt that you look incredibly delicious in Allayan uniform," she whispered to him.

That made him laugh, completely out of protocol, which required them to stand apart, eyes forward, on quiet display for nobles, guests, and commoners alike for a good half hour before they could relax and begin the party. The idea was that all involved could judge them, come to an opinion about them, and then let it be known how they felt about the union to come.

But in his amusement the Tarian threw off protocol and lifted the hand that was threaded with their queen's to his lips, pressing the most sincere of kisses to the back of it and looking so baldly into her eyes that there was not a person in sight who couldn't see the love for her that was radiating out of him like a storm.

Every woman in range released a collective sigh.

It was only a moment after that that he was ringing her around the waist, drawing her up close in a romantic sweep, her dress with its brocade and platinum panels sweeping around his strongly braced legs. He did not kiss her. Did not need to. He touched his forehead to hers as their eyes met and held.

"I want to invite my friends to evening meals. Frequently. I don't wish to grow apart from them," he said to her, brushing back the red and gold cape of her hair.

"Anytime you like. Does that include Justice?"

Rush frowned. "I will invite her, but it doesn't follow that she will accept. She's still sore at me."

"She's here," Ambrea whispered.

Ambrea, in this case, didn't mind being thrown over for another woman. Her husband-to-be jerked to attention and his eyes swept the room. There she was, leaning out of sight, trying her best to not be where she was and definitely not stand out in the process.

He grinned. One thing Justice had never understood was that she was too much woman and too much Tarian to ever successfully blend in with non-Tari-infused cultures like this one. She was wearing her dress uniform, although she had not been asked to come in an official capacity. A little bit of protective armor, he supposed.

"She's coming around," Ambrea noted softly. "And whether she wants to admit it or not, she misses you."

"I miss her as well," he said deeply.

"You miss all of them," his bride-to-be said a little sadly.

He smiled at her then, drawing her into his warmth once more.

"I'm far too busy to miss them most days. It's when I stop and stand still like this that I realize it." He touched gloved fingers to her temple. "I don't regret my choices, Ambrea. I'm far too content for things like regret to show their ugly faces."

Her lips turned up. "Even when I force you to dress in uniform and parade you in front of the entire continent?"

"Even so. But I do regret not being more social with my friends."

"Then we will remedy that, Rush. I never wanted you to completely cut yourself off from your family."

"I know." Rush shaped the curves of her face with the gentlest touch of his fingertips, wishing he could shed the dulling gloves he wore and actually feel the softness of her skin. Time had only proven to more strongly bond his heart to her, and, he had no doubt, hers to him. It was ridiculous how much delight he took simply in watching her go about her daily business. And Rush knew she often took time out of her busy schedule to come down to the headquarters of the Imperial Guard and watch him train soldiers to a proper way of thinking and acting. A fair and legal way.

"I love you terribly," she breathed suddenly, her free hand coming to grip his wrist where his fingers revered her face. "And once we are done settling this country, I want to start a family with you."

Suddenly Rush recognized that there had been a tinge of longing in her earlier observations of Ravenna. A whole new anxiety gripped him down the length of his breastbone, but it wasn't the paralyzing and adamant denial he had always felt when faced with this concept in the past. It was no longer about his genes, or even her genes. They both had risky material to play with, they knew.

"I think I might make a terrible father," he admitted to her.

"Liar. No one knows better the importance of true family. I, however, might make a terrible mother."

"Liar. No one has a better example of what not to do to a child than you do."

She smiled.

"Then it is settled. We will start a family."

He gave her a dirty look.

"Trickster," he accused her.

"Perhaps," she breathed as she leaned against him. "But I have never known you to fall for anything you weren't willing to fall for."

Rush had to agree with her. She had known him such a relatively short span of his life, and yet she knew him so incredibly well.

"Aye," he admitted on a whisper, before he totally blew protocol out of the water and drew her mouth to his for a soul-defining kiss.

The cheer that went up around them was powerful enough to shatter that bright protective glass.

It pissed him off royally, but Commander Bronse Chapel couldn't help stumbling once again as the sand shifted from under his fast-paced footing. He corrected himself with a hard, jolting body movement in order to keep his balance, and the jerking motion elicited a soft, barely discernable groan from the burden on his back.

"How goes it, Chief?" he asked, pausing in his stride to request the answer and to allow his fellow soldier a few beats to grit out the agony that had to be washing through him by then.

"Just waiting on my encore, sir," Chief Trick Hwenk responded with the traditional gung-ho attitude of an ETF officer, his young voice sounding suddenly much younger and far weaker than it had two miles back.

Chapel hesitated and then shifted the weight of his human burden up a little higher against his spine and shoulders, wishing that the grip Trick had on him was not getting so obviously lax. Bronse could smell the injured soldier's blood just as easily as he could feel it soaking through his gear where the man was slumped over his back. The commander had a well-powered grip around the younger man's thighs and knees as the soldier rode piggyback. But if the kid couldn't hold on to his shoulders, they'd be in deep shit, and Bronse felt that fact clear to his straining bones.

"All right, Chief. Just hang by your grip for three more miles and we'll be in the nest. Of course, that means you'll have to listen to the medics bitch at you for a few days," Bronse noted, using the jovial reminder as a cover for restarting their staggering progress across the ever-shifting sand. Bronse narrowed his eyes behind his goggles, peering at the west sandline. The wind was getting antsy, but he couldn't yet see a cloud forming on the line. *That* was a blessing, at least. Provided it stayed that way. The last thing they needed to contend with was a sand hurricane.

Bronse went back to concentrating on where he was putting his feet, and how fast he could risk going without jostling his precious burden too dangerously. His every muscle burned from the exertion, but he welcomed it. He preferred being soaked in sweat, working himself to the limit of his endurance and pounding out whatever was necessary to see a certain goal achieved. He'd always felt the most in control when he had that kind of dedicated focus, and he supposed that was what had gotten him the command position on the First Active squad of the ETF in the first place.

Then again, he had wanted to be an Interplanetary Militia soldier since . . .

Well, his *matra* would swear it was since they cut the cord, and his *patra* would have proudly boasted that it was set down in his very genes, but Bronse remembered the first time he had seen a BioVid of the history of the Interplanetary Militia's ETF when he was six years old. The IM was an intra/interplanetary peacekeeping and defensive military outfit, and it had existed for well over a century. The IM had been created as a joint military effort among the three inhabited planets in the system: Tari, Ulrike, and Ebbany. It had more or less succeeded in its charter of keeping the treatises of coexistence among the three entities, as well as managing missions of peace and humanity on and among the individual planets.

The IM had several specialized branches, but nothing compared to the Special Operations sector known as the Extreme Tactics Force. To a six-year-old the ETF had sounded deadly, dangerous, and exciting as all hell. Watching the BioVid had only confirmed what Bronse had already dreamed of. Being in the ETF was a good way to get an adrenaline rush and have an opportunity to do things with nothing but your balls and your skills to get you out of hellish situations. Not to mention that it was an excellent way to get important body parts blown off.

Unfazed, Bronse had known right then that he was destined to be one of those elite soldiers, and nothing would stop him. Learning that kind of goal setting and determination at that young an age had served him well. Now, here he was, commander of the crack team of the First Active ETF soldiers. First Active meant they were the lead team and were always called first for an assignment, and it meant that his team was the best of the best. They were the ones who went to do the impossible in the worst situations, maintaining a no fear/no fail/no fatality motto that was rarely betrayed.

That motto was balanced on Bronse's back at the moment, losing blood too fast for what remained of a three-mile hike. But Bronse was doing his damndest to make them the fastest miles ever to be hiked on sand. He'd never lost a team member in the field, and he wasn't about to start with a rookie communications officer who had balls the size of jumbo adder crystals. The kid had more than proved his grit today. Trick might be their newest and youngest member, but Bronse had known the minute he'd laid eyes on him that he was the perfect fifth for his group. They'd been searching for a communications officer for a whipsnout's age, going through three washouts before Trick had sauntered onto the base, fresh out of the grueling ETF training program.

Trick had those blond boy-next-door good looks that you could see a block away, riveting blue eyes that penetrated at every glance, and the disarming manners and engaging charm to go with them. He'd been in the mess hall hardly ten minutes before he'd had a small harem of female officers and noncoms all around him. They had been laughing and flirting with him like they weren't already surrounded by a cafe overflowing with virile, accessible men. Keeping in mind that militia women were not something one toyed with lightly, or at all for that matter, Trick's magnetism was impressive.

Bronse had turned to Lasher and said that any boy who could communicate that well with IM women deserved their team position as communications officer. Lasher had agreed, looking mighty impressed himself. Another recommendation in and of itself because very little impressed Bronse's second in command. So Trick had joined Bronse, Lasher, Justice, and Ender's First Active ETF team all of two months back, and this had been their third mission out since the team had been locked in. The first two missions had been sterling. Chief Hwenk had proved himself capable of jacking into everything from TransTel satellites to the antennae of a Flibbean ground slug. The boy was a damn miracle worker.

The third mission, however, had run into a bit of a snafu.

Bronse had to stop again, this time so they both could toss back a few gulps of nutria-treated water. The sand and sun, not to mention Bronse's labors, were sucking the hydration right out of his body. The Grinpar Desert on Ebbany was merciless in that respect. Actually, it was merciless in all respects. Only the Great Being knew why anyone would want to fight over the right to live on such a forsaken piece of hell-acre. The sand hurricanes alone could rip solid stone out of the ground. A person caught aboveground was as good as dead, or at least scoured to a bloody stump.

To make matters worse, the sand was black.

That meant it soaked up the rays of the sun all day and could melt or burn the hell out of anything that touched it, stumbled in it, or outright fell down looking to bake their face. Only the special protection of the soldiers' boots and clothes kept them from this type of fate. That and Bronse's impressive sense of balance.

The faster they were out of that hostile environment, the better, Bronse thought as he began to trek off again.

For this mission, the team had split up to do reconnaissance at two separate locations. Bronse hadn't recommended or approved of that plan. However, due to the sand hurricanes and an awkwardly timed insert by their command center, they hadn't had the time to recon their target sites in succession. Their limited circumstances had meant hitting the recon objectives simultaneously, which meant either aborting to a later mission or splitting up a single team right then. Abortion meant doubling the danger of detection, doubling the risk to lives. Bronse had given in to his upper command and split his team. Justice, Lasher, and Ender had taken the north site, and Bronse and Trick had taken the northwest target. Bronse and Trick had been filling PhotoVids with recon information when they'd been made. Bronse still couldn't figure out how it had happened. They'd been silent and—wearing black—all but invisible. The Nomaad patrol had jumped them from behind, six to two, and the indigenous life-form's guards had been very skilled in hand-to-hand fighting.

Still, nothing compared to ETF training. Especially when it came to hand-to-hand fighting. Bronse and the kid had moved like lightning to eliminate their threat, working silently so as not to alert any other patrols. Trick hadn't even cried out when he'd been pig-stuck by a wicked Nomaadic knife with a dual edge and hooks in the hilt meant to either hold the knife in, or rip flesh violently away if the wielder recalled the blade. Trick had done the smart thing, bracing a hand to hold the knife in place as he cut off the Nomaad's hand at the wrist. No small feat that, Bronse knew.

Though he rarely made a sound to reflect it, Trick still had the six-inch blade stuck deep in his gut, the hilt of which Bronse could see if he glanced past his arm on the left-hand side. Removing the blade would guarantee Trick's death. Moving Trick, every step and every slide in the sand, jiggled sharpened metal against the fragile pink tissue inside the young soldier's belly. But Bronse had no choice. The area been too hot for a pickup with the light transport ship they'd brought for the recon. Plus, covert reconnaissance produced little advantage if you announced you'd been there with the screaming engines of a flight ship.

With luck, a sand hurricane would hit within a couple of hours and the patrol that had jumped them would be considered lost to it. There certainly wouldn't be any traces of bodies or blood. Bronse had already seen to that. In and out like ghosts—that was how ETF preferred to do their work. It was such a habit for Bronse to cover his own tracks that he could cook a four-course meal in a stranger's house and leave them none the wiser for it by the time he'd finished. His ex-wife, Liely, claimed he'd done the same thing to their marriage. She'd insisted that, for the two years they had been wed, she had hardly known he was there.

He'd never understood why she'd been so surprised by that. What had she expected it to be like? He'd been ETF born and bred—ate it, breathed it, practically made love to it—and she'd always told him that this was a major turn-on for her. *She* had sought *him* out, not the other way around. Having a relationship had been nowhere on Bronse's radar. He'd learned years ago that the Extreme Tactics Force and long-term liaisons did not mix. But Liely had come on strong, oozing attractive enticement, hero worship, and a hell-acre of wild and adventurous sex. It wasn't often that a soldier argued with that kind of easy fortune. She'd been smart, witty, and sizzling hot, seemingly with a good head on her about what it meant to hang around with a First Active soldier who shipped off in a heartbeat when called. With the volatile politics and disturbances of three planets to manage, that tended to be fairly often. Hell, she'd waved him off and hugged him hello every time without a single complaint, and after a while he believed that he'd found the rare fortune of a woman worth asking to marry. She'd said yes before he'd even finished popping the question.

And that was when everything changed. Or nothing changed, according to his discontented wife. Liely had bitched and moaned nonstop about his "inaccessibility" and how lonely she was all the time. Why wasn't he home more often? He had a family now, so why didn't he change—work a desk, get promoted so he'd make more money. Her logic was lost on him when she told him she'd expected it to be "different" once they were married. He'd been dumbfounded. He'd never once intimated that he saw himself changing for any reason. Still, Liely thought he should make concessions to coddle a whining wife—just because.

Grounds for a segregation? Yeah, inevitably it had been. Like every other fight, he'd done it quickly and quietly, putting an end to his mistake as soon as he legally could.

Bronse wasn't introspective at heart. He had a very basic makeup and that never required much self-discovery. However, he moved better when he kept his mind occupied with a lot of things at once. He kept his attention on the terrain, checked the sandline, and kept an ear out for any agony on Trick's part, but the rest of him did whatever it took to make travel through the awful conditions fly by faster.

The transport was waiting another mile and a half away now, the closest they could get and stay undercover. Justice and Lasher had wanted to trek out to meet him, but he didn't want them in the sand so close to a hurricane event. Bronse's equipment had read the storm forming an hour ago. By now it was fast approaching, and he'd soon see it on the sandline. He wouldn't risk them as well as himself and Trick. He knew that his decision had burned them, knew they were furious with him, but they'd obeyed and would continue to obey unless he said otherwise.

It rubbed them the wrong way, though—this group who lived by the motto no fear/no fail/no fatality—to be coddled by their commanding officer like a father protecting his children.

Bronse looked over to the distant sandline. The sky was becoming obscured with swirling black and violet clouds, and ground lightning was illuminating the funnels and downdrafts of the approaching hurricane.

"Hey, Boss," Trick spoke up in a rasp of repressed pain, "not that I'm complaining, but I hope I won't be washing sand out of every crack and crevice for the next few weeks."

"Can you think of a better way to encourage you to take a bath once in a while?" Bronse retorted breathlessly as he tried to pick up his pace and keep jostling to a minimum. "Gonna need a sand hurricane to scour the stink off you, boy."

"That's just—" Trick broke off his riposte to grit a low sound of agony through his throat. "Arrrhh!"

"Hang on, kid. Last leg. And I'll beat the storm with at least a minute to spare."

Trick's forehead fell limply against the back of Bronse's neck. The pain had to be horrible, Bronse knew, even though Trick had barely made a sound. The pain was communicated in the feel of the boy's skin—both clammy and hot—and in the slackening of Trick's strength and grip. He was losing consciousness, and Bronse wasn't sure that it wouldn't be the kinder thing, as long as the kid didn't slip off his back. Bronse leaned into his trek, keeping Trick pitched forward against his spine and balancing him even more as he went limper, finally falling unconscious.

Deadweight.

Trick was out, and Bronse could feel it in every ounce of the body on his back. He had always been fascinated by why that made a difference. It was a balance and weight distribution factor, he knew logically. The person wasn't awake to best center himself on the person who carried him. Still, it was remarkable how consciousness, or lack thereof, made such a difference in the feel of their weight.

Bronse realized he was grasping for thoughts. Practically babbling in his own mind, really. But he had to do something to make himself move faster, maintaining burden and strength, beating out the storm, and not second-guessing himself about why he wouldn't have the rest of the team come out to meet them.

"That was cutting it close!"

Justice made the declaration seconds before she yanked and banked the transport away from the approach of the storm. She pitched up toward the higher atmosphere of Ebbany, the gravity decks working hard to compensate so the team didn't end up spilled across the flooring. But it wasn't Justice that Bronse was worried about. All of his concern was aft, in medbay, with Trick and the medic. But because he needed to hear his team's report, he had to fulfill command first and let the others get back to him as to Trick's progress.

"I sure hope we don't have to find another nav/com officer," Justice quipped over her shoulder. "They come and go so fast around here; I'm getting tired of wiping the butt streaks off this chair." She nodded to the empty chair behind her and to her right.

"That isn't funny, Captain," Bronse said sternly, looking up from his VidPad, where he was recording his portion of the report before transmission.

"You're right, sir. I'm sorry, sir," she agreed quickly.

Captain Justice Mulettere was looking straight ahead, piloting them out of the atmosphere and into the starred darkness of space, but she was also glancing in her back-view disc. She kept the little shiny disc clipped to her console so she could see the activity behind her. Not having to turn around to see what her crewmates were up to made for better piloting. The ship's designers could have set the pilot's chair farther back, she supposed, but she preferred models like the transport which let her feel the nose of the craft around her rather than the pilot's chair being muffled in its mid-section.

So she could clearly see Commander Chapel's reflection in her shiny disc as he sat sprawled in the command chair behind her. He hadn't even paused to breathe after dropping Trick on the medbay table and ordering her to get the transport out of there. The commander had come forward, sat down still drenched in sweat and blood and caked black sand, and gone right to his report. The trek had been brutal on him, and she could see the tremors in his overexerted muscles, even via the disc. She wasn't one to second-guess her commanding officer, but she hadn't understood why he wouldn't let them meet up with him so they could help bring Trick in. Was Bronse protecting them? They were ETF, for Great Being's sake. They were *supposed* to stick their necks out. But she'd known her superior officer for a while now, and she suspected that Bronse had been a little wrecked up about letting the new kid get tanked. The commander got very strict after one of them got hurt. His personal motto, they had learned, was no fear/no fail/no fatality, and no fuckups.

Justice sighed. The episode with Trick meant they'd be running rigorous drills and extreme training again during their next downtime. Not that she minded, because a girl had to do something to keep her figure, but she did wish that Bronse would parallel that way of thinking with other things sometimes. Like snapping a bootlace would mean a day of intensive shoe shopping. She chuckled noiselessly to herself, trying to picture the hulking men she was teamed with sitting in a shoe emporium, eating canapés and sipping Lathe wine, while salers slid the latest in fashionable shoes onto their feet, one after another. Actually, Lasher was a mighty fine fashion plate when he was out of uniform, Justice mused. He would probably get a kick out of a day of shoe shopping.

But Commander Chapel was plainly not in a mood to appreciate her humorous ideas on these matters, so she kept them to herself. Perhaps she would share them later with Lasher. And Trick would get a kick out of them for sure.

Justice frowned, hoping that Trick would be all right. She had faith in their medic; he could hold the kid over until they returned to Ulrike. The best medical care in the tri-planet system was on their base planet. Once they got the kid there, he would be good as new.

Of the three worlds, Ulrike was the most advanced and civilized in many ways besides medical care. The ETF was based there, as was IM headquarters. Although the planet was half land and half water, most of the landmass was settled and there were few uninhabited areas.

Not like Ebbany, the planet they had just left. Ebbany was mostly landmass, with little in the way of water and oceans. That made for a high percentage of deserts covering the face of the planet. However, the Ebbanites had managed to eke out an impressive civilization along the edges of the waters. Yet the bane of the peace seekers were the barbarians of the wilderness areas and the Nomaad populations wandering the desert highlands and the lowlands of belowground caverns that stretched for hundreds of miles in all directions. The endless squabbles and arming for war, especially in the Grinpar Desert, had begun to make Justice feel like she would be wearing black camouflage for the rest of her life.

If Ulrike and Ebbany were polar opposites in civilization, however, Tari had to be the middle ground. Living there was rough, whether you chose jungle or desert, city or country, or life on the many colony platforms sharing the planetary orbits and sight line between Tari and its forested moon of Adia. The platforms were situated in a line from Tari to Adia like metallic stepping-stones, each one housing tens of thousands of citizens. They had the best advantages and technologies that life had to offer, their supplies often coming straight from Ulrike, where they got first dibs on imports before they even filtered down to the planet itself.

The trouble with Tari was that each colony was a faction unto itself, and they were always squabbling over trading rights or imagined slights from another colony. Feuding was frequent, and policing the colonies was difficult because it was hard to blend in on a floating piece of metal where everyone lived in close quarters and was wary of strangers. Planetside wasn't much better. Trading rights were a bone of contention there too. Traders figured, why spend time flying all the way to the planet surface when they could simply go to the nearest platform colony. This meant that by the time goods filtered down the line to the planet, the prices were exorbitant. Only half the planet was settled; the other half was a wild frontier that drew adventurers, troublemakers, and a serious criminal element.

Tari was one of Justice's favorite places. She had grown up on one of its platforms—a middle-class upbringing in a place that, to be frank, had been flat, cold and gray. Still it had had more than its share of dangers for a young girl. A contrast to platform life, the wilderness on Tari held a wild, colorful appeal for her. It was a matter of honesty, she thought. At least when you went to the Tari plains and rises, you knew you were headed into blatant dangers, unlike space colony life, where you thought you were safe, yet good faces held hazards in camouflage. Justice had always preferred the honesty of knowing you were in constant jeopardy.

Rather like her career choice.

She had enlisted in the IM right out of school, letting them teach and train her, letting herself be the perfect lump of clay for them to mold into the perfect soldier. Now she was one of the top five pilots in the Special Forces communities; she was one of only ten female ETF officers, and she was on Commander Bronse Chapel's First Active ETF team. Chapel was a legend in his own time, and there wasn't an ETF soldier who wouldn't give his right arm to be on his elite team. Justice had been in her exalted position for three years now, and she had thrilled in every minute of it.

"Out of atmosphere; out of orbit traffic, Commander," she reported automatically as they pulled away from Ebbany and headed fast toward Ulrike.

"ETA?"

"Thirty-two hours, sir."

"That long?" came the sharp demand.

"This is only an XJL transport, sir," she reminded him with gentle respect. "I don't have any zip. Just handling for best travel and evasion on the planetary surfaces. I can do only thirty-two hours at top mach."

Bronse's jaw clenched, and Justice could see a nerve tick angrily in his temple. The one thing none of them ever had to doubt was that their best interests and safety were at the heart of Commander Chapel's every motivation. The entire team trusted their lives to him, and with good reason. They had seen Chapel do much more miraculous things to save the lives of his crew than humping out a kid with a six-inch blade in his belly, over black sand, in hostile territory, and a sand hurricane nipping at his heels.

Justice tired of watching her commander in the disc. Now that they were in the void of space, she flipped on her autopilot and swung out of her chair as if she were dismounting a horse. She strolled back to the supplies chest secured against the rear deck plates, and unlatched it with a hiss as it released its airtight seal. She fished out a first-aid case and resealed the chest. Then she walked up to the commander, who had gone back to typing his report, the blunt tips of his fingers dashing over the electronic keyboard of the handheld VidPad. She opened the kit and, without bothering to ask for permission, she began to tend the wounds he had sustained in his fight.

He had a cut over his left eye that would need knitting, a

great deal of generalized bruising that a heal patch would take care of over the next twenty-four hours, and a bitching case of sunburn that was already beginning to blister. He had apparently lost his protective headgear in the fight, which had left him exposed to the sun. Justice would bet he had a hell-acre of a sun-induced headache as well. He had the misfortune of having coal black hair, and, like the black sand, it had absorbed every ray of brutal sun that had beaten down on him. Justice selected two heal patches from the kit and slapped one on Bronse's left arm and the other under the hair on the back of his thick neck. When she pulled back, he was looking at her, a brow quirked up in curiosity. A light scar cut through the peak of his brow, accentuating the arch.

"Two?" he asked dryly.

"Yeah." She grinned, pausing briefly to nibble on the gum between her back teeth. "One for reabsorption and swelling reduction."

"And the other?"

"To cut the pain of the headache and sunburn."

She looked studiously into the first-aid case as she spoke, so she could only feel the narrowing of his eyes on her at first. Not one to give in to cowardice, not even in the face of Commander Chapel's disapproval, she smiled sweetly at him as she looked up.

"You gave me a narcotic?" he growled dangerously, reaching for the patch on the back of his neck. He looked up in surprise when she caught his huge fist in her palm, staying his actions. "Back off, Captain," he barked shortly.

"Uh . . . with all due respect . . . bite me, Commander," she retorted with lazy, unconcerned wit. "It's only a low dose, meant to counter the dip when your adrenaline plummets. Which will be any minute now. When it drops, your pain will kick in. I've been around this block enough to know. If you want to stay lucid, you have to let me cut away at your nerves a little. Otherwise, you won't be able to focus and stay alert with us."

"I don't like my reflexes being diminished or my perceptions screwed around with," he argued predictably.

"That's why it's a low dose," she reiterated. "And that's why I used a patch and not a hyperspray. If we run into trouble, you just yank it off and you'll be right in ten minutes, fifteen tops."

"I know." She held up a hand to forestall his coming argument. "A lot can happen in ten minutes. But you have to trust me. I'd rather you be half-narced without pain than blinded by the agony that we both know is coming. If I let the medic look at you, he'd lock you in medbay. At least this way I can tell him I gave you first aid and he can focus solely on Trick. Don't you think I know that's why you ran out of medbay—before the medic could get a look at you?"

"Fine. I'll leave it for now," he acquiesced as if it were a heavy travail. "But next time, ask and present arguments before just doing it, okay? I'm not ignorant. I can listen to reason."

"Yes, sir. Sorry, sir."

"Jus, I want you to stay at the stick for a while. I know you're tired and the autopilot could get us there in its sleep, but I have . . . I have a strange feeling. Let's just keep alert, okay?"

"Roger that, sir."

Justice put away the case and slung herself back into her seat, keeping her eyes on her monitors.

Despite Bronse's worries, they reached Ulrike without mishap or event. Justice swung into port on the IM space station that rotated in Ulrike's orbit with smooth grace in spite of its enormity. Thousands of troops moved in and out of the station, known as Station Zero, every day, at all hours, and the time of their approach was no different. Since IM acted in the role of law enforcement as well as militia, personnel were constantly shifting. Station Zero was a major exchange port, situated equidistant from Tari and Ebbany and practically on top of Ulrike.

Shortly after the XJL landed on the tarmac, the doors of the cargo hold lowered to reveal the entire squad standing at the ready. Trick was supported on each side by two team members, their arms linked to form a human sedan chair of sorts to support their injured comrade. Justice and Lasher stood on the right, Bronse and Ender on the left. Bronse was, of course, in front, his thick wrist and forearm linked beneath Trick's thighs with Lasher's equally powerful grasp. At a soft sound from their commander, the team strode forward in a perfectly timed march, cushioning Trick, yet precise and proud in step so no one could mistake them for anything but the mighty warriors they were. Wounded team members of the ETF had always been brought home in such a manner, their heads held high, keeping them from being the object of pity or dismay, something every soldier dreaded in moments like this.

Silence fell over the soldiers crowded around waiting for their departing flights. A respectful silence. All braced their legs and linked their hands behind their backs in honorable attention as the ETF officers carried their injured man past them, heading for the station medical facilities.

Don't miss
the next exciting installment in
Jacquelyn Frank's seductive
Three Worlds series

SEDUCE ME
IN SHADOWS

Coming soon
from Ballantine Books